SEASON OF PREDATORS

Mark Fulcher
Annet Libeau

For more information and other books published by the authors, visit our website:

http://seasonofpredators.com

ISBN 978-0-9852095-3-7

Published by Sun Day Consulting, Inc.

1

Kryger listened to the hypnotic thrum of the scout's powerful twin Stardrive engines for any break or change in rhythm. They had taken a longer jump than any previously recorded attempt for a two-man scoutship; already more than twelve hours in subspace at the mind-numbing speed of twenty-five light years per hour—a little less than eight parsecs per hour or a light-year in less than two and a half minutes.

In subspace, a transit-computer controlled faster-than-light spacecraft. The pre-set course couldn't be altered before the ship left subspace at a predetermined point. Spacecraft were programmed to correct, or temporarily bypass problems, since human minds and reflexes were far too slow to respond in a vital split second when a malfunction occurred. If a serious fault developed, the computer would immediately start exit procedures into normal space.

So, there wasn't much one could do when cooped up in a two-man scout during a long distance jump. After the initial gut wrenching, sickening lurch into the dull, unending gray blindness of the subspace dimension, and then the fierce acceleration to achieve faster-than-light velocity, there was no awareness of movement. The sensation of speed existed only in one's imagination; the mind nudged to the edge of sanity by the visual isolation and the nearly soundless, far-off whispering of straining engines.

In a small ship, such as the scout, you put your trust in technology to look after your welfare; and those who wanted to make light of the scary reality joked that you didn't have to be mad to be a scout-pilot, but it sure helped to keep you sane. There were no recorded accidents, and the theory was that the subspace dimension was a complete void. Still, nobody wanted to become a statistic.

Kryger arched his back to stretch his powerful two-meter body in the confined space. Shortly after they had entered subspace, Quarr—the astrogator accompanying him—told him that due to months of inactivity of their enemy, the Bikans, she'd obtained permission to visit a far-off system; of which the coordinates were given to her in early childhood. Unfortunately, she wasn't sure whether her recollection was factually accurate. She told Kryger that she was trying to determine if her colony still existed, and if so, to locate her people, get reacquainted, and establish if they would permit her to return after countless years of forced exile.

Other than Kryger's parents, no one knew that Quarr was a shape changer. Kryger found out when he questioned why she resembled his mother, believing she might be his sister. He was told the tale of how, many years before, his parents rescued a rare, brown leopard cub that was close to death from starvation. After reviving it, they were taken by surprise when the withered cub slowly changed into a small copy of his mother, cat face and all, except for her eyes, which stayed the same yellowish-brown color with round pupils.

After she had recovered, Quarr told them—via decoded translations of images and feelings through mind communication—that she didn't know how to hunt in the shape her mother had helped her and her baby brother change into to hide when the hostile Bikans were on the verge of capturing them. She only remembered that she was four years old, and that her brother had subsequently died of thirst and starvation.

Kryger had sensed the purity of her thoughts and accepted her as normal. Kryger and his brother had inherited the outward appearance of their Thrassar mother, and they were accepted by the colonists as normal human beings even though their eyes and the shape of their heads were catlike.

Amazingly, Quarr disliked her own voice and preferred to use mind-speech. With such a beautiful voice, she couldn't even utter a determined "no" to uninvited advances without conveying the impression that she actually meant "yes," even when accompanied by a negative headshake and a serious face.

On the rare occasion that she did laugh out loud, everyone within audible range stopped in their tracks to listen. It was so spontaneous, so merry and contagious, that everyone joined in because it felt like the right thing to do. Kryger fervently wanted to hear her sing, but she always firmly declined such invitations. Her voice always sounded amused and full of suppressed laughter, even when in serious disagreement with Kryger while they were being briefed for a mission during which protocol required the use of voice-communication.

Quarr was hauntingly beautiful and known as the finest astrogator and navigator on the planet. Some pilots tried to woo her away after such serious-seeming disputes, because they thought that Kryger and Quarr were lovers, which was the exact opposite of the truth. Only the odd esper among the pilots sensed that Quarr lived an asexual life. The non-espers just couldn't understand why all Kryger and Quarr's missions were successful, since they conveyed the impression that they detested one another. Yet, they were quiet and efficient when they entered the cockpit, trusted each other wholeheartedly, and would lay their lives on the line for each other without knowing why. They were experts in their respective fields and dedicated to the safety of Nevus; and they depended on each other to stay alive in perilous situations.

Kryger reminded himself to test the MAG at the first opportunity. He groaned softly and abruptly slapped both cheeks with the palms of his hands in exasperation as he remembered the offhand remark made by the scientist of the Golden People, who'd installed the puny looking little weapon in place of the heavy beam-cannon in the scout's nose.

"It's a new pocket sized, secret weapon, and more deadly than the beamer it replaces. It was developed by your twin sisters, and is entrusted to you for field-testing. We call it a MAG, short for Matter Annihilator Gun. It creates neat, round holes through anything that gets in the bolt's way. The crazy Bikans and their sponsors would sell their corrupted souls, if they had any, very cheaply for possession of this little toy if they ever got wind of it. If you crash land the scout—as you usually do at first opportunity—disconnect and take the MAG with you. Otherwise, destroy it with the scout.

"Remember never to pull the trigger with the shields on. A force-shield isn't matter, and it's the only thing we know of that can deflect the bolts. In theory, a bolt will ricochet inside closed shields until the craft and/or the shield-generators are destroyed. The effective range could be hundreds of kilometers in space. We haven't tested its range in space yet, but it's a hundred and seventy eight kilometers on Nevus. Barriers in between don't impact the range. Before you ask, I can't reveal how we tested the effective range on Nevus…it's classified information."

The scientist then explained, step-by-step, how to change a magazine, and how easily it could be converted into a deadly hand-weapon. He helpfully supplied the handgrip to convert it into a small, light gun that could be carried in a trouser pocket.

3

"The twins, geniuses that they are, thought of everything, for one never knows where *you* will end up, because of your tendency to wreck craft when you play games with the enemy. Talk to your sisters if you want an explanation of how it works. Maybe you can even finagle an extra magazine or two out of them," he had finished airily with a wave of his right hand, as if lecturing a four-year-old child.

Kryger loved his eighteen-year-old sisters with all his heart, and they were very close. They didn't inherit the cat-like characteristics of their Thrassar mother, only her striking beauty, golden skin, odd golden hair streaked with cross bands of red, and the dark emerald color of her eyes. Unlike other kids their age, they were more interested in applying themselves to invent useful, albeit destructive, gadgets than in participating in teenage frivolity. These weapons were so sophisticated that they were used to keep the Bikans from rediscovering Nevus. The twins had many admirers, but politely discouraged those who expected more than just a casual friendship.

"So, how come this so-called 'toy' of yours doesn't destroy itself," he had asked his sister, Amok.

"How can I explain it to a destructive numskull like you?" Amok replied with a seemingly serious look on her face, but gave him a powerful, sisterly hug. "Let me try though. When the trigger is pulled, a momentary pipe-like shield, about a meter long, is generated to protect the gun and to give the bolt accurate direction—which was Bir's brilliant idea after our first attempt almost ended in catastrophe. The miniature inner mechanism takes about a second to regenerate the required power and to advance the special wire for the matter-destroying bolt…until the coil-magazine is depleted of course, but we managed to cram enough wire around a coil-magazine for sixty bolts. Nothing natural stops the bolts, except distance, so mind where you point the device before pulling the trigger. To be on the safe side, we'll try to make the next MAG a little bit bulkier for a hundred or so shots, and we're thinking about ways to eliminate the one second delay."

Kryger sighed heavily and yawned loudly. The conviction that he had erred in not testing the MAG before the jump concerned him. The twins had said they had tested the weapon a couple of hundred times. It was experimental and the only one in existence. The scientists of the Golden People were careful, for Nevus was the planet where their race came into

4

existence and developed. *But there was always the possibility of an unintentional mistake, such as misalignment,* he thought gloomily.

The thoughts about the MAG made him recall and consider the scout's other weaponry, for it wasn't armed for prolonged battle as fighting craft were. The most devastating were the two small, pre-armed nuclear-type missiles in the nose, right under the pilot's position, which, when activated, locked onto the target pointed to by the crosshairs on his faceplate. The missile tubes could swivel as far as he could turn his head to take aim at a target—up to a hundred and sixty degrees on either side. Then there were four rear-facing tubes; each tube containing twelve intelligent missiles which could be dispatched up to four at a time to destroy homing missiles or powerful pursuers. The only other weapons were two rear-facing, medium-heavy beam weapons, one on each side under the half-extended wings. Not much in the way of self-defense, but thought to be enough for a craft that's notorious for its stealth and speed.

Quarr had been silent for most of their journey, which was unusual. She also, uncharacteristically, was feeling apprehensive. She idly amused herself by following Kryger's silent musings through a wispy thought-tendril created by her unusual brain. What she didn't tell Kryger was that when she was reunited with her people, it would be time for her take up her duties as hereditary ruler. She would have to face expected disputes and challenges to her fitness to rule. At least that was what she was hurriedly told just before the Bikans began to torture her mother; just because she obviously belonged to a different race and wasn't the color of an overripe orange, Quarr thought bitterly. But rumor had it that the Bikans even killed their own kind if they thought they could get away with it. They were mentally deranged, and unbelievably suicidal, which made them an incredibly tough enemy to take on in any kind of battle.

As was a navigator's prerogative, Quarr claimed Kryger as her pilot even before he had finished his training. She was bitterly criticized by other jealous pilots, because, in a way, Kryger was family. Quarr had known him from birth, and was always convinced he would develop into the best combat pilot that Nevus could produce. As expected, he graduated very early at the unprecedented age of seventeen. It wasn't really surprising, because he took after his father, the legendary Torak.

Kryger developed into the most successful, though somewhat unorthodox, fighter pilot Nevus had. His only weakness was his intolerance of selfish, arrogant, greedy people, which too often led to severe reprimands from superiors.

After he graduated, Kryger had been sent on countless missions, even though he was still considered an adolescent; presumably to prepare him as a penetration scout, but perhaps there were other, more obscure reasons. He never talked about his experiences, except to report them officially as required, and mentioned only the facts that were essential and had direct bearing on the mission. She became aware though, through peeping into his mind, that he'd witnessed horrible atrocities on many planets, and she thought that those incidents were the cause of the haunted look in his brilliant, green, cat eyes during unguarded moments. She admired his self-control when she witnessed these rare moments.

He developed a devil-may-care attitude toward life in general, but wasn't careless or reckless in a cockpit, or in battle. It was as if his restless soul urged him to go farther and do things that no other known mortal had done before, but she sensed that he knew his limits and capabilities. She always had the inner certainty that he would keep her safe, and eventually take her home—or at least to a colony of her people.

Nearly twenty-one years ago, her mother's spacecraft had crash-landed on entry to Nevus. Miraculously, it crashed in a wild region, the same continent occupied by the colonists from a planet called Earth. She recalled that her mother had commented that the explosion that had occurred just as they had entered the atmosphere was too convenient to be a coincidence. If her mother had been a less experienced pilot, they would have been killed, but she experimentally touched the atmosphere and immediately bounced back into space before attempting to land. That act saved their lives, although for two of them, it was only temporarily.

In her dying moment, her brave mother still tried to impart essential information to Quarr. She cautioned her to find her people, and to prepare herself mentally and physically before she headed home.

It had been busy, eventful years since Quarr was rescued by her foster parents. She was now as prepared as she would ever be, and had promised herself that the person or persons responsible for the cowardly sabotage of her mother's craft would die an agonizing death if found.

While waiting for Kryger to summon the courage to present a joke to break the monotony, the cognitive part of her powerful, far-reaching mind scanned normal space at the approximate exit point. She had cultivated this habit when, about three years ago, she and her former pilot had popped out in the middle of a stationary Bikan battle fleet. Her pilot was so stunned that he couldn't react, and only the momentarily stunned surprise of the appreciative Bikans, together with her fast reflexes, had saved them from certain death. Navigators were also qualified pilots, serving as backup in case of emergencies, and dual controls at the navigator's position were standard on scouts and two-man fighter crafts.

Quarr suddenly stiffened and withdrew her tenuous wisp of a feeler from Kryger's mind to focus on what she had just perceived. Was this a repetition of what happened three years ago?

You'd better find out fast, old girl, she thought fleetingly.

2

The fifteen-minute ping-pong sounded slowly but sharply. It served as both a wakeup call and a warning that they were slowing down for exit into normal space, but as usual, there wasn't a noticeable sensation of reverse-thrust being applied.

Space should have been devoid of life at the exit point, Quarr thought, *but there's an intense, purposeful concentration of thought, amplified by an assembly of minds all concentrating on the same thing, and it doesn't feel like a friendly homecoming committee. The gravity-analyzers would not allow exit near anything with a heavy gravitational field, so the groups of hostile minds must be in a big ship, a fleet of smaller ships, or perhaps a combination of both.*

Kryger caught a glimpse of deep worry that was not quite as quickly shielded as Quarr had thought.

The five-minute chime warned that the craft was entering the final stage of slowing down for exit and the now rapid deceleration shoved him forward. He secured the cross-straps around his upper body. *What could bother her now that the jump was just about over?*

Just as he shrugged his shoulders every-which-way to ease the discomfort of tired muscles, the thirty-second double chime sounded sharply and deceleration became intense. Quarr's harsh and urgent mental bark abruptly terminated the action.

GET READY, KRYGER! DO IT NOW! HURRY! I'm picking up impressions at our exit point, but can't isolate individual thoughts yet. It appears to be an anxious reception party with unfriendly intentions. I'm webbing up. Quarr engaged the crash webbing that supported her body, head, arms, and legs. She could easily snap her neck or break an arm or leg when she inevitably lost consciousness during the severe gravitational strains they were subjected to during violent maneuvers.

Kryger winced and gritted his teeth. He sometimes regretted being a Sensitive. Quarr didn't realize that her mental yells always reverberated inside his head, leaving him somewhat dizzy, nauseated, and confused for a split second.

Her mind must be incredibly powerful to be able to sense thoughts in normal space from subspace at such a distance, he thought. Her senses had never been wrong and he became alert, despite the momentary disorientation. He connected his helmet to the weapons-guiding system, and the optical crosshairs became part of his vision as he closed the faceplate. He started to breathe rhythmically to force his body and mind into combat readiness. He felt the heady surge of adrenaline pumping into his blood, and was ready to take on as many adversaries as cared to come looking for trouble when they popped back into normal space. *Let them come and swallow their medicine,* he thought fiercely. At twenty years old, he had the confidence of youth, tempered by bitter experience, and a finely trained, analytical mind.

Quarr was subjected to artificial adaptation as a child, to allow her to move around on heavy gravity worlds without too much strain and uneasiness. She never took chances or complained about discomfort. Kryger respected her for it, because no other navigator—whose skills he had to test from time to time when they were deemed qualified—was as fearless and comfortable with his combat methods when their lives were the price to pay for a wrong move, a moment's distraction, or indecision.

Kryger didn't need to web up as his constitution could withstand more gravities than Quarr's. In addition, the aiming device connected to his helmet was synchronized with the crosshairs on his faceplate in line with his eyes, but would be ineffective if he couldn't turn his head to retaliate. His head, arms, and legs had to be free, otherwise the scout would be a sitting duck for appreciative enemy fighter pilots and gunners.

Quarr wondered if they were merely in the wrong place at the wrong time. How could anyone have known of their visit from three hundred and seventeen light years away? To her knowledge, subspace-scanner gadgets were in their infancy. Therefore it would be impossible to detect a small scout in subspace and determine its exact exit point from light years away.

It was inconceivable that hostile forces were waiting to ambush or destroy their ship. This was supposed to be a secret destination, unknown to even Kryger and the Council of Elders. Impossible as it seemed, they *were* expected, that much she could glean from a stronger and somewhat isolated thought

9

source. As far as she was aware, no human or other creature could read her thoughts unless she deliberately opened her mind, which was something she never did. She was absolutely sure that there were no spies on Nevus, so how could anyone have known that she would arrive here at this moment?

Navigators entered the destination coordinates into the jump-control computer only when they were out of the gravity field of a planet, and a ship would never emerge anywhere near a planet for the same reason. No one else on Nevus could have known the coordinates. She barely remembered the information relayed to her by her mother while in extreme agony near death.

Quarr was familiar with Kryger's all out behavior during evasive action, and she'd always lost consciousness during the high gravities generated in the first extreme maneuver to outwit the opposition. She abhorred the often-repeated experience, but preferred to stay alive, so she had to prepare since she probably had less than thirty seconds to gather information after entry into normal space.

The exit warning sounded sharply three times indicating that "pop-out" will be exactly ten seconds after the last bleep. As the usual, momentary, gut wrenching, nauseous exit sensation—which made one feel as if you were being ripped inside-out—started, the collision alarm shrilled harshly and almost made the ping that signaled release for manual control inaudible.

The scout popped out into normal space at the scientifically calculated "safe" speed of ten kilometers per second. This particular scoutship was capable of achieving more than twenty times that speed when pushed to the limit.

Kryger's trained reflexes were incredibly fast and the scout was designed to be superbly nimble, responsive, and tough. He had less than a second to avoid a collision with a stationary battleship that was parked sideways about ten kilometers away, directly in front of the exit point. His reaction was instinctive. He forcefully jerked the joystick between his knees as far back as it would go and just barely lifted the scout over the enormous ship. There wasn't time to sum up the situation or think of suitable names to characterize the miscalculating commander of the battleship.

As the scout flashed closely past the gigantic hull, he let out an involuntary pent-up breath. *I saw the traction-beam operator duck sideways in his seat just as we were about to scrape his bubble turret off the ship—as if that would have saved him if we were successful. I suppose it was too much to hope for that he didn't tighten up with fright before he ducked,* he thought wistfully as he took stock of the situation.

His traction-beam was pointing way off target, as if he expected us somewhere else. He couldn't even have caught our shadow if we had one. I'm guessing it's only experimental equipment, that somehow they can now trace a ship in subspace, so this is all new stuff and not too accurate yet. Very interesting, I must say. Perhaps we have run into more intelligent humanoids than the Bikans, or perhaps the Bikans have stolen yet another invention.

Quarr didn't know how much time there would be before Kryger was forced into serious evasive action to dodge traction beams, or into a battle in which she would inevitably lose consciousness. She hastily scanned the shocked, wide-open minds in the battleship, identifying the commander and ruthlessly invading his mind. She gained the knowledge she sought within a few seconds—including a nasty, unexpected surprise.

Perhaps it was by design or just fate, but as the scout's trajectory carried them past the battleship, a cruiser loomed up almost directly in their path, less than a hundred kilometers away. As Quarr calmly told him that fighting craft were already pouring out of the battleship like innumerable, scattered fish eggs, he watched a turret on the cruiser swing their way while a traction beam was being powered-up. Perhaps a long wait had dulled their reflexes, or they'd thought that one traction-beam was enough to snare an unsuspecting, surprised quarry as it emerged from subspace. Kryger thought it sloppy, amateurish planning, and weighed their chances of escaping from the trap by running. He realized that he'd have to fight his way out when the faintly red-glowing traction beam shot out sooner than expected from the turret on the heavy cruiser, now only about fifty kilometers away. No ship, however fast, could outrun traction or beam weapons unless it had a head start of a few hundred kilometers. And the farther one was away, the easier it was to be accurate with beam weapons.

While casting a hasty glance at the rearview monitor for fighters on his tail, Kryger evaded the grabber-beam by looping the nimble little scout sideways and then underneath the faintly visible beam. Still heading toward the cruiser, he briefly straightened the scout's flight-path to lure the beam-operator. The beam wobbled jerkily as the operator made adjustments to follow, but the scout was too fast and elusive for the outdated, manually operated mechanism. Pushing the throttles forward for more speed, Kryger lifted the craft in a wide, seemingly lazy loop over the beam to make it difficult for the operator, then straightened the flight path for a moment to align the crosshairs and trigger one of the nuclear missiles.

It was overkill, like shooting an annoying predator with an explosive missile that would normally be used by ground troops to destroy barriers. Then he chided himself for allowing his mind to wander any which-way on irrelevant thoughts. Their opponents, perhaps caught by surprise after a monotonous, long wait, should not be given time to wake up and anticipate his reactions. He had to retaliate fast and furiously.

He was too close to the target, and as the missile flashed away, he looped below the ascending grabber-beam and banked the scout sharply away as he stabbed the master switch to simultaneously activate all force-shields to protect the scout from the expected vicious blast and accompanying debris.

A moment later, he felt the initial, slight slowdown as the traction-beam locked onto the scout just as the cruiser exploded in a brief, soundless flash of blinding light. The shockwave tumbled the little scout violently and seemingly out of control for what felt like an eternity.

He felt disorientated, but couldn't afford the luxury of taking time off to recover if he wanted to escape this elaborate trap. As if to remind him to pay attention to his whereabouts, a beam from a fighter bounced off the half-extended left atmospheric wing, briefly changing the color of the shield to a reddish tint.

Another quick glance at the rear-vision monitor showed a number of fighters spread out in formation close behind and edging out to his left, as if trying to herd him somewhere or away from something. He briefly wondered how they had escaped damage, but it was irrelevant. He felt the familiar, heady surge of combat acceptance, which made his body feel slow in responding to commands from his brain.

They must be feeble-minded! They can't be Bikans, for their behavior and methods are different, but I hope they too can't take the physical punishment of high gravities. They give the impression that they are novices, and it seems that they don't know much about battle formations. I've already shown them that I can bite viciously and that this fight's for real; not a precise formation-flying show-off, he thought. *They act irresponsibly. Are they trying to impress me into meek submission, or are they just playing dumb as a ploy to sucker me into some other kind of trap? I'll use the MAG, but first I have to get behind them for a test shot. Then I'll see how they behave in real combat.*

He slammed the twin throttles to maximum power and executed a sudden, fairly tight head-over-heels flip-roll to turn the scout to face them. The heavy gravities tore at his guts, but as expected, the enemy pilots weren't prepared for this unusual, confusing maneuver. Kryger thought that if the scout was to survive, he had to determine the top speed their craft were capable of, because they were too close on his tail.

He once again executed the tight head-over-heels backward flip-roll to get behind them. He came out of the flip-roll in line with the leftmost fighter—which was much farther away than it should have been in comparison to a Bikan fighter—and lined up the visor-sight for the MAG just as they started a belated, slow, precision turn, still in neat parade-formation, to come after him.

They must be fresh-out-of-training recruits, and their instructors know sweet-blow-all about warfare, he thought. But he was in a position to retaliate and it didn't make any difference that they were obeying senseless orders. They would realize soon enough that they couldn't capture the scout by doing show-maneuvers and thus leave themselves open to retaliation. They should know that they have to disable the scout first, but he would appreciate it if there weren't a single independent thinking entity among them.

He heard a very faint click when he activated the trigger, which was linked to the joystick, but there was no recoil or visible indication that the weapon was functioning at all. He thought that he must have missed, which he found hard to believe. His score with any weapon was faultless. He had a natural aptitude for any weapon, however strange, and the helmet-aiming device was finely tuned for accuracy. *Did it malfunction?*

Anger replaced disappointment. Now he had to turn tail and run, and hope that the scout was fast enough to outrun them. *It was catastrophic for this untested weapon to fail. It must be misaligned, or a dud, a cruel joke which can only end in disaster.* The bitter thoughts took no time at all, but a moment later he had to bank sharply to avoid crashing into the fighter, which suddenly lost power and was not participating in the slow turn. He realized that he had expected an immediate, visible result, such as a spectacular explosion, and not just a quiet cessation of life and activity. He should have remembered that not even beam weapons were instantaneous.

Savage satisfaction replaced anger, and he thought elatedly that the invisible bolt must have gone from the rear end all the way through the cockpit, via the ill-fated pilot of the hapless fighter, because there was nothing to stop the matter annihilating charge.

They must be quite an unimaginative bunch, Kryger thought as he followed the formation in their somewhat slow, copybook turn. He remembered being told that the weapon was still experimental and that it took a second to recharge, but by now it should be ready again. *Fifty-eight bolts left,* he reminded himself as another fighter and pilot died quietly and unspectacularly.

Still confused by their quarry's unorthodox maneuver, the squadron belatedly realized that they were being attacked from behind. They suddenly panicked, scattered helter-skelter, and three fighters collided, dying silently as they broke up into debris. Kryger killed five more in as many seconds before the arena became temporarily empty. He looked around, wondering what had happened to the rest.

Perhaps he kept the scout steady for a moment too long. When the scout was suddenly grabbed, he realized that he had been suckered, at a heavy price, into ignoring the battleship, which could be seen clearly less than fifty kilometers away to his left. The Bikans—the only enemy they knew of, and had fought until now—used enormous carrier ships to transport a host of fighters, with no escorts of any kind. Kryger had automatically reverted to the norm and had ignored the fact that this wasn't a confrontation with the maniacal, suicidal, predictable Bikans.

No one knew why the Bikans and their sponsors did not develop their own weaponry. It was well known that they were avid collectors of other civilizations' inventions, always on the lookout for new weapons, and even destroying entire civilizations in an effort to get their grasping hands on useful weapon technology. Maybe they were too lazy to think and just too fond of the mayhem and destruction that accompanied their savage raids. He was all too aware that his deadly little weapon must not fall into enemy hands, and that the scout must not be captured with their shielding technology.

While these thoughts flashed through his mind, he noted that the scout was gripped with the nose pointing toward the battleship at an angle of about eighty degrees. Under normal circumstances, resistance wouldn't alter the final outcome, but the scout had one bite left. If that failed, the only alternative was to self-destruct.

A locked-on traction-beam couldn't nullify the normal operation of instruments or weapons, but it would pull a power-assisted missile directly toward the traction-tube generator much faster than a craft, which would be applying reverse thrust for resistance. He couldn't activate the force shields with the traction-beam gripping the scout, because the generators would overload almost immediately and melt or explode, but the missile would kill the beam-generators a split-second before the battleship exploded. *A pity that the shields cannot be activated automatically the moment the traction ceased*. The realization hit him that no one had thought of it before.

He activated the side-thrust boosters on the locked-on side to resist the pull—not that it would make much difference, but it might just buy them that little bit of extra time and distance by pushing them away in the final moment when the traction-beam generator was destroyed. He hoped that his reflexes were fast enough to activate the shields in that split-second, which might give them a slim chance of survival. As the scout strained to break away with engines screaming, he aligned the remaining missile and sent it on its way without hesitation. There was no other option.

If the missile malfunctioned and the MAG couldn't turn far enough, he would trigger the self-destruct mechanism the moment they were pulled alongside or inside the ship. To him, death was not important, but how he died was what counted. He faced death in every battle, and forced self-destruction was not so much different, especially if it was the only alternative to a slow death by torture. He had seen too many cruel atrocities committed by the Bikans, and wouldn't let any enemy touch, let alone torture, Quarr.

The unconscious watch his brain always kept on Quarr's welfare registered that she had regained consciousness

15

a moment before the scout leapt free—a mere instant before the battleship blew up spectacularly, which he only saw for a moment before his visor blackened. As his finger was ready on the shield-power master-control button, he instinctively stabbed it the moment it felt as if the scout hesitated. There were a number of dull thuds against the outer hull an instant before the shields flashed into existence.

The explosion was violent beyond imagination. The little scout was blown away with an unbelievable force that sent it spinning and tumbling into the vastness of the space-sea. Kryger briefly had time to wonder what the ship had carried that caused such havoc, because the warhead in the missile wasn't *that* powerful. The scout wouldn't break up easily, and he hoped that the armor plating and shielding around the engines' nuclear power converters weren't damaged, since it wouldn't be good if they woke up in a radioactive wreck in the middle of nowhere with help unreachable, light years away. It didn't register that the mighty engines died when the debris hit the scout, because he felt smothered and crushed, unable to catch his breath due to the astounding rapid acceleration. He fought the exceedingly increasing gravities and the blackness that threatened to engulf him with every iota of his willpower, but there was a limit to what any being could endure. For the first time in his short life, he lost consciousness.

As quiet as a tomb, the slowly tumbling, spinning scout sped away from the awful havoc—by sheer coincidence—in the general direction of the distant sun, which was Quarr's intended destination.

3

As consciousness reluctantly returned, Kryger noted, with wry amusement, that the scout was completely silent. The only light in the cockpit was a faint reflection from the life-support instruments. He wasn't fully conscious yet, and it took some time for his bemused brain to register that the ever-present growl of the engines was absent, which explained the loss of the little bit of gravity that made life so much more comfortable. When a spacecraft's engines quit, non-life-supporting devices automatically switched off after a short period. Only vital equipment received emergency power in the absence of human intervention.

The half-lucid thought that nagged at his dull-functioning brain was that he had to go outside to check the damage and try to repair whatever he could before reporting the ambush or calling for help, which would arrive too late to be of use if a few of the enemy fighters had miraculously survived the awe-inspiring explosion.

He shook his head to clear the grogginess, then winced and regretted that he had been so enthusiastic. It felt as if the little bits of brain-matter that were left sloshed around in his cranium. A vicious headache throbbed as if someone were using a sledgehammer inside his head with every heartbeat and threatened to explode out of his eyes and forehead. He functioned in a dull sort of way and realized that he had better get his lazy rear-end into gear and do something meaningful about their predicament. He needed to determine the scout's status and start repairs.

He managed to mentally check his body, and was relieved to feel nothing broken or out of place. He assumed that he could live, as always, with sore muscles and bruises where the harness had bitten into his body.

Although he was concerned about Quarr's welfare, his first duty was to scan for company before he could check on how she had fared. Only then could he look for painkillers in the emergency-aid box. She might need them even more than him.

It felt as if his eyes were throbbing rhythmically with the terrible headache. He blinked a number of times before dimly discerning the instrument panel. He fumbled for the scanners' switches before flipping them on. The instruments came to life, but it seemed that there was nothing worth detecting in a sphere two million kilometers across. Either he was seeing what he wanted to see, or the instruments had been damaged. Then he did a perfunctory check of the automatic locator instrument, but the readings were different from what he had remembered. They were millions of kilometers away from their point of emergence from subspace, and if he were able to purse his lips for a whistle, he would have done so.

As a matter of principle he tried the engine-start switches, but there was no response, not even a click. He checked their course. They were drifting more or less toward a faint, far-away, orange-green sun. He grinned fleetingly, but only in his thoughts, as he once again wondered what the battleship had carried that could have caused such a great-grandmother of an explosion. He wondered if the commander had awakened to realize that his physical body was just scattered atoms, together with his ship and his command.

He ached all over and desperately wanted to go back to sleep, but forced himself to release the harness straps. This was the critical time; a time when some people would take the lazy way out and perhaps lose their lives. After all, it's easier to lapse into comfortable sleep than to force awareness and action. After disconnecting his oxygen line from the main supply, he plugged it into the emergency container, a permanent part of his lightweight space suit.

He shifted in the narrow seat, fumbled the small sliding door on his left open, and slowly pulled his weightless body through into the navigation compartment. *At least the door wasn't jammed,* he thought dully, *and I don't have to cope with gravity in this nauseous condition. I hope this never happens again. Now I understand what Quarr must endure after a dogfight.*

Although he realized in a dim sort of way that it was caused by the excruciating, throbbing headache, the rational part of his mind worried about his mental tardiness and inability to focus on one thing at a time. He couldn't afford to allow his mind to wander.

He found Quarr still unconscious, but breathing normally, as if she'd lapsed into sleep. The web was intact and her neck and limbs seemed to be at their normal angles. He hooked a foot under the navigator's seat to keep himself anchored, fumbled, and released the harness as dizziness threatened to overwhelm him. The weightlessness was a blessing, since it wasn't necessary to support her body and thus expend energy he didn't have. He lifted her slowly and gently out of the seat, moved her to the pull-down sleeper in the narrow compartment behind the seat, and strapped her down again.

Gently but rapidly, he felt along her backbone with three fingers held tightly together through the silky material of the tight fitting space suit. Her vertebra felt intact on the surface. He then checked her ribs by running his fingers along both sides and gently applying pressure. He checked her arms and legs for obvious breaks before glancing at the cockpit-pressure gauge.

The reading seemed normal, so he sat down sideways on the navigator's seat and opened his faceplate, then slammed it shut again in reflex to the unexpected voice in his head as his aching stomach muscles tightened simultaneously from shock.

You delude yourself, brother. You'll need plenty of practice to develop a gentle touch. If you're truly that concerned—I hurt all over from head to toe. There's no internal damage that I'm aware of, but my ribs ache a little; perhaps from your "gentle" touch, but more likely from your vicious maneuvers and the blast. Yikes. You really played havoc with our adversaries, and almost succeeded in destroying us at the same time. I didn't even have time to feel sorry for myself, or them, for that matter. Let me know well in advance the next time you contemplate suicide, so I can at least compose myself for the inevitable. Then again, I should be used to it by now. Wow! You look as dreadful as I feel.

He felt more alert after the sudden shock, but his head now throbbed with a terrible vengeance. He didn't explain or apologize, for he sensed that Quarr was just talking to gather her wits.

"You scared the daylights out of me, Quarr. Don't do that again! Your comment on my looks is a deliberate understatement to dupe me into thinking that I feel better than I am. If I look the way I feel, I must be a tragicomic sight. It's just as well that there aren't any mirrors in the scout to add to my misery. I feel as if I've been trampled by a herd of vengeful mammoths, and they're still enthusiastically playing football with my head, or in my head—I'm not sure which. Anyway, I couldn't check for a broken back, ribs, and bones by caressing you."

Quarr gently removed her helmet—being careful not to shake her head in an attempt to clear the cobwebs, since she sensed the possible consequence in his mind.

Silently he handed her some restoratives, headache capsules, and a squeeze-bulb of water before he opened his faceplate again to gulp down double the prescribed doses of both, as if twice the normal dosage would double the effect or make him feel better twice as fast. It wasn't necessary to talk or send thoughts to Quarr, because she always kept herself well aware of all his thoughts, even the intimate ones. She felt no compunction at all to read his mind whenever she felt like it, which was most of the time. It didn't bother him, as he didn't have improper thoughts or a guilty conscience, and he knew that she would never use or repeat any information she gathered. To her it was the most practical way to be ready for whatever he had in mind.

Intercepting what he was thinking, Quarr thought, *He only needs time to develop. Let him think that I can always sense his thoughts for the time being. He doesn't understand that I can't read his thoughts all the time; that there are moments he instinctively shuts his mind so completely that I can't even penetrate his public mind…it's quite remarkable.*

She sent a calm, unrelated thought into his mind. *I'll check and repair damage inside. You get the engines operating again—quickly—before you check the hull. We may not have enough time for all repairs. I sense a couple of surviving fighter pilots scouring space in all directions, hoping that we survived the horrifying explosion "we caused." Very considerate, isn't it? I can sense their resentful thoughts. They have some nerve. We didn't ask to be waylaid. They've signaled for help, which they are hoping would arrive in about half a standard day, if at all. We must finish repairs sooner than that, because it's just a matter of time before they head in this direction to go home.*

I wasn't able to determine how they knew, but they were after our shield-generators, which they hadn't been able to steal as yet, because we're the only civilization that has such technology. What really stunned me was that the late commander of the battleship was expecting me, personally, as part of the booty, although he had no idea what I looked like. What I did find out though, is that the ship had experimental subspace-scanner equipment on board to determine where we would pop out. It was developed by a traitor, one of my own people, and close family to boot! It could detect a ship some light years away and calculate an approximate exit point.

Quarr paused as she was struck by a sudden realization. *By checking our line of flight, they could probably determine where we came from. I just hope both the battleship and information were destroyed before the data could be passed on.*

She shivered. *I also gathered that an alleged immortal being—a very powerful entity by the name of Gorrel—ordered the ambush. The commander deduced that it had been at the request of the developer of the subspace-detector unit. This Gorrel may well be one of the ancient enemies my people fled from a few centuries ago. I can sense the evil thoughts of the creature, and it is chuckling with glee at this very moment in an attempt to ruffle my feathers. Keep a constant, tight shield around your mind, Kryger. Don't let it slip for an instant! Don't succumb to the urge to send out a call for help, either.*

"How are you able to sense thoughts without knowing the person, or their personal mental wavelengths?" Kryger wondered out loud. The range of her powerful mind never ceased to amaze him. He was no slouch either, but as his mentors had told him long ago, he had a load of untapped potential that could only be developed by his own efforts, at his own pace, and in his own way. No one else could do it for him or even give him a clue as to how to go about it.

Quarr replied with laughter in her thoughts. *Easily! You've been a good boy and I'll try to teach you sometime…even how to hide your thoughts from me. Mike and your parents trained you. They did an excellent job, but they didn't have enough knowledge. Okay, they trained me as well, but I have a different makeup, and young as I was when your parents found me, I had already undergone intensive, advanced instruction. You can be trained too, but it won't be easy on either one of us, because you have a stubborn streak, which is an obstacle. Now go outside, headache and all, and repair what can be repaired before they head this way, or we'll regret that we've wasted time on social chitchatting.*

Kryger didn't need to see her shiver again to believe that Gorrel existed, and that it was an utterly evil creature. His own talents were still relatively untrained, as his mind was mostly occupied with developing new tricks and methods to beat the odds in the survival game. Mike—which was an abbreviation used for the Main Artificial Intelligence Center on Nevus—had urged him to make an effort to develop his unique talents and potential. He sometimes had intuitive flashes of that potential, but never took the time to follow through. *Perhaps it's time to make time for it,* he thought as he closed his faceplate before exiting through the one-man airlock. As soon as he was outside, he attached the oxygen and safety lines to his suit, since the emergency bottle wouldn't last another twenty minutes without requiring a refill.

The tough outer hull was severely dented in more places than he cared to count. The dents wouldn't impact the scout's performance, but a sizable chunk of debris had smashed a large hole through the tail section just underneath the atmospheric rudder, partly severing the bottom of the rudder where it was anchored to the top of the curve above the twin thrust tubes. Closer inspection revealed almost catastrophic damage inside the gap. By a rare million-to-one chance, the nexus for the subspace-inverter on top of the twin engines had been in the path of the debris. They were stranded in normal space unless they could replace the nexus.

Damn, he thought, *the one thing that's too big to carry a spare for. It may be lucky for us that the damage wasn't worse, but we'll see. No wonder I felt it an instant before the shields came on.*

As his headache gradually disappeared, almost unnoticed, so did Quarr's admonishment to keep a tight shield around his thoughts. Not feeling the presence of anyone trying to intercept his thoughts, he tried to get hold of Mike, his parents, twin sisters, and brother in that sequence, on a beam as tight and as narrow as he could make it, but he was unable to establish contact with anyone. Perhaps they were out of his range. There never before was a need to mind-call them from light years away, so the limit of his sending power was still undetermined.

His brain felt dull and drained of all energy and he felt the numbing chill of deep space through the sophisticated space suit. *Damn this depressing feeling of impending disaster,* he thought. *But while I have some life left, I will fight. I should have swallowed a few ration tablets before I ventured outside, but when one has to exist on those tasteless, unappetizing pills, sometimes for weeks, normal eating habits and hunger are quietly suppressed. Why can't they at least have different flavors?*

Spacecraft always carried essential spares. Navigators and pilots were trained to repair minor damage. The instrument he was holding didn't indicate radiation leaks, but even if it did, he would've had to bypass the inverter by disconnecting what had remained of the nexus and connect the engines directly to the starting mechanism. Luckily, the tight fitting, flexible gloves of the seemingly flimsy space suit didn't hamper normal working methods and were almost impossible to tear as long as one avoided sharp objects and ragged edges.

He worked swiftly, but carefully, to repair and reconnect conduits and electrical cables that fed and controlled the armor-encased engines. Their lives were at stake and he had no idea how much time they had. Quarr had very fast reflexes and could handle scouts and fighters as well as anyone—if not better—but she didn't have the ruthlessness to kill without considering the lives she would be snuffing out, which was why she became a navigator instead. Anyway, he knew that she wouldn't leave him to die in space to save her own life. He was surprised to note that he had been working for more than three hours already, and he was almost frozen, despite the insulation and built-in heating. He hadn't slept for more than thirty hours, and wasn't surprised that his thoughts were as sluggish as cold treacle.

At last the repairs were completed, and used to always being monitored by Quarr, he asked on a tight, narrow beam, *How are things at your end, Quarr? I'm nearly finished, but there's nothing I can do about the nexus. I can't reach anyone to report our problem and ask for help. Could you try, please?*

He received no reassuring or even caustic reply, which was cause for concern. He tried again, but she remained silent. When he really concentrated, he couldn't even sense the presence of her mind. *It was rather unusual for her not to comment caustically on my slow progress from time to time,* he thought dully. *Did she lose consciousness again, or did she have an accident?* Quickly, but meticulously, he replaced the access plates, and after a last look around to check that everything was in place, anxiously made his way back to the airlock, concerned about Quarr's wellbeing.

4

Kryger disconnected the oxygen and regulation safety lines, made sure that their storage compartment was locked, and hurriedly entered the airlock. He saw Quarr motionless on her back, underneath a pullout panel, but she moved her head to look up at him as the narrow airlock hissed open. She spoke even before the inner hatch closed. Her melodious voice was beautiful, merry and lilting—in total contrast with her serious mien—as if her vocal cords were meant for wondrous melodies and not for something as common as ordinary speech.

"So, Kryger—" he imagined that she sang the words, "—did it register on your stunted perceptions that we're mentally isolated? The enemy must have raided a civilization that had developed a solar-system-wide damper that prevents mind-to-mind communication. I doubt they were smart enough to develop the technology on their own, even if they had combined all off their brain matter, and had thrown it together in half a grass-warbler's egg. This thought-exchange inhibitor is not the same kind of intelligence-destroying suppression that we—I mean your parents and I—experienced in the Bikan city. We have to get away to report this new development.

"The malignant thoughts I received earlier were a deliberate slip to make me panic and do something dim-witted—like signaling for help or returning to base. This entity has too powerful a mind for such a blunder. I have a feeling that this Gorrel and its kind might be the power behind the Bikans.

"Did you repair the damage outside? It took you long enough—just over *four* hours. Did you fall asleep or did you have too much fun out there?"

Quarr's conversation was to bring him up to date, since he obviously had not experienced the same phenomenon. He replied with a negative shake of his head. "Try working out there for an hour or two sometime. It's a freezing, lonely experience, and to gulp down a shriveled stomach every few seconds isn't my idea of fun. Yes, I repaired the damage to the engines, but the nexus of the subspace-inverter has been destroyed, so we won't be returning home in a hurry," he informed her without any sugarcoating. "I disconnected what was left of it and connected the engines directly to the starting mechanism. It's up to you to find the planet the enemy originated from. We're going to have to raid them for another nexus, or another FTL craft if possible. If we can't, we're stranded until we can locate and destroy the suppressor and call for help.

"It may sound incredulous, but I thought of something out there in the deep-freezer. If we had the ability to jump into subspace for a second or two with the push of a button, the damage may have been avoided or it could have been less severe. If we make it back, I'll ask the programmers and engineers to look into such a possibility. And if they can, they should make the nexus smaller so that a scout could carry a spare, or they should, if possible, enclose it in armor as they do with the engines."

"We're in a bit of a precarious situation," Quarr said in a tone of voice so vibrant, leaving the impression that she was laughingly looking forward to the experience. "It was inconceivable that a nexus could ever malfunction. We couldn't very well signal for help before we'd assessed the damage, and my mother told me that it's too dangerous to use mind-send between the stars, because it can alert our old enemy if they, by chance, are looking for another planet to add to their larders. They are predators and they prefer humanoids to any other prey.

"I've warned the Council, and they've in turn warned all espers—including you—to use very short bursts in code, on a narrow beam, on the predetermined wavelengths—and only when it's *absolutely necessary.* I hope you hadn't forgotten." She squinted at him.

"Ah! You tried to, didn't you? I saw you wince! We have to accept that we're on our own. I'm afraid, Kryger…dreadfully afraid. I've never ever encountered such a powerful, cruel, *cold* mind. The Bikans at least enjoyed it when they tortured my mother, but this creature is so coldly pitiless and devoid of feeling that I've no words to describe it. I'm sure the words *compassion* and *pity* don't exist in its vocabulary."

Kryger smiled. He couldn't help it. Her melodious, cheery voice would encourage the worst pessimist in the most hopeless situation. "I'm sorry, I forgot. There's no way we could return home in our lifetime without a jump-craft, unless we learned how to teleport to a destination light years away." Something vaguely nagged for recognition in the back of his mind, but he was tired, dull, and hungry, and couldn't concentrate.

25

"I agree, but we won't give up based on a little setback like this," Quarr replied, banishing the thought that was about to penetrate Kryger's consciousness. "I only found one planet in this solar system that can support oxygen breathers. Let's see if the engines will start. I saw three blips at the extreme limit of our detection units about twenty minutes ago. They're heading this way on a zigzag course; acting very innocent, as if they're out for a leisurely, early morning sightseeing flight. But I'll bet anything that they will go to max as soon as we power up the engines. They will be here in about an hour and a half at their present speed, and I think they're under the impression that they are sneaking up on us."

"Okay. We can run and fight on one engine if we have to. The hole under the rudder was too big to repair. It's possible that there could be internal damage. Which way do you want to go?"

"That way," She smiled and pointed a finger a fraction to the left of the distant sun. "I'll give you a precise course shortly."

Kryger checked the relevant instruments, then flipped the first of the two engine-starting switches to the ignite position. He listened to the faint whine and carefully checked if there were abnormal sounds or vibrations when the engine started. He let it idle for a few seconds and then started the other engine. The emergency power switched off automatically, and the normal tenth of downward gravity-pull and all instruments were restored. While he listened attentively to the growling engines, he gradually increased power.

"A couple of fighters are now heading directly this way under what seems to be full power and they're accelerating like mad." Although she tried to be level, unemotional, and matter-of-fact, her melodious voice sounded amused over the intercom. "Perhaps they only detected us when you started the engines and they may be broadcasting our location. I can hear excited chattering on the radio, but I don't understand the lingo. It's not Bikan, and not remotely similar to any other language we have knowledge of. It's a pity I can't pick up the thoughts behind the gibberish. On the other hand, I think I detect a note of disappointment in their voices, as if they thought they had fooled us."

"They're suckers for punishment. Or perhaps they are suicidal like the deranged Bikans. Do they have a built-in 'death or glory, wish, or are they just chasing us because we seem to be running in the direction they'd like us to go? Okay, to please them, I'll go to full power. It's the best way to see if the engines can handle it and whether those guys can keep up. I know they're fast, but I'd like to know exactly how fast." He didn't have to tell her that they would either be dead or captured—which meant the same thing—if the engines cut out completely and he didn't have enough time to check and repair the problem. He decided that if the engines quit or malfunctioned, he'd go outside immediately and detach the deadly little weapon. It was easy enough.

Kryger pushed both throttles forward slowly with a sincere prayer in his mind that there was no damage he had missed. The engines responded with a deep-throated, joyful growl of power and the little ship seemed to leap forward eagerly. As far as he knew, no known spacecraft could catch a Nevus-built scout at full thrust in normal space. *I wonder if there's a reason why they don't protect the nexus. I thought it irrelevant and never asked, because we are taught that it didn't even need maintenance checks,* he thought as he listened for irregularity in the far-off, throaty song of power.

"They're losing the race. If both the engines quit now, you'll have a little less than half an hour to fix the problem," Quarr said after fifteen minutes.

"Then let us outdistance them completely. I'll be magnanimous and let them live to die another day, since we've already scrapped a fortune in spacecraft for them."

Quarr didn't comment, because she was thinking of something else. After she handed him a packet of rations and a bulb of water, she spent the next three hours fiddling under panels and behind plates. He assumed that she was rechecking repairs, because she never took chances. He occupied himself by listening to the engines and watching the instruments. The dots on the detector-screen quickly dwindled until they disappeared. He thought that these fighters, although astonishingly fast, couldn't even smell the exhaust fumes of a Nevusian-built war-craft.

Quarr returned to her instruments and made a small course correction.

"We should reach the planet in about eighty minutes at current speed," she informed him. "It has a single moon—which is big and could almost be a smaller planet—coming up in forty two minutes. By a strange quirk of fate, it is directly between us and the planet. I'll do some instrument scouting. Why did you keep full power on all the time? We've lost our pursuers hours ago."

"I'd like to enter the planet's atmosphere without a fight, if possible. For a while I entertained the foolish notion that we could perhaps catch them half prepared. I'm worried that the structure under the rudder is weakened because of the hole, and that it might not be strong enough to withstand the severe buffeting if we entered the atmosphere at high-speed. I'd prefer to slow down quite a lot when we reach the planet. As you know only too well, we can't bail out at high speed or use the gravity neutralizer too high up in the sky. I was ordered not to abandon the new weapon, and I'll crash-land alone if it comes to that. My gut feeling is that the same little weapon may be the only thing that will help us overcome extreme dangers on the planet, because we only have the big needle-guns as hand weapons."

"I've done something to help you if the rudder misbehaves. I connected the side, upper, and lower thrusters to the atmospheric controls. You'll still have directional control with the thrusters if the rudder tears off. The scout will be more frolicsome in the atmosphere than you're used to, so be careful not to be heavy-handed or you'll have us doing spectacular, weird, and dangerous aerobatics without appreciative spectators. I don't know why the designers didn't think of doing it. It's logical and easy enough."

"Perhaps they did think of it, but abandoned the idea as too dangerous, impractical, or unnecessary. Thanks Quarr. You're a genius!"

"I know. I studied hard enough while you played the lonesome hero. You've become a danger to yourself, which is why I'm your navigator and guardian angel," Quarr retorted, seeming angry, but her tone softened immediately. "I've also made a slight change so that you can use the MAG without disabling the forward shield. When you press the button to activate the trigger, the shielding mechanism will instantly generate a small opening in whichever way the MAG's generated tube is pointed, and just long enough for the bolt to pass through. Of course I didn't test it, but I've used the same technique for making openings for side-thrusters and the main engines. I wonder why they didn't think of it for all weapons. It's so obvious."

28

"That's brilliant, Quarr! Exploiting the overlooked obvious." His voice conveyed a sincere tone of admiration.

She continued as if she didn't hear him: "I should have told you before, but when the Bikans captured my mother on Nevus, she implanted the location of this planet in my mind in the hope that I might survive and find a way to return. A colony of my people settled here about fifty years before our craft crashed on Nevus. My mother suspected that we were ingeniously sabotaged with the intention to murder us.

"I suspect that your race and mine have a common enemy—a force that drives races under its control to conquer and eventually destroy planets with intelligent life. My knowledge is incomplete, but if I remember correctly, we've been fighting this destructive enemy for much, much longer than you have, because your people arrived more recently in this part of the galaxy. It seems that we were always on the run. It destroyed our home planet two or three centuries ago.

"I suspect that Gorrel's race controls and manipulates the mad Bikans, and many other races on hundreds of planets. I don't know our history, for I've been out of touch with my people for a little more than twenty years, and only vaguely remember my mother. Family members are sort of a blur. As a matter of fact, I can't even remember my *true* shape. I've been relying on you to take me back to my people when the time comes— assuming my race survived."

Kryger sensed that she wasn't telling him the whole story; that there was information she wasn't prepared to share with him. "Does that explain some of the out-of-the-way scouting trips we secretly undertook, or were we truly looking for signs of enemy occupation on those planets? If you'd asked Dad or me, we would've made it easy for you to find your people. Why didn't you tell us?"

"Those special trips you are referring to were legitimate, ordered by the wise, but dried-out old prune-faces in Command Council. I know that I could've asked, but there were reasons why I couldn't. Increased search activity and mind-messages between the stars can draw inimical attention to Nevus, and I don't wish that on the people who saved my life and befriended me. Once the enemy knows about Nevus and its location, the planet may be destroyed, or worse, laid to waste as unconquerable and dangerous. Fortunately, the Bikans seem to have mislaid the location of the planet they call 'New Bika,' or

29

they deliberately withheld the information from their sponsors, which is something to be grateful for. Anyway, I chose the best fighter pilot on the planet, so I've all the help I need and want."

Kryger distrusted compliments from her and he never fell for it. It was usually a prelude to a sarcastic comment about something he did not do quite right. It must be frustrating to be sad or angry, and sound cheerful about it. In retrospect, she didn't have a large pool of pilots to choose from, for Nevus was still sparsely populated, and many women were fighting as gunners and pilots. Although Nevus was quite heavily defended by planet-based installations, spaceships always returned home via the nearby Great Cluster to throw would-be trackers off their trail—which may soon be a waste of valuable time because of this working subspace-scanner invention.

"Thank you for the compliment…I think. I saw a shadow flash out briefly from behind the moon and then make a rapid U-turn. Did your instruments register anything, or were you concentrating on dishing up underhanded compliments so that you can insult me?" Her compliments made him very uncomfortable if he couldn't sense her real feelings.

"I was serious, and I know what I'm talking about. Believe me, Kryger," she answered in a quiet, preoccupied tone of voice, though it still sounded like repressed laughter, which told him that she was serious, but that her mind was elsewhere. "I noticed the shadow. I think it was a deliberate move to attract our attention. There's more than one shadow behind the curve of the moon. It was fast, so it may be interceptor craft waiting for us to come closer."

He knew her well enough to know that this compliment was actually sincere. There had always been an unbreakable, inexplicable bond between the two of them, which wasn't obvious to outsiders except—his own family, of which she was a well-loved, unofficially adopted member.

5

Unaware of the train of thought her compliment provoked, Quarr calmly continued, "I think that brief flash was a ploy to divert our attention away from the camouflaged observation station on this side of the moon, which seems to be in communication with them. My surveillance equipment indicate that there's more hidden than revealed under that innocent-looking dome—which, by the way, is not a force field like our shields, but a real, transparent, manufactured dome to keep air inside. Puncture it with our peashooter as we pass over it, although I suspect they'll shoot first.

"I detect six pairs of Interceptors behind the moon, but there may be more further back; I'll keep an eye on them while you take care of this fake observatory. Here's your target identification."

She pressed a key to transfer the image and the coordinates to the target-panel in front of him, so he could adjust the flight-path of the scout. She could have done the course correction herself, but that meant that she would momentarily take the control away from him, which could be a fatal mistake while within reach of the enemy. Her reactions were exceptionally fast, but she couldn't match Kryger's reaction time.

"The shields are on full power for the eventuality that they take a pot shot or two at us as we come into range. Thanks to your brilliant idea, I just have to dip the nose to give them something to occupy themselves with."

The commander of the force manning the camouflaged battle station had been told of the failed ambush and warned to be on the lookout for the invaders who destroyed their only large ship and a host of fighting craft. The lonely little ship had been detected an hour before, and he could only believe that it was a hostile, advance scout when it didn't reply to the command to identify itself. He immediately ordered three heavy beam-weapons to be readied. To him, it was logical that such a small craft couldn't create the havoc the invaders were supposed to have caused, but he decided to play it safe and destroy the spy-craft, rather than catch it with a traction beam. As it came within range, he ordered two of the beam canons to fire simultaneously.

31

The commander knew nothing about shields, or even that such things existed, and couldn't be blamed for misjudging the toughness of the tiny ship and the fortitude of its occupants. In his experience, one direct hit by a single heavy beam was enough to blast a small ship like that to fragments.

Kryger was thoroughly aware that the impact of a direct hit, even with the shields on max, could kill them even though the scout would suffer only minor to no damage at all. He had a moment to dodge the two beams, but the third, fired a split second later by a nervous finger, struck the overlapping shields on the left side, which flared brilliantly as it deflected the force-beam. The scout shuddered, groaned in protest, and tipped onto its right side.

The brilliant flash blinded them for a split-second before their visors adjusted. Kryger's teeth ached and he thought he felt something bounce loosely inside his skull again as he shook his head in an effort to quickly clear his vision, but the salvo had pinpointed the heavy artillery for him.

If the shields didn't allow the MAG's bolt to pass at the precise moment it was triggered, he thought with grim humor, all their worries would be over, and they wouldn't even know that they were dead until they woke up in the afterlife. But if Quarr said something would work, then it definitely would.

He did some nimble sidestepping to dodge the all-too-accurate follow-up salvos. They were close to the dome when he hastily dipped the nose of the scout, aimed, grimaced, and triggered the MAG as they sped over the lonely battle station. It felt very wrong to engage the deadly weapon without first deactivating the forward shields, but he was grateful that Quarr had made the change, otherwise he would have had to return to attack at low level with the shields powered down, which was a chancy thing, but would have had to be done, because the enemy had long-range weapons and missiles.

"Your change worked perfectly," he calmly praised her.

That was the only recognition she wanted for a job well done, which was not normally in her line of duty. She didn't expect praise and she wouldn't give any for piloting brilliance. It was their respective functions; what they had trained for.

On her monitors and instruments, Quarr saw a surprisingly large explosion. An unexpectedly large area erupted on the airless moon as the scout sped on. She surmised that the bolt must have pierced a huge ammunition dump or a nuclear generator—very effectively destroying the entire base. She checked the analyzers.

"The explosion was nuclear," she commented. "I'd give a whole peanut to know what they stored there other than ammunition."

"Here they come like moths drawn to an open flame, again in copybook formation. They obviously have no battle experience," Kryger interrupted. "I haven't seen this type of interceptor before. Judging from our recent experience, they don't fly and fight as insanely as the Bikans, but their craft are exceptionally fast." He was careful to keep his voice unemotional and matter-of-fact, for his ego still smarted from the raspberry he was rewarded with not so long ago.

Close pursuit will be annoying when we enter the planet's atmosphere, he thought. *I must reduce the odds a little while I can do something about it.* He banked the scout to meet them head-on. The best defense, in his experience, was to do the unexpected.

He kept his attention on the interceptors, wondering how they would react. As he put out a hand to switch the forward shield off, he remembered that it wasn't necessary, unless he had to use the laser if the MAG emptied. He aimed and fired the MAG twice before they were in laser range, and almost immediately destroyed two. They seemed to be caught by surprise or indecision and didn't break formation, but the scout's belly-shields flared briefly from a near-hit by a belated salvo as he approached head-on. He lifted the scout slightly at the last instant to avoid a collision as he flashed over the still almost perfect formation.

Raw novices, but they have courage and discipline. I mustn't get too confident, because they might not be as dense and unimaginative as they appear, he thought as he executed the usual, thoughtless, tight flip-roll to get close behind them.

His heart skipped a couple of beats as the scout turned more sharply than usual and shuddered in protest under the awful gravities. He felt a loss of power, and immediately aborted the head-over-heels maneuver. *That was stupid on my part,* he thought viciously. *I was reacting out of habit and now we really have to run—if we still can. I hope it's something we can live with. Oh boy, Quarr must be out again.*

He'd preferred a dogfight to even the odds somewhat, but now it would have to be a running fight, with him trying to be an elusive target. They had to be well away by the time more combat craft could take off from the base, now clearly in sight at the far edge of the moon's curvature. He slow-looped the scout toward the relatively nearby planet, then pushed the twin throttles forward for all the speed he could get. The scout responded sluggishly. He glanced sideways and saw the interceptors turn to gather on his tail, but in a raggedly spaced, haphazard line, trying to outrace each other in pursuit.

Now each individual wants to be first to kill us, to be known as the one who avenged his fallen comrades. They're fast, and there could be crack shots among them with enough brains to think of ramming a beam up the thrust-openings, he thought grimly as he started a slight, erratic weaving run, to present a constantly shifting target. He watched them in the rearview panel.

They were gaining, but did not waste shots with target practice for which Kryger was thankful. Perhaps they wanted to be closer for a kill—a sure sign that they were not very good marksmen. As the leading craft came close and a beam from it narrowly missed, he applied side-thrust and went into a wide loop. The enterprising pilot of the interceptor overshot and was killed as he passed, but Kryger had paused a moment too long to take aim for a certain kill. The scout shuddered as something heavy slammed into the rear shield. He wished that he were able to use the rear laser, or the missiles, in the same way as the MAG. It was something to remember and worth recommending if they ever made it back to Nevus.

"Why are we running away from a fight?" Quarr asked as if the shock had shaken her into consciousness, but she might have come to before that. She usually kept her silence during a fight and only uttered a warning when it was necessary, because his full concentration had to be focused on adversaries.

"Have to," he replied after checking the closeness of the next interceptor. "I'm sorry. My problem is that I've developed a dangerous habit with that reckless flip. I was reverting to habit and something gave way. The scout lost some power during the second flip, but it still responds fine, although it won't speed up. I should have kept the damage to the tail foremost in my mind. I've been careless, and I now realize that it may be a predictable maneuver if used too often during a single

34

fight. I don't know what went wrong, but the rudder's still there. These interceptors are astonishingly fast, and we have to run as we fight, or fight as we run, whichever. They are the best fighting craft we've ever encountered, but fortunately the pilots aren't. They don't appear to learn from mistakes made by their comrades."

He rolled the scout away in a side-loop as another beam scored a glancing blow on a side-shield. He took the interceptor out when the pilot overshot while he looked for too long a moment to check whether his score had done any damage, for of course, the shields were invisible in space. Kryger liked what he saw, for that was the sign of a novice who had never been in a serious struggle before.

"See what I mean? After my ridiculous flip-roll, the scout won't develop full power for some reason. Please check how many interceptors are left. I didn't keep count of the fatalities." He again side-looped the scout to dodge a beam he saw coming in the rearview panel and thought that he was becoming predictable to loop to the same side every time a beam comes near. The interceptor passed too fast and close for comfort. He sighted the MAG, hit the trigger, and swerved quickly as the scout nearly collided with the suddenly powerless interceptor.

"Now there's only three left, and two of them are close behind, a little below us. I see another group or two scrambling from the moon-base," Quarr announced calmly, as usual.

Not daring to fiddle with the throttles in case he'd lose more power, he took a chance and executed a wide loop-roll to the opposite side to let them pass. He found the two craft exactly in line—one following behind the other—almost straight in front of him. The other interceptor was far to the right and more or less level with them. Kryger only had to dip the scout's nose slightly and then level it to be right behind them. He triggered the MAG without hesitation and both died simultaneously. He banked the scout a little to avoid them while the remaining interceptor executed a hasty about-turn to avoid the same fate, as the scout coincidentally pointed more or less his way.

Kryger sighed regretfully and said, "Pity we won't be able to make at least one orbit, and slow down to check things out. We'll have to dive directly into the atmosphere with them likely biting our tail, but I hope we can stay far enough ahead to avoid another fight, because I can only side-loop to either side to avoid a bolt or a beam, and they will now predict such a move. I hope I haven't used up all our luck, since our guardian angel might have given up the job as nerve-wrecking?"

"I seem to have inherited the job of being our guardian angel. The shields must remain on when we hit the atmosphere, and therefore you can only use the MAG in an *emergency*. Keep the shields on for as long as necessary, because they will help prevent the overheating problem that accompanies speed-entry. It will appear as if we're burning, but the shields won't overload, I promise.

"Those interceptors are accelerating like bats out of a freshly-stoked hell—as if their lives depend on catching us, or maybe they have a pooled wager on us, and the one who bags us is the winner. Compared to our present speed, they're really fast! This dependable old scout sounds unwell, and we must try to avoid serious combat. We'd better get to ground level fast and head for the mountains as fast as we possibly can, for we'll have to play hide and seek with any craft they can muster on the planet."

As if protesting against being called old, the scout picked up speed, and Kryger dared not touch the throttles. It took just over two hours to reach the planet, but they were well ahead of the pack. Only then did Kryger dare to pull the throttles halfway back before he applied reverse-thrust. Speed must be down to a relatively safe level. Otherwise they would be killed by the impact when the scout hit the atmosphere.

Quarr melodiously told him that the pack hadn't gained on them, but wasn't slowing down either. It didn't bother him, for any kind of missile fired at the scout from space would quickly burn up once they were in denser air, and bolts or beams fired from a long distance would disperse too quickly to cause damage or reach them.

Scouts usually didn't have the instruments to test the density and composition of air, or the gravity of a planet, but it wasn't possible to dive headfirst into atmosphere anyway. They would be dead before the scout was ripped to pieces, shields and all, and if they and the scout miraculously survived the impact, the terrific heat build-up would fry them within a very short time even with the shields on. It was safer to let nature take its course and to feel one's way down, using the upper, less dense atmosphere to break. He could use more reverse-thrust to reduce speed rapidly, but the pursuers were coming too close and too fast for peace of mind. Time was in the enemy's favor.

These irrelevant thoughts flashed through his mind as he pulled the throttles back most of the way before he put the scout's nose down in a shallow dive to skim the upper fringes of the atmosphere. It would rapidly reduce some of the still excessive speed, and if they were deep enough into the planet's atmosphere by the time the interceptors arrived, the enemy could only do the same or go into orbit.

6

Keen eyesight allowed Kryger to see a rugged-looking continent bathed in brilliant sunlight receding far below. He wondered if Quarr remembered this mountainous continent. *It was worthy of being considered as a refuge for the hunted,* he thought as he fought to keep the wildly jouncing scout under control and as steady as possible.

They were already far past the continent and over a deep-green ocean when they reached denser air. Quarr reported that, using the far-scope, she could see another continent on the horizon, but that it was mostly flatland and there were no signs of any cities. Entering a planet's atmosphere at speed wasn't exactly the scout's forte, and it was very difficult to maneuver even with the assistance of the side-thrusters, but somehow Kryger managed to gradually turn the misbehaving scout in a shallow curve back toward the rugged-looking continent without bending the joystick or wrecking the craft.

The scout was still turning when an unexpected air pocket caused its nose to dip sharply. The sudden fall and nosedive into denser air made the jouncing incredibly rough, and the scout shuddered with a violence that threatened to rip it apart. The forward shields were taking the worst of the punishment, but Kryger was anxious, because he knew that anything could give way. He could apply some reverse thrust, but he thought it unwise as Quarr may not survive the extra pressure, and he might lose consciousness long enough for it to prove fatal for him as well.

The scout streaked down in a more or less forty-five degree trajectory in a cocoon of flame. Sight was obscured, except directly above them, and the increasing heat on the exterior hull made instruments totally useless. The shields flared brilliantly as if the scout was burning. The brightness almost cost them their lives.

A cultivated instinct—or perhaps some sort of clairvoyance he wasn't aware of—warned that their lives were in danger. The same feeling of imminent disaster had saved their lives on numerous occasions and he never disregarded this odd intuition. He instinctively squinted upward—because it was the only direction not totally obscured by flaring flames—and saw a rapidly approaching contrail far above and slightly to the left.

Leading the now downward curving contrail was a small, black, pencil-like craft with a flaming tail. It was too small and traveling much too fast to be a manned aircraft, so he assumed it to be an intelligent, heat-homing missile.

There wasn't time to think, as death was seconds away. He pushed the throttles forward for full power and miraculously got it, then banked and lifted the nose of the scout into a climb to meet it head-on. There was no other way and the downward pull of the planet's gravity was incredible, but the craft withstood it. He had no other choice if he wanted to survive. The missile was approaching faster than sound, and the scout's response was heavy and sluggish, because it was falling like a brick in the heavy air-pressure buildup.

Years of practice helped him judge the speed and distance correctly and he pressed the trigger of the MAG as soon as the crosshairs aligned at the correct distance in front of the missile. He hoped that it was possible to penetrate the shield despite the fierce heat. *It worked!* He banked slowly to the right and dropped the nose of the scout sharply to avoid debris from the exploding missile.

Deceleration was incredibly abrupt as the spherical shields hit denser air at high speed, and the scout's tough structure creaked audibly under the unbelievable strain. His forehead slammed into the transparent faceplate as his head snapped forward. *A bleeding nose or blackout is all I need to write the final chapter of our short, eventful lives.*

Even though the hard encounter with his faceplate disorientated him, he managed to pull the throttles back sharply and haul the nose of the scout up to decrease the angle of descent. He noted that two disintegrating interceptors—one following the other, and disguised as flaming meteorites—flashed by overhead. *Nah,* he thought, *those dumbasses copied my bad example. They don't have shields, so I might as well take it easy.*

The sudden deceleration had slowed the scout so much that the shields were now just a faint blue color—almost normal—so he turned them off. The scout still shuddered and bucked like a wild horse, and wasn't easy to handle by manual control, but he dared not engage the "safety first" auto pilot, for their speed would then drop too much to get to ground level fast enough to escape additional attention.

He couldn't make use of the built-in antigravity either, for he would have to switch the engines off, and the craft would then spiral down slowly like a falling leaf into the ocean instead of gliding toward land. They would also lose momentum too rapidly, which may be appreciated by parties interested in erasing them.

He judged the speed low enough to level out the glide, so he flipped the switch to extend the wings. The slanting drop changed into a jouncing glide as the wings slowly deployed against the air-pressure. At that instant, he felt a powerful questing probe touch his busy mind. He felt the cold malice as the entity behind it arrogantly tried to force entry into his mind, expecting little or no resistance. Without conscious volition, he irritably told the would-be invader, *Piss off, Gorrel.* He pushed the probe aside as he closed his mind to outside interference so that he could concentrate on maintaining some control over the still rebellious scout.

He was unaware that he'd casually brushed aside a very bewildered, confused entity, which for the first time in a very long, unopposed life, was unable to penetrate and take control of a mind undoubtedly focused on a difficult task. It smarted under the casual brush-off by an inferior creature, and its rage mounted when it finally figured out what "piss off" meant. It promised the arrogant little freak a very painful and messy end if it was captured instead of destroyed. It then ordered all efforts to be increased to destroy or disable the invading craft, and to capture the occupants for questioning. *Perhaps I should use the link to the others and attain the added power to subtly take control of the presumptuous little creature and learn its secrets*, it thought.

It reclined in order to calm down and think about the practicality of the notion. It couldn't simply admit to its linked contacts that it was completely baffled, for the story would be passed on quickly, as usual. Perhaps, it thought, it should tell them that it may have found another species equal to the elite of the Gwarra, because it must be careful not to damage its carefully nursed image and it must not, of course, admit that the creature very easily dismissed it from its puny mind. Yes, that may be the best way to persuade his peers to join the exploration and invasion, but right now it first needed a snack to replenish expended energy.

Quarr, on the other hand, captured Kryger's attention immediately. "Wow! I'll just pick up my limbs and be off." Due to the mind-to-mind communication damper, it was impossible to keep track of his thoughts as was her wont, and she couldn't even begin to guess what his intentions were. "What the hell were the antics for and what in the blazes do you think you're doing to the scout and us? I was out cold again and I will have a web pattern all over my body for a week." She tried her level best to sound angry.

Kryger was unrepentant. "There was no time to warn you. If it makes you feel better, you can inspect the goose egg on my forehead as soon as we touchdown. I saw two interceptors flash past, disguised as meteorites, just before I told Gorrel to take a hike. Do we have other company around?"

"Ugh!" she exclaimed when she checked her now normal-functioning instruments. "Yes, there are another two heat-hunters rapidly closing in on us. They're all yours—with compliments!" She could have fired two rear-guarding missiles herself if she chose to do so or if it was a matter of urgency.

"Very kind of you." He could use all weapons now that the shields were down. He checked the rearview panel and triggered two of the small homing missiles at the scout's tail end to intercept them. They functioned with intelligent software and would interrogate each other so as not to select the same target if there were more than one. Both targets exploded a few seconds later.

"They don't like us very much, do they, Quarr? We only came for a social visit and it's downright uncivilized to make us feel so unwelcome. Are there any more coming our way?" he asked innocently. Quarr didn't bother to reply, as he knew that she would inform him in time, or if it mattered, take care of immediate threats herself.

Their speed was now down to a manageable Mach three and dropped further as they descended rapidly. The jouncing eased and he manipulated the throttles now and then to maintain speed, while he mentally kept his fingers crossed for the scout's continued health. He was surprised that the tail section held together after all the rough handling and buffeting, but this was a war-scout, designed for rough use and built sturdily for endurance to get its occupants home under extreme conditions.

Quarr interrupted his musings. "We're clear…for the moment at least. Get down to ground level while you can and as soon as you can, but be careful not to rip this abused wreck into little pieces."

"That's what I'm trying to do…I mean, getting down to ground level in one piece as quickly as possible. I hope there's no more outside interference with my intention." He dropped the nose of the scout into a fairly steep dive, but eased the throttles back to reduce speed and to ease strain on the scout's tail. *The thrust-connections Quarr made must account for the scout's survival up to now,* he thought gratefully and then told her so.

When he could distinguish individual features on the ground below, he gave a long whistle of surprise. "Take a look at your mountains, Quarr! I've never seen such an awe-inspiring sight. The entire continent is just one vast panorama of unimaginably high mountains and deep canyons. One will take forever to get anywhere on foot, and I'd hate to footslog it down there. Did you remember them when you told me to head for them?"

"No, it's an idiom, numskull! But I agree, they truly are magnificent. Even from up here they make me feel like a microbe observing a deeply ploughed field from high above."

"They have that effect on me too. There are canyons you can fly a whole squadron in, side by side, and the canyon floor is shaded by its high walls when the sun is not directly overhead," he added unnecessarily. "And I'm just an unimaginative warrior, not an intellectual giant or a stool-pigeon who paints magnificent, enticing pictures of the glory of being a heroic space pilot—to lure simple-minded suckers like me into joining the miscalled elite-of-the-elite, and get mauled or killed for falling for the well thought-out drivel."

Quarr didn't reply as she realized that he was blowing off steam to ease the terrific tension of the last hour or two. The constant alertness to keep the scout from breaking up and under control was a strain she happily left in his capable hands. Being an experienced pilot herself, she was convinced that less than a handful of pilots possessed the necessary stamina and instincts to have survived the last hour.

They were easing off into level flight well below the high peaks when Kryger frowned. Something was out of place in the shallow canyon they'd just flashed over, or was it just an impression magnified by that unique, eye-catching, pencil-thin-looking pinnacle that stuck up into the sky like a derisive middle finger, mocking mortals who only glanced at its lonely existence in passing? He'd received the fleeting impression that shadows or moving objects changed suddenly, but it could have been his imagination.

"I feel uneasy. Let's get out of sight, anywhere where we can temporarily hide and inspect this wreck you're nursing so considerately, before it decides to quit on us for good in plain sight of every passerby. Pick a deep, narrow canyon and look for an overhang—a cave or anything suitable. There seem to be a series of narrow canyons up ahead. Any one of them will do for the time being."

"I obey your command with gusto, oh mistress-who-must-be-obeyed," he mimicked, and thought, *I'm way too fast and high for a sudden turn down into a narrow canyon.* He drastically reduced power and eased the scout still lower. The anomaly he had noticed in the shallow canyon promptly faded from his conscious mind as more immediate matters required his undivided attention.

He'd passed two canyons when he too suddenly felt the urge to get out of sight, and right away. The intense feeling prompted him to bank the scout left into the next canyon, which like the rest of them, seemed to be meandering southward. To him it was south, for his magnetic compass now pointed directly behind them, and before he turned into the canyon, it pointed to his right side. The scout responded very sharply with Quarr's modifications, so he slowed down to less than six hundred kilometers per hour since he didn't want to terminate their existence on the first sharp bend. But the feeling persisted that they were being watched and that they must get well away from the point of entry. The nervous feeling caused him to keep the speed higher than was safe.

Kryger wasn't aware that he began chanting an ancient power-song he was taught by the wizards of the Golden People. His voice was a warm, melodious tenor, which gave the chant a strange kind of compelling power.

Quarr was reassured when she heard the chant start, and she immediately felt the rejuvenating power flowing around them. He sometimes unconsciously chanted this ancient, beautiful song when death was just a heartbeat away. This stirring melody restored mental vitality and power of concentration in moments of extreme stress. It reassured her to

43

know that, whenever he unconsciously sang this song, the whole of his being was present in the cockpit. The chant affected her too, and as he relied on her to do her part, she took her attention off his acrobatic flying to concentrate on her instruments. She was just in time to see the rear-scanner flicker to life.

"Uh oh!" she exclaimed in dismay. Her jolly voice betrayed her again, but she knew that Kryger would hear her even though his concentration was wholly centered on not crashing the scout around a turn. "Two fighters are on our tail, and they were dim-witted enough to enter the canyon to chase after us." The chanting ceased the moment Kryger took a quick glance in the rearview panel.

"I've had it with this lot!" he exclaimed in disgust, and reduced speed drastically so that he could divide his attention between the aircraft and where he was going. "This could have been a peaceful, friendly visit, but no, Gorrel and company wouldn't allow it. I'd prefer to kill the warmongering perverts themselves, and not the minions who have to pay with their lives." Prophetic words; but he didn't know it at the time.

If Quarr had the time or inclination to take her eyes off her instruments, she would have had the most breathtaking, hair-raising flight of her life. He weaved the crippled scout erratically from side-to-side to amuse and confuse their pursuers, sometimes narrowly missing a jutting overhang or barely negotiating a sharp bend, forcing the pursuers to concentrate on not crashing their aircraft. He didn't want to waste the limited rear-defense missiles unnecessarily, and he could still climb above the canyon and take them on, but decided to wait until he was forced to fight, for he might lure them down low enough for them to destroy themselves.

Quarr grunted when he suddenly banked and swerved sharply to take a very abrupt bend in the canyon an instant before a hastily fired missile exploded lower down at the turn. He took the scout lower.

"Damn idiots!" he said derisively. "They barely made the turn, but they still followed us lower. They act like intelligent robots. Either that, or they have a built-in *death* wish. Hold on! One is steadying his craft to fire a missile."

He noticed that the canyon narrowed ahead and then angled sharply to the left. He reduced speed and simultaneously dipped the nose sharply and leveled out four hundred meters lower down. He divided attention between the rearview panel and where he was going, and saw them taking the bait by following him. As they leveled behind the scout, one of them senselessly fired a missile. Kryger dipped the scout sharply and stood it on its left wing. The missile passed overhead and exploded against the cliff. The scout's belly almost scraped against the perpendicular wall of the abrupt bend, but they were past in time to miss the shower of detritus. Kryger barely took the scout around an unexpected, second sharp turn to the right.

As the scout cleared the second turn, Quarr's instruments registered a double explosion. *Their pursers must have flown into the debris and then crashed into the canyon wall even as they, presumably* she thought, *desperately tried to swing their speeding aircraft upward or downward into the tight, narrow bend.* She managed to feel sorry for them, but just fleetingly. They wouldn't have made the second turn.

"I don't detect any satellites up there, but that's not to say there aren't any. Those geniuses must have reported our position, and we'd be sitting ducks if they locate us and decide to attack from above. My instruments are useless inside this disguised gully and can't pick up anything out there."

"Gully? My dear lady, you can hide a cruiser in that trickle of water down there, and this scout would be mistaken for a water bug. Okay, it may be a bit narrower in places than our much-vaunted Great Fissure, but its more than three kilometers deep, not just a measly one. I feel like a gnat flying above a twisting irrigation canal."

Quarr kept her silence. She too felt overawed by the grandeur of the canyon, and she wished that they had time to slowly cruise along so that she could take it all in. It would take half a lifetime to explore just this one canyon on foot or by boat.

The narrow canyon now twisted sharply at more frequent intervals and Kryger was forced to reduce speed even more.

Quarr felt a sudden urge to be away from this place. Perhaps they'd already overstayed their welcome. She did a quick mental calculation: they had dived into the canyon an estimated three thousand kilometers from the coast and they had traveled for about twenty minutes at an average speed of five hundred kilometers per hour. She came to a decision and told Kryger:

"It will take us perhaps four or five hours to reach the coast, but I have a feeling that our luck won't last that long, and I don't feel comfortable in this canyon. Ascend to just above the rim so that I can take a peek at the world outside."

"I also have a strong urge to be elsewhere right now. Such a premonition is usually a sign of a nasty surprise waiting just around the corner. The scout seems to be fine and we can perhaps risk a dash to another canyon, if you like."

7

Kryger increased speed as he lifted the scout's nose. He checked his instruments and took quick peeks at the sky above to verify that the instruments were accurate and reliable. It paid to be careful. At times like this, Quarr would be glued to her instruments, which had a wider range, but their immediate safety was his responsibility. As the scout rose above the canyon, he thoroughly scanned the sky with a practiced eye, but it seemed to be devoid of aircraft.

Three hundred meters above the canyon Quarr commanded, "Hold it here."

Other than being blocked by a few high peaks, they had an excellent, all around view. After a long moment of cautious inspection, she commented, "I see nothing unusual, but I feel as if I'm sitting on a bomb with a burning fuse. The sky is clear and I think we should head west again to the ring of huge mountains that will conceal us from any type of ground-based detection gadgets. Keep as low as possible and run as if the devil is after us. Dive into the nearest canyon if I give the command. Keep your fingers crossed that the scout's tail holds."

Quarr never got to find out that her intuition was spot on or that this was a very wise decision. A little more than four hundred kilometers south, the canyon gradually widened into a deep, vast valley. Anything that could be used to give the invaders a warm reception was being readied in a feverish haste since contact with the jets was lost. It was an old city, built randomly with rock from the same area by the ousted inhabitants. It would have been neatly camouflaged were it not for the new spaceport, runways, and a few gray concrete buildings built by the conquerors. Two ultra-heavy traction-beams—each capable of downing a battleship—were powered up and centered on the mouth of the canyon in anticipation of the scout's arrival. There would have been no escape.

"Okay," Kryger replied. "I hope this crate can still take it, but we can always walk if necessary. We just might have all the time in the universe to find their base. Web up and brace yourself for the scariest flight of your life."

As he banked the scout to the west, he engaged the computer-controlled anti-collision gear for automated flight. At high speed near ground level, even his superb reflexes might be too slow to avoid a head-on collision with a peak or outcropping. The automatic pilot—or ape as pilots called it—took over when he pushed the throttles to one-tenth power. The scout hesitated for a moment and then surged forward eagerly. The terrain became a flat blur and the flight was anything but smooth as the equipment constantly adjusted the flight-path and height of the scout relative to the projected ground level. Kryger felt scared, but forced himself to relax as much as he was able to, while he fought the inclination to close his eyes, even though it would have been quite safe to do so.

He extended his hand to reduce speed. Suddenly the scout slewed violently from side-to-side, which instinctively made him pull both throttles back past the idle position, but the computer had already recognized an emergency situation and had switched the antigravity on, which automatically disengaged the ape. The scout's hectic momentum checked immediately to what felt like a standstill as it slowly floated to the ground. The rearview panel showed the upper tail section still flapping slowly as if it was waving goodbye, and the entire tail was bent at an awkward angle.

"Oh hell! The tail collapsed, but it's not torn off, so at least we won't be leaving debris behind. It seems that the ape isn't programmed to understand the changes you made. I guess we hide for a few days and hope that we aren't discovered. Are you okay, Quarr?" he asked belatedly as he pushed the throttles a fraction past idle to keep them moving forward.

"Yeah, but mad as hell that I didn't consider the ape when making the adjustments. Get into the first deep canyon, and look for a deep hole. If we get back, I will recommend that they build you a special one-man fighting scout that can withstand your *insane* piloting. I've had enough scary missions to last me two or three lifetimes."

"That's illogical reasoning. May I remind you that it wasn't my piloting that created the damage in the first place? Forget about your recommendation, if you quit on me, I'll take up farming and forget about fighting the war, because life will be boring as hell without you. Just think of it: no Quarr to sneak a peek into my mind, and no one to disagree with! Missions just wouldn't be the same."

"I've had a bellyful of constant peril. The worst always seems to happen to us. Right now I'd prefer a dull domestic scene to the predicament we're in, and there are plenty of boring admirers to choose from. I have absolutely no idea how, where, or when we're going to repair this scout, if it can even be repaired. It's a miracle something didn't go wrong before."

Her words created an inexplicable sense of loss in Kryger, but he didn't know why he felt so, because it wasn't jealousy, and he was used to fighting or scouting on his own. *She can't be serious,* he thought, as she had shown no interest in starting a relationship with anyone, but it hurt for reasons he couldn't explain. To keep his thoughts away from the subject, he forced his attention on the sky and the rough ground not far below.

Dear, honest, precious Kryger: if I find my people, you may have to go it alone anyway, she thought as they slowly approached the nearest canyon in line with a bare, precipitous peak she couldn't see the summit of, because it was above the cloudbank, which seemed glued around it. *I'll miss your daring audacity, but if I find my people I have an obligation to fulfill…although I'll think long and hard before making a final decision. If there's another way, I'll opt for it, because I can't imagine my life without you to make it miserable, yet exciting, at the same time. Life is full of surprises though, and one never knows what's around the next corner.*

The engines were idling fast to provide power for the anti-gravity unit and to keep the scout moving forward at a relative crawl. He could go faster, but he didn't want to leave the tail behind for anyone to find, since he was quite sure that all metal detection gadgets on the planet available to the enemy would be airborne by the next morning.

Kryger was tired, and he had had enough of mad plunges for the time being, so he gently eased the nose of the scout over the edge into the canyon. When they reached the bottom three kilometers lower down, he slowly applied more power. The rudder was bent at an angle that made the scout difficult to control at a crawling fifty kilometers per hour, even with Quarr's ingenious modifications. He didn't want to speculate, but it would take a complete workshop with the right equipment at least a week to repair or replace the tail section. What was important, for the moment at least, was to get the scout out of sight. Fighting was out of the question. They were

49

vulnerable and virtually a sitting duck, for he could only control and maneuver the scout slowly on manual.

The kilometer-wide, strong, flowing river covered the bottom of the canyon, and he found numerous caves along the almost sheer walls on both sides, but they were either too narrow, too shallow, or too small altogether to accommodate the scout. After what seemed like an eternity, but was actually just short of an hour later, they hovered before a promising cave on the eastern side of the mighty river. The entrance sloped into the river at a fairly steep angle, but the opening seemed wide and high enough to allow the crippled scout to enter. A fairly strong brook, close to the right-hand side, flowed through a naturally carved-out trough, which could make the cave an unacceptable hiding place if it was too wet, but since they had to get out of sight for a few days until the pursuit quieted down, he had to check the inside for suitability.

Kryger drifted the scout closer and then inside. The floor gradually sloped upward, and he thought that, if it was more or less level at the back and didn't show flood-marks, it would be ideal. They probably would have to swim out if they decided to abandon the scout for a few days, but that would be acceptable, as it seemed an unlikely place to hide a spacecraft. The river was a murky green and flowed strongly, though slowly. They would have to be wary of the unknown denizens, but they wouldn't be in the water for long—just a few minutes to swim around an outcropping, which also disguised the entrance from downriver.

He kept the scout hovering just above the water, and switched the landing lights on to illuminate the colossal, domed cave for a thorough examination. Slowly and carefully, he floated the scout into the cave using only minimal power. The more or less level floor at the back was spacious enough to park a dozen scouts. To get an overall impression, he eased the scout around in a half-circle until the nose pointed toward the entrance. A waterfall—not quite high enough to conceal the scout—poured slowly and thickly over an overhang on the now left-hand side of the cave, gathered briefly in a pool, and then overflowed down the ancient, water-excavated trough. There were no tracks in the sand and mud at the entrance.

It seemed that the cave had never been used, which wasn't surprising. He lowered the landing gear and reversed the scout toward the back of the cave before he switched the engines and lights off. The craft settled onto its landing gear with a soft groan of straining metal. Their ears were attuned to the lazy growl of the engines and the sudden silence was deafening.

Since they did not have to go through the airlock on a planet with breathable air, he popped the canopy open. They listened carefully for a few minutes, but the wonderful silence wasn't interrupted by any sounds except the creaking of the scout as the engines cooled.

"At least we have breathable air and water." The lack of light wasn't much of an issue for them—they had the natural ability to see fairly well in the dark and it lessened their chances of being spotted by passing craft. Kryger suddenly felt lost. "To be on the safe side, I think we should abandon the scout for a few days—at least until things cool down a bit. We could explore the highland above for two or three days until we're reasonably sure that it's safe to continue. After that we can return and try to use the craft to reach the coast. It would take months otherwise."

Quarr had come to the same conclusion. "I agree. Let's take our survival kits, along with anything else we might need if we had to *completely* abandon the scout. I'll have to use a small light inside the cockpit to remove a little used instrument that could be converted into a portable life-detector. I'm assuming only the landing lights would be visible outside during daylight, because of the twilight down here. In addition, due to the dangerous wind-shear conditions, I don't anticipate early morning, late afternoon, or night flights in pursuit of us in these canyons."

"What do we need the detector for?"

Quarr responded with a counter-question. "How do you propose we find inhabitants, even if we didn't have to abandon the scout? It would be a dead give-away if we used our seeking-senses—an open invitation for our enemy to come and get us at their leisure."

"Okay. I owe you a peanut. You're the thinker. I'm just a weary, intellectually-challenged driver. Anyway, I can't think with a complaining stomach. Let's take some tablets. We're going to have some meat for supper tomorrow—if there are any suitable mammals on this planet. We'll have no choice but to live off the land when our supply of rations is depleted—might as well see if anything will poison us."

"What if something is poisonous?" She was referring to the doctrine on Nevus—to test anything new before eating it.

"This planet has a humanoid population and you also believe that you came from here. Your people wouldn't have settled here if the environment were inimical; and our attackers live here as well. They must be human enough for us to take that chance. We know that the Bikans are omnivorous and thrive on our food, therefore we can assume their sponsors have the same kind of constitution."

"That's not scientific thinking, but I hope you're right. Otherwise our problems might be over after our first local meal."

Their survival equipment was in a pullout chest below the sleeper. Kryger went in first to dress in tough, imitation leather shorts, with a jacket and soft shoes of the same material. Boots were an integral part of spacesuits and couldn't be removed without damaging a spacesuit. There were a dozen arrowheads, a length of strong string, fishing hooks, a small reel of tough, thin fishing line, his hunting knife, and a needle gun with a forty five centimeter barrel that was called a needler. He decided to take everything, for he might need it when ammunition for the needlers ran low. He also pocketed the special handgrip for the MAG. He thought that he might as well play it as if the scout would be found while they were away.

While Quarr dressed for travel, he dropped down to the ground and opened a panel underneath the nose of the scout. A special tool to remove the MAG was concealed in the compartment. Once detached, he fitted the little gun to the special handle. He now had a devastating hand-weapon, but it looked like a toy in comparison with the deadly needler.

After they had taken the unappetizing rations with some bottled water from Nevus, he unenthusiastically explored the cave. Now that the responsibility of getting them down safely was over, the accumulated stress and fatigue nearly overwhelmed him.

Quarr remained in the cockpit to remove the instrument she wanted to modify. Under normal circumstances, they wouldn't have needed it since their trained senses could detect any warm-blooded life forms in a roughly estimated five kilometer radius, and they would have sensed any sentient thoughts on the planet if it weren't for the mind-to-mind communication damper. Their chances of finding any kind of civilization, including that of the enemy, were slim, unless the enemy pursued them on foot or in ground-hugging vehicles, in which case they could follow the tracks back to their origin.

Kryger dully tried to think about what they should do if they lost the scout. Lost in contemplation, he inspected the miniature waterfall. Behind it was a deep, smooth hollow, spacious enough for a dozen people to sleep in without being crowded. It seemed cozy, private, and dry enough.

Suddenly the thought occurred to him that the organized search and interceptions were not really for him, that it was all a tragic mistake, because he was no one's enemy. He should get rid of his weapons, as nothing on this planet could or would harm him. Then he should walk in a southeasterly direction, where friendly people would be waiting to welcome him with open arms and explain everything. Or he could make a bonfire on the nearest peak and the people would come to him, thus saving him a long and tiring journey. Weapons were so unnecessary and uncomfortable. He didn't need them.

Kryger unbuckled his weapon belt and threw it through the watery curtain. Yes, that's the right thing to do. Now he could leave. He started walking toward the river. A remote corner of his mind wondered why he was walking instead of lying down when he felt so desperately tired that he wanted to collapse, but he dismissed the thought as unimportant. Why should he bother to sleep when friends would fetch him shortly? He would rather go and start a fire so that they could pinpoint his location; then he can sleep soundly until they arrived.

His mind was closed to external stimulation and he didn't see or hear Quarr when she appeared in the open cockpit and yelled, "Hey, Kryger! I need some extra muscle! Say, where are you going without your weapons?"

Kryger kept on walking without giving any indication that he had heard her.

"Hey, stupid! Come back here and give me a hand, NOW!" She was annoyed, but not yet alarmed. He seemed preoccupied—not quite his usual self.

When he walked unheedingly through the mud and the shallow rill to the riverbank, it was so out of character that she realized that something was seriously wrong. Alarmed, she called out at the top of her voice, "KRYGER! COME BACK!" She jumped down and ran to stop him, but he was already descending the steep slope into the slow-flowing river, as if in a trance—or under control. Now her instincts really screamed. In turn she screamed as well and went full-out after him, but Kryger was already down the short decline and out in the river—and immediately sank out of sight.

8

Kryger popped up some distance away, coughing and spitting—a confused, bewildered look in his eyes. Then the water splashed into showers of droplets as he furiously swam back into the cave, scrambled out of the water, and ran up the incline as if the devil was close on his heels with a white-hot trident. His eyes were out of focus and he seemed to be fighting a mental battle. His wet face was ashen, as sickly gray as his golden-brown skin allowed the pallor to show.

He stopped on top of the slope where Quarr was waiting. She was too scared to open her mind to find out what was going on. She anxiously watched his face.

"You look sick. Were you walking out on me or was it the rations?" she tried to joke, smiling outwardly, but desperately suppressing the rising panic inside. "What's wrong, Kryger?" she yelled when he didn't respond.

Her words only vaguely penetrated, because he was struggling desperately to repulse another vicious attack from a furious entity trying to forcefully regain control of his mind. A single thought was knocking for attention, and he tried to exclude all else without relaxing the rudimentary block he was so desperately trying to maintain, to let it register, for it might save his life.

"Water?" he seemed to be asking himself in a whisper. As his embattled mind finally comprehended, he shouted, "Water!" to an uncomprehending Quarr. He stumbled to the curtain of water and fell through, intuitively rolling in a break-fall as he landed. He sat up, hugging his knees and shuddering as if he was freezing, but the awful clamp and pressure on his brain was gone again, and the relief showed plainly on his face.

A mystified Quarr quickly followed him through the icy curtain. She asked anxiously, "What's wrong, Kryger? What happened? What's this thing about water?"

Kryger took a deep, shuddering breath before he was able to reply. "I'm sorry I scared you, Quarr. That sneaky Gorrel implanted thoughts in my mind instead of trying to grab it directly as he had previously done. The water clearly creates a barrier to mental control, because the influence was abruptly cut off when I went under in the river, and the same thing happened again just now when I came through the cascade. I felt the arrogant *pest* trying to continue the mind-control as if nothing was wrong as soon as my head popped out. Bless this river, but I sensed approaching danger even in my panicked state, and it prompted me to get out fast. The water saved my life, and I suppose I subconsciously realized that most of the area behind the cascade should be soaking wet."

He grinned tiredly, but began to shake as if he had the ague. "Did you watch me churn the mighty river into a shower of droplets?" Then his face turned serious, "I'm afraid, Quarr... more afraid than I've ever been in my life. I felt the frustrated, terrible anger of a completely self-centered, heartless, evil entity that regards other life forms as existing only for its own selfish pleasures. When it controlled my mind, it let me feel its evil glee and what misery it intended for me, for by then I was powerless to resist. It didn't exhibit even the faintest trace of compassion." He suddenly paused as if something had just penetrated his befuddled mind. "I just realized that its power must have been augmented somehow by one or more of its own kind, because it was substantially stronger than before. Didn't you feel them questing around?"

"No, my mind's thoroughly shielded. We have more immediate concerns though—do you think that Gorrel was able to pinpoint our location?" It would relieve his uneasiness if she could keep him talking awhile, but safety came first.

"It doesn't take a genius to deduce that we're close to the water in one of the canyons, and it may be able to calculate the approximate direction, because of our last contact with the two fighters, but based on the fact that it wanted me to light a bonfire and walk to a specific destination more or less south-southeast from here, I have to assume that it was unable to pinpoint our *exact* location. The minds felt non-directional. They were unaware that something as common and simple as water could disrupt their coercive persuasion. They were baffled and furious that I was able to break away from their control."

Quarr noticed that the pallor had left his face, but he still shivered. "Go on, get it out of your system," she urged. Talking about it would ease the guilt he experienced.

"They were so persuasive, Quarr! And they so subtly convinced me to discard personal weapons that I truly believed the thoughts were my own. Fortunately, I didn't think about the MAG at the time, so they aren't aware of it. We can't let ourselves fall into the hands of this utterly callous Gorrel. It'll be the end of us—my people, and perhaps yours as well. We have too much scientific and military knowledge that it must *not* have access to. If it grabs my mind again, use any means to restrain or kill me if you have to, please!" His voice was stronger and he wasn't pleading. He was stating the obvious as politely as possible—what they were commanded to do when caught without any hope of rescue before being interrogated.

Quarr could see the calm determination on his face, and she suddenly had an almost irresistible urge to giggle hysterically, but fought the panicky response. One person's life, however dear or valuable, could not outweigh that of a nation's, or an entire planet's population. She swallowed hard and almost shouted, "If it has to be done, then so be it, but that will only be the *ultimate* recourse. We haven't been captured yet! You can hold out, because you have the discipline to resist being controlled again. While I work, I will think what can be done to help you. Perhaps I can show you how to maintain a shield for a long period. Unfortunately, I also think that we must get away from the scout as early as tomorrow morning to be on the safe side."

Her determined and almost angry words calmed the turmoil in his mind completely. She was right. He mustn't allow himself to succumb to fear of the unknown, for he knew quite well that if you feared or expected something, your mind created the circumstances for that very thing to happen. He felt rather shamed by his weakness, because he once repulsed an attempt by Gorrel to take control of his mind. So why couldn't he do so again, even if Gorrel's mind might be augmented by its own kind? He realized that only fear prevented him from giving it a go with his stubborn, Samurai spirit. He had to overcome that fear.

"They'll find us—and very soon," she said. "You have to know how to create a permanent, reflective, mental shield, and maintain it before we can leave this protected sanctuary. Otherwise we'll have a constant struggle to fight Gorrel and his equals off. You won't be able to keep it up for very long. I know that you already have such a shield, but you obviously don't know it and can't use it consciously, which is a requirement."

Her subconscious mind must have worked out the solution for the wish she'd expressed to herself while they were in flight. There was a solution that should appease her people. It was so obvious that she hadn't thought of it consciously until now that her hand was forced, so to speak. They didn't really need her hereditary leadership, since they could rule themselves by following the example of the Nevusians. She only had to explain the principals and see that it was done while, for the time being, keeping hereditary control from a distance. She made up her mind, but it took a while to thoroughly think things through. She dropped her mind-shield little by little and tested carefully with her senses, but their sanctuary was a void. No outside influences intruded.

"This is as secure a place as any that we'll find at short notice. The water seems to cut off outside influences, as you've observed. It's chancy, but I'll have to try and merge our minds to imprint my type of mental control on your memory cells. Unfortunately, we'll be totally helpless while I'm doing it. I owe your parents a blood-debt, which perhaps I can repay this way. It's the only way I can think of right now, because there isn't time to teach you by the usual methods. Even under hypnosis it could take weeks, but we both have blocks against hypnosis, and we may not even have a day, let alone two."

He stammered, "The idea of merging with another mind—even one as *pure* as yours—seems a drastic method to me, too, and somehow repulsive. I might become half-female and you half-male, but I will do it if there's no other way you can help me."

She thought it through and decided it was the right thing to do. He had tremendous potential, but his brain was underdeveloped in some areas. They would both benefit—if it didn't turn into a truly horrible nightmare, because she didn't have proper instruction and only a vague memory of how it was done. There was no other way to save them both. On her own, she might as well give up and die with him, because she didn't know the ways of the wilderness. Kryger was an expert, taught by the very best on Nevus.

She returned to the scout, trying to recall what she was hastily told about mind-merging so long ago. Time was their greatest adversary.

Quarr returned to the sanctuary within minutes with some tools and other things that were part of their survival gear—the portable heater and their sleeping bags wrapped in waterproof covers. Kryger was shivering in his wet clothes and was grateful when she turned the heater on.

"You still okay?" When he nodded, she said, "I'll be back as soon as I get the life-detector working and have set up security precautions." She stepped through the waterfall to continue her tasks, and to contemplate the sudden choice forced on her without warning or preparation.

Kryger was warm and dry by the time she returned. The area behind the waterfall wasn't cold anymore, and he was lying on top of the sleeping bag, clad only in shorts, which had dried quickly, because they weren't genuine leather. As always, she admired his beautifully muscled, golden-brown body. He was big and muscled like his powerful father, but he had the face, the emerald catlike eyes, the short, bi-colored hair and hairy, pointed cat ears of his mother, although he hadn't inherited her soft, golden skin. His eyes regarded her with an odd, trusting look, which she found awkward to return as she suddenly realized that she didn't want to be separated from him for any reason.

To cover her embarrassment, she said, "I'll set the perimeter guard at the entrance—the heat and motion detector we were so sure we'd never need. Now we need the warning, because we'll be busy and unable to scan with our senses. I'll be back in a few minutes."

When she returned, she was all business. "Let's swallow these disgusting dry rations, because we need to maintain our strength and energy—the only useful function they serve." Quarr tried to act nonchalant, but she wasn't very successful in hiding her nervousness.

He sensed that she was uncomfortable, but couldn't understand why she would feel that way. "There was a time dad thought that these rations were the ideal fare for a scout—that is, a human scout on an exploration trip on Nevus, when he and my uncle discovered the artificial intelligence systems. He changed his mind very quickly when he had to live on them for a few days. We flyers have to exist on it for weeks at a time…but hey, we'll never gain weight while dashing around in space."

"Yeah?" she was a deep red in the face and didn't turn in his direction. "Well, anyway, back to our immediate problem. I don't have any experience in, or much knowledge about, merging minds. I remember that we must be secure and not subjected to mental influence from an outside source. I remember being told that it's a dangerous undertaking, and that we may not be able to separate our minds and therefore our thoughts, afterward without expert help. We could end up as one helpless person in two separate bodies. That much I remember. Having warned you…do you want to go through with it?"

"I have a feeling there are large, dangerous, aquatic life-forms in the river. I can't stay under the water for long even wearing a space suit. So unless you can quickly dream up something like a mechanical shield, I'm out of ideas."

Quarr was over her initial embarrassment and turned to face him. "I also felt that mind in the singular, remember? If there are such gadgets in existence somewhere, I'm not aware of them. The merging of minds need not be a sharing, or transfer, of all accumulated knowledge when one knows how to do it properly. That's also something I remember vaguely, but I don't know how to go about it. The ritual has its origin in marriage-merging, which is supposed to be a characteristics-only transfer, both ways, so that the couple can be more or less compatible for life. As you might have been wondering, this is more than merging minds—it also involves merging our bodies physically.

"Merging minds with you is not at all revolting to me, it's the possible failure that scares me. We are from different species and there is a possibility that you may become a partial shape changer or I may lose some of the ability. I just don't know. You may have to put up with me for the rest of your life. I'm five years older. Also, there is a very real possibility that we may become totally helpless if we can't separate our minds afterward. Consider it very carefully."

Kryger knew that it was his only hope to resist Gorrel. "No, Quarr, I don't have to consider. We took to each other from the very beginning, and I can't imagine my life without you. This is not a declaration of undying love, but perhaps a successful union would benefit both our races. Only time will tell."

"Yeah, and perhaps my people will kill us both, a task I don't envy them. But let's cross that bridge when we get to it."

Kryger had one last thing to say. "Now I understand why you weren't interested in men. I sincerely hope that this sacrifice, if you want to call it that, is worth it and that it works."

Having made up her mind, she undressed quickly, as if it was the most normal thing to do. She was beautifully proportioned—her skin was a soft brown from hairline to toe. When, as a child, she'd changed into human shape, she'd automatically copied Lerra's, Kryger's mother, outward form, but her supple muscles were earned, not copied. She always trained hard at every opportunity, for she had realized at a very young age that imitation muscles were not strong and therefore quite useless. Then she stood upright as if waiting for his approval, but her nose wrinkled in disapproval.

"You're beautiful, Quarr." He was short of breath and danger was forgotten. He suddenly understood why men kept pursuing her, and why scout pilots never gave up having her as their navigator. It wasn't merely for her skill.

9

Instinct took over. "Relax completely as you've been trained to do, and do not resist me entering your mind when I do so," Quarr commanded self-consciously.

Kryger blushed furiously. The first part was easy enough, but he couldn't control his breathing, and it was difficult to relax with a racing heart. She pushed him gently onto his back, then quickly raised herself, straddled him, and linked fingers with him. He was happy to oblige and she heard him groan as she slid him all the way into her. While he automatically concentrated his mind on her velvety softness he relaxed, and was distracted enough for her to reach inside his mind and synchronize.

As they climaxed together, his mind went blank and there was no resistance. She opened her mind to him and was astonished. She found wealth, joy, horror, and the reason why merging with an undeveloped alien mind was forbidden.

She found amazing courage, an indomitable fighting spirit, knowledge, and a wealth of experience she never even suspected he had accumulated through hardships. He never let on that he knew more about astronavigation than she did, and she suddenly realized why he was chosen to check out new navigators. She was vigorously trained in empty-handed combat by his great-grandfather, but she now found that she really knew very little. She realized that he was the most deadly empty-handed fighter on the planet of his birth, even superior to his infamous father. She learned of his respect and love for all forms of life, and a fearlessness that defied all logic.

She could not understand his philosophy of life: that one should learn to live and make the best of life; that death was inevitable and therefore not worthy of consideration. She now understood why his peers regarded him with an awed mixture of respect and jealousy. He had a reckless kind of courage, tempered by an inborn sense of responsibility and an implacable determination—he never gave up, no matter what the circumstances.

The joy she found was a deeply buried love and respect for her; her uncomplaining courage and her total acceptance of his judgment when piloting a fighter or a scout in deadly combat.

She shared the horror of atrocities he had encountered committed by the Bikans and their allies, which had changed him and made him who he was. She realized that all her inner, closely guarded secrets were now part of his memories too, but the real horror was that she couldn't extricate her mind from his—she went in too deeply and had stayed too long. She shared with him his somewhat wry thought that they were as confused as two cats rescued from a vigorously spinning tumble dryer, but she couldn't find the same amusement in it. What she had feared had come to pass. She accepted the fact that they now were one mind, sharing all actions and thoughts. They would interfere with each other's thoughts and actions unless they could develop a way of shielding their minds individually. She struggled to make sense of which thoughts were her own, and being the unique person that she was, she partly succeeded.

A deep feeling of immense calm and gratitude transfused what little she could still call her own mind, banishing the confusion and the rising panic.

Right now it might be for the best, for we have doubled the power of our brains and our thinking power. Excuse the sickly pun, but it's true that we are now able to fight those evil entities off as one mind. We still think our own thoughts, although we share them all the time, and it's confusing. All we have to do is to discipline ourselves to suppress our own thoughts when the other one is thinking or acting for our welfare—for the present at least. We can learn to do so, as we are doing right now—instinctively. We're still two entities, princess, and yes, I have access to memories you've either suppressed or had shoved aside. I can hear and feel your mother's frantic transfer of her knowledge as she died. She definitely was a human being. I will share it with you again to refresh your memory. The loss of your brother in such a tragic way was a traumatic experience, which suppressed vital memories. Experiencing the incidents again with me as an adult participant will let you see it as it really happened. Accept them, and live with them. What is past can never be changed. His thoughts were utterly tranquil, controlled, reassuring, and totally devoid of apprehension.

Her earliest memories came flooding back as he examined them dispassionately. She could no longer distinguish her own mind, or his way of thinking from hers. His passionless

63

examination of her long suppressed memories gave her a true perspective. She no longer felt embarrassed about her exposed innermost memories. She somehow, gratefully, realized that he was exceptionally perspicacious for his age.

Kryger's thoughts became sluggish. It was a taxing day and he was desperately tired. *I have the same problem, Quarr, but why should we be embarrassed? It serves no purpose. Thank you for your sacrifice, my princess. You're an incredibly brave woman and I'm proud to be part of you. I don't think that I would have had the same courage if our positions were reversed. When we leave this sanctuary, we must be capable of independent action, because we cannot both sleep at the same time, regardless of the perimeter-guarding device. It can only warn, not defend. We may already be in danger, but we must take the chance and sleep; to give our subconscious minds a chance to work through our predicament without interference.*

She was sleepy as well, but she had a last thought to air. *This thought-damper could be a blessing in disguise. It may help to separate our minds if we're not close together, but we'll see tomorrow. For tonight, let's both sleep in peace while we can—if we can.*

They slept the sleep of the dead. As had been drilled into them, their senses, although restricted to the cocoon of safety created by the little waterfall, kept watching periodically for anything out of the ordinary. It was a trained, unconscious process, and only if real danger threatened would their conscious minds awake.

10

Although limited to a very small area, the intense concentration of thought-power when Quarr merged minds with Kryger attracted the attention of the ubiquitous consciousness of an incredibly ancient entity. She examined the brains of the two mind-mergers and immediately became interested. These, at long last, were the children of those who called themselves humans, and the event she had been awaiting for ages beyond memory. She had grown used to the loneliness, but she felt sadly joyful that her isolation was nearly over, for when the rescue and transfer of selected knowledge was over, this very night, she could bid this material dimension farewell with a clear conscience, and join those of her kind who had long, long ago gone on to the next plane of existence.

But a thought intruded: perhaps she should wait for the test, which was to take place in the very near future—not even the blink of an eye in the eternity of time. It will only be a few short days longer, and it would be appropriate to report initial results, she decided. She might as well wait to see the outcome of the first event, for success would mean the end of her exile. Only then could she be sure that the transfer of the pre-selected knowledge was adequate for the pair to survive, and for the male to succeed in the penalty imposed on him at the dawn of time for this particular three-dimensional galaxy. His task would be harsh and perilous, so she might as well make sure that he was properly prepared.

Her elongated humanoid body was imprisoned in a life-preserving stasis unit that kept her alive, but her mind was free to roam the universe, and she passed the long ages by checking the evolution of the different creatures on planets in solar systems far apart. That occupied her until recently, when the malicious, questing thought-searches of the insensibly cruel entity intruded, and the wasteful slaughter of innocent creatures began. She was annoyed with the careless slaughter and thoughtless cruelty, and considered terminating the entity and its slaves, because their ruthless killings interfered with, and rudely disturbed, her lonely vigil and peaceful contemplation on this, the ancient planet of her birth. But on reflection, she realized that the arrival of the malignant, artificially created entity was the event and task she had been charged to wait for all these long millennia beyond memory ago, and that the time of her release was near. And now the two humans had arrived as predicted, and the event that was foretold so long, long ago, was unfolding at last.

The male of the two human beings must undergo at least one test so that she could be sure that he was adequately prepared to rid the galaxy of this vicious being and its equally pernicious brethren. She could kill them easily enough, but the development of this male was necessary so that mankind could learn by his example, and later on by his teachings. But he must survive the first test without her help. If he was not adequately prepared, she would have failed and would have to prolong her stay in this weary, material existence.

The ageless entity quickened her thought processes to synchronize with the humans, and she participated in the process as part of both minds, but only as an observer, for she realized that it would be catastrophic to interfere while they were fully conscious. She shared their memories and was pleased by the boundless courage and total honesty she discerned from both.

The old prophecy proved to be accurate in every detail, but that was expected, since her kind predicted the probable destiny of this physical universe correctly many millennia ago; including the unfortunate development of the evil, almost indestructible insect-like predators with the unique but unorganized brain-capacity for storing information. She could have put a stop to the irresponsible experiment, but her punishment was not to interfere as the species that called themselves mankind must learn its own lessons in order to develop and fulfill their designated role as guardians.

Her kind had passed on to a higher realm, but the different seeds of life in this universe, which they had carefully nurtured, must be preserved, because the remorseless predators with their rudimentary developed brains, if unchecked, would eventually destroy all life; including themselves. The appointed task of this unique humanoid male and his mate was to destroy this species whose premature, forced development, corrupted their intended role in the scheme of things. In the process, the different sentient species of this universe would mature through trial and suffering, ultimately guided by this unique pair and their offspring.

She must save both from their necessary folly, without their knowledge—for the present at least—until the male's potential was fully developed by his own efforts. Her task was to restore their entangled individualities, and then to nudge the male on the way of development so that he could preserve himself, the female, and ultimately all other species. It was a task she didn't envy them, but was part of the overall plan, designed by a much higher power than that of her own kind.

She waited for them to go into the sleeping state so that she could separate their thoroughly entangled personalities. She was encouraged by the mental discipline shown by the male as he forced himself, and by association his companion, to sleep. This was a brain worth stimulating to develop, she thought as she went to work.

She gently disentangled the hopelessly enmeshed brain-processes, but left a tenuous link that might prove useful to both in the near future, and which would force them both to develop. As they developed and their brain-frequencies started to differentiate more and more, the link would dissipate. The link also served to make them think that their subconscious minds did the separating, and it would force them to keep their shields on most of the time, thus concealing their whereabouts from the creature known as Gorrel and others of its kind.

It would be better to call the two humans by their given names, she decided as she removed certain inhibitions from Kryger's brain, and cross-linked other clusters where she engraved knowledge that would help him survive impossible odds. The know-how was there, requiring only relevant circumstances or appropriate thoughts to access the knowledge. He would think that his own enhanced brain—because of the merge—devised the solutions that would pop into his consciousness in times of extreme stress.

When she was finished, she created a cocoon of safety for the bodies of the humans while they slept deeply to rest their overtaxed bodies and brains. Then she invited Kryger's soul to come with her to see his legacy left by the ancient, hidden civilization that flourished on this planet at the dawn of time, after this universe was created. She gently helped his soul to disengage from his body, and took him on a very strange journey.

Kryger's soul—his inner-self—accepted the out-of-body experience with awed wonder. He instinctively trusted the strange being of light that took him by the hand in what felt like a strong grip, and bade him come with her. To Kryger's surprise, they passed easily and rapidly through the solid rock to emerge on top of the mountain. He would have had misgivings of the subsequent swift flight through the air if the being didn't have him firmly clasped.

She perceived his doubts and quickly reassured him. *You mustn't confuse your tenuous soul with your material body, which can't travel this way without mechanical gadgets, Kryger. This body, your soul, is the real you which survives and goes on to the next existence after the death of your physical body on the material plane. The physical body is only a temporary vehicle. Your soul is the repository of all experience and knowledge you accumulate during your temporary three-dimensional existence. You can fall if you think it so, but you can't get hurt. As you have just experienced, it goes through solid rock and it will go wherever your consciousness directs it. It will even fall right through the planet as easily and as fast as it will go around it, even though this body feels solid to your touch. Your soul is merged with your physical body, but it can be separated under certain circumstances, or with a little help. You can also do it consciously if you know how.*

In no time at all they arrived at a truly enormous mountain range. They hovered before an impressive, sheer precipice. *This is solid rock on the material plane, Kryger—the highest mountain in this canyon continent and on this planet. Down there at the bottom is a huge double door—the dark blue-black stain in the otherwise black-brown surface. It can only be opened by a certain series of words uttered aloud in a certain pitch of voice; knowledge I've already transferred to you. Of course you may remember this journey vaguely as a dream, but in the far future, certain words—also engraved on your brain— uttered by another being, will joggle your memory to remember this journey and make you return to our ancient city, to see it again and learn more about our physical and mind sciences. I'm taking you inside our hidden city to show you around. The entire city is kept in working order by robots that will repair each other, and even themselves. They, and the city, have been functioning for billions of years, and will keep functioning until this planet is destroyed. You are the inheritor of our sciences, and hopefully, our wisdom. You might live long enough to make use of all that you inherit, and pass your inheritance on to advanced beings worthy of receiving it; not necessarily your own offspring. It was the sincere wish of my people when they departed this existence that you carefully observe and train worthy beings to inhabit this city again.*

They passed through hundreds of meters of solid rock without hindrance until they arrived high above the domed city, which was carved out of the hard rock and reinforced. She pulled Kryger to a walkway cut out of the surrounding rock, and set their spirit feet down on the smoothened ledge.

We can see the entire city clearly in our spirit state, but you will remember that, when you arrive at some future date, you must envision the city illuminating when you are inside and the double doors are closed by your command. Your brain has been sensitized to the controls of everything in the city so that you can safely enter anywhere. Now think of the city being lit up, and you will see an unsurpassed sight that would take your breath away, were you in your physical body.

Kryger did so and watched in awe as the impossibly vast dome lit up as brightly as if it had turned into a shining reflector. From their vantage point more than two kilometers above, he saw that the city was circular, with a diameter of around ten kilometers. From the center, which was a blindingly bright, gigantic ball-like dome, circular roads were spaced at regular intervals. They in turn, were intersected by straight roads starting at the center, which gave the city the appearance of a gigantic wheel.

The outer rim consisted of a smaller brim and two storied dwellings; obviously homes occupied by long-gone elite. The buildings toward the center were progressively larger, taller, and more colorful. The five inner rings were connected by slender, flimsy-looking walkways over the roads, and in-between buildings on different levels. Kryger surmised that it was some sort of control center. The brilliant ball in the center was surrounded by a circular, outward-leaning high wall that was reflective on the inside.

Kryger thought that he looked down on a multi-colored fairytale city, and that the ball-like hub emitted the light for the dome above to reflect over the entire city.

You are quite perceptive, Kryger. Yes, that is so, for it consumes less power, and the outward-leaning wall around the power generator is to reflect the light and heat upward, otherwise those in the science center would have been fried and the buildings set aflame. The five inner circles are, or rather were, the administrative, research and control center: in short, the Science Center. It became more or less deserted after my people attained freedom from physical restrictions, and was only used periodically to record our special experiences, new attainments, or to rejuvenate an injured or old body. Freedom from physical restriction meant that we still had bodies that had to be looked after and nourished at regular intervals, but we could go anywhere at will, and learn anything by detaching our consciousnesses—our souls—from our physical bodies.

By the way, it would take a million entities hundreds of this planet's years to review our records. It covers time immemorial.

When she was silent for a few moments, Kryger observed, *I don't sense sentient life of any kind in the city and you indicated that you were the last of your people. Presumably you still have a physical body somewhere. What happened to your people? I also assume that a regular night and day cycle is still maintained, otherwise the exotic plants and blooms would have died long ago.*

You are quite right and I am very pleased, young Kryger. You are everything the foretelling proclaimed, and much, much more. This three-dimensional universe will suffer greatly if you ever become a rogue, but I sense a great love and respect for all forms of life in your mind. I know that you will never become greedy and selfish, but I have nevertheless implanted a safeguard against such an unlikely eventuality. In my unfortunate experience, I have learned never to take anything on face value.

We've had a few million years to develop and evolve without interference, although we were not the only species in this particular universe. We eventually inherited the role of guardians, and our task was to see to it that each species had the opportunity to develop and evolve without outside interference. We too continued to evolve, and eventually were able to leave our physical bodies and check on our wards without their knowledge, because in the spirit form as we are now, only the very gifted of so-called civilized beings could detect us. The beings we consider lowly animals could sense and see us all the time, of course. It's a natural ability of the so-called lower forms, because they don't have the intellectual ability to doubt their natural gifts, as do alleged civilized entities.

I eventually came across a humanoid entity that was exceptionally intelligent. It was a male from a fairly primitive culture, and he'd built a spaceship without any training or knowledge of the subject. He staked his life on the supposition that he would find an advanced race on another planet, where he could satisfy his burning hunger for knowledge that wasn't available on his own planet. He had worked out the principles of spaceflight and what was required to stay alive. He set out alone in his primitive craft, but had miscalculated the duration of his journey, the amount of sustenance, oxygen, and propellant he would need to stay alive and on course.

Kryger wondered why this seemed to be a familiar story, but the entity continued.

By chance, I found him drifting in space. He was near death with his food and water depleted and his air supply nearly exhausted. I admired his extraordinary resolution and courage, and because his abnormal intelligence interested me, I suspended his life and quickly organized a rescue mission. We took him back to his planet, but I was curious, because such intelligence was rare at that stage of evolution. I thought that I'd at last found an evolved creature of exceptional intelligence and courage, and I visited him often in the flesh to talk to him, advising here and cautioning there. What I did not realize in my trusting stupidity was that he was also exceptionally cunning, and could hide his inner thoughts from me.

He applauded my knowledge seemingly sincerely, and I innocently lapped it up like a trusting child. I ignored our policy of non-interference, unless a very destructive war was brewing, and the fact that he was a-far-from-evolved entity. I ignored the fact that he was still primitive and could misuse advanced scientific knowledge for unscrupulous, selfish purposes. I taught him things that he, at that stage of his evolution, was not ready for and could therefore not use wisely for his people's advancement.

Owing to my teachings, he became powerful...then greedy and hungry for personal glory and wealth. First, he and his followers subdued the people of his own planet, then they set their solar system aflame with war. Next, they started with nearby solar systems, for I'd taught him interstellar travel as well. The elected supervisors of my people were alarmed and became very angry, and told me to bring an end to what I had started. It took me years, but I eventually succeeded in destroying him and his followers. Unfortunately I couldn't undo the damage that was done.

That's my sin in a few thoughts. The time came when our supervisors realized that our guardianship of this universe was coming to an end. We all came together to participate in the final forecast for the future of this galaxy. The bare facts, or essentials, were this:

In the far distant future, a few foolhardy scientists will discover a long-lived, almost indestructible, omnivorous creature with, to use one of your terms, a computer-like brain that never forgets what it hears or learns. And, like a computer, without the intelligence to make use of stored information unless it's cross-indexed and linked by an intelligent agent or by pure chance, they would be denied the time to develop naturally over thousands of years. To crown their idiocy, the scientists will instead of developing better mechanical devices, artificially enlarge the creatures and use them as repositories of knowledge. The mechanically inclined part of the population would realize the danger and depart their planet.

The prognostications indicated that the enlarged creatures will require a tremendous amount of energy to stay alive and will become wholly carnivorous. They will devour their creators and other life forms on their planet, and then spread into the universe and set themselves up as deities while unthinkingly destroying planet after planet without regard to the consequences. They will realize too late that they should have preserved something to feed on, to prolong their existence.

Some centuries after this catastrophic experiment, a hybrid humanoid will be born on an out of the way planet. He will be a great warrior with a mind capable of withstanding and defeating the merciless mind-power of these seemingly undefeatable predators. The problem would be that he will not have had time to develop his unique mind, because he will be engaged in an interstellar war with slaves of these prematurely forced-developed creatures. During a lull in the war, he and his future mate will visit this planet to look for a remnant of her race, but become entangled in each other's minds when the female tries to save him from one of these creatures, for she will have a better trained brain.

To atone for my sin, I was charged to wait for this event and separate the minds of the two, and then to stimulate certain centers in the male's brain. I then was to imprint certain

72

advanced knowledge on the brain of this being—which he could have developed on his own in the course of time if he had stayed away from this planet. I was to ensure that he was capable of defeating the nearly indestructible predators.

With my mind-power, I could have stopped the experiment, or destroyed the creatures, but the other inhabitants of this universe must evolve, learn to stand together, and take control of their own destinies. They have to learn to think before they act, and to look after themselves. Impulsiveness must be eradicated from intelligent beings, for therein lies the seeds of destruction.

You were born to give the various creatures a chance to develop by destroying most of these predators, and to teach others to continue when you and others work together to find easier ways to defeat them, other than intense mental conflict followed by death. Only then will the words be uttered that will let you remember and make you return to this city.

Now, follow me down to the dark blue building in the second ring from the hub, and I will show you my physical body. It will be destroyed when I depart to join my people. This was another test, although she already knew that he was fearless, and that he was also a fast learner. She floated slowly down toward the building.

Kryger hesitated a few moments to recall her teachings, and then thought of standing in front of the building. The next moment, to his surprise, he was there. His tutor arrived and said with a smile in her thoughts, *You definitely are worthy of being taught, Kryger. I'm proud of you. There is no need for you to see my physical body, but I have this primitive urge that you must see me as I am.*

No, lady, it's my need you are picking up. I would like to know what your people looked like, and I want to remember you in my later years. I admire your fortitude in staying sane after being on your own for millions of years. There ought to be a statue to remind us of your heroism. I understand the reason to let me think that I'm developing on my own, but please don't erase my memory of you.

Thank you for your kind words, Kryger. Now, follow me, please.

She walked through the closed door with Kryger on her heels. She could have floated if she wanted to, but he sensed that she never did anything without a reason.

73

Quite right, Kryger. Walking is natural and doesn't require attention. When you are in the flesh, just think that you have a right to enter any door in this city, and the door will open and then close, unless you want it to stay open. We walk, because I want to explain the workings of this place. It is a place of healing; of preservation of life. These boxlike coffins you see along the walls are stasis units where physical bodies were preserved until they could be treated. In later years, bodies were kept alive in these boxes while their owners were away on a long visit. Although physical life is suspended when a body is incarcerated, it is massaged, fed, and looked after until the owner returns, or until the energy cord that connects it to the soul is severed when the entity decides to depart this life. My body is right at the end, and it will immediately turn to dust when I sever the connecting cord as I leave.

As if his eyes had been opened by her last remark, Kryger now noticed the thin, pulsating, silver-blue cord emanating from the top of her head and continuing to a stasis unit at the end of the row on his right-hand side. He also became aware of his own cord disappearing into the distance.

Again, Kryger, most animals can see the cord while in their bodies, but very, very few so-called civilized beings can do so, unless they are trained from a very young age. Before we look upon me, let's step into this room on the left.

They did and Kryger saw a small, deep, empty pool. It was more a hole than a pool, because there was only standing room for three or four persons of his size at arms-length from each other. There was a narrow ladder with handrails to climb in or out of the hole. It didn't look as if his body would fit between the rails, but his feet would fit the steps.

When a person, or persons, were physically injured, they were lowered into this pool if they were incapable of using the ladder. Sensors released a healing liquid up to the neck of the shortest entity, and the healing began. Sometimes the process itched so much—especially when that person or entity had been severely injured or had multiple wounds—that he or she had to be lifted out awhile. The knowledge is inside your head so that you can bring severely injured persons here to be healed when your sciences lack the ability, but as I had indicated, that will only happen in later years, because you and Quarr will not need it. Now let's go and see me.

74

Kryger looked at a long, slender, naked, woman of indeterminable age. Her body—he guessed that she was three meters tall—was suspended in the transparent box and it floated upright as if she was in a zero gravity field, but held upright by invisible means. There was a faint golden tinge to her entire body, as if she had been out of the sun for a very long time, and she was hairless except for high, thin, brown, arched eyebrow-lines and long brown eyelashes. Her enormous head tapered down to a small, firm mouth and chin. Her rather large eyes were closed and her long, quite beautiful face was serene. She was lovely in an alien way, and he said so.

That is the most sincere and loveliest compliment I've ever been given in my rather long life. Thank you, Kryger. I will remember you with fondness. Now, let's get you back into your body. It's near daybreak and my task is not quite over yet.

As she gently showed him how to get back into his physical body, she blocked his memories of the night, but many years in the future, when certain illogical words were uttered, he would remember everything. Then she left to implant the words into the brain of a very young entity who would meet Kryger under very unusual circumstances many years into the future.

11

They awoke as one when a harsh, whistling sound reverberated between the canyon walls. A glimmer of light, reflected into the cave by the river, informed them that daylight had reached the bottom of the deep canyon.

Her hearing was not as keen as Kryger's, who took lonely excursions into the wild, mostly unexplored wastelands of Nevus whenever he could take a break from the harshness of active military life. Quarr wasn't sure what she had heard as she had never heard that particular, ear-deafening sound before.

"It must be midday at least. What's that dreadful noise?" she asked.

Kryger was startled by how much better and stronger he felt, as well as the fact that their minds were not as hopelessly intertwined as the previous night. "It sounds like a primitive, fuel burning jet, flying slowly down the canyon. There may be hundreds of them out there crisscrossing the continent searching for any sign of us. I don't feel safe here. I'm guessing the aircraft is equipped with advanced detection apparatus. How are you feeling?"

She ignored the question as the realization hit her that they were operating as individual entities again. She still felt somewhat groggy and hadn't thought about their ordeal.

She stretched luxuriously, and although she was still naked, quickly got out of the warm sleeping bag. "Get up, lazy bones! Yes, I too don't want to stay here the rest of the day and perhaps another night. I think that it would be unwise." She took a quick splash under the icy cascade, dried herself, and hastily dressed. She glanced at the watch imbedded in the broad, clear bracelet around her left wrist. "Wow! We slept for almost fifteen hours."

"Cheerful, aren't we? Thanks for not asking, but my head hurts too. No, it's not what you think! Perhaps it's from too much knowledge crammed into the confined space between my adorable cat ears.

"However, my thoughts are clear and my senses keener than ever. I woke up in the early hours of the morning, since my senses automatically kept watch when we went to sleep and vaguely sensed that malicious chum of ours searching for my previous mind pattern, but it was just a baffled, angry thought that didn't penetrate our sanctuary. It was then I realized that I had started to develop some kind of shield to separate my mind from yours. Thank you for what you did, Quarr. I only hope I can repay you someday."

What he didn't tell her was that he felt that the new kind of shield wasn't fully developed yet. He didn't know how he knew it was different from hers, and didn't think it prudent to let her know until he was quite sure what it was. He still shared thoughts with her, but during the sleeping period, his subconscious mind had apparently developed some sort of block that enabled him to isolate his thoughts from hers. He would experiment cautiously and slowly to develop this unique reflective mind-shield ability. Whatever it was, it still required conscious action to maintain the shield, and control could slip any time his full attention was focused elsewhere. He felt the nagging thought that he had forgotten something.

While those thoughts flashed through his mind, Quarr took up where he left off. "Look, forget it, will you? I told you why I did it, but I wasn't prepared for what happened. No regrets however, and I know that there are none on your end either. We were a team before and now we are a united, formidable unit…I hope," she added as an afterthought.

Kryger stepped under the icy water, then retreated and swept the water from his body in front of the heater. Quarr again admired the play of muscles on his body as he dressed. *He's beautiful,* she thought. *His body is all hard muscle and he earned it the hard way, just as I did. It's worth the effort to look like that, and to feel confident and healthy because of it. Mind and body must always act as one.*

Kryger's back was turned toward her so she couldn't see the smile and the blush. It was flattering to "hear" such a sincere compliment, and to also know that their roles were reversed, albeit through her own voluntary sacrifice. She would never again be able to peep inside his mind unless he allowed her in.

They packed their rucksacks and stepped through the watery curtain. Kryger activated the scout's self-destruct mechanism and then sealed the canopy. The mechanism would only respond to his and Quarr's voices or palm-prints. If an intruder forced his way inside, the scout would self-destruct after the standard ten-second shrill, frantic warning to deactivate the mechanism, destroying half the mountain with it. Kryger grinned wolfishly.

He distrusted the river, as did Quarr. They didn't know what dangers lurked in its depths, as they had no knowledge of the planet's fauna and flora. He was in the water for only about ten seconds the previous day, but had received the strong impression that something inimical reacted to his immersion. His mind and senses were finely tuned to danger and had never been wrong. He felt uneasy, and turned to face Quarr as they reached the edge of the water.

"Do you sense that something is waiting for us? Or am I imagining things?"

"I do." She scanned the rough surface of the rock around the exit. "There are a few protrusions on our right-hand side. It leads to a ledge about six meters up. Let's go that way and see where it takes us. I'll go first, but cover me with your peashooter."

The needler was deadly, but he wasn't going to rely on it. When Quarr's life was at stake, he'd destroy half the planet to ensure her safety. He drew the MAG and kept his eyes on the river as she ran the few steps through shallow water to gain momentum for the jump to reach the lowest handhold.

He didn't see her overshoot the handhold and save herself by grabbing the second protuberance just below the ledge. As she scrambled onto the ledge, a flat, broad reptile-head, attached to a long, finely scaled neck, popped out of the water below the ledge, followed by a huge body. The neck stretched upward to grab Quarr and the fanged jaw opened in anticipation. Kryger targeted the head and saw it flopping over backward. As a precaution he put another bolt through the whitish, scaled, streamlined body just below the neck, even as he estimated that the creature was larger than half a dozen heavy draft horses attached in tandem. The strange creature thrashed its brief death-dance with webbed feet, churning the water at the entrance into shiny droplets, while its short, rudder-like tail beat the slow-moving water into choppy waves. Then it flopped over, belly up, as the current grabbed hold of it.

"Nice shots," Quarr commented. "What an ugly creature! It's bigger than two fully-grown mammoths. The two of us together would have been just a small bite." Quarr's voice was filled with loathing—at least as far as she was able to express in her unusual voice. Her needler hung from a shoulder by its strap, so she took it off in case another monster made an appearance.

"I misjudged the gravity of this planet, which is weaker than that of Nevus, and I jumped too high for the first protrusion. I thought yesterday that I seemed stronger than usual, but ascribed it to my worry over you."

"I was too disturbed yesterday to notice anything, but the lesser gravity will make our climb so much easier. We might as well go to the top. That will make it easier to see what's around us." He jumped and easily landed on the ledge beside her, the MAG clutched between his teeth. He wanted it within easy reach. After a thorough look around, he put the gun away and said "Let's get a move on. This ledge is too easy for the longnecks to reach."

From the somewhat flat ledge, it was almost easy to climb to the next higher ledge where the steep upward-slant began. Accustomed to the heavy gravity of Nevus, they scrambled up like monkeys. On a convenient ledge, about a half a kilometer up, she stopped and asked "Why do you think we should go south?"

"Because Gorrel wanted me to walk southeast. We might be able to find…HIDE!" His keen hearing detected a faint whistle that did not belong in the silence of the canyon, and was therefore suspicious. He did not know what it was, but it was out of the ordinary and definitely not natural. They squatted side by side under an overhanging rock just large enough to accommodate both of them.

Ten seconds later, a small, silvery jet appeared, flying up slowly from downriver, slightly below them. The pilot was concentrating on keeping the rocking craft steady, slow, and level in the middle of the narrow bottom of the canyon, and the passenger beside him was peering intently at what could only be detection equipment.

"That's a strange kind of craft," Quarr whispered as if the fliers could overhear.

"Not really," he replied in a normal voice. "It's the kind of aircraft we heard earlier. I read about them in one of the Terran history books and I've seen and heard them on other planets. They use fossil fuel, and were called *jets* by the historians, but they are atmospheric craft only, since they need a massive amount of oxygen to burn the fuel to convert it into thrust power. They have a limited range, because of the amount of fuel they can carry, and must be refueled after each trip. If you're interested, you can search your memory. It's all there, now. I hope their detection equipment is as primitive as their aircraft. If they find us, I'll have to kill them, and that might lead others right to our scout, which only the most sensitive metal-detectors would normally be able to find."

"We're dressed like hunters to blend in with more or less any terrain. If they see us, they may not associate us with the scout." Quarr seemed to be laughing about it.

"I won't take that chance. We don't know what's normal on this planet. If you can judge them at all by the behavior and persistence of the fighter and interceptor pilots, they will take a closer look and maybe shoot at anything that moves. From what I could gather, the occupants of the jet seemed somehow different from us, and we will immediately be recognized as strangers. We must put some distance between us and this place, because they surely noticed the dead reptile. It won't have floated very far yet."

The jet continued seemingly unperturbed up the canyon, still rocking unsteadily in the turbulent air. When it was out of sight around a bend, they scrambled up the mountain faster than mountain goats. They were panting by the time they reached the top. They found themselves on a vast, uneven, grassy highland, dotted with rocky hillocks and stacks of jumbled boulders that gradually sloped down toward the east. Further south there seemed to be a high ridge across the way.

The sun had completed three quarters of its daily journey. At this high altitude and latitude it was quite cold and the sweat on their brows cooled rapidly. Kryger remarked, "We're not that out of condition, Quarr; it's the altitude. We should look for a cave or sheltered place before dusk. It will be freezing at night." He turned and looked around. "I want to fix this location in my mind just in case something messes up our direction finders. Wow! These mountain chains around us are really high. We must be about five kilometers above sea level, and it looks as if we're in one hell of a vast mountainous valley surrounded by higher mountains. What kind of primeval cataclysm created this continent?"

They stared in awed fascination at a panorama they would never forget. Far away to the south, the orange-green sun glinted on rivers of a dozen lower canyons. Mountain ranges stretched away on every side. Here and there, as far as the eye could see, were slender, lonely peaks clad in perpetual snow, and the ghastly silence was deafening. Only in the harsh Thirstland—the wild, predator-infested half-desert of Nevus—did Kryger experience a vast, lonely silence such as this. As if to emphasize the quietness, a far away, wary call of a seemingly forlorn creature was quickly suppressed, as if the caller was embarrassed to break the eerie silence, or perhaps it was alarmed by something.

Awed, Kryger could only gulp. "I feel lost. The scout picked one hell of a place to quit on us. We'll have a very long, difficult walk ahead of us if they locate the scout. It can only be repaired in an adequately equipped workshop, but we can still go somewhere with it if they leave us alone."

Quarr, too, was almost overwhelmed, but she tried to be practical. "We'll see within a day or two. The jet that woke us up might have found something, and the one that just passed may be here to pinpoint the find. I recommend that we move further away tomorrow, and fast, for I don't want to be near if the scout blows up. It's too risky for them to try and fly in at night, because that pilot was already fighting to keep his flyer steady."

"I owe you another peanut, Quarr. You are quite right, and its logical reasoning. Let's hunt as we go—if we can find anything—and look for a place to spend the night. Who knows what terrors this godforsaken land holds in store for the unwary stranger."

"Yeah, okay, if you say so." She sounded weary. "Keep reminding yourself to maintain your mental shield all the time, especially when you concentrate. Gorrel and his connections may suddenly decide to switch the thought-communication-suppressor off to catch us off guard. Don't take anything for granted."

"Uh, yes Quarr, but perhaps they can't switch it off, and Gorrel doesn't need it off." He decided that it was time to confess. "You know that it's not a habit, but I lied to you this morning, because I wasn't sure. We're still connected, as far as I can tell, but I've developed, or my subconscious has developed, some kind of solid, reflective shield. I think I now have the principles under control."

At that moment, as if Quarr's words had served as an open invitation, both felt the inimical touch brushing past their mind-shields. It was baffled and angry. Kryger grinned. "It's good to feel their perplexity. They weren't even aware that we're still

81

alive, and they brushed past us without feeling our presence. I sensed six minds linked together. No wonder they were able to overcome me so easily before. But they don't seem so hot now that I have your sophisticated abilities merged with mine. I don't know if you felt it, but they are leaking thoughts like a sieve and I picked up on most of it. They suspect I may have drowned and are mentally kicking Gorrel's butt for not considering such a possibility. They haven't found the location where our scout went down yet, but Gorrel is still waiting on a few aircraft to report back."

Quarr was awed by his rapid development. "It's almost unbelievable that you can glean so much information from such a brief brush of minds, Kryger. You are now more powerful than me, but you always had that potential and I'm glad I did what I did. Both our brains have more or less doubled in power. I would ask for nothing more if we could truly be individuals again."

"I'm sure it will be so again—given enough time. As we learn to control our thinking, we'll go out of sync. I felt your reaction to our uncontrolled merging, but don't worry, Quarr. Our age difference won't be of any concern to my family or myself. They love you and will be pleased that things worked out this way. What difference will five years make fifty years from now, or when we are a hundred years old? We have each other, even if we aren't able to ever leave this planet."

He slapped his forehead angrily. "Damn! There's something I should remember, but I can't think clearly in this mind-mucking fog with the thought-damper. What is it, Quarr?"

"I also have the feeling that there's something we should remember, but I've been so busy that I haven't had time to work it out. I don't think it's important at the moment, though." She suddenly embraced him tightly. She'd felt the urge to do so a few times during the past month, so perhaps her decision to merge minds with him wasn't as sudden as she thought the day before. Now she accepted the urge and was happy. She felt safe in his powerful arms.

He held her tightly. "Hey! You are almost as strong as I am, and you can now survive on your own if something happened to me." He spoke into her hair. "Speaking of survival, my stomach is growling with a not-going-to-take-this-anymore vengeance and I have to find something esculent. Let's move away from each other to hunt as we go, but make sure that we keep each other in sight all the time. Step as lightly as you can, and look where you put your foot down before you take a step forward."

Their needlers were ready when they separated by about twenty steps. They flushed rodents, which seemed to be plentiful. Near sundown, Kryger killed something that resembled a mountain sheep. As he gutted it, he remarked, "It bleeds red and it smells like a goat; therefore its edible—I think."

She smiled beautifully. "Yeah, I think the same way, which shouldn't surprise me. Let's go to the edge of the canyon and look for a cave or some shelter. We won't find anything from up here, so you carry our food, and I will check below the rim while you play the alert lookout."

The weathered rock provided plenty of shallow hiding places and she soon found a narrow cave with a low entrance. She called out to him to come down and take a look. When he arrived, he dropped the carcass at the entrance and warily inspected the cave. He judged it deep enough to give them a chance to meet a sudden attack, but went inside with his needler, ready to check for signs of recent occupancy. He found none and told her it was safe, a good choice. Because of the high altitude and the iciness, they were both very hungry at this point, and Kryger only skinned the sheep-like creature where he wanted to cut the exposed meat into easy-to-fry portions. There was no need to look for firewood because the little heater functioned as a small fryer as well. While he busied himself with that, Quarr set the safety precautions at the entrance.

The evening breeze took the enticing aroma of frying meat up and over the rim of the canyon. They were unaware of the suddenly curious, shadowy creature that paused and took a deep sniff; then decided that the tantalizing smell must be carefully investigated, for it meant the presence of enemies. Then the breeze carried the smell of man—the hateful creatures had lately come to capture and kill his kind, without reason or compassion. The weird creature shivered with deep hatred. Perhaps he could catch the wanton killers unawares and kill them. They did not deserve a quick death, but he didn't have the time to make them suffer.

12

As he put the first two portions aside on their thin, lightweight plates to cool down a little, Quarr, who felt a bit uneasy, told him, "I've set the perimeter guard. We don't have room in this excuse for a grotto to dodge an attacker, but we'll have a second or so to shoot if anything tripped the alarm. Unfortunately, it's far from secure. We might want to continue where we left off last night, but we'll have to keep our mind-shields tight all the time, which I don't think will be easy, at least not for me."

Kryger wished they'd been able to use their senses to scan the immediate area for threats. Why did someone, with such obvious premeditated intention, invent an infernal machine capable of isolating an entire solar system to suppress the use of the finer senses? *What was the purpose behind this invention, or was it just a bad case of xenophobia?* he thought viciously.

I'm not leaving this planet before I disable the invention, together with its creators. Kryger did not take a vow lightly.

The big, shadowy creature stole stealthily down toward the cave, but he distrusted the faint, steady glow of light reflected against the rocks in the gathering darkness. He would dash in fast and kill quickly, he decided. Hated man was meat and he could feed his injured mate with one carcass or more. He felt his fury mounting. That was good. In a killing frenzy, he was as fast as a thunderbolt that killed the unlucky without warning during heavy thunderstorms. He reached the flat rock above the entrance, but there was an overhang that prevented him from seeing inside, and he couldn't just drop down recklessly. It would be unwise, for if he were killed, his mate would slowly starve to death.

He retreated, tested the wind direction as a matter of precaution, and stalked his prey from the downwind side. He wasn't particularly concerned, since it was common knowledge that the Killers' noses were as inadequate and useless as their feeble strength, but he couldn't take a chance when his injured mate depended on him for sustenance and protection. Man depended on his weapons, for without them he was as helpless as a newborn stinker-rodent baby.

At short intervals, he paused to rear on his powerful hind legs to sniff and scan the area around him for signs of a trap. His mate was caught in an ingenious snare not so long ago, some distance from here. He used his powerful four-fingered hands to silently lower himself from a ledge as he stole closer. At last he was close enough and level with the hideout so that he could peep into the opening from behind the safety of a boulder.

The seemingly peaceful, unconcerned scene puzzled him, and distrusting what he saw, he opened the third eye in the center of his broad forehead. Yes! It was a trap, just as he had suspected. Lines of power crisscrossed the entrance between two devices placed on each side. The alert male, with a rather small weapon clutched in one hand, was looking directly at him, as if he sensed his presence but wasn't really seeing him. A Sensitive among the Killers, he thought. Very strange and disturbing!

Cocoons of power surrounded the slender devices. They, therefore couldn't be touched, for it was rumored that even a thrown missile, such as a rock, would be deflected and set off alarms which could get him killed. He couldn't know that these particular beams, when broken, only caused the devices to shrill a harsh warning. To his knowledge, those kinds of beams meant writhing, agonizing suffering, and a slow death. Before the thought-communication-damper came into operation, he had shared the exquisite agony of members of his faction when they tried to penetrate the barriers of light-beams around their old city, which was taken over by the Killers. He thoroughly loathed them. Perhaps he could exterminate them as he did with Krivvers, the river-dragons, by accurately throwing rocks, but such machines captured missiles as they did living bodies, and there was no sense or satisfaction in killing from a distance if he couldn't collect the bodies.

He didn't want to waste any more time on this. His mate was hungry and in pain, so he decided to let the enemy know that a stalker was nearby and watching. They would rush back to the old city in fear, which would make pursuing and slaughtering them that much more pleasurable. But he didn't take into consideration that his enemy had to cross the mighty canyon rivers, nor did he think to wonder why they were separated from their transport. He roared his anger and frustration as he jumped away from the opening, expecting a volley of bullets.

He was mystified when there were no panicky shots. Were they afraid, or perhaps low on ammunition? He couldn't take the risk to find out. Now that he thought about it, they looked different from the others, and when he smelled them, he didn't detect the faintest trace of fear. On the other hand, they may not be the type that panicked easily, and that may be why they were out here by themselves. What was also perplexing was that they were not dressed like the Killers, and the eyes of the male looked similar to those of the small, clawed rodent hunters who hunted mostly at night, and both had the same type of feline ears.

Something was not quite right, and it disturbed his peace of mind. He decided that he would feed his mate and then return to spy on them. If his mate felt up to it, they would follow and wait for an opportunity to slay them. He roared his frustration again. If the thought radiation suppression wasn't there, he could have divined their thoughts to know their plans and intentions. The two-legged creatures were as dense as prey animals and not nearly as vigilant. He stopped his grumbling and scented the night air in search of suitable prey.

They had just finished their satisfying meal when Kryger sensed intense hatred and the intention to kill from a source outside the cave. He wasn't surprised that he could detect strong emotion through the mind-inhibitor, for his powers were developing at an astonishing rate without conscious volition. He could have reached out with a feeler to the source of hatred, but wasn't quite ready to draw the attention of those inimical beings. He warned Quarr and readied the needler while he kept his eyes on the entrance in anticipation of an attack.

He could just barely make out shadowy movements near the big boulder that half obscured the entrance twenty steps away. His eyes somehow couldn't focus on anything definite, but perhaps it was because the feeble light emitted by the heater affected his sight. When the unwelcome visitor roared and jumped away, he had a momentary glimpse of the weirdest looking creature he had ever seen.

"That creature must be as big as a draft horse," he exclaimed, "but I could only make out a bulky shadow when it moved. Strangely, it was almost invisible, but I could see the gleam of three eyes and white fangs when it faced this way and roared. It might be a vicious killer, but why didn't it attack? I don't think that I'd want to meet one without weapons, even in broad daylight, because it will be an ugly customer."

Quarr took it calmly. "So, we have unexpected company. Where there's one, there'll be more. I guess we'll have to sleep in shifts."

"Well," he pretended to think deeply. "I hope I can sleep with the block on my thoughts firmly in place. Otherwise, after what happened last night, you'll have to share my erotic dreams."

"Why dream?" she remarked as she removed her shorts.

When they touched each other, even with mind-shields firmly in place, they found that thoughts flowed freely between them. They had amazing chemistry together and shared incredible moments, memories of which would last forever.

As they relaxed later that night, Quarr remarked with a smile, and her usual laughing voice, "Now you look all in. Anyway, you've had the training to stay awake or sleep at will, so I'll take the first watch 'til about what I think might be the local midnight, which should be about five hours from now, or when I can't keep my eyes open anymore. I somehow know that our visitor will come back, and I have a feeling it's more intelligent than we can imagine. Don't kill it unless you're forced to. Its frustrated roar may have been an unintended warning. An ordinary predator would have attacked mindlessly if it were hungry, because the opportunity was there. We'll have to be on the lookout all the time."

"I agree. Do you realize that your senses are beginning to function in this muck with your shield on?" As she shook her head in wonder, Kryger smiled. "I thought not. I felt that monstrosity's inexplicable hatred, and a needler may not stop it in time if it decided to attack. Here, take the MAG and keep it in your hand all the time, pointing to the entrance. There are twenty-eight shots left. I don't care if you drive a dozen tiny tunnels through the planet, as long as you don't shoot upward and possibly bring tons of rock down on us. Goodnight, dear." He turned over on his right side and was asleep within seconds.

Although it felt as if he had only slept for a few minutes, he awoke instantly when she touched his shoulder. He washed his face with a handful of water from his canteen to drive the last vestiges of sleep away. Quarr was already starting to breathe deeply and he thought that she must be really exhausted, and that she must have a will as strong as the mountains to have kept awake for five hours. He watched her fondly for a short while and then turned his full attention to the entrance as his keen ears detected a faint scraping sound. While he was sleeping, Quarr had turned the heater off in an effort to stay alert, so there was no glow to affect his eyesight. There was now also a silvery-green moonlight, although not very bright, but he could see as clearly as in daylight.

Just before daybreak he saw the hideous, shadowy form materialize cautiously from the deeper shadow of the nearby boulder. Its color was a curious kind of mottled gray that blended well with the wan moonlight, and it was as big as a two-year old horse, but more powerfully muscled in a peculiar sort of way. He saw the rippling muscles on its shoulders and hindquarters. The animal, if animal it was, looked sleek, fast, and deadly despite its size. In contrast to its body, its face was a nightmare of protuberances and fangs. Two of the three eyes glared intense hatred as it looked toward the cave, but Kryger wasn't sure that the creature could see him in the dark grotto. For a moment he was tempted to kill it, because it was a menace to their safety, but innate respect for life mixed with curiosity withheld his finger from pulling the trigger. In his mind he clearly heard his father's often repeated admonition:

Son, you must always keep in mind that some people kill without thought because they can do so without retaliation, or just to indulge in personal pleasure, because they can get away with it, or out of fear. They fear the unknown and kill to remove their own fears. Some kill for trophies to impress other people, because they think that proves their fearlessness; and some just kill out of curiosity. Once taken, a life cannot be restored, and we must learn to kill only out of necessity for food or in self-defense. If and when you are sure of yourself and what you can do, you won't feel the need to prove anything to yourself or others. First try everything else before you resort to useless demonstrations for the amusement or envy of others, or killing unnecessary just because you can. A savage face doesn't necessarily mean an evil nature, and neither does an angelic face represent a benevolent soul. With an animal, try this for instance. He then demonstrated the very high frequency call sign for friendship, and the mind-bolt he had discovered by chance to discourage a stalker.

Kryger only killed for food when he was hungry, and afterward silently asked the prey to forgive him. Right now, he and nightmare-face apparently stared at each other, one curious, the other full of hatred and indecision. Kryger noticed the muscular arms with three-fingered hands and opposing thumbs, much like the claws of a raptor. He filed the picture away in his memory, and decided to send the mind-signal for peace to see if the creature responded to it, but just then he felt the penetrating brush of the combined minds again. It reminded him to be careful.

The shadowy creature, by opening its third eye, could clearly see the odd-looking Killer in the dark shadow, but he was puzzled by its behavior and he was ready to take off the moment it lifted the small weapon. Also feeling the mind-search, he gave voice to a frustrated growl and slunk away into the shadows. Why did the evil Gorrel, search for these creatures with its powerful mind? Were they really being hunted, or was this just another deception? Something was amiss. It didn't quite fit. These creatures looked like the Killers, but their heads and attitudes were different. He distrusted anything concerning Gorrel and the Killers who arrived with it, and this just seemed to be a bit too coincidental. He decided to follow them and see; and kill when the opportunity presented itself. It was always better to be safe than sorry.

He would go and discuss this with his mate. She seemed to be in a bit less pain now and perhaps she might be able to travel without too much inconvenience and suffering. He rapidly climbed to the plateau and then broke into a racing gallop. The Killers might be able to search with their noisy machines and he didn't want to be caught out in the open.

13

When the night began to fade, Kryger started to fry portions of the mountain sheep, and the smell woke Quarr.

"Ah! This is the life! Breakfast in bed," she jested. "Did anything happen while I was sleeping?"

"Yes, our visitor was here when you woke me up. Its body, including its neck, looks as if it is a cross between a grey horse and a spotted tiger, but the head is a nightmarish, crazy mixture of that of a horse, a warthog, a wolf and some other weird creature; complete with thick fangs half as long as my fingers. To add to the confusion, it seems to have three eyes, and two long thick arms protruding from overly broad, muscular shoulders. We had a good look at each other, but I couldn't see whether it had hoofs or claws, because it has a peculiarly camouflaged coloring that makes it blend with its background when it's motionless. I think it must be a Sensitive, because it took off like a scorched dog when our self-elected enemy tried to trace me again. It must have claws or something similar, because it ascended the steep incline to our right very fast without making a sound. If it's as intelligent as it seems to be, we could try to make friends if we come across it or its kind again."

"I agree. It would be useful to have an ally or allies with local knowledge, but let's take it one step at a time. This canyon, like all the others we saw from the air, runs in a southerly direction. To go east and south, we probably have to cross a few canyon-rivers and other obstacles. But first we must get as far away as possible from the scout, as quickly as possible. I have a feeling that something really crazy is about to happen. I have the urge to panic and run like a scared antelope. For all we know, they have detected the scout and are on their way in force."

Kryger agreed, but first he wanted a satisfying breakfast. When they finished, they packed quickly, and he reluctantly left the carcass for scavengers. They climbed to the top of the canyon again and managed to maintain a good pace, staying near the ragged edge, as it provided some cover should highflying aircraft appear. Two hours later, they reached the high ridge, which continued on eastward, and then, in the far distance, turned north. It looked as if the river ate through a connecting ridge in ages past and that the natural bridge over the canyon had collapsed with the passage of time, leaving ragged, weathered precipices on both sides of the river.

They slowly climbed the steep ridge in the rarefied air and reached the summit around mid morning. On this side of the canyon, it wasn't a ridge as they'd thought, but a high, bleak plateau, and a cold wind was blowing. Kryger's practiced eyes noticed occasional little dales and that the highland was sparsely dotted with stunted shrubs and an occasional boulder—some of which were just big enough to conceal a predator or a human being—and clumps of tough grass with raspy-rough sharp blades.

They did not look back the way they had come as their eyes were drawn to a clear spring some distance away. They therefore did not see the two creatures on their trail as they filled their canteens and started to jog slowly with the cold wind in their faces, still along the edge.

Pushing worrying thoughts aside, Kryger kept his eyes darting and ears open, for the strong breeze made it impossible to test the smells of the area. They'd covered about a kilometer when the wind brought a faint buzzing sound, which he immediately associated with racing helicopters as he had encountered the same type of aircraft on other planets. Quarr did not ask silly questions as she followed closely on his heels when he raced for the cover of a stunted tree next to a boulder.

The two shadowy stalkers had just reached the edge of the plateau, and they too hurried to inadequate cover with very unkind thoughts aimed at the pernicious Killers. The female was slower and walked with obvious discomfort, but she was as determined as her companion to be present when they met their quarry, but for a different reason than her mate. She saw their quarry race for cover as well, and the act confirmed her suspicion of the night before when she was told in detail about the two odd-behaving intruders. They could kill possible allies. She growled her observation to her mate, but he spit an angry reply. "It is better to kill in error than to perish in betrayal. The two-legged ones are not worthy of trust, as had been proven time and time again."

"As you can see for yourself, they are wary and hide from the Killers. There must be a good reason for it, and you said that they look a bit different. Let's wait and observe. We have time on our side. Their confidence tells me that they can kill, but choose not to. How did they kill the prey animal you smelled?" She sensed, even in this artificial mind-murk, that things were not as clear-cut as her mate wished them to be, and there was this nagging feeling that they were not using their weapons as freely as the Killers for a perfectly valid reason.

The male, Ycagabys, didn't want to argue as it might upset her, and she had a biting sarcasm that he strove to avoid whenever possible; but she was making sense. "Agreed," he growled. "We'll follow and observe for a few sun-circuits. I will hunt at night when it's safe for you to rest. They are slow and cunning, but it doesn't make any difference to me. I promise that I will not act rashly." He muttered an untranslatable curse-word: "...this mind-talk barrier. We could have divined their thoughts and caught them off-guard, or otherwise confirmed your suspicion."

She was totally dependent on him for survival until the festering wound allowed physical activity and kept her silence, as she was not about to start an argument. There might be a perfectly valid reason for their quarry to travel in the direction of the enemy base, but her species was being decimated and they had to survive at all cost, even if it meant killing innocent beings. She had to protect the new life beginning to stir inside her, for it would be ready for release into this harsh world in another moon-cycle.

The deafening noise of six fast-moving helicopters lower down in the canyon made them stay in cover a little longer than necessary, to wait for the noise to dissipate. *They must be on their way to the scout, hoping to trap us with it,* Kryger thought bitterly. He was just about to leave cover when he faintly heard, and then saw, a small, strange type of aircraft half a kilometer away where the canyon made a left turn, which he thought might be a one-man helicopter-type gunship trying to lift over the edge onto the plateau. The icy wind seemed to be creating a dangerously strong downdraft, for the small, silenced aircraft kept dipping and swerving violently, as if it didn't have sufficient power to overcome the downdraft. After a number of attempts, the pilot gave up, and turned to move slowly down-canyon again, as if seeking a safer place to lift out, or return to base.

"It is a type of spy-craft I have not encountered before," he told Quarr, "and the downdraft must be fierce. It must've been silenced, because I almost couldn't hear it, which may account for the power deficiency. From now on, we must stay close to cover and avoid open spaces whenever we can, even if it takes a day to go around an open space. I have no idea how severe the explosion will be if the scout self-destructs, so let's run to put more distance behind us, or until we start gasping for oxygen. I have a nasty feeling that those helicopters weren't racing for dry beans or for the fun of it. They're trying to catch us asleep, and they are going to be very disappointed when they find us gone."

They started off at a pace that baffled their pursuers. Ycagabys thought that he could easily catch up with them, but he had to consider their weapons and his mate. There was no hurry, since they didn't have to sleep like other creatures and could follow their trail by scent at night.

Kryger and Quarr had hardly run for ten minutes when the plateau swayed beneath them and they stopped in their tracks so as not to trip on the waving ground. Almost as an afterthought they heard a not too distant clap of thunder.

"Oh damn! Damn it to hell! Those bastards couldn't wait to break the scout's canopy open." He was really angry. "Now we're stuck here forever."

"You're not thinking, Kryger! They always come from down-canyon and they have spacecraft. All we have to do is to stay alive, find their base, and confiscate the best we can get our hands on. By the way, we've got uninvited company. I happened to look back the way we came to check if there's anything to see of the explosion, and saw a big grayish shadow duck behind cover way behind us on our trail. It must have exceptional eyesight to see my head turning at such a distance, but with three eyes it is to be expected."

"If it can think at all, it had better think twice before attacking us. We've got enough trouble as it is and I'm angry enough to tackle it with my bare hands." But he thought that he should make sure that they were indeed being followed, because if one knew what to expect, one could be prepared.

"This oval depression ahead of us runs eastward, and there's a reasonably shallow gully down the middle. Let's follow the gully, pass a few easy-to-cross places, and then cross at an angle about six hundred steps from here and head south again, in line with the jumble of boulders on the other side, about half a kilometer away. It should provide a good vantage point if we can sneak back behind them—" he grinned and indicated the direction with his chin, "—but we'll play cute and pass them a little way to the right. If the beasts are following our tracks, they will leave the gully in the same place. Oh…I'm just sharing my thoughts," he hastily added.

Quarr nodded, and without looking back, they jogged unconcernedly, as if they had all day to cross the dip, which was about a kilometer in width. After they passed the jumble of boulders about a hundred steps to their left, the ground sloped away sharply to the south, allowing them to double back without trouble as soon the dip was out of sight.

They were just in time to see the two grayish, weirdly horse-like creatures pause to sample the air in the same place they too had paused when the ground heaved. The creatures seemed to listen intently as they carefully scanned the surrounding area and the sky. Then they looked at each other as if they discussed something before they slowly followed the tracks. The second creature's left hind leg was almost useless and its progress was visibly painful as it hobbled along on three legs, but the other patiently kept pace with it.

Kryger's anger had abated. "Hand me your backpack. I'm used to hard running and can carry the extra weight without much discomfort, even in this rarefied air. Let's go southeast to put some distance between those shadowy creatures and ourselves. The crippled one will delay their progress, but we won't be able to lose them, since they can obviously follow our scent, and yes, you were right. Only intelligent creatures care about each other as those two obviously do."

Quarr didn't argue. She knew quite well that he had thrice her stamina and was used to long hours of hard running. She exchanged the pack for the MAG, which she carried in her hand.

Kryger set the pace and they ran for hours, as only persons adapted to the high gravity of Nevus could. They drank a mouthful of water every now and then and only stopped to replenish their flasks whenever they found water, which wasn't very often.

He took his hat off for Quarr, as she kept pace without complaining. She was fit, but didn't have the relentless training to detach her mind from her body. Perhaps she was unconsciously drawing the principles from *his* memories. Also, the lesser gravity of this planet was a boon for both of them. It was late afternoon when he sensed that she was nearing exhaustion. He slowed the hard pace down to an easy jog.

They topped a rise to find that a deep river barred their way. Kryger was surprised to find such a big river on the upland between canyons, but the evidence was there to prove that the unexpected was always possible. They slowed to a walk and Quarr continued to breathe deeply.

"The river's too deep to cross without swimming, and we know only too well what kind of eager denizen might be waiting. There may be other strange, hungry inhabitants that we haven't encountered yet, but I hear water falling some distance away to our right. There could be space behind the fall to overnight, and even if it's cold and wet, it might be safe from Gorrel's interference. Let me have the MAG back and let's proceed carefully, as we may come across something to eat. Have your needler ready, because it's your turn to provide supper." She was a crack shot and they had hunted together before.

Perhaps the prey animals were nocturnal and their kill of the previous day was just pure chance. They reached the falls without finding a thing worthy of being called supper, except the ever-present rodents. The water thundered down into a deep chasm and talking was nearly impossible.

He studied the sheer precipice, then took hold of her hand. Thoughts flowed clearly between them as he pointed down. *There's a ledge more than halfway down. Let's investigate; we may be in luck.* She could see that the weathered and cracked face of the cliff was almost perpendicular.

You lead the way and catch me if I slip, she joked.

It was a difficult descent, but they reached the ledge without mishap. The fairly wide ledge tapered rapidly until it petered out, but the other way led behind the fall. It became slippery under the fall, and they were delighted to find a deep, spacious cave behind the water about halfway through to the other side. In ages past, the river must have poured through a fault in the rock, smoothing the oval cave before the water was blocked off. The sides, bottom, and top were smooth and rounded, and the cave smelled clean. The back still showed signs of an ancient cave-in, and the only access was the way they had come. It narrowed and ended some ten steps farther on in a sheer drop to the watery depths some sixty meters below.

The rush of the fall was muted at the back of the cave and it was easier to talk normally. Quarr rubbed his arm. "I'm afraid I can only offer a choice of rations, so let's get on with supper," she joked. "We'll be safe tonight, I think, but let's activate the perimeter guard in any event, before we turn the heater on."

14

Far behind, the mottled grey creatures stopped for the female to rest. She was tired and in tremendous pain again, but determined to be present when they caught up with the two-legged ones. Her curiosity was aroused, and although the chances were negligible, she hoped to find a way to communicate with them before her vengeful mate could have his way. She was convinced that it would be a grave mistake to kill them for the sake of an easy, empty revenge, without even trying to find out why they too, hid from the Killers. She didn't know how she could stop her mate, but she would give it a try when the time came.

"Find us some food, Ycagabys," she requested in their growling language. "I'll rest to ease the pain so that we can continue after eating. It will be safer to sniff out their trail in the dark, since the Killers don't hunt at night. Also, the morning dew may wipe out their scent."

"I find it curious," Ycagabys replied as if he picked up her thoughts, "that they also hide when the Killers come, but they are running in the direction of our old city. It does not make sense. Okay, I'll go now."

He returned four hours later with a buck slung over his muscular shoulders. As he handed her the prey, he explained, "I hunted on their tracks to find out where they went in the event that we lose their scent for some reason. They didn't cross the river, but have gone down the cliff above the place of the wild white waters where we cannot follow. We will watch from the top of the cliff, and when the sun comes up we'll see where they go. They may find a shallow ford above the white water to cross the river and then follow along the canyon-river, which no one can cross by swimming. We'll catch them long before they reach the salt waters."

It was their name for the ocean, and they had learned from the Gwarra that there were other continents, separated from each other by a vast ocean. Some of them had even seen pictures of their planet floating in space, which was hard for them to fathom. Of course, all such information had been transmitted from mind to mind across the continent, so they weren't as ignorant as one would expect from predator-looking, but unexpectedly intelligent, beings. They didn't know that the tremendous explosion that rocked the table-land earlier had permanently blocked the flow of the great canyon river, and that it would be easy to walk across to the next canyon if their quarry decided to head west, away from the old city that now was the enemy's stronghold.

The female, Pgabys, made a decision. "We'll go on after midnight then. Do you want to share the prey with me?"

"No, I've killed for myself. How are you feeling?"

"Not much better, I'm sorry to report. The bullet lodged in my haunch makes it very painful, but I will manage on three legs, as I've done up to now. I have no choice, because the Killers might find me while I'm out in the open, as I cannot hide as quickly as I might need to. We must walk slowly, for we have more than enough time to find a good place to keep watch before daybreak."

"It will be as you want, and I will rest with you until it's time to go."

She ate, her powerful jaws crushing bone with apparent ease, while he made himself comfortable. They never slept as humans did. It was just a relaxed, restful doze for the body to recuperate while their senses remained alert—their heritage from a perilous past.

They were in hiding on the edge of the cliff close to the river long before daylight. There was no way of knowing that their quarry had left an hour before they had arrived.

Kryger and Quarr woke after midnight. With the isolation provided by the water, they found that they could mind-talk without touching each other, but deemed it too risky and agreed to do so only in an emergency, and to keep it very brief if they had to warn each other outside such protection. Feeling rested and restless, they deactivated the alarm and went out onto the icy ledge. The waning moon was up, and the illumination was enough for them to see as clearly as in daylight. They decided not to wait for sunup and went back inside to pack up.

The descent was precarious, but they took it slowly and reached the bottom after about half an hour. The high waterfall poured down thickly into an enormous, turbulent pool with deafening noise, but left a wet, slippery passage of almost twenty meters. They slid their way through a thick, ages-old green carpet of tricky slime and moss, and were thoroughly

98

drenched and shivering by the time they reached the opposite side.

Quarr spoke close to his ear. "It's a unique, fun way to cross a river—underneath. At least there were no monsters waiting to take a bite out of us."

They walked on the rocky bank at the edge of the deep, roaring river to find an easier way than climbing straight up out of the deep, perpendicular ravine. After about a kilometer, the canyon walls closed in on the river, leaving no ledge or beach for walking, which explained the absence of animal life. The water accelerated at this point and they could hear the dull, intermittent thunder of hair-raising rapids just a short distance away around the first bend.

That left them no option but to climb, which soon warmed their half-frozen bodies. The top of the high mesa and the surrounding peaks were already bathed in the rosy, green-tinged light of dawn when they reached the summit. The cold, profound silence made them feel like trespassers in the lonely, vast panorama of canyons and mountain ranges. It really brought home the fact that they were totally isolated. They could see as far as their remarkable sight could reach, and they felt as insignificant as insects on an enormous, uneven surface. It was an exciting, vulnerable sensation because they were more used to the close confinement of a cockpit.

Ycagabys was getting fidgety. From their vantage point he had a clear view of the massive waterfall and the deep chasm where the river continued, but there was no sign of his quarry. "The sun will soon be above the mountains, and no sign of them!" He growled impatiently. "I'll check along the chasm."

"Ycagabys, be careful! You should know that there's another life inside me who is also dependent on you."

He stiffened in surprise and scrutinized her body. Yes, she had a swollen belly. He felt proud, because it was their firstling. This was unexpected, as they had been under severe strain for many cycles of the moon. They'd been running and hiding for as long as he cared to remember. An offspring would be an extra burden, but since it was there, it was his responsibility to care for them both. He looked into the far distance across the river toward the southeast, and grunted with surprise. The quarry was scrambling up the escarpment as nimble as mountain goats.

"Look there, Pgabys," he growled urgently and pointed with a hand. "I don't know how they crossed the dangerous river down there in the dark, but they certainly didn't sleep as long as the Killers normally do. They are stronger and nimbler than I thought, but I won't underestimate them again. We have to kill them. We can't take any chances, especially now that you are with young."

Pgabys knew that stubborn look. His mind was made up and he wouldn't budge, even if he were wrong. She didn't know how, but it may make a difference if she could get a chance to convey to those two by signs that they wanted to be friends before Ycagabys attacked, for she was afraid that he might be killed. She could use that argument to approach them first, for without him she and her offspring wouldn't survive.

"Painful as it will be for me, we'll have to cross the river. Look for a suitable place," she instructed as she rested her head on her forepaws. It eased the pain a little when she rested half on her left side, with her wounded right buttock relaxed by stretching her leg out backward.

He scanned the sky carefully for highflying aircraft and strained his keen hearing to the utmost. It was quiet and seemed to be safe, so he took off at a gallop. He would use the time-honored way to outwit the local river beast. They were fiercely territorial, but not too smart, and he expected that one would be waiting in a pool close to the falls for drifting carrion. He found the monster lazing in a deep, rocky pool where the river seemed to hesitate before it rushed the short distance to spill headlong over the edge.

He turned and ran upstream along the riverbank. This close to the falls, the riverbank was solid rock, but he found a belly-deep ford a few hundred steps farther on where he could cross in a few leaps, but Pgabys was crippled and not capable of jumping. He had to make sure that she had more time than usual to cross at a slow pace. He returned, explained what he had in mind, and led her to the spot.

There was a copse nearby where she could hide if aircraft arrived, and large boulders on the other side, but she waited patiently on three legs at the ford while he galloped upstream. It was too much trouble to move closer to the hiding place, for it was early yet, and she doubted that the Killers would arrive this early in the morning. It would be out of character.

Ycagabys picked up two oval rocks along the way, each weighing about five kilograms, but which he handled as if they were mere pebbles. He lost sight of Pgabys before he found what he was looking for—a separate slab of rock that extended into the river, and which should amplify sound in the water. He began to beat a peculiar rhythm with both rocks just below the waterline. The water would carry the dull-booming sound-vibrations downstream, and depending on its state of mind, to the river-beast it would sound like an invitation to a fight over territory.

Pgabys whistled a piercing warning when the river beast stormed past her like a powerboat in its eagerness to investigate the source of the all too familiar sound. When it was past, she started to wade cautiously, because the beast's primitive brain would be totally focused on the imitated challenge.

Ycagabys first saw the fast approaching patch of agitated ripples, then the pale body when the long neck and nearly flat head emerged to utter a confused challenge to the invisible challenger that should have been nearby. Ycagabys tensed his body and rapidly threw both rocks, one with each hand and harder than required, at the reptile's head a few steps away. Both rocks smacked accurately on target, because it was an activity often practiced with deadly intent.

After such abusive treatment, the unfortunate recipient usually woke up shortly after with a splitting headache that probably lasted for days, or it drowned without being mourned. Ycagabys thought that he really didn't give this one a choice. The current this close to the falls was swift enough to carry it over the long drop before it could recover. He sprinted for the ford and was across before his victim had drifted thirty meters.

They knew the area well and took a shortcut by means of a broad fissure in the high mesa to get ahead off their quarry. They thought that the two-legged beings would travel above the river, because the fast and dangerous rapids prevented crossing until it swung around the upland toward the east. They couldn't imagine that the humans would first head east and then south across the tableland.

Although her progress was slow, Pgabys took to the nearly level low ground gratefully, and plodded on. It was extremely unlikely that aircraft would fly along this fissure, as it was extremely narrow in quite a few places. As the day progressed her hunger increased, and it took her thoughts away from the throbbing pain as she hobbled along on three legs.

Kryger froze and took hold of Quarr's arm. He slowly pulled her into the cover of a stunted bush. *Our pursuers must know the area quite well, because they are ahead of us. Look down, a little toward the left. There!* He pointed.

Yes, now I see them. They look like shadows with those dotty dark grey splotches on their lighter grey hide, and the way they move and blend with every kind of cover. They remind me of our sand-cats, which are almost invisible on the desert sand. Hey! They have tails like lions—it looks pretty funny on those bulky bodies

The shadowy hunter had decided that it was close enough to its unsuspecting prey. It charged silently and with deadly swiftness, then jumped up into the air, very much like a wolf or a jackal hunting small prey in high grass or snow. As it came down, it grabbed the buck with both hands and swiftly crushed the neck with its huge jaws. The buck only had time for a short, startled bleat. The Shadow swung the buck over one shoulder and returned to its companion where they shared the kill by tearing it in half, the bigger portion going to the injured one.

They could hear the crunch of bones as the Shadows quickly devoured the deer, bones, hide, head, everything but the horns and perhaps a few drops of blood.

Kryger whispered, "It takes strong jaws to crush bones that easily. Must be one heck of an adversary. The way they share the kill tells me that they are rational beings, although still a bit on the primitive side, perhaps. I'll go down and see if I can make the uninjured one listen to my side of the argument."

Quarr patted his arm and nodded agreement. He slipped the pack from his shoulders and stood up in clear view of the Shadows and began the steep descend. They didn't see him, so he kicked a loose rock down the slope to see their reaction. As it started to bounce, he smiled and noted where the Shadows had disappeared into cover.

When he reached level ground, he tried the high-frequency friend-sign, which was met with blank stares. He then held his arms up in the air at shoulder level in what he thought was the universal token of peace and surrender.

"What's the perverted creature up to?" Ycagabys growled. "Hah, the puny little thing is asking to fight for you... I can't believed it, but I'm seeing it with my own eyes! Why does he want you? That sound must be some weird kind of speech, or a death-song. Anyway, I intended to kill it, so now the only difference is that I'll be able to laugh about it."

He stepped out of cover, raised his hands and growled acceptance, showing his fangs in a horrible grin. He walked to an open space where the ground was level and free of obstructions, and kicked dust into the air with his hind feet to show his scorn.

Kryger was nonplussed. The Shadow obviously was aggressive, that much was very clear, but why didn't it attack outright? Kryger held both hands forward, palms up; the show of empty hands as a placating gesture.

To Ycagabys this was an invitation to attack first. He gladly roared his acceptance and launched himself into the air in a powerful jump. He would crush this creature in no time at all, he thought. He was astounded and confused when the man-creature took an astonishingly swift step forward, and stooped underneath his body while he was still in mid-air. The only thing he would remember afterward was that, in the fast-flowing movement, one foreleg was grabbed and pulled down and rearward with unbelievable power. He tumbled and landed flat on his back with an agonizing groan.

As the Shadow hit the ground with a satisfying thud that temporarily winded it and raised the dust, it lifted and turned its head in reflex to get back onto its feet again. Kryger delivered a devastating punch behind an ear where the head joined the thick neck. The Shadow's neck flopped limply back to the ground and its body relaxed as if in death. It showed no further interest in combat. Kryger quickly stepped away and immediately went into a ready stance, expecting its injured companion to attack as well.

He was somewhat astonished and mystified when the injured Shadow limped from cover with its hands folded over its head, which was bowed as if in submission. The beast came to a halt in front of him, and waited. He wasn't sure what would happen, but he put out a cautious hand and touched a hairy hand on its head.

The beast shuddered but stood its ground, and he "read" a stream of strong thoughts as she growled softly in her own language. *What manner of creature are you? My mate is full of hate for Killers like you, but you challenged him for me and killed him in fair combat. Now I'm yours, but I cannot imagine what use you have for me.*

Kryger was stunned, but he replied without hesitation. *I'm not a Killer, and your mate isn't dead. He'll wake up in a while with a bit of a headache. I wanted to talk, and thought that holding my hands in the air to show that I held no weapon was a sign that I came in peace. We have many questions, but those can wait as you are clearly in a lot of pain. Let me see what we can do to make you more comfortable.*

He looked up toward the mesa, but saw that Quarr was almost down to the level ground. She must have started down as soon as the fight began. When she joined them, he took her hand and told her to take the other hand of the noticeably pregnant Shadow. He projected a thought. *I'm Kryger, and this is my mate, Quarr. We came from the stars and are hunted by the Killers, as you call them. What is your name? Please explain what causes your pain.*

I'd been hoping that I could talk to you. I am Pgabys, and my irresponsible mate is Ycagabys. The "bys" were added when we become bonded. It is to tell that we have a mate, and it would be impolite to address one of us just as Ycaga or Pga. I have a piece of soft metal imbedded in my left haunch and it's crippling me. I was shot by one of the Killers when they hunted us five sun-cycles ago. Can you help me? She pleaded and looked Quarr in the eyes.

The bullet is poisoning your blood and your body is trying to reject it, Quarr acknowledged. *I have to cut it out, but you will not feel the pain. Let's go to the shady spot where you hid. Your companion should be awake soon. Will he attack again?*

While they walked the short distance, Pgabys talked, *I do not think that Ycagabys is that stupid, but I will talk to him when he wakes up. We thought that you were Killers—at least my mate thought so, but your behavior left doubt in my mind. Your mate said that we'd talk later. This is a good hiding place if the Killers come.*

They were trained, and equipped, to do small operations in an emergency. Taking the size of the Shadow's body into consideration Quarr injected a liberal dose of local anesthetic around the septic wound. When Pgabys said that feeling was gone, Quarr probed the inflamed wound with long tweezers until she found the bullet. After cleaning the wound thoroughly, she applied antiseptics and stitched the inflamed hole; knowing that it would help to speed up the healing process. When she was finished, she touched hands with the beast.

You must not run or put strain on this leg for ten days, otherwise the wound will reopen. Try to rest as much as possible, and when you walk or move, do so slowly. The wound must have time to heal.

At that moment Ycagabys staggered drunkenly to his feet. Pgabys glared at her mate and growled warningly for a few seconds. He steadied and growled back. The growls sounded like the prelude to a fight between the creatures, and Kryger was a bit uneasy because he couldn't understand what was going on. Quarr, however, still had hold of Pgabys's hand. She understood, and smiled.

Quarr told Kryger to relax as Ycagabys would not attack again, and to cross his arms to show his peaceful intentions. He blushed furiously when he was told that the thrusting of arms upward was a challenge to fight for a mate. Palms down and arms straightforward meant an invitation to squat down for a serious discussion. Placing both hands on one's head meant surrender, which seemed to be a universally accepted gesture.

Ycagabys placed both hands on his head in a token of submission before he held them out to Kryger, palms down. Kryger was wary of trusting the beast, but his suspicions vaporized when he touched hands and felt the innate gentleness of the creature's thoughts. He relaxed completely when he received Ycagabys's wry and humorous thought.

I saw your empty hands, so what'd you hit me with? You have the eyes and ears of a rodent hunter, yet you are built like a Killer. Why is this? And you are not as weak as they. You're as strong and fast as two of me put together in a small body. Thanks for sparing my life and helping Pgabys.

Before Kryger could reply, their keen ears detected the chopping sounds that indicated a number of helicopters rising out of the canyon less than a kilometer away. Ycagabys hissed his hatred, but did not immediately let go of Kryger's hand. *They're approaching rapidly and have instruments that can detect body heat at a great distance. They have been after us*

105

for a long time.

15

Three helicopters were approaching around the curve of the mesa like vengeful hornets. Kryger stood beside his chosen refuge in plain sight, ready to duck behind it, and held the MAG in his hand, pointed down.

He was waiting for the approaching party to show their intentions, and their attitude would dictate future responses. The helicopters fanned out in a half-circle and slowed down to a weaving hover about three hundred meters away. Seeing no overt weapons capable of killing at long distance, and expecting no opposition, they halved the distance. Kryger saw huge grins on brown-purple faces, and the crews made gestures to indicate that he should run.

He noted that each helicopter was equipped with two antiquated cannons; the kind that still fired solid, explosive shells. He wondered what use they had for them, as beam cannons were much more destructive. He found out as soon as the thought entered his head. A gunship swiveled its cannons in his direction and fired.

Even as the canons lined up in his direction, he stepped and squatted behind the huge boulder and pressed his hands over his ears. He made it just in time. He was showered with chips and dust as he cringed, feeling helpless and terrified that the onslaught would not end before the boulder was reduced to gravel. But the boulder withstood the salvo.

Are the Shadows so elusive a target, so hard to kill, that they need cannons to do the work of a single half-decent sniper. Clearly they wanted to create panic and horror for the sheer pleasure of it. They most probably laugh as they describe the terror they induce, he thought viciously as he remembered their huge grins. Kruger became deadly calm.

When the firing momentarily ceased, he stepped out from behind the remains of the boulder. "Having fun, are you?" he hissed between clenched teeth as he aimed for the propeller shaft of the offending gunship and fired. The blades stopped and the engine revved to an ear-splitting pitch as the craft dropped down. Continuing the same movement, he shifted aim to another craft and fired simultaneously with the gunner, which made him dive behind the boulder again even as he pulled the trigger. He heard Quarr yell as salvos of shells almost ripped his refuge apart. Partly dazed from the intense barrage, he realized that she was shooting at the remaining craft, that the noise had stopped, and that Ycagabys was making a beeline for the nearest helicopter, which had crashed less than a hundred meters away.

The needler was ineffective against the machine, for the tiny needles exploded uselessly against the transparent windscreen, but the accurate shots in front of his eyes made the pilot panic. Without thinking, he turned the helicopter to flee, thus giving Quarr a clear shot at him through the open side. The helicopter went out of control, and kept spinning crazily until it crashed halfway up the mesa in a ball of flame against the slope.

"It's the proper way to wipe the smirks off their ugly mugs, Quarr," Kryger praised.

She gave him a beatific smile. "Glad to have had a piece of the action. Why must you always hog it all? Anyway, I've got to protect my mate, don't I?" This time her voice fitted the words.

Ycagabys was starting to pull screaming victims out of the crashed helicopter, and ripping them apart one by one to give vent to his long-nurtured anger and frustration. He wasn't about to let the chance for vengeance pass him by, and quickly dashed toward the second helicopter. His mottled grey fur was streaked with blood and gore before he was satisfied. Not a single survivor was overlooked. Regretfully, he tossed the mangled body of his last victim into the air and expertly kicked it up into the air with both hind legs.

The screaming engines were a source of annoyance and danger. Kryger sprinted to flip switches one by one until the engines of both helicopters powered down.

Kryger put a hand on an un-bloodied part of Ycagabys's arm. *Do you know how to use their weapons? It might be useful if you and Pgabys can fight back next time.*

The unlovely face with the yellow wolf-eyes looked pleadingly into his. *No, but if you do, you can teach us. It would be brilliant to use their weapons against them.*

Okay. We should get away from here before more Killers show up.

Ycagabys loped away to a sandy patch and rolled around like a dog joyfully rubbing his back. He squatted on his haunches to rub sand into the remaining wet spots. Satisfied, he returned, touched Kryger, and explained. *I'll clean up later. There's usually a second batch of machines after an interval to surprise any survivors of an attack by the first team, but a storm is approaching rapidly. We will have to go to a place of shelter very soon, for these storms are dangerous. I will tell Pgabys to go to the nearest safe haven now.*

Kryger looked up, and for the first time noticed the ominous looking dark clouds rushing rapidly toward them, driven by a strong wind in the upper atmosphere. *Thank you, friend! We're collecting undamaged weapons and all the ammunition we can carry, but not the small weapons used in one hand. I don't think we'll have a need for those.*

Quarr looked after Ycagabys as he loped away to Pgabys. "It looks as if he's anxious to tell her the good news." She smiled secretly as she followed Kryger into the nearest helicopter: "Just imagine yourself, of all things, fighting for Pgabys's favors when you have no such intentions! By the way, they are more than just intelligent animals. Pgabys told me that they built houses and villages out of stone ages before the invaders showed up."

Kryger had blundered out of sheer ignorance, but he still felt the heat rise to his face. To hide his embarrassment, he combed the second wreck's interior for weapons. He immediately came across a heavy, undamaged Blaster-rifle. One bolt from it, placed in the right spot, could cripple a huge spaceship. It could also blast a stone fortress open, and he wondered what need they had for something so modern and lethal in a gunship.

He checked it carefully for damage, sniffed at it, and detected the distinctive odor of recent discharge. Were they so afraid of the Shadows that they would use it against them? It seemed unlikely. Maybe they had used it to destroy something big, like a cave they were too scared to enter, for instance. He searched the wreckage carefully and found half a dozen unused recharge magazines for the Blaster.

He appropriated a couple of medium caliber rifles, as they would be ideal for the Shadows. There were enough boxes of undamaged ammunition for the guns to start a small war, and he carried it some distance away since he intended to blast the helicopters to atoms. The scars that would be left by the blaster-bolts couldn't be easily concealed.

109

Percussion type bullet-guns were museum pieces on Nevus. They were taught the principles of their operation in school, and he had the uncertain privilege of firing a couple of rounds with one during training. Although warned beforehand, the recoil was unexpectedly violent and unpleasant, but the guns had been effective killing instruments in their time. The noise they made sounded like a close thunderclap to his ultra-sensitive ears.

Both helicopters had carried a crew of three. He surmised that it would have been the pilot and two gunners. The mutilated corpses looked human enough, but they were not the deep orange color of the Bikans. The dark brown skin had a distinctive purple tinge—a color he had not previously seen or heard of. Their kinky hair was a rich yellow, but their faces were flat, with broad noses like an inverted "v," as if, during infancy, each individual had been dropped hard on his face.

Quarr found one undamaged rifle and plenty of ammunition for it in the other helicopter. Kryger requested her to throw the pistols back, as they had no use for them.

At that moment, Ycagabys returned. He'd told Pgabys to take an easy path down to the river to a shelter they had previously used, and now he again drew their attention to the ominous storm, which would be on them at any moment. He helped to carry the boxes of ammunition a safe distance away and then volunteered to quickly return the corpses to one of the helicopters.

Kryger blasted the helicopters from a safe distance, to remove evidence that ammunition and a few weapons had been removed. *Let investigators—if they find any surviving pieces— scratch their heads and take wild guesses as to what had really happened here,* he thought. The one that had crashed against the slope was too far away to reach in the little time that was left before the storm broke. The debris was scattered over a wide area, and it would be obvious that it had crashed and exploded.

Kryger looked up at the sky as a dark shadow obscured the sun. He didn't like the look of the thick, ominous-looking, racing black cloudbank that was approaching from the southwest, and which rapidly obscured the landscape as if night was falling. And all of a sudden, the deafening thunder started, and awe-inspiring, almost continuous sheet lightning, began its display. His sensitive ears suffered, but there was nothing he could do. Rain, and especially a storm as threatening as this, wasn't welcome at this particular moment, but it would obliterate signs of their presence, which otherwise would be plain enough to read for anyone with a little tracking experience.

16

Ycagabys, his arms full, led them by the shorter, slippery way over the corner of the mesa, and then down again. The thick cloudbank now hid the sun completely. It was as dark as midnight, and bitterly cold. The continuous thunder-cracks made hearing impossible, and the white lightning flashes almost blinded them at times when it illuminated the gloomy sky. They hurried down the mesa as fast as they could in an eerie glow cast by the sheet lightning. As the strength of the wind increased, the chill became more numbing to the humans.

The ferocious wind that preceded the storm made the descent terrifying. Quarr was concerned about Pgabys's welfare, because the howling wind grew stronger by the minute and threatened to blow them off the narrow path. Slipping and sliding, they eventually reached a high overhang above a smooth, sloping shelf that ran into the river some ten meters down about fifty meters away. In the southwesterly direction where Pgabys must come from, the area next to the river widened, and they could make out a somewhat flat area for quite a distance.

As they progressed, the overhang became lower and deeper. It seemed to be just that—a powdery red, dusty overhang. Kryger was disappointed. He had expected something better, like a cave for instance, but beggars couldn't be choosers and it was better than no shelter at all. The overhang would keep the rain away, but the icy wind swirled the red dust around in thick, choking clouds.

Ycagabys didn't stop, however. He stepped onto the smooth shelf into the dust cloud and continued for another fifty meters or so, then disappeared as if swallowed by the rock. Kryger and Quarr had no option but to follow. They turned around a corner and found a narrow, inverted u-shaped opening, just a crack in the overhang, but high and wide enough to permit passage for the huge Ycagabys. After just five or six steps, the seemingly narrow crack abruptly ended in a huge chamber, half as big as the one they had hidden the ill-fated scout in. Only accidental discovery, or a careful search on foot, would give the cave away. The red powder reminded Kryger of iron ore, with which he was quite familiar. He put his backpack, guns, and ammunition down, then touched hands with their guide.

Friend, you have chosen well. This red dust means the area is just about pure iron ore and will defy penetration by instruments. Only the evil, questing mind of Gorrel can penetrate it, if we permit it. We will have to be careful in the open area during the day when I teach you to use the weapons.

That open area is a fairly large valley for hunting, friend Kryger, and we must not scare our prey away. We must go in the other direction if we're going to practice with loud weapons; I'm off to see what's keeping Pgabys. He stooped a little to enter the short passage, then took off at a gallop toward the south—the hunting ground.

Once their eyes were adjusted to the darkness, they inspected their temporary home. If they remained undiscovered, they would reside here for the next fortnight, or until they were reasonably sure they could continue their journey without harassment. The rough walls were broken here and there with large, dusty hollows, which could be cleaned for sleeping rooms to give them privacy. A small, clear fountain bubbled from one of these pocketsize rooms and ran a few meters into a large pool on the river-side of the main chamber. The pool overflowed into a crack that probably provided drainage into the river.

"He must know this canyon like the back of his hand, because he chose better than he realized, Quarr. I will gather some grass and leafy branches when we go out to hunt tonight—assuming the storm is over by then. The main room is sandy and not so dusty because of the pool. We can settle here for the time being. Let's put our things in front of this pocket so that we can claim it for some privacy."

They returned to the entrance just as the deluge started. The rain came down in almost solid sheets and Quarr pitied creatures caught in the full fury of the storm, especially Pgabys. She need not have bothered, as both Shadows turned up right at that moment, already drenched to the skin and looking like half drowned comical horses without hoofs. They shook the water from their hides, like dogs, but Pgabys was limping badly while she shivered uncontrollably.

Concerned, Quarr rushed to her side to find out what was wrong. It turned out that she had slipped outside on the wet rock, but had suffered no obvious injuries, for the stitches were still intact. Pgabys explained that she was almost frozen and that it was the reason she had slipped on the wet shelf.

Knowing that unfamiliar gadgets might alarm the Shadows, Quarr explained the use of the small heater before turning it on. The heat would also ease the pain of Pgabys's wound. The four of them sat down around the heater to soak up the heat, linked hands, and exchanged information.

The Shadows were surprisingly intelligent and knowledgeable. Kryger and Quarr learned much about the planet, which the Shadows called Okrion. They were semi-civilized, but didn't use fire at all, as they were flesh eaters. The growling sounds for the name of their race were untranslatable, even though the meaning of it was accompanied by thoughts. At Quarr's suggestion, they accepted being called Shadows, and they were amused by the reason for the nickname.

They'd learned about flying machines and guns, which killed at a distance, when the Killers arrived a little more than half a year ago and appropriated the old village previously occupied by Ycagabys's faction. The Shadows were rounded up and pressed into slavery. Those who managed to escape were ruthlessly hunted down, and attempts to free those inside the compounds always ended in failure and agonizing death. A few semi-wild factions still roamed the mountains and deep canyon. They quickly learned, after being warned, to hide their thoughts and to stay as far away as they possibly could from the location of the newly built spaceport.

As the conversation petered out, Quarr thought about her reason for visiting the planet, but before she could ask about other inhabitants, Pgabys told her.

I sensed your thoughts about people who came here long ago from space. My faction used to live in the cold north, on this same mountain-land between the two great canyon-rivers. Hairless two-legged beings, not unlike you, but without the rodent-hunter's ears, came there in a huge ship in my grandmothers time, about eighty or more hot seasons—or years as those people taught us—ago. I see you also call it years. They were peaceful and friendly, and we mind-talked with them and learned much. They did something to their ship and it came apart into houses, in which they lived when they started to excavate a huge cave inside the mountain as a permanent dwelling.

They could change into other shapes when they wanted to do something that required a different body construction, which fascinated my people. My mother and I

114

*didn't see this marvel, because the north became too
snowbound and cold for our kind to find food during the cold
season. My faction wandered south long before my mother was
born. If I remember correctly, my grandmother said that the new
people called their faction the Gwarra, or something like that.
She told us many tales about the wonderful things they learned.
That is where we learned about space and that the lights in the
night sky were other suns with planets that floated around them.
It still seems strange to me, but I'd like to see it for myself.*

The name stirred Quarr's memory and she was filled
with grateful joy. She vaguely remembered the name, but had
forgotten what it stood for. Now she remembered and was
happy. Perhaps her people were still free, and she and Kryger
could help keep them that way. She was a hereditary ruler, a
princess. It was time for her to begin her tenure of regency; to
take the responsibility of guiding her people, but she had already
formulated another plan.

The Shadows watched with some alarm as Quarr set
the perimeter guard over the entrance. Kryger saw the
expressions on their unlovely faces and went over to explain:
*The little machine creates beams of invisible light across the
opening from one rod to the other. When something breaks the
beams, an alarm will ring and wake us up.*

*We never really sleep, friend Kryger, but we see the
advantage. The warning will give us time to get ready if our
attention is elsewhere. We can see the beams when we open
our third eyes, and they look the same as what the Killers have
to guard their spaceport, but theirs is lethal. We assumed yours
were as well.*

*If it weren't for that infernal machine that suppresses
mind-talk, we wouldn't need this mechanical guard. It's too small
to kill or stun, but a bigger one will be too heavy to carry around
with us. We only need a warning so that we can decide what to
do about the intruder. Some intruders might be friendly,* Kryger
replied.

If one of us goes out, will it also make the alarm go off?
Pgabys asked.

*Yes, even a small rodent or a snake will set the alarm
off, but not a small insect.*

*Then we will use one of the chambers for the calls of
nature; that one on the other side.* Pgabys pointed to one
furthest away. She didn't intend it as a joke, but she was so

115

serious that Kryger laughed. They would get used to the serious nature of the Shadows. Although they never joked about anything, they did have a talent for seeing the grim humor in bizarre situations.

Despite their unlovely faces, the Shadows were unusually intelligent. They were well above beasts, although they were descendants of predators, and they only required decent explanations and some training to master new physical skills. They lived in communities and build dwellings of stone, some of which were destroyed, but in the case of the spaceport, the whole village was taken over by the Killers when they arrived. The breeding herds of large, tame, prey animals of the Shadows were either slaughtered on the spot, or carried away for use by the conquerors. They earned the name *Killers* by never leaving anything alive behind that could be utilized by their enemies— should any have survived after the raid.

A question had been nagging at the back of Kryger's mind for quite a while. Before they broke the connection to go to sleep, he asked, *You say that your people lived in the city where the spaceport is now, and that it's impossible to cross from canyon to canyon due to the infested, strong flowing rivers. How did you two get here?*

Ycagabys uttered a series of barking coughs, which Kryger interpreted as chagrined laughing. *Mostly by running and hiding, friend. I came north more than a year ago to hunt creatures that wander south during the cold season and prey on our herds. I got lost and didn't want to return to my village after I met Pgabys. We decided to stay together. We exchanged information with my faction and other individuals by mind-talk before the thought-communication-suppresser prevented us from doing so. That was how we were warned, and the way we warned other factions about the Killers. We lived in Pgabys's village far to the south near the great salt waters.*

One afternoon—I can't remember how many moon-cycles ago—the Killers surrounded our village to capture slaves. Many of us were out hunting and escaped the ensuing slaughter. We have tried many times to reach the beach to escape to another highland between canyons, but the way south is blocked solidly by the Killers. Their usual technique is to work from the ocean up to the cold north, because they know we can't cross the canyon-rivers without being devoured by the primitive river beasts. We cannot swim fast enough. And no, friend Kryger, the Killer's so-called god cannot mind-search for us, unless it knows our individual thought-patterns. Even then we know how to close our minds and shield our thoughts when we feel the Iñyo's search.

Sensing their puzzlement, Ycagabys explained that Iñyos were small, stinking, disgusting rodents with a life span of about thirty days. They fornicated almost continuously from puberty to death, or until caught in the act by a certain type of small rodent hunter for which it was an abundant source of food. Comparing someone with an Iñyo signified utter disgust. He continued.

The so-called "god" of the Killers looks like a giant insect, and goes by the name of Gorrel. The description we have is that Gorrel is big—three or four times our size. It looks like a giant ant, but unlike an ant it moves upright on four legs that are attached to its underbody. It has four tremendously strong arms mounted on the separate chest, and it likes to crush or tear other creatures apart with them. Gorrel has a very strong mind and if a Killer or a slave is disobedient, its mind is invaded and destroyed before it is slowly crushed to a seemingly agonizing death to discourage others. Gorrel's strong mind has very little effect on us, unless we are known to it. We fear it, but even if someone gets close to it, it cannot be killed. The people of many factions have tried many times, but it is said to be made of metal from which even bullets bounce. We don't know if the creature is male or female. It is rumored that agonizing, screaming pain amuses it.

Near midnight, they bade the Shadows goodnight and retired to their own chamber. Although they were tired, they had a lot to discuss and think about.

"Perhaps the two of us linked together might be strong enough to overcome the creature. It, or its race, seems to be the power behind all this, as well as the Bikans. If so, it's our duty to find out where the creatures came from and how powerful they really are."

"I don't want to think about it right now." Quarr's voice was weary with fatigue. "I doubt if I have the courage for a face to face confrontation. I have a feeling that the thought suppresser was launched to prevent messages being sent across space by my people, and not to prevent communication by the Shadows. The field's too strong, and it reaches out past this planetary system for goodness knows how deep into space. We were tens of millions of kilometers away when it was activated, remember? They could be about to launch an all out offensive against my people, and perhaps they don't want the genocide to be broadcasted. The noxious monster described by Ycagabys could have found out about them and their place of refuge by forceful interrogation of the Shadows."

"Yes, that could be, but it serves no useful purpose to worry about it now. It's cold and you left the heater for those two to share so that Pgabys would be comfortable. Will you share my sleeping bag?"

"Sure." It was irrelevant in which bag they slept. It was just one of those little things that had to be agreed upon—as if it mattered.

Knowing that the Shadows also kept watch, they relaxed and slept soundly for a change.

The hideout was well chosen and they stayed inside the cave whenever they heard the characteristic buzz or whistle, which was echoed by the nearby canyon long before an aircraft appeared. In the days that followed, slow moving search-flights came over regularly during the mornings. Sometimes a flight of heavily armed helicopters stopped, and the site of destruction was thoroughly inspected, but Kryger was sure that the remains gave no clues as to how they were destroyed. Ycagabys quickly learned to use the bullet guns of the Killers, but his accuracy left much to be desired. When Pgabys was well enough, Quarr trained her as well, and perhaps her female intuition served her well for she soon became remarkably accurate.

Kryger and Quarr practiced the ages-old fighting skills and formal exercises of karate every morning while they waited for the predictable reconnaissance flights to pass. The Shadows watched in awe and astonishment at the full out, lightning fast kicks and blows that seemed to connect, but stopped within millimeters of contact. Both were skilled at judging distance and controlling their blows.

After ten days, only a dull ache remained to remind Pgabys to be careful for a while yet. Kryger had kept the skins of prey, which he dressed and fashioned into suitable bags for the Shadows to carry on their backs. They stowed the ammunition and guns into these saddle-like sacks, and set off across the grassland early on the eleventh day. The Shadows felt confident that they could tackle the enemy and come off best, and if the humans had doubts, they didn't let on.

Midday of the second day out, they found an overhanging cliff on the eastern side of the canyon-river, which was large enough to block the water, if it could be knocked down. Kryger and Quarr performed careful calculations. They did not want anything to go wrong and perhaps collapse the cliff on top of themselves or some unfortunate animal, except one of the river beasts, which was perhaps unavoidable unless they instinctively fled at the first sign of danger.

The Shadows seriously assured them that the vicious creatures were an oversight by the Creator and not worthy of being considered. Kryger had to smile since, of course, the Shadows thought themselves quite attractive. *In the eye of the beholder*, he thought. He remembered the smooth, streamlined shape of the Saurian, and classified it as beautiful in its own way, although it was a deadly kind of beauty.

They were still far away from the spaceport, but there was a possibility that late reconnaissance flights might spot the possible dust cloud and rush to investigate, because they routinely scoured the canyons from midmorning to midafternoon. Kryger suspected that dangerous air currents developed during the late afternoon and at night that the Killers had to take into account. He asked the Shadows if it was possible to find prey anywhere near, since he didn't see any tracks as they approached this place, and they wouldn't find any prey within ten kilometers after the cliff came down.

The Shadows seemed to have a special sense for detecting prey where he thought none were to be found. They returned soon with adequate prey, ate under cover, and waited for late afternoon.

When he thought it safe enough to bring the cliff down, he told the others to take cover about five hundred meters away, because there was no way to prevent detritus from scattering all over the area when the cliff crashed down. After making sure that they were behind boulders, Kryger went back to the edge of the river where he could see the base of the cliff where it met the water. He aimed the Blaster and fired twice at different points before there was an ear-splitting crack of breaking rock, and the cliff started to break loose with a continuous thundering noise—slowly at first and then with gathering momentum.

When it started, Kryger turned and sprinted at full speed to the pre-selected hiding place, wondering whether he would make it in time. The ground shuddered as the cliff thundered down into the river, making it difficult to keep his footing on the sloping, uneven ground. As he dived behind the cover of a giant boulder, he was showered with detritus and muddy water. Then he was inundated by a great blob of muddy water, which seemed to home in on him alone as if in revenge. He felt and looked like a half-drowned cat.

"I'll be more careful with the next," he told Quarr a few minutes later when she managed to stop laughing. "From now on, you'll have to take cover farther away to one side, and I'll have to examine the way a cliff will fall before I choose a hiding place. As soon as the wind blows the dust away, we'll go and check whether we have made a decent bridge."

They didn't expect the cliff to break smoothly, and it didn't. They clambered around and over immense obstacles with razor sharp edges. It wasn't easy, but they took it slowly and managed without mishap. They were across by nightfall. After they crossed, Kryger aimed the Blaster at the middle, triggered a blast, and the river roared as it started to slowly push the temporary obstacle apart. He thought that by morning nobody would associate it with a temporary bridge.

They climbed to a flat, rocky undulating upland with scattered, wind-scoured stunted trees and clumps of low bushes. It offered no shelter against the icy wind, and they didn't rest before early morning. Just after sun-up, Pgabys found a hollow beneath a low overhang next to a rivulet where the freezing wind did not penetrate. The temperature was somewhere below zero, as was usual for this time of the morning, and Quarr lost no time in activating the heater. There was no feeling left in her or Kryger's exposed legs. Even the hardy Shadows were grateful for the little warmth.

17

Kryger and Quarr were just about to doze off when they heard the far-off whistle of a slow moving jet aircraft.

"They will see the remains of our bridge that isn't washed away yet, and may decide that it should be investigated. There could be Killers on our trail by midday," Kryger growled in the Shadows's language that he and Quarr were beginning to understand.

"Sleep and rest, friend Kryger. We will watch. If they come, they will not catch us asleep," Ycagabys promised solemnly. He didn't realize that his remark was humorous when they smiled, for he was pleased that Kryger and Quarr could talk to him in his own language, even if it was not quite perfect. He promised himself that he and Pgabys would learn to speak their language in the near future, even if it came out sounding mutilated, since their vocal cords were different.

The Shadows kept their slumbering watch, and it was early afternoon when they sensed they were no longer alone. Ycagabys quietly left the shelter to investigate while Pgabys woke the humans. He was back within ten minutes and apprehensively reported that a team of Killers was quite close. Four handlers were leading a vicious snuffer animal, which, reportedly, was strong and fast enough to catch and kill a Shadow. These weird animals were brought in from off world to hunt escaped slaves, and to discourage others from taking off into the wilderness. The few big predators on Okrion were not as strong and vicious as these creatures were reported to be.

Kryger was glad that he understood the growling language well enough to follow what Ycagabys was saying. He sensed the growing urge for panicky flight, even without touching them. The Shadows were not prone to fear, so this beast must be horrific.

He touched both Shadows to transfer his confidence and calmness: *This is a good opportunity to face the enemy and see how well you can use your weapons. Leave the animal to me this once. This time I will kill it for you, but you must remember that you can kill it with the guns yourselves. Take your weapons and go with Quarr. Do only what she tells you and nothing else, because you must first learn how to engage the enemy from a distance. Of course it is very easy to panic and*

*start running, but that will not kill the animal or the enemy you
are afraid of, and that is exactly what the enemy wants you to do
to make it easy for them.*

He turned to Quarr and told her, "They are mortally
afraid of the tracker-beast. Our needlers will suffice, but take the
bullet gun along for some practice. I'll whistle when things
become too hot to handle, or when it's time to depart, then we'll
meet back here to gather our things. If it comes to that, I'll keep
the enemy at bay while the three of you retreat."

"Okay, let's go and prepare the reception." Quarr, too,
wanted to see how the Shadows behaved under attack with
bullets whistling past their ears like angry hornets.

Kryger pointed to a knoll to the right, about eight meters
high. They slunk toward it, making use of boulders and low
bushes to keep out of sight in case there was an advance scout.
They could hear the enemy a distance away. They were so
noisy that Kryger thought they wanted to scare anything in the
vicinity away, or perhaps they were not used to being out in the
wilderness where silence and stealth was the only thing that
counted. The hunters clearly were not expecting their quarry to
lay in ambush.

The approaching troops did not know what they were hunting,
but they were expecting entertainment with a few panicky
Uglies—their name for the Shadows. The troops nearest to the
hound were reluctant to watch it closely, laughing and joking to
hide their fear of it, and thus didn't notice its odd, confused
behavior because of the unfamiliar scent it picked up, mingled
with that of the quarry it was trained to run down and kill. It's
muscular handlers expected it to hoot in excitement when it
detected the fresh scent of an Ugly, but were too busy trying to
control it to notice anything unusual in its behavior.

They crept to the top of the knoll and selected hiding places.
Quarr supervised the Shadows while Kryger studied the
advancing troops. They were bunched in a sloppy v-formation—
weapons slung over shoulders as if they didn't have a care in
the world. Leading in the middle—with four handlers looking as if
they were hanging on for dear life—was the dog-like beast
sniffing the ground seemingly a bit confused. It was as big as the
Shadows, but built narrowly as if it were developed for
squeezing through fissures or between densely planted trees.

The beast and its handlers started the slight ascent about eighty meters away. Kryger lifted his arm above the boulder to take careful aim, because he didn't want to miss the shot or wound the beast. Although narrowly built, it was unmistakably muscled for power and speed. His instincts told him that he couldn't deal with it if it were let loose; that it was a beast he couldn't take on without a firearm and not from close-up either. Kryger shivered involuntary. It was a new experience to feel apprehension for the perceived physical power of an unknown creature.

The beast must have noticed the slight movement, because it lifted an ugly fanged head in his direction and its light-orange eyes seemed to look straight into Kryger's emerald eyes. It didn't have time to sound a warning even if it intended to. It died with a startled grunt when the carefully aimed needle exploded in its brain. Its handlers only had time to look startled, for all four died a second later. Kryger was a fast and deadly shot, and the needler was a weapon developed for close combat, although it had a range of almost a kilometer.

As the beast and its handlers dropped in their tracks, Kryger's companions fired rapidly into the unpleasantly surprised company of Killers. A few died, mainly due to Quarr's trained marksmanship, before the rest woke up and dived for cover, not knowing what they had encountered, but acting instinctively.

The troops were trained, but were unprepared for retaliation. They were totally surprised and confused. They were too used to an unarmed quarry desperately trying to get away, or charging blindly to a wasteful death. They rallied under the threats and curses of their commander and began to retaliate after a fashion, shooting randomly at an unseen enemy.

Ycagabys became trigger-happy and overeager now that he could fight back. He saw the enemy fall, and in his eagerness to check on the gone to ground enemy, he exposed himself needlessly. Luckily, a bullet only clipped his shoulder. He growled a curse in his own language and dropped back into cover so fast that the Killers thought that he had been killed. A few cheered happily. Taking courage now that they had scored, and having seen the approximate position of the ambushers, they began to fire more accurately.

Bullets began to hum like angry hornets and clipped the foliage from the stunted trees as they ricocheted among the boulders. Knowing that the Shadows were too inexperienced for a prolonged skirmish and that they might make disastrous mistakes as Ycagabys almost did, Kryger gave a piercing whistle for the retreat. He kept his eyes on the enemy's position, however, and killed another one who was dim-witted enough to pop up to check what the whistle was about.

Ycagabys slunk up and growled, "We are killing them. Why do we run now?"

Kryger did not know the language well enough yet to express himself clearly. He touched the Shadow's shoulder, but kept his eyes on the enemy. *We cannot kill them all right now. They are rallying now that the surprise is over and may have means to summon more troops. We must go quickly so we can stay alive and fight later when the odds are in our favor. Gather our packs and go upstream. I will keep them occupied to give you time to get clear, and I will follow when you are well away. We must discuss tactics, as this is a new way of fighting for you, and you must learn to fight with guns from a distance. Go now, please, and help Quarr carry my packs. Carry the Blaster and don't leave anything behind.*

Very well, friend Kryger, I understand.

Quarr immediately realized why Kryger ordered the withdrawal, and that he would be in danger if they dawdled. She motioned Pgabys to follow and without looking back, ran crouched and silently to the temporary shelter. She hurried, but made sure that nothing was left behind. Ycagabys's wound wasn't serious and could be treated later. It would hurt awhile, and hopefully teach him to be more careful.

Kryger moved from cover to cover as silently as a shadow and fired at the slightest movement, killing the overeager and wounding the incautious. They had to think that a dozen well-trained men with silenced guns were waiting for one of them to stir. The object of the exercise was to teach them to stay as still as rabbits in hiding, and to be afraid to blink an eye without written permission. He doubted that they were familiar with the silent needler or this kind of tactic.

He was right. The commander, who had wriggled halfway under a boulder, was shocked out of his wits and in a quandary. He couldn't decide whether he should call for help and be punished severely for losing a valuable tracker-hound, or whether he should order a discreet withdrawal, even if the terrain below this knoll was devoid of decent cover. He was used to making what he called "sports," with unarmed, panicky Uglies, and couldn't come to grips with this unusual situation. He felt incapable of original thought and the silenced weapons were adding to his panic. He knew all about silencers, but the accuracy and rapid fire was uncanny and nerve-wracking. There must be a dozen or so highly trained marksmen in ambush, and they could only be the invaders they were told to capture or kill, but which up to now nobody believed existed.

He clutched a stinging hand with a tiny hole in it and cursed silently. What kind of weapon was this that could kill instantly but left such a tiny, painful hole in flesh? He really didn't want to know at this moment. He wished merely to be left alone so that he could think in peace long enough to make up his mind.

He shouted a command. "Hold your fire! Don't waste ammunition, and don't move if you value your lives! There are too many of them and they are well camouflaged! Shoot only if you see one clearly!"

But how can they see someone when they couldn't move? The remaining troopers didn't dare question the bizarre order, but they took it literally and were only too happy to comply.

Kryger didn't understand the language, but had heard the command and deduced its meaning as all movement abruptly ceased. He smiled, waited a moment, and then withdrew quietly. As he backed away, he kept watching the top of the knoll, but didn't see movement of any kind. When he was well away and thought it safe enough to turn his back, he ran silently at almost full speed to put distance between him and the knoll.

18

The little creek his companions had followed to its source bubbled merrily from underneath a fairly high cliff into a clear, moss-edged pool before it started its sluggish struggle down toward the canyon-river.

They had been running hard and Kryger only caught up with them at the foot of the high ridge, which seemed to mark the start of the downward sloping grassland.

We'll go south along this ridge until we find a place that offers protection where we will not easily be spotted when we climb. I will go over the ridge first to check if it's safe and watch our back trail. Pgabys will climb after me with Ycagabys right behind her, followed by Quarr.

Kryger didn't know why he had the sudden impulse, but as Quarr passed him, he handed her the Blaster again, and said, "Give me your rifle and some ammunition. Be prepared to lead the way to the top if we're attacked and have to get away fast. If Ycagabys and I are separated from you, climb the ridge and go on. We'll catch up when we can.

On the outside, Ycagabys looked like a hideous beast, but inside the unlovely exterior was an intelligent, loveable character, eager to learn to defend himself, his mate, and his people.

There was a sudden clattering buzz of racing helicopters from above the ridge, and they scurried for the nearest cover, which was a boulder close to the ridge, and hoped that the females had reached cover without being detected. Clearly help had been summoned and had arrived in record time.

Kryger kept the MAG ready. *I have to play cornered rat, not cat and mouse,* he thought wryly.

The helicopters came into view well away high up over the ridge, and raced toward the northwest without pausing. He didn't hear shots and was relieved that the females were undiscovered. They landed close to where the skirmish took place about forty minutes earlier. Ycagabys growled his thoughts. "There are only two of them this time, friend Kryger. They brought more Killers."

They would never know whether it was intentional or purely accidental. The helicopters, having discharged their troops, were heading straight toward them and not rising to lift over the ridge. Perhaps they were following the plain trail Quarr and the Shadows had left. The bolt from the MAG would be invisible in the sunlight, and Kryger aimed at the clearly visible pilot of the leading craft. He shot the pilot and then shifted his aim to the other pilot and shot again. Both craft gave an almost imperceptible shudder, but flew serenely on.

"Run as fast as you can to another hiding spot. They're going to crash right where we are," Kryger growled urgently.

They sprinted like scared antelopes along the side of the ridge. They were sixty meters away when the leading craft crashed a little higher up against the ridge. It exploded in a ball of flame a second before the other helicopter crashed next to it.

Kryger was in front and he grabbed Ycagabys's partly extended hand and pulled him behind a convenient boulder. He growled, "Stay a few moments. The debris can kill or injure."

Even as he spoke, a heavy piece of metal clanged against their shelter, showering them with detritus.

"I see what you mean, Kryger. What do we do now?"

"The enemy will look at the explosion with distance glasses that can see clearly far away, so we must try to remain unseen while we get away from here. Get on the trail of our mates, but keep low and behind cover from down there. Move slowly, as if you were stalking alert prey. Movement attracts the eye. There is a place in front of us that is not so steep. Our mates may have taken that way up."

The sudden *wwharrup* of the Blaster being used on top of the ridge made him disregard his own advice. He sprinted up the incline, leaping from one projecting rock to the other as if he were on level ground, leaving an astonished Ycagabys to scramble up as fast as he could.

He growled to himself, "By all that is sacred, these human friends are beyond understanding. They are such powerful beings! I'm glad that Kryger wanted to be a friend. We're learning so much from them."

He didn't know it then, but this casual vow of friendship would have far-reaching consequences for both races in the far future.

Kryger reached the top of the ridge in less than a minute, and he wasn't even breathing deeply. He heard the *wwharrup* rapidly twice more in that time, and almost fell over Quarr and Pgabys where they crouched behind a ragged, almost flat bank of solid rock at the edge of the precipitous slope.

"What took you so long?" Quarr asked innocently.

"That's irrelevant, damn it. What did you run into?"

"Oh, not much, really. Only a few hundred troops," she tried in vain to sound casual. "Take a look at what's left of them. It's not my fault they supplied us with such a devastating weapon. They were obliging and assembled in three tight groups to listen to what sounded like inspirational speeches, which is a dangerous habit without reconnoitering first and posting sentries. See what it got them!"

He thought that, for the first time, her voice almost suited her utterance, but ignored the flippant remarks and took a careful peek. After he looked, he stepped out into the open. Quarr didn't play games with an enemy. She could be ruthless when she had to be. There was nothing left, just a few scattered lumps of flesh, charred scraps of clothing and metal, and three deep gouges in the ground.

What looked like a ridge from below was a rugged escarpment to another highland or mesa, which wasn't as flat as the plain they had crossed. All around were gullies and ragged, rocky hills, interspersed with scrubby trees and bunchgrass. Southward, almost at the edge of the plateau, the rock-bank behind which the females had hid gradually rose to form a sheer, bare wall that widened as it gradually rose. *What a mess nature can sometimes create,* Kryger thought as he calmly surveyed the area, *but it's a beautiful mess.*

Seeing not a single body, he dryly commented, "I'm sure that you don't need my assistance, and I'm quite sure that I'd never want to be your enemy. If that ever happens, I'll escape to another galaxy, because you would likely use a heavy beam-weapon to get rid of me." Then he said, seemingly severe, "Give me that Blaster and take back your rifle. I can't trust you for one minute out of my sight. The poor bastards never stood a chance." He smiled. "Good work, princess. I couldn't have done it better." He gave her a brief hug.

Ycagabys arrived, breathing hard, and Pgabys growled an explanation.

Kryger wondered aloud, "I don't understand it." He looked at Quarr. "Why are you so important? It doesn't add up.

Why would this giant insect, or being, whatever it is, send so many troops to capture or destroy the occupants of a single scout-craft? It doesn't make sense. Are we missing an important clue?"

Quarr shrugged her shoulders. "All I know is that someone wants me alive or dead—remember? But how could they have known about me and that I would arrive here at this time? I wouldn't know, Kryger. I sure wish I had some sort of explanation. Perhaps we'll find out in time."

Kryger had a sudden inspiration. "Maybe we can capture one of them and find out. Let's see if we can create a bridge tonight and then we wait for them to cross. We can cross downstream later to get behind them when the river is almost dry. We may be able to grab one of them and extract information."

"What do we do with the captive afterward? Kill him?"

"It depends. Perhaps the Shadows might be able to do it, but I can't kill in cold blood. I'll likely let him go so that he can inform on us. We'll see when the time comes. The Shadows may have to stay out of sight, as we don't want to give the enemy too much information. Okay, will you tell them? I'll check our back-trail."

The survivors of the first skirmish didn't seem to be in a hurry to catch up, but they were on their way. Perhaps they were waiting for the fresh troops on top of the ridge to take the brunt of the expected confrontation before they joined the action from behind. *They couldn't know that the troops were completely wiped out,* Kryger thought. The enemy must realize that their quarry was en route to the spaceport where the odds were in their favor. Perhaps their security wasn't up to scratch so that they had to try and stop anyone as far away as possible. Maybe they just had some kind of paranoia about strangers. He couldn't even guess what they were hoping to accomplish by chasing them all the way and trying to kill them, when all they had to do was to wait, and perhaps beef up their security. He didn't like riddles when their lives were the price to pay.

He knew well that all this was purely speculative, and the only way to know for sure was to obtain firsthand information. The chances were good that they would capture one that didn't have a clue of what all this was about, so he must make sure that they isolated one of a higher rank. He hoped that they carried insignia on their shoulders or somewhere in plain sight so that they could be distinguished from ordinary troopers.

Ycagabys could watch them until after sundown. When they were asleep, it might perhaps be possible to spirit away an individual without alerting the whole group.

He was grinning when he rejoined the others. Kryger was still too inexperienced to realize that even the best thought-out plans could go disastrously wrong if every angle and possibility was not thoroughly examined and planned for.

19

The Shadows, not having been at war with anyone as far back as they could remember, found the idea of capturing an enemy for information exciting.

Kryger couldn't formulate a plan before he saw the set-up in the camp and the number of sentries. He envied the Shadows their ability to see lines of force with their third eyes.

They followed Ycagabys and wished they also had the ability to blend so completely with the shadows as to be almost invisible. The camp was oddly silent. The normal banter of men camping together was absent. They had chattered like excited monkeys before they were ambushed, and perhaps it was an enforced stillness. Kryger distrusted the silence and wondered if it was a setup. He felt apprehension stir and began to question the wisdom of the spur of the moment plan.

There were no fires. It was as if they had not expected to camp out at all. Only one sentry sat dejectedly on a rock—now and then staring out into the darkness in token watchfulness—apparently waiting for the commander to go to sleep, for he glanced over at an isolated figure at the edge of the hollow more frequently than looking into the darkness outside the camp. The others were curled up, looking very uncomfortable and cold without any blankets or sleeping bags. Kryger touched his companions.

This isn't normal behavior. Something went wrong for them. They're miserable and cold. He looked at the figure who sat at least thirty steps away from the others.

He is shunned by everyone. He must be the commander. Ycagabys projected amusement.

There were only ten men, excluding the commander. He wondered where the other troops who had disembarked from the helicopters were. Perhaps they had taken the blind trail.

It's the loneliness of command by force that makes him an outcast. It will be easy to take him, but you'll have to do it. We'll watch the other men, because we can kill without any noise. You have natural camouflaging, which makes you difficult to see, and you move silently. Give me your hand. Feel this place on my neck? Don't do it to me, but if you deliver a fairly hard blow with the edge of your hand on that spot, you can render a human unconscious.

Move up behind him, like this, Kryger demonstrated on Quarr. *Clamp your hand over his mouth, and at the same time, slam the edge of your other hand into his neck. Then bring him here.*

Kryger watched the sentry, who didn't seem to be worried about enemies or predators. The other ten, including the commander, now lay silently on the cold ground, curled up in fetal positions. After an hour or two, the darkness became tainted with a soft silvery-green luminance as the moon made its imminent approach known. The sentry still sat on watch, but his head rested on his chest, and he snored fitfully through his nose. It was time to put the plan into operation.

Kryger saw the Shadow creep up behind the commander, then some sort of noiseless activity, then only a deeper shadow moving cautiously away. He let out a pent-up breath. He was grateful that the abduction came off so easily. He thought that if a Shadow could spirit someone away so noiselessly right under the noses of his companions, a dozen or two would make a formidable commando after some intense training.

Ycagabys slung the unconscious commander over his back the way he did with prey, and they set off at an easy walk along the ridge-like wall. They did not go far before they found a suitable place. The commander was still out like a light. Kryger asked Ycagabys to make his victim comfortable against the rough rock wall.

Kryger sat in the lotus position next to the unconscious commander. He was relaxed and thinking about what he had to do and how to go about it. The man was already in the state that bordered on wakefulness, so Kryger implanted the thought that he was reminiscing on past events. *It's very cold and I must try to sleep on the hard, icy ground. So where are the troops that came in with the helicopters?*

The commander shivered and curled into a fetal position. He accepted the thought as his own and continued where Kryger left off. *They said that they would go over the ridge further up along the tracks left by the enemy agents to reinforce the troops that were waiting to intercept the enemy. They were supposed to flush the quarry and drive them into our arms. As if that fooled me! Where are they now? I hope that they are as miserable as we are. They were pissed off that both helicopters crashed. The pilots didn't expect the quarry already on this side*

132

of the ridge, so the bastards destroyed the troops that were supposed to have our equipment for this ridiculous chase. For all I know, the enemy agents could have been responsible for the destruction of the helicopters. We're chasing an enemy and we don't even know the damage they can do. We should have been given more information. Now my life may be forfeited, because I lost the Snuffer and a few careless men. What am I supposed to do? Let the enemy escape without contact so that I won't lose men?

The commander rambled on and on about his woes and Kryger thought what he could do to obtain the specific information he wanted. He didn't want to force direct questions, as the subject may remember that he was interrogating himself and question it. As the commander paused, he threw in a supposedly random thought. *I wonder what the enemy agents are doing here and why we must stop them before they reach the spaceport.*

Now, why didn't that thought occur to me before? Are we so indoctrinated and fearful that we never ask questions, or are our thoughts controlled by our immortal god? No! I mustn't think such thoughts, for I'll be severely punished...but they could be after the Gwarra. The jerk thinks he is the immortal Gorrel's partner. Perhaps they know about the subspace ship-detector and the mind-to-mind talk-inhibitor invented by that brilliant, fool of a Gwarra—Pupaul. I almost feel sorry for the poor, deluded idiot. He'll have a rude awakening when he's of no further use to Lord Gorrel, but the imbecile is so full of hatred and self-importance that he is totally blind and deaf.

Again the commander rambled on, giving his opinion of an arrogant man who thought that he could dictate terms to an immortal deity. *The Hullenii were the indestructible rulers who dictated who did what and how, and nobody dared question their actions or decisions. It had always been so and will always be. No one could remember when the immortal deities came or where they came from. They cannot be harmed, because beams and bullets bounce off their bodies, which was demonstrated often enough when someone went crazy with fear or lost their head and rebelled.*

When the captive paused in his ramblings, Kryger interjected other thoughts. His idea was that if the commander ever thought about this episode, he must believe that it was his own subconscious musing, dreams, or nightmares caused by hunger and the numbing cold.

He noticed the commander's nose twitch as if he smelled something that bothered or annoyed him. Kryger was too inexperienced to think it significant, and he ignored it as he wanted to extract as much information as he could.

What Kryger gathered with his unsubtle, inept method of questioning was that the thought-communication-damper was at the spaceport and the experimental subspace-scanner had been lost with the Destroyer. Pupaul invented both devices. He had arrived when the spaceport was completed and offered his services to Gorrel in exchange for unknown favors. It was common knowledge that Gorrel was amused by the audacity of the Gwarra-traitor, while the latter was ignorant of his inevitable fate once he outlived his usefulness. Gorrel played with him, as it saw an opportunity to prevent off-planet mind-calls for help. The Gwarra extermination would start when Pupaul failed to be of any further value to Gorrel.

The commander was getting restless and Kryger decided he wasn't going to get any more useful information, so he erased the memory of the dreamlike self-interrogation and supplanted it with a dream-memory of fearlessly chasing the enemy agents. He believed that he owed the man that much—if he lived to reach his base. He was still indoctrinated with the idea that another person's private thoughts were sacrosanct, and because he himself was blocked against hypnotism, he didn't even think of hypnotizing the commander to impel forgetfulness or for direct questioning. Instead, he induced deep sleep and withdrew his mind.

In the Shadows language he said, "He doesn't know much. We have all the information we're going to get out of this guy, I think. Let's hope that his absence hasn't been noticed. Let's take him back, but we have to be extra careful, because the moon's peeping over the mountains. If some are awake, we'll leave him as close to their camp as we can. I've another idea that we can go and try out." He took the Blaster from Quarr.

The camp was asleep. Even the guard had become inured to the chill and was still snoring gently where he sat upright on the flat rock. Ycagabys deposited the commander on the same spot and then blended silently with the moonlit shadows.

Quarr elected to return to the hideout to rest after she heard what Kryger had in mind. He explained to Ycagabys what he wanted to do, and after seeing Quarr safely to the temporary sanctuary, led the way in a fast run toward the next canyon-river an unknown distance away.

The nearly full moon was higher by this time, and to them the terrain was brightly lit, showing every pebble and unevenness clearly for their nocturnal eyes. They reached the canyon-river uneventfully after an hour's run, and searched along the high cliffs for some time before they found a suitable place to collapse. Kryger supposed that the sound of the commotion would wake the sleeping enemy, but he didn't think that they would come before daybreak to check the cause of the crashing noise. He assumed that they would think that the enemy agents had crossed over during the night.

They could take turns to watch the enemy and follow when they left, but Kryger decided that it would be a waste of time. They might as well go back to the overhang and get some sleep, or rest in Ycagabys's case. They could cross later in the day, lower down, and seek the tracks of the enemy before removing the blockage. He thought that it would be easy and safe enough, but it was a thought he would remember very soon and regret bitterly.

20

They reached the empty riverbed about midmorning, some distance downstream from where Kryger had collapsed the bridging cliff. They paused in the middle of the wide riverbed to study a monstrous river beast from close up. It was trapped in a small, deep pool and it swam forlornly in circles. Apparently it was not equipped to move in very shallow water or on dry land. Kryger and Quarr hadn't had the opportunity to study one before from this close up. It was sleek and streamlined, and its long jaw was lined with rows of sharply pointed teeth. They wished it better luck next time and started up the slippery incline.

In the prevailing silence, the sudden, sharp, explosive crack and grinding together of gigantic boulders upstream, echoed like the crack of doom down the deep, drained riverbed. A thunderous roar reverberated against the canyon-walls as the weight of the accumulated water finally pushed the barrier aside.

The Shadows took off immediately at a hard run. They realized what was happening, for they lived close to nature and had experienced flashfloods before. Kryger hesitated a second, realized what was happening, grabbed Quarr's hand, and chased the fleeing Shadows.

"Run like hell!" he shouted to her. "I didn't expect the dam to break so soon. It must have rained up north, or the cliff I collapsed wasn't as high and solid as it appeared to be. We didn't inspect my handiwork, because we ran like blazes to get away from the debris!"

They scrambled frantically up the wide, overgrown old ravine to reach high ground as the thunderous rumble rapidly became louder. They stopped and turned when they heard the flood arrive behind them. They were just high enough. Two meters below them, a solid wall of brown water raced down the canyon, tumbling and roaring as if cursing the impudent beings it had just missed by not more than a second or two. The rumbling-roar impaired Kryger's normally keen hearing, and his eyes were focused on the picturesque display of ever-changing tumbling water below them.

Quarr laughed. "It sounds pretty furious, doesn't it? I pity the river beasts, fish, and other denizens. Many of them will be crushed. This highland leads to the spaceport, doesn't it? I mean, we don't have to cross another canyon, do we?"

"No, we don't." They turned away from the river and moved a few meters higher to be on the safe side. "Ycagabys told me last night that when he carried the commander back to the camp, he heard him dreaming. He was hoping, in his dream of course, that the enemy agents would create a bridge, for he had a suspicion that no airlift would be arranged for them. He had sinned in not capturing or killing us and by losing a lot of his men, even though they were fighting against overwhelming odds. Now he can tell his master truthfully that he chased them, but lost their tracks somewhere as they, perhaps, veered north without leaving a sign to join the Gwarra. It seems that Gorrel and his sidekick don't want us to arrive intact at headquarters."

Immersed in the wonder of the spectacular flood like over-protected children, they didn't scan the nearby ridge as closely as usual, and therefore didn't see the danger. Deafened by the flood below them, their usually keen ears didn't detect the footsteps of the surviving troops, and they didn't hear the warning hiss from Pgabys. She realized that they were oblivious to the danger and growled a warning to her mate, who scurried back to warn them.

As the humans looked for their companions on the upward slope, they saw Ycagabys gesticulate with one hand to hide quickly, the other hand pointing to the ridge. They didn't need a second warning. Unfortunately, there wasn't a suitable hiding place nearby. Ycagabys tried to blend with the scanty shadow of a scrawny bush, but they had no other choice but to stand motionless so as not to attract attention.

It wasn't a moment too soon. Kryger and Quarr remained motionless, partly in view of the soldiers. Kryger saw that the soldiers on top of the ridge were looking at the flood and not down into the deep gully where they were, but he was ready to explode into action if one of the soldiers spotted them.

After a moment, there were angry shouts from beyond the ridge, followed by silence. The soldiers scooted back from the edge without a downward look. Presumably the commander was taking them to task for wasting time on sightseeing in plain sight of anyone who cared to look their way. Although he was an old hunter and had been drilled in the fundamentals of basic warfare, Kryger—because he mainly fought in the emptiness of space—badly underestimated the seemingly inept troops. He waited a moment, took a deep breath of relief, joined Ycagabys, and thanked him for endangering his life to give them a timely warning.

"It was nothing, Kryger. What are friends for?" Ycagabys gestured to Quarr and growled, "Pgabys would like to talk to you."

The worried commander didn't admire the spectacular flash flood, but searched the area with distance-glasses, and then saw them as he looked down into the old cutting below. When Kryger interrogated the commander the previous night, he didn't realize that the purple people had a sense of smell as keen as that of the Shadows and his own. The commander remembered that he smelled the strong odor of an Ugly sometime during his dreams, and detected the odor on his uniform. It made him suspect that his reminiscence was anything but real. Now, he quickly stepped out of sight and angrily called his troops back from the edge to get them out of danger, scolded them thoroughly for being so unobservant, and ordered them to quietly crawl back to the edge of the gully and destroy the couple of enemy agents and the Ugly.

Pgabys was still out of breath from the frantic scramble to get out of flood's way, and remained in the shade of her hiding place where Quarr quickly joined her to get out of the glaring midday sun. As Kryger and Ycagabys came closer, a volley of shots rang out above the thunder of the raging flood. Both males fell down like pole-axed pigs, looks of utter surprise and incomprehension on their faces. They all heard the cheers of the enemy soldiers above.

Kryger lost all interest in the world around him, for he was paralyzed and couldn't even move so much as a single finger. He couldn't hear the surprised grunts on top of the gully as Quarr's needler silently decimated the exposed troops, but he was aware in a curiously detached sort of way that the Blaster was plucked out of his nerveless fingers. He didn't hear or see the furious, raging females storming the ridge like two she-devils out of hell in utter disregard of their own safety, obliterating anything that moved.

He wasn't conscious of pain or any other sensation—not even of the sun toasting the back of his neck—just a curious inability to move and think coherently. The realization gradually sunk into his shocked and barely conscious mind that he had been caught like a trusting, three-year-old. It was an unforgivable blunder. He tried to roll over onto his side, for the side of his face was party buried in the dirt and made breathing difficult, but his muscles didn't respond to the panicky commands of his brain. He felt like jumping upon himself, but he couldn't even find the strength to close his eyes.

He faintly heard Ycagabys groan softly next to him. He was conscious of time that went by, and was still experimenting on moving his big toes when he recognized running feet. *Are they coming down to inspect their victims? Are they that confident when they should be approaching cautiously? I'm sorry about the MAG, but I'm helpless to do anything. I hope my people can forgive me for the loss of it…*

Gentle hands removed the heavy pack from his back, turned him on his side, and then on the other side to remove his jacket. "Oh! You're still alive and conscious, are you? I thought you'd bought it for sure this time." Quarr's voice had a musical matter-of-fact tone. It didn't betray her relief at finding him alive. She whistled in surprise when she saw the damage to his back.

It upset him, but knowing it to be a joke, he tried to grin, but found that, too, impossible. He wondered if he still had a voice, but he wouldn't know until he tried. He tried, but it only came out as dumb sounds through slack lips.

Quarr immediately created a mental cocoon around them. *Your back is a real mess,* she told him.

I'm paralyzed all over. Can't even close my eyelids. What's the hell's wrong with me?

She disregarded his injuries and turned him onto his back again with the intention to get some water down his throat. She lifted his head and held her canteen to his lips. To his surprise, he swallowed, but almost choked as the water went down his dusty throat. She saw a gaping wound on his left upper leg, but it wasn't bleeding much. Perhaps the dirt had clogged the wound. She turned him onto his stomach again and took a look at his back one more time.

Thank the Powers that look after our well being that these troops were lousy shots, or perhaps they just weren't used to shooting downward. One bullet went through the lats just below your left shoulder. You were lucky. It may have nicked your ribs, but none are broken. Just one centimeter higher and your shoulder-joint would have been smashed. Another bullet cut your upper left leg's muscles open without touching bone.

Your backbone was nicked twice just above the hips, but it's odd that the wounds aren't bleeding much. Just two or so millimeters made the difference between recovery and permanent paralyses. You'll keep awhile because you're not bleeding much. I have to treat Ycagabys before I clean and bandage your wounds. He's worse off than you and bleeding copiously. I'll have to stem the flow somehow. I wish I knew more about their constitutions. She left him on his stomach, but made sure that his head was turned sideways.

That means he's still alive! Thank Heavens. What kept you so long?

You both went down like cattle shot in the brain, so we just went nova…the avenging females and all that, you know, thinking that our mates were killed and all. It took us a while to hunt them down one by one—they scattered like quail. They were running so fast that bullets and blaster-bolts took a while to catch up with them. They weren't running straight, more dodgy, like jackals or hares. She didn't collapse the cocoon, but knelt at Ycagabys's side and tactfully sent the keening Pgabys to find a decently safe shelter to get her out of the way.

Why chase them all the way to hell? Kryger persisted.

Don't you remember the first rule of medical treatment? First remove the cause. The commander didn't run. Maybe he didn't have a chance to decide which way to run. He probably doesn't know that he's dead. The Blaster left only his feet intact inside his smelly boots. She managed to conceal the anguish she felt when she thought Kryger mortally wounded.

I never want to fall out of favor with you! Kryger was serious.

Stop talking. I have to drop the shield. Are you able to create that shield over us? He's in serious condition and lying in a pool of blood. I need to focus in order to clean and stitch his wounds while he's out. It's a miracle he's alive. Unfortunately, there's not enough local anesthetic left to ease the pain in his huge body.

Kryger created the shield. *Go ahead. Let me know when to drop it.* It wouldn't take too much concentration and energy, and even if it did, he owed it to his friend to make up for his ignorant blunder. He cringed at the mere thought of his unforgivable negligence. Feeling a need to punish himself, he thought: *I should not have been so confident that our enemies were inferior cowards. I—*

140

Shut up, will you? Quarr snarled impatiently in his mind. *We're a team, and it behooves all of us to be responsible for each other's safety. Now, be quiet! Please,* she added as a polite afterthought.

She concentrated on stopping the bleeding and cleaned Ycagabys's wounds as quickly as possible. The first aid kit was limited and she had to use everything sparingly, because Kryger's wounds, although not bleeding profusely, were rather extensive. She assessed the damage to the Shadow: a bullet went through his neck between the vertebra and the windpipe—miraculously missing both. Another went through his chest muscles and one though his hindquarters, missing bone, and there were numerous creases from near-misses. The bullet that knocked him out had grazed the top of his head; leaving a deep furrow in the thick bone. He too, had been lucky, with no obvious broken bones.

When she was finished, she remarked, "You can discontinue the cocoon awhile. Either you were both lucky, or these guys were too trigger-happy to aim properly. At least one of you should have been dead."

He shrunk the shield. The water had lubricated his throat, and he replied in a croaking voice, "You sound happy about it, either way. I can't move anything except my head and jaw, but I'm quite happy to be *only* wounded. How come you ladies came off scot-free?"

"How should I know? Perhaps they thought we weren't dangerous, or they didn't notice us in the shade. At least we were able to keep the two of *you* alive." She knelt at his side to clean his wounds, and was pleasantly surprised. "What's happening to your wounds? They're healing almost noticeably! Do you have some healing magic that I don't know about?"

"The wounds may only be closing on the outside. Perhaps I'm subconsciously using your shape changing methods, or maybe, in my panic at being helpless, I triggered something. I must have fallen on my face. My teeth hurt. My lips feel swollen, but I can't lift a finger to touch them. I can only feel it with my tongue, which seems to be the only thing I can move, other than my eyeballs."

"You're way too loquacious for someone who fell on his mug. I only see gritty dust on your face. Here comes Pgabys. I hope she found a decent shelter. I suppose we'll have to drag both of you by the feet."

"I won't mind, as long as you do it slowly and cheerfully. Perhaps I'll be able to use my legs when the shock has passed. In the meantime, drag or roll me into some shade and leave me there while you see what you can do with Ycagabys. He'll be too heavy to drag. Perhaps you can cut some brush to cover us until we can be of some help. It will camouflage us and could fool passing helicopters. Predators won't be a problem, as long as you're around."

"Okay, that may be the best *temporary* solution. I'm reluctant to move Ycagabys. We'll have to wait until he wakes up to find out how he really is. In the meantime, I'll do as you say, but I'm keeping the Blaster. It's a quick and permanent solution to any threat."

"Just use it as sparingly as possible. We don't have many charges left. If you can, hide any bodies so that they're not visible from the air. It might be somewhat embarrassing if a helicopter lands nearby to investigate."

"If one arrives, the pilot won't have time to regret his arrival," she promised grimly. " Let's get you into some shade."

21

Ycagabys regained consciousness near sundown. After complaining about a splitting headache, he growled for a few minutes at Pgabys. Then he painfully struggled to his feet and slowly followed her to the hideout. Every few steps, he stopped comically to ask if his wounds were still behaving.

By this time, Kryger was able to move his arms and to roll over slowly by contorting his upper body, but although he could feel his legs, there was no strength in them. He was about as strong and active as a baby at six months, but not nearly as cute. His wounds were completely closed, but they throbbed, even without movement. Quarr picked him up and unceremoniously draped him over her shoulders like a sack of potatoes, only a bit more gently. Thus they proceeded to the shallow cave, which the females had visited earlier to store their paraphernalia.

Quarr passed the other two and reached the hideout long before them. She made Kryger as comfortable as she could.

After Ycagabys was settled with much grunting and complaints, Kryger growled, "How are you feeling, my friend?"

As was typical, Ycagabys thought of his belly first. "I'll feel better once I've eaten. The wounds are painful, but they're not bleeding. I won't be able to run or fight for some time, but I'm alive. We are in debt to our resourceful mates."

"I agree," he replied, "but our mates are tired. Share some of our ration tablets. It's not tasty or filling, but it gives energy and it sustains life." Kryger had to smile at Pgabys's comical grimace of distaste, but agreed with the sentiment.

"No thank you, friend Kryger," she growled. "A full stomach is much more comfortable, and I can hunt for us with this outlandish gun. I sense enough prey in the vicinity."

"My needler is silent and won't frighten prey animals away like that noisy gun. It's also easier and more accurate to use at night. Let's go," Quarr declared. They left without further ado.

Kryger regained the use of his limbs on the second day, and lost no time in moving about to regain his strength. Although there was no trace left to show that he had been wounded, the areas remained painful and sensitive to remind him that his body was still recovering. An inexplicable restlessness had taken hold of him and he felt that time was running out rapidly, but he couldn't explain the urge or the why of it. There was an uncontrollable, pressing need to get to the spaceport.

There had been only one searching over-flight by aircraft on the first day of their convalescence, but no troops had landed. They linked hands for a group discussion.

They decided that it made more sense for Kryger and Quarr to continue the journey alone the next morning. Kryger and Quarr felt a responsibility toward the loyal Shadows and didn't want to continue to put them in harm's way. They needed to deal with Gorrel on their own. Kryger decided to entrust Pgabys with his needler. It was silent and deadly, and she was an accurate marksman. Quarr instructed her in the use and maintenance of the needler, showing her how to destroy it if they were captured, or if death seemed inevitable.

They set out very early in the morning. Like an animal, Kryger had the ability to disregard pain, or at least, was able to push it to the background. Quarr had fashioned a sling for his left arm to ease the tension and pain on his Latissimus Dorsi muscles.

It took three days and two nights to cover a little more than an estimated hundred kilometers. Kryger was obviously in pain and limped badly, but he refused to rest for long periods, because a restless urge drove him on. As a consequence, they slept very little and rested only when Kryger was about to keel over from exhaustion. Quarr also started to feel an urge to reach their destination, and they pushed on as fast as was possible under the circumstances.

They set foot in a vast, uneven, grassy valley with deep dales and very few hills sometime during the second day, and followed an old, broad, once well-trodden game trail, which ran more or less southeasterly, in the direction they wanted to go. It was easier going than the broken terrain, which was mostly high grass interspersed with trees and hidden rocks, which made the going difficult and slow.

Sometime during the third night, Kryger removed his arm from the sling. Except for a few mild twinges, his body was just about back to normal—except his left leg was swollen to almost twice its normal size and it throbbed with a vengeance whether he was walking or lying down. He did not complain, though. He accepted the pain as payment for his stupidity and wrote it off as a valuable experience.

The eastern horizon was brightening when they ascended a low knoll that was covered with sparsely leafed shrubs and clusters of stacked boulders scattered haphazardly in the sparse, long grass. They disturbed a colony of early risers that looked suspiciously like a lost colony of ordinary rock rabbits, but they had fur almost the same yellow-brown color of the grass and their legs were longer. The group fled into burrows under and in openings between boulders while they chattered abuse at the strangers who prevented them from welcoming the sun.

Ignoring their noisy, angry chattering, Kryger sat down on a convenient flat rock a few meters off the trail and awkwardly stretched his leg out straight on it to make it easier for Quarr to examine the swollen, inflamed upper leg.

She whistled softly through her teeth as if she was shocked when she pulled up the leg of his shorts. It put him on edge as her mind-shield was tightly closed. He couldn't see the smile on her face as she had her right shoulder against his chin, as if she wanted to prevent him from looking.

"You're giving me the damn creeps again, Quarr," he said angrily. "Why do you take pleasure in my pain and discomfort?"

"Oh, it's nothing serious, I hope," she said seriously. "You should've swallowed your stubborn pride a few days ago and let me have a look at it from time to time. It's inflamed and festering, as if there's something lodged underneath the skin. I'll have to cut it open. The problem is that I have no local anesthetics or painkillers left after treating Ycagabys."

"So stop talking and cut, but do it quickly. I have enough self-control not to pull my leg away. Give me a moment while you get your torture instruments ready." He changed his breathing to a special rhythm and focused his mind on feeling detached from his body and to feel no pain. After about a minute, he nodded for her to go ahead.

She looked intently at his face. He had a blank, detached look in his eyes that indicated that he had more or less isolated his mind from his body. She made the incision fast and deep enough to expose the damage inside. Kryger didn't even flinch. Pus and blood ran down his thigh. She pressed around the incision with her thumbs to open it and to make it bleed, and found a few grains of sand and a small pebble. The bleeding stopped almost immediately as she washed the incision with water from her canteen. She had nothing left to treat or to sew the cut with, so she wrapped the last clean bandage tightly around his leg.

She shook his shoulder to get his attention. "Now, don't go and interfere again. It could have been half-healed by now, so leave it alone."

"It would have been healed completely if I hadn't panicked. I had a few scratches on my forearm after my fall this morning. I saw the blood, but after about half an hour, there was nothing to show but dried blood and a bit of an itch. I think you have the same ability. It may be something caused by our unconscious memories. Check my back and see for yourself." He removed his jacket.

Quarr checked, but didn't whistle in mock surprise this time. "It looks fine, as if you've never sustained any wounds. If one knows where to look, one can see only faint scars. If you ever break a leg or something, you'll have to set it immediately, since it may start healing automatically."

It wouldn't do to exert the leg too much before it healed by itself. It was marvelous to have a self-healing body, and he wondered what this would lead to. Different abilities led down different paths. In the case of his father, his short distance teleportation ability had led to the opening of a portal to resurrect the Golden People, and later to the destruction of a couple of Bikan fortress-ships. Only time would show him the purpose of this peculiar ability. Perhaps he should ask Quarr to test whether she now had the same ability.

Quarr wiped the instruments and repacked the first-aid kit. She took up the packs and started to rise, then froze and sank down slowly. She whispered, "There's a patrol about fifty meters away." She drew her needler.

He made a quick decision. "Let's hide and see what happens." To get into a struggle with a patrol so near the spaceport would be unwise. He pointed to another flat rock about six meters from the game trail that was more than a meter high.

"Lie flat behind that rock with your back pressed against it. It's the least obvious place, so it might be overlooked," he whispered.

He drew the MAG, but wished for his own needler. It would be a waste of irreplaceable bolts, but it was silent and wouldn't set the grass on fire.

"Don't shoot unless we're discovered. I'll take cover behind that bush so that I can see what they're up to," he whispered close to her ear.

Quarr found more than enough space behind the rock, and their packs were well out of sight.

Kryger crawled half on his undamaged side and half on his stomach until he was behind the not-very-dense bush, and then half-underneath it for some sort of camouflage. He could hear the patrol talking loudly, as if they didn't expect a living soul within ten kilometers. He hoped that they would be too talkative and inattentive to take notice of tracks in the game trail.

His feet were partly exposed and would be seen if they looked back after they pass. If they paused and looked back for any reason, he would have to kill, and quickly. He prayed that it wouldn't be necessary and stayed motionless when the wound started to throb again. The slightest stirring, or even the fall of a leaf, might draw their eyes to him.

The three-man patrol was relaxed, as if they had gone over this route countless times before and that the patrol was just a means to get out from under the eyes of a bullying commander. Short rifles and backpacks were slung casually over their shoulders.

Kryger stiffened and was ready to shoot when the leader stopped near the rock he had sat on during Quarr's treatment. The purple man didn't look around, but fiddled with his trousers and then urinated noisily into a burrow where some of the pseudo rock rabbits had scurried into earlier. The other two kept on walking and passed him while he was emptying his bladder. They laughed at a comment from him. Kryger almost sighed with relief as the man zipped his trousers and hurried to catch up with his companions.

He didn't stir as he listened to the gradually diminishing voices and laughter. When they were gone, he rose stiffly and hobbled to where he could see them to make sure they weren't going to double back, but they were almost immersed in the tall grass a few hundred meters away, still gesticulating and looking at each other instead of at the trail. *Well, so much for a patrol that strolled on routine orders instead of taking it as a serious duty on which their continued health may depend,* he thought.

"What a sorry patrol!" Quarr exclaimed as she joined him. "They might as well have stayed in their barracks to play cards or something. A child could have taken them."

"Yes, they're a disgrace, but I like it that way. It's an advantage to us that they're so loquacious and unconcerned. It would've been bad for us to take them out so near the spaceport. They would be missed by tonight if they didn't return. This part of the canyon would have been very unhealthy by tomorrow morning."

"I agree. How's your leg?" she asked as she shouldered their backpacks.

"Better already. Thanks. We'll see how it is in about an hour's time."

He frequently looked back over his shoulder as they walked, but saw no indication that the patrol was returning early.

22

After two hours, Kryger wasn't limping anymore and he stopped to remove the bandage. The wound was completely healed and there was no pain, except a sharp twinge when he pressed lightly on the still visible cut. He put the bandage in a pocket and donned his jacket. He caught up with Quarr and asked for his backpack, telling her that his leg had healed in record time.

"It's about time," she replied with an irritatingly merry voice. She had been thinking, and now put those thoughts into words. "We've seen no flights by any type of aircraft for the last two days. I wonder if that means our fleet has arrived. I know Mike keeps tabs on us, but it might just be a coincidence. We can't assume anything and their ground troops might be about, in addition to normal patrols. We should be alert and keep close to cover when we're out of this long grass."

"I have a specially padded pocket inside in front of my trousers— behind my belt—that will effectively conceal the MAG, unless they strip us naked. I'm telling you about it, because I'm going to conceal the MAG there before we enter the spaceport. I don't think that we'll be able to enter by stealth, because they'll be more alert than usual. Anyway, we'll cross that bridge when we get to it, after we reconnoiter and plan thoroughly."

"Yes, but I think we have to be bold. It would've been easier if our forces had arrived a few days later. Now we'll have to bluff our way in or resort to trickery." She paused while she gathered her thoughts. "You said something about a theory as to what caused this newly found ability to self-heal automatically. What are your thoughts?"

"I think that our subconscious minds have a memory of how every individual cell of our bodies is constructed in the overall pattern, otherwise we would look different every few years. Mike mentioned that mentally developed people tend to be healthier and therefore live longer. To keep the explanation short, I think it's our subconscious memories that do it. If the brain cells don't deteriorate, the subconscious mind remembers the construction of our cells, and repairs or replaces them whenever they're damaged or old.

"I've been experimenting with shape changing on my own. I was sure that I could do it, because the ability should've been transferred by our bond. When it was in the sling, I changed my left hand into a claw, but as soon as I took my attention away, it changed back. That has to do with memory, and so I figured this healing capability must be too. I think you have the healing ability too, and perhaps you can no longer shape-change voluntarily or maybe only semi-permanently."

"I will do so tonight, if we can find a hollow behind a waterfall. Ycagabys said that there was a river this side of the spaceport. Maybe you can change to look like one of them and hold the image long enough to get past the guards. I think I'll change into a young Shadow cub and enter the spaceport that way. Now, cut me with your knife so that we can see if your theory works."

Kryger cut her arm quickly. It was only a shallow scratch that oozed very little blood, but it healed within a few minutes and left no mark. Quarr was speechless and also a little apprehensive. "It feels weird, but it means that we may no longer need the usual first-aid kit. I don't regret having merged minds with you, even if it means losing my shape changing ability, but changing only a part of the body may not be the correct way. Let's see what happens when I change my entire body."

"Okay, but first, if it's safe to do so tonight, I want to attack your mind with all the power I have to see if your shield holds. Then you must do the same to me. Before we enter its den, we should know if we have a chance to withstand Gorrel's mental onslaught, because we must *survive* to eliminate the rest of its kind. Otherwise there will be never be peace until most planets are lifeless. I'm sure the MAG will kill it, but we must be able to confront Gorrel and its kind without succumbing to their mental powers first."

"You don't have to spell it out. Judging from the attitude of the patrol we saw earlier, the spaceport shouldn't be too far away. If that's correct, we should reach the river long before noon."

As if responding to her words, a flight of noisy jets took off about ten kilometers away toward the south. The jets circled with their landing gear lowered and then landed again one by one.

"There's your confirmation, Quarr. I just hope our luck's in, and that we can find some sort of waterfall that can be used as a hideout, otherwise we'll have to go in unprepared and untested, which would be utterly foolish."

"Correct, but as you said earlier, there's nothing else to do except go on."

They walked alertly and in silence until they came to the river. They continued downstream along the riverbank, making use of cover whenever possible. They moved slowly and carefully. The enemy to fear most was the enemy unseen.

The river wasn't wide or fast flowing, just deep enough to possibly accommodate the dreaded river beasts, although they doubted any had survived near an old Shadow settlement. They were well prepared for them since Ycagabys and Pgabys had made them practice the peculiar beat to provoke the beasts. They came across a few insignificant rapids opposite the spaceport, but no waterfall. Night overtook them when they were nearly past the spaceport, and they spent the night coldly between boulders. They continued along the bank at first light.

Three or four kilometers past the spaceport, at midmorning, they found what could be called a fall, but it wasn't vertical enough to offer space behind the massive cascade. The river poured over a nearly vertical drop of about sixty meters, but the steep slope on both sides offered more or less easy access down to the shallow, extensive, short-grassed, treeless valley that could have been the former grazing ground of the Shadows' prey-herds.

As they stood indecisively halfway down the slope next to the fall, they heard a fast approaching jet aircraft from the spaceport. There was no cover, so they squatted with their heads against the steep, rocky decline next to the fall, hoping that they resembled small outcroppings. As the aircraft flashed by close overhead, Kryger made up his mind.

"It was accelerating. I doubt it, but let's assume that we were seen. I'm going to blast a hole behind that fall. There's nowhere else to hide and we won't find a place in this shallow valley. We want to stay close to the spaceport to check things out."

"Go ahead. I'll keep watch for troops," Quarr agreed and climbed back to the top. She had seen the possibility of carving a hideaway as soon as he did.

He chose a spot less than halfway down where there was an almost level shelf of solid rock that continued for about a hundred meters on the other side of the fall, and which would show wet footprints only for moments. Logically, any hideout would be expected right at the bottom. Inspection of the rock face on the nearside of the stream showed only a few horizontal cracks a meter or so above his head. He moved some twenty steps away, and then pointed the Blaster at the black rock underneath the fall. *The angle is just about right,* he thought as he pulled the trigger. Steam and murky water spewed out on the other side of the stream and were immediately overwhelmed by the thick, powerful cascade, as the flow of water resumed its normal appearance. He pulled the trigger twice more while aiming at the same place.

He stripped naked while he waited a few minutes for the rock to cool down. He stepped through the watery curtain to inspect the still steaming hole. There was now a big, long hollow space behind the fall, but spray from the bottom edge of the hole filled it. It wasn't deep enough to keep them dry. He stepped outside, aimed directly inside the newly created hole and pulled the trigger again, but there was no discharge of devastating power.

He checked the Blaster and saw that the charge was depleted. He ejected the empty clip and threw it into the middle of the river and then rummaged in the rucksack for a replacement.

Having replaced the charge, he repeated the process until the hole was high and deep enough to his satisfaction. He carefully inspected the damage to the rock-face and roof on the other side of the fall. Assured that both would not give way unless assisted with undue violence, he triggered the Blaster from inside to make a concealed-by-water exit on that side as well.

The fall looked the same as usual from outside, but the slight alteration in the flow might puzzle an observant onlooker familiar with the falls. The newly created cave could not be seen behind the thick curtain of water during the day, and they would have to be careful that the faint illumination of the heater didn't discolor the waterfall at night.

When the temperature of the rock had cooled down to normal, he carefully inspected the deep, newly created chamber. The space was big enough and it seemed solid and dry, so he moved his pack inside.

Outside, he donned his pants and climbed up to where Quarr was keeping an eye on possible approaches. "You can move in whenever you like, but prepare to get wet on entry."

152

"Okay. Try to get us something for lunch and supper. I'll watch awhile longer until I see you return. We might as well wait until tomorrow to check the spaceport."

"The water dampened the noise, and it wouldn't have been heard from more than a few hundred meters away. That jet may have scared wildlife away though. Either way, I'll go and investigate."

He gave Quarr the MAG in exchange for her needler, and set off down the valley at right angles to the stream. Ycagabys had taught him how prey-animals on Okrion behaved, and he had a good idea of where to find a few. He returned a little later with a large deer carcass slung across his well-muscled, naked shoulders.

Quarr had a last look around to make sure that they were still alone, then started down when he started to ascend the incline. "Nobody came looking for us, so we can assume that we weren't seen, or they're being kept too busy elsewhere. I didn't hear any strange noises issuing from the rock, so I assume it's safe to move in. Let's see what you've created."

She removed her clothes and stuffed them into her rucksack to keep them dry, then quickly stepped through the thick, icy water curtain. Quarr made a show of thoroughly inspecting the hollow when he moved inside and put the antelope down in the far corner. The sight of her naked, shapely posterior splendidly on display while she was disappearing into the watery curtain, made him tremble with excitement. His throat suddenly became dry at the sight of her beautiful skin.

Kryger noticed how tight and firm her body was. He wasn't paying attention to what she was saying. "You're the most beautiful woman I've ever seen." He was naked in seconds, eager for her to see his lust for her. She motioned for him to come closer and he complied instantly.

"Yes," she breathed, looking up at him with gorgeous eyes, smiling lovingly and taking in his expression. They both gasped as he slid into her. He could feel her contract all around him as she moaned, her orgasm tearing through her. He leaned over and kissed her gently, and she smiled against his lips.

23

Being young and full of energy, time went by without them being aware of its quick passage. They were surprised to notice that dusk was falling when they at last started supper. Kryger passed naked through the water to check whether the dim light from the heater was conspicuous. Grateful that it wasn't, he returned and dried himself quickly, for the air outside was already as chilly as the water, and a strong wind was blowing. They dressed and ate. It was time to seriously test their capabilities to withstand the mental onslaught they expected in the very near future.

It took Quarr almost an hour to change into the form of a young Shadow cub since she couldn't add bulk she didn't have. Kryger inspected her and couldn't find fault. He wanted to whistle and jokingly comment on her ugly countenance, but desisted. She tried to speak to him, but her vocal cords were no longer capable of human speech. Then she mind-spoke to him on a very low frequency, which they suspected was too low for Gorrel and his kind to detect or intercept. When it searched for them, it used the middle and higher ranges of thought channels.

That was really difficult, but what do you think? Will I pass muster?

"You look ugly enough to pass any test. Don't expect me to fall in love with that form, but look out for young Shadows. You don't smell like one though, so you can sleep next to me the rest of the night. I suppose you *can* sleep, since you're not a true Shadow."

Yes, of course I'll sleep. I don't expect to fool a real Shadow, so I'll growl at them if I encounter any, and explain that I'm in disguise. They'll see the difference before they can even smell me, since my eyes aren't the same as theirs. Help me into my bag, please. Sweet dreams, my love.

"Same to you, my ugly little darling," he said as he held her sleeping bag so that she could back into it. She snorted through her nose.

He woke up in the early hours of the morning, looked at Quarr, and smiled when he saw that she had resumed her normal form. Whatever her real form should be, she would forever retain the general features of his mother—with the exception of her own superbly developed body and eyes, of course. Her ears and hair must be her real face, because they were somewhat different from his mother's.

When morning came, Quarr wasn't happy to find that her effort had been in vain, but Kryger assured her that it didn't matter. He had a plan...sort of. It depended on circumstances and the early morning patrol.

"We must waylay the patrol not too far from the spaceport, but not where there's a chance of anyone spotting the encounter. I assume that it's a regular three-man patrol that leaves early in the morning—small enough for us to influence them to ostensibly capture us peacefully. One of us should create a cocoon, and the other must control them to prevent them from getting sporty ideas. The rest of the situation we can only tackle as it develops...until they proudly present us to Gorrel. We must act as quickly as we can, because we have to get rid of Gorrel before our forces arrive. I'm sure that it will link up with its chums to turn our unprepared fighters against each other."

The falling water concealed both openings completely, which made the newly created cave a safe storage place. They left their weapons and backpacks wrapped up in their sleeping bags and groundsheets. Quarr's needle gun was deactivated and wouldn't explode if handled by another person. They would come back for their equipment if they could.

Kryger secured the MAG in the special pocket behind his belt where it could be reached without wasting too much time, and then put a packet of emergency rations in his back pocket. With clothes and footwear clutched in a small bundle tightly against their bellies to keep them as dry as possible, they stooped through the waterfall on the spaceport side of the river.

They really felt naked and exposed without the burden of packs and weapons, but dressed again and set off at a hard run to generate some heat in their icy bodies. They ran for less than twenty minutes before they came within sight of the spaceport. They crouched and stalked closer behind available cover.

They identified a large number of ground-to-air and ground-to-space missile installations among other heavy beam-weapons, and thought the security and heavy defense of the spaceport almost foolproof. It would require a couple of Battleships to neutralize the weapons from long distance, but the losses to the attackers would be phenomenal. A bombardment from space with nuclear missiles would be much easier and perhaps less costly in manpower and equipment, but it would be a last, desperate measure.

Scores of fighting craft were parked and manned, ready for immediate takeoff. Kryger assumed that the smaller, winged-craft were the atmospheric jetfighters. They looked sleek and deadly, and he wished for an opportunity to fly one of them, to see how they compared with the antigrav-fighting sleds back home. He was itching to have a go at it. His first love was flying machines and all things associated with them. *Get back to reality*, he scolded himself.

The perimeter fence, as he remembered it from Ycagabys's description, was out of bounds. It was electrified with a killer voltage, and it was regularly patrolled by troops accompanied by the narrow-bodied snuffer-beasts. He assumed that the fence would be floodlit at night as well. *The only safe way to gain entrance is as prisoners,* he thought wryly.

They watched the activities until after midday, but found no clue of where the damper was hidden. Kryger murmured that it was time to find the trail used by the patrol and be captured. They crept away until out of sight of the watchtowers. He steered Quarr in the general direction of where the trail that was used by the day-patrol should be. They made use of every available cover, because they didn't know when the patrol would return. The only thing they were sure of was that no patrols circled the spaceport at intervals.

There were several hummocks—some bare, some with boulders, and others with trees and rock-protuberances scattered around on the undulating, bushy flatland. They made use of them to look around to check that they didn't run into surprises.

It was late afternoon when they carefully ascended a grassy knoll. Quarr happened to look in the right direction and pointed quickly. The three-member patrol was way past them. It was too late to do anything about being discovered. The patrol acted tired, so Kryger assumed that they must have left at dawn, unless they were putting on an act for the benefit of a dictatorial commander. He quickly checked the route they had followed with a practiced eye, and memorized it as they made a beeline for a gate near a cluster of low buildings inside the fence.

Although it wasn't necessary, he whispered, "We may

assume that a daily patrol uses the same trail to the river, for they must have some means of crossing it. We'll return before dawn to that knoll with the clump of low bushes and a big boulder. We'll check to see if I'm correct in the morning. When we see them leave, we make sure they take that trail, and then we lie down in the trail and pretend to be near death. I'll grab their minds as soon as they spot us."

"Are you sure you can do it, and that it will work?"

"I wouldn't even think of trying it if I weren't sure that we have at least a ninety-nine percent chance of success. The chance that humanoid curiosity is more or less the same on any planet is about fifty-fifty. You're the scientist, so why must I be the one that does all the planning and thinking?"

"It's because you've changed beyond measure since our merging. I'm not sure I can keep up with your development." Quarr's left hand was resting on her hip and she was making prolonged eye contact, as if teasing him.

Kryger leaned forward and gently kissed her on the forehead. "Mike pointed my mind in the right direction, but I was mentally too lazy to take him seriously about developing my true powers. Now it happens almost automatically, and you *do* keep up, you know. I think that destiny has something unpleasant in stall for us—like hunting and destroying the scum of this galaxy, for instance. Speaking of the galaxy—in the whole of this galaxy, at this moment, the two of us may be the only ones uniquely qualified to do such dastardly deeds. Let's move out of sight of the sentries before we start running. It won't take more than ten minutes to our place if we run full out."

They skulked away until they were out of sight of the watchtowers, then ran like gazelles in the lesser gravity of Okrion.

24

They slept very little and were in place long before dawn. Both had a distinct and unsettling feeling that this day would decide their own destinies as well as that of humankind, and that the fate of mankind depended on whether they succeeded or perished.

Quarr had examined her innermost self during the night, and she felt confident that her own abilities, pitted against that of any other human, would prevail. The two questions were: how powerful was Gorrel without the augmentation of mental-power from its fellow beings; and how could they defeat it if it got the chance to link with others of its kind?

She and Kryger resembled his mother—the last of the Thrassars, a race that had perished more than ten thousand years ago while she was kept in suspended animation by Mike. Even if they failed today, anyone searching for their race would search in vain. Even death would be some kind of victory, but with Kryger and his MAG in close attendance, she didn't expect to die today.

She could fight as well as any man, excluding those of her adopted family, and she had almost, but not quite, Kryger's terrific mental power. The difference was that she wasn't quite as adventurous as he was, and she lacked his uncompromising relentlessness, tenacity, and raw physical power, but she came close in mental and physical endurance. She was as prepared as she would ever be and not afraid of dying. Death was inevitable, sooner or later; it could not be avoided forever.

As the sun came up, Kryger whispered, "It's a five-man patrol today, but I can handle them."

They crawled onto the well-trodden footpath and sprawled as if they had collapsed from hunger, thirst, and exhaustion. They half closed their eyes to pretend to be near unconsciousness. Quarr created the well-practiced cocoon when the footsteps paused and then cautiously approached, accompanied by the sound of rifles being un-slung and cocked. Both of them remained relaxed. Kryger seized their minds one by one as they entered the cocoon. Each of the five repeated to themselves with Kryger's guidance.

So, these unarmed creatures are the notorious enemy agents everyone's looking for? Half-dead and helpless from hunger and exhaustion. What a laugh! They have no weapons. It's a miracle that they're still alive. They're harmless and to be pitied. We must leave the female alone until we hear what Lord Gorrel has in mind for them. Let's revive them with some water and take them to Lord Gorrel. We're lucky that we are the ones who found them. We may be rewarded. Let's take them in and feed them; then see what he decides to do with them. There will be no senseless slogging it in the sun for us today.

When Kryger was sure that every member of the patrol accepted that he and Quarr had been thoroughly searched, he released their minds. Quarr sensed it and collapsed the cocoon, as she thought that it might be detected if kept active for too long so close to Gorrel's lair. It was doubtful that the communication-suppresser affected the bastard in any way, because they had felt its searching mind, and sometimes the combined minds, quite a number of times during the last twenty days.

Kryger kept a pinprick-sized opening in his shield so that he could keep track of the men's thoughts. He would close it immediately if he couldn't deflect the probe when anyone tried to penetrate the shield.

The leader delegated two of his patrol to attend to the captives. They kneeled next to Kryger and Quarr, lifted their heads and clumsily poured some water into their mouths. Kryger pretended to choke, cough, swallow painfully, and feebly opened his eyes while allowing some of the water to dribble past his slack lips in the process. They should now be quite convinced that he and Quarr were not a threat.

As if she'd picked up his thoughts, Quarr coughed violently and convincingly, as if she'd inhaled some water. Kryger had to control himself with all his might not to laugh. He managed to turn his head away and coughed feebly, although his body shook and he had to hold his breath until the laughing fit passed. *Damn it*, he thought angrily, *I hope Quarr doesn't overdo it. This is ridiculous, but it seems they're accepting it as genuine. I think they are inherently decent people.*

They were lifted to their feet, accompanied by grunts of exertion. Kryger sensed that the man lifting him was not strong enough to fully support his weight, so he helped a little. The man was a head shorter. Kryger intercepted the thought behind the chatter when the man spoke in his own language. "Hell! This guy is as heavy as all of us thrown together! He must weigh at least a ton—he's solid muscle. I wonder where they came from."

"The woman is just as heavy. I wouldn't mind if she fell on me, but gently, because I'd like to survive the encounter. If they're all as attractive as this one, I'd like to meet them on friendly terms—I mean, the whole race. We must try to find out where they come from so that we can go and visit them sometime, hopefully as friends. As enemies they will be too strong."

"Cut the chatter! That is Lord Gorrel's business, not ours. He'll find out where they come from when he interrogates them. Let's take them in. Patrolling seems pointless now. We'll feed them first so that they can look stronger and make a better impression." The leader laughed.

Kryger pretended that he was wobbling on his feet, trying to walk on his own, and saw that Quarr was doing the same. He pointed to a water flask and swallowed a few mouthfuls when it was presented to him.

He convincingly staggered the few steps to Quarr, and decided not to wink at her, for she might start laughing. He held the flask to her mouth. She took the cue and swallowed, then pretended that it was what she required to regain some strength. They bowed slightly to the men to indicate gratefulness, and Quarr managed a shy smile.

Quite the actress, Kryger thought admiringly. He detected admiration from the purple men as well. *They're not bad. It's a pity that we're enemies.* He took the flask from her, took another gulp, although he didn't need it, and handed it back to the man, bowing again to show his appreciation. The man smiled.

I like you too, but I'll kill you if I have to. Sorry, Kryger thought as he pretended to be unsteady but somewhat stronger. He started to walk when the leader barked an order and pointed to the spaceport. He didn't understand the language, but the accompanying thought indicated that they should proceed to the gate about a kilometer away.

Kryger took Quarr's hand so that they could share thoughts. He told her that he had a minute opening in his shield, just enough to get a thought-tendril through, so that he could keep tabs on the men's thoughts, and that the opening would close instantly if an outside thought brushed his mind.

Now why didn't I think of doing the same thing? It's the logical thing to do. Like this? She showed him a mental picture of an opening as big as a pinhead.

No, that's much too big. If Gorrel gets in, and if it is as strong as reported, it can force your shield open. A pinprick-sized one big is enough and is not easy to detect—like this. He showed her. *We don't really know how strong we are, because we've had no experience in protecting ourselves, and the only practice we've had is the night before last. The problem is that we held back somewhat, because we were, unconsciously, afraid of causing damage and death to each other, but we'll find out today what we are capable of. I'll watch you and you must watch me. We can link immediately if something goes wrong.*

I'll watch you as anxiously as a tigress watches her first cub. I gather that these men think that we're holding hands because we're husband and wife, and they are laughing at the fact that we were thought of as dangerous enemy agents. You should be ashamed for influencing them so convincingly. I almost feel sorry for them.

Yes, I like them too, but they're enslaved by Gorrel, and are probably allies of the murderous Bikans. That, unfortunately, makes them our enemies. Perhaps we can free them if we defeat Gorrel. I'll certainly try. They're not inherently bad, just perverted by cruelty and terror. Oh well, here we are. They're going to feed us first. Decent of them, don't you think?

Definitely…assuming their kind of food doesn't poison us.

When they entered the gate, Kryger memorized the way they were taking to the barracks. He assumed that the newly erected building was part of the mess hall. They were seated and fed a decent, fine-tasting meal amid the gathering of inquisitive men and cooks, and then led through a maze of streets to a huge concrete building some distance from the runways. Kryger and Quarr still let their shoulders sag as if they were overtired, because they had agreed that it might make their powerful bodies less noticeable to the casual observer. He memorized the shortcut they were taking and hoped that Quarr was doing the same in case she had to lead the way if they had to escape in a hurry.

The building looked very alien. It was cast in meters-thick grey concrete, which was in sharp contrast to the town on this side of it. The Shadows used native rock in the construction of their dwellings. It was obviously built to be an impregnable fortress, and therefore must house the laboratory where the thought-communication-suppresser was constructed and put into operation. This close to the source, Kryger felt the heavy oppression was almost unbearable, but he was strong and managed to pierce the mental fog at will. He was thankful that the mirror formed by their shields deflected the numbing rays, and he was sure that long exposure would slowly numb any powerful brain. Hopefully Gorrel's brain was being affected, unless it has a natural resistance to its influence.

25

They passed through an astonishing number of unnecessary security checkpoints—one at every intersection of major passages, or so it appeared. Did Gorrel fear sabotage from its own people, or was there another reason for the multiple checkpoints? What did it fear? Or was it just dictatorial harassment to make the big brass feel important? Ycagabys had indicated that Gorrel rather enjoyed physical and mental confrontation, so the checkpoints could be to keep his so-called partner from escaping, or to protect the damper. Kryger gave up quickly, for speculation interfered with his attentiveness to every little detail.

Merry laughter greeted them at every checkpoint when they were introduced as "the unarmed enemy agents who destroyed our troops and flying machines." Kryger and Quarr easily followed the boisterous conversations, because the alien speech was accompanied by natural, unsuppressed thoughts and images that any Sensitive could understand. All non-Sensitives broadcasted this way without ever realizing it.

They were delayed at the last checkpoint. Gorrel was having an "audience with his partner." There was sneering laughter at the mention of "partner." It seemed to be a tremendous joke that everyone shared. They somehow knew that this "partner" lived on borrowed time, arrogantly unaware of his inevitable fate. They all seemed to know that once he outlived his usefulness, his last moments as a living being would provide a few moments of messy, cruel entertainment. The cause of their amusement was the anticipation of seeing the surprise on his pompous face.

Kryger managed to feel a small measure of momentary sympathy for the self-deluded traitor. What was the purpose of this mockery? Was it a token gesture of tolerance for amusement purposes, or was he being pumped for knowledge? He shrugged the sympathy away. A man reaps what he sows. It was a universal law. The traitor should know that.

A haughty officer who almost burst with self-importance hurried up as soon as the news of the prisoners began to spread. Kryger and Quarr still maintained the tiny openings in their respective shields, to follow the leakage of uncontrolled images and thoughts behind the incomprehensible words. The officer angrily addressed the checkpoint guard who told the captors and their prisoners to wait.

"Makozonke, you fornicating, slow-witted idiot! You know that we have standing orders to take the captured enemy agents *immediately* into Lord Gorrel's presence when they are brought in! What are the reasons for this delay?"

"Sir!" the guard sprang to attention. "That was weeks ago. Lord Gorrel is in conference with his *partner*. From what I hear, I think that mister high-and-mighty Pupaul is about to be kicked in his contemptuous backside." This was accompanied with a wink and a sneer.

The officer went red in the face and bristled with fury. He didn't like to be treated as an equal by a lowdown, disdainful trooper. "Wipe that silly smile off your face, asshole! What our MASTER does or does not do is none of your damn business! Report for correctional treatment, NOW!" He jumped with fury to emphasize his last words.

The guard's face was suddenly ashen. He quickly saluted and departed at a run. Kryger almost felt sorry for him.

The officer looked sternly at the leader of the escort. "Have you searched the prisoners?" His voice was still angry and he bristled with self-importance, and he seemed to be perpetually angry.

"Yes sir! They were almost dead from hunger and thirst when we found them. As you can see sir, they have not yet recovered from their ordeal. They had no weapons and offered no resistance. We let them have a meal, but they will need time to build up strength and recover. We brought them for interrogation by our lord and master as soon as they were able to walk unassisted, sir."

He knows how to stroke a superior officer's over-inflated ego, Kryger thought with admiration, and suppressed an urge to pat the guy on the back.

"You did very well, trooper. I'll commend all of you. Follow me." He turned away and marched very correctly and importantly to the huge double door.

"Thank you, sir!" the squad replied in unison, coming to attention and clicking their heels. They winked at each other behind his back and waved the prisoners forward, then followed the officer in military precision. Kryger liked them. He appreciated a sense of humor and wished that there was some way he could save them if his plan succeeded.

The jack-in-the-box officer pushed the doors open theatrically, and marched swaggeringly into the presence of "Lord Gorrel". Gorrel was in the process of berating and placating his "partner", both at the same time, in a gravelly, gargling voice.

A sudden ominous silence greeted their entrance. To Kryger it was like a thundering applause. The officer went down on his knees and bowed his head in reverence, but the detail bowed to their master from the hips. Kryger had a powerful urge to step forward and kick the officer from behind onto his face; then bow mockingly to the weird being, but suppressed the sudden sense of gaiety. Instead, he squared his powerful shoulders and pushed his chest out. Like hell would he bow to a self-appointed deity!

He immediately felt a tremendous mental clamp of power around his mind-shield; as if the so-called deity wanted to crush his head in an attempt to take control of his mind. It both shocked and angered him. With the tiny opening in his shield, he was hard pressed to withstand the onslaught, but he was determined to maintain it as long as necessary. This was the first real test and he had to pass.

While he resisted, he summed up the situation. Their presence had perhaps interrupted an important conference, or merely postponed the fate of a self-deluded power-seeker. Kryger didn't care. They were fighting to bring peace to the galaxy so that ordinary people could have a chance to develop their particular potentials, which were going to waste in this perpetual war. There could never be peace as long as greedy power-seekers subjected nations, or planets, to their will by war and violence.

Kryger's experiences led him to believe that the purpose of his existence was to strive to help attain that so-often-fragile peace. He came to believe that this was the reason he excelled in anything connected with combat. He was born with unusual talents, which enabled him to develop rapidly when he put his mind to it and exerted effort.

Because he and Quarr made such a successful team, he sometimes intuited that she was part of that purpose when he contemplated their well-charmed successes. This belief was confirmed by the unique outcome of the forbidden merging of minds, which strengthened them both mentally. He was quite sure that he was strong enough to confront these self-appointed deities one by one, and he now was convinced that they were the instigators of the evil that destroyed entire planets. He wondered if there was more to their seemingly wanton carnage than he knew about.

The mental-onslaught ceased as suddenly as it had begun, and then concentrated on Quarr. She winced once, but stood her ground and ignored Gorrel's onslaught on her mind. She even managed to grin at the suddenly pale scientist in front of Gorrel, which caused his face to go ash-gray.

Kryger, free from concentrating on mental defense but expecting it at any time, was able to study the weird being in detail. It looked like a monstrous escapee from a science fiction horror movie. He had seen lots of huge insects in his time, but this one resembled nothing he had ever come across. It made him think of a three-way cross between a gigantic ant, an equally huge praying mantis, and some unknown bug. The only thing remotely resembling a mantis was the head, which swiveled on a short neck that was attached to an unbelievably big chest. The chest, in turn, was connected via a short, thick, swivel-waist to a big belly with a chopped-off-looking behind, which enabled it to walk upright on four, thick, double-jointed legs that were attached to its rounded-off under carriage.

It's about four meters tall, or long, he corrected himself. Four thick, swivel-type arms—two on top and two at the bottom—were attached to the overly-large chest. They could reach every part of its body, even its back. It was *huge.* He was sure that it weighed more than a metric ton. Its entire body, from head to tarsus and claws looked as if it was made out of shiny, highly polished, deep-green tinted metal armor plating. Kryger doubted that this weird creation ever became physically tired. He wondered from what strange creation this monstrous being and its kind had escaped.

It was seated on a weirdly-shaped, cushioned couch, as if weary from carrying its own weight on those thick, stump-like legs, which was bent at the knees on both sides of the sofa.

Kryger shifted his attention to the "partner." He was about the same size of the purple people, and powerfully muscled. His face and features were humanoid, and his eyes showed intelligence, but his brown, conceited face was now shockingly pale, as if seeing an unexpected ghost.

Gorrel must have given up trying to take control of their minds. It said something to the scientist in a voice that seemed

166

choked with phlegm. Kryger widened the opening in his shield so that he could follow the conversation. He was confident that he could drive the being from his mind if it pounced unexpectedly. He intercepted the last part.

"...when you have a conversation in my presence, use speech or open up your mind. There must be no secrets kept from me. I won't tolerate such impudence, Pupaul."

Ah! So this despicable creature is powerful enough to keep its thoughts from Gorrel, Kryger thought. *Curious, indeed! This self-elected deity is not as powerful as it tries to make its subordinates believe.*

"I'm sorry, Lord Gorrel," Pupaul replied. "I apologize most humbly. This enemy, who should have been destroyed in space, mind-spoke to me and I replied without thinking. This woman is of my race and must be eliminated *immediately.* She is dangerous and means us harm. As you already know, she evaded the trap set for her, and she circumvented all subsequent attempts to kill her, which means that she is very powerful."

"Ah-hah! So she can mind-speak to you without me knowing? Come off it, numskull. That's *impossible!* I tested both of them and they are naturally mind-deaf. I'm very powerful, and you know it! She's the one that you've dreaded will return at this time to claim the rule of your people, Pupaul?"

"I do not fear her, Gorrel! No! She's but a *female,* a daughter and look-alike of the one I hated. Her shape is like mine, but she prefers to look like this...this *other* creature." his voice dripped with grimace and distaste. "She has mated with this impure creature and both must be put to death *immediately.* I will not tolerate their presence! Kill them *now!*"

"Shut up, Pupaul! You've gone too far this time! You presume to be disrespectful and *order me?* You are afraid of two brain-dead creatures Pupaul, but I'll be lenient with you and not kill you outright for your disrespect. I declare that you will fight her for my amusement. You may kill her slowly, as you usually prefer. Do it! *Now!*" Gorrel imitated Pupaul. "If you win, you will fight the male creature. I'll let the winner live...for a while. I don't think that she's an enemy agent, or of the attacking forces, as you've led me to believe. She may be a danger to you, but she's come to claim her inheritance; or what might be left of it after I've made your people my slaves. The only partners I have, or need, are my own people, you arrogant fool! We are the respected gods of this galaxy and we prrr…ah…use lesser beings as we like. You amused me for a while, but your usefulness is at an end. We'll duplicate your work and conquer the stubborn fools who resist us. You will fight right now, and without weapons, as I do. If you like, you may resort to your teeth like my hounds, feeble man-being."

To Kryger, its laugh sounded as if it was gargling with slime-coated gravel, but he took note of Gorrel's near-slip. In its arrogant rage, it almost said, "We *prey* on lesser beings like your kind." He also noted that Pupaul was now white in the face. The fool at last realized that he had been played, and would fight like a cornered rat to stay alive just a little longer. Quarr was superbly fit, and could fight like a tigress. She was used to fighting in gravity nearly twice that of this planet, and was trained to perfection in fighting arts, which should be quite unknown by the Gwarra and other races not of legendary old Earth. Kryger should feel sorry for Pupaul, but he couldn't. The arrogant twerp had walked into a trap of his own making.

Pupaul retained some of his dignity by not replying to Gorrel's taunting. Instead, he scornfully looked Quarr up and down. He was impressed by his own powerful body and wanted to intimidate her in spite of his own confidence. He couldn't see her lithe, powerful body covered by her loose-fitting jacket and knee-length shorts, but he could see part of her beautiful, well-shaped feminine legs that belied their awful power. Kryger could almost feel what Pupaul was thinking—a female never is a match for a trained male—although it was plainly written on his face.

This one is a match for any man, as you'll soon find out, Kryger thought. He decided to throw caution to the wind. Gorrel's mind was powerful, but it was limited in quite a few ways. It couldn't access the lower frequencies of mind-communication and, as a matter of fact, it didn't even know that such frequencies existed. Kryger cautiously probed Gorrel's mind and defenses with a thin tendril of thought on the lowest frequency he could manage. He gathered quite a lot of useful information.

Gorrel's attention was now fully focused on a few moments of pleasure by an amusing fight between two creatures it considered so low that they were not even worthy of contempt. It had no feeling for creatures of any kind, and not much for its own kind either—only a kind of racial loyalty, which it couldn't identify with. Its mind was powerful, but primitive.

Just to see if it would work, Kryger quietly planted a suggestion in Gorrel's mind that it send its lackeys out of the hall, and that they should close the door, because the fight would only remind them of their own mortality. They might spoil this performance by their lack of appreciation, and the fight between these lowly creatures was for Gorrel's private amusement only. It could handle Pupaul and the prisoners, for its own strength was beyond anything these lowly creatures could even begin to imagine. Gorrel accepted the thought as its own and gargle-barked an order. Within seconds, the place was evacuated and the door quietly closed.

While Pupaul was busy stripping down to his underpants, thinking that he would impress Quarr with his powerful physique and make her cringe in fear, Kryger subtly entered his mind and extracted the formula for the subspace-scanner and the damper.

So it is called an Inhibitor, Kryger thought. *Perhaps it can be altered to use against Gorrel's kind. One never knows how canny scientists could manipulate an invention.* He also found a quiet satisfaction in Pupaul's thoughts, which he heartily approved of and gave the man credit for. He had planned to double-cross Gorrel. Now he was quite elated that he had, and thought that he could use it as a lever to escape when the fights were over. The plan for the Inhibitor and Subspace Scanner he had provided Gorrel with would result in a satisfying nuclear explosion as soon as power was fed into a contraption built from his description. *He tried to safeguard himself, but in the wrong way,* Kryger thought. It can only be called revenge, for that was what it amounted to. It was always a pity when such brilliant minds were perverted and used for selfish purposes. He couldn't feel any sympathy for Pupaul.

He felt a kind of gratitude toward the man, since he could now destroy the Inhibitor with the knowledge that this insect-deity and its kind couldn't duplicate it. The ugly bugs deserved to be blasted to atoms if they were stupid enough to follow every step in the assembly of such machines, but he didn't think that they were that industrious or inquisitive. They were predatory destroyers, not builders or preservers, and they sadly lacked the ability to think logically. The only question was, would one of them be present when the machine was being powered up, or would it be far away when power was applied? The unfortunate part of Pupaul's revenge, and what he didn't take into account, was that it could happen only once.

Quarr had not moved, but she now touched Kryger's arm. *Pupaul is my mother's half-brother. He's the one who sabotaged my mother's ship, because he wanted to rule my people. He doesn't even know why or for what purpose; it's just something he wants. I'll tell you the story I extracted from his mind later. He doesn't even know that you and I were in his mind at the same time, using different frequencies to extract different information. I'm going to kill him. I owe my mother and brother that much. It's a pity that I can't torture the despicable, arrogant murderer as the Bikans tortured my mother. Gorrel will certainly be amused by what's about to happen.*

Bloodthirsty little beauty, aren't you, my love? Feel free to start anytime, and take your time, but be careful and watch out for dirty tricks. I know that you don't need my help, and I won't interfere—I'll be gathering information from this insect's mind. It's bored and starved for amusement, and will therefore concentrate on the fight. I'll take it on when you finish-off your uncle, or whatever he thinks he is. Be prepared to back me up if necessary.

Okay. Surprise the primitive bug whenever you feel like it. Pupaul might have a few dirty tricks up his sleeve. I'll be alert and keep my distance, and don't be surprised if I enjoy it. I owe the bastard.

Pupaul seemed to be warming up by flexing his muscles and doing weird distortions of his upper body—either to impress or intimidate Quarr with the play of his massive, over-developed muscles. In Kryger's experience, ponderous muscles slowed a man down, although it denoted exceptional strength—at least for this planet.

Quarr wasn't impressed by the display, and threw a few derisive suggestions his way to annoy him, but she excluded Gorrel. It would only have uttered that horrible, gargling noise that was supposed to be a laugh, and she wanted to avoid the noisome ordeal as much as possible.

What you're doing is a waste of time, and it's not impressive in any way, uncle. I've seen better muscles before. I'll do you the honor of miscalling you by that undeserved title for the few minutes that remains of your long, treacherous life, you miserable, low-down scumbag. Why don't you just do a few push-ups and sit-ups, uncle? It might be good for your shoulders and your flabby stomach. Perhaps it might even warm up the rest of your fake muscles. Just be careful that you don't overexert yourself and get out of breath. You really look unfit, uncle. You've got a fight with a weak female on your bloody hands, remember? You're wasting time to live a few seconds longer, and that really is cowardly, even for you. Where's your pride, old man?

She was trying to make him angry, and the undisguised mocking tone of her thoughts succeeded beyond her expectation. He jumped up, his face red with fury. He sputtered as he addressed her in a language she had more or less forgotten, but she picked up the furious thoughts behind the words, which flowed like curses from his mouth.

"Shut up, bitch! You've got a vicious mouth, which you must have inherited from your bloody mother. I'll crush you, screaming, into pulp, whore! I'll spit in your pussycat face and piss on your remains. I have yet to see a whore that can put up a decent fight, other than with her dirty mouth. I've prayed for this chance. I foresaw long ago that you would show up just before your twenty-fifth birthday to enjoy your undeserved power over my people. You will die screaming, whore, and so will your pussy-faced bedfellow after you."

Quarr was deadly calm and gave him an unconcerned smile, which further infuriated him. *Then come on. See if you can impress your smelly bug-bedfellow with your best performance. You seem overly familiar with whores, and you convey the impression that that's the only type of women you spend your time with. Stop wasting time with your silly exercises, dear uncle, and come and get the last surprise of your perfidious existence. Your boss is waiting impatiently. You don't want to annoy it further, do you?*

She moved casually away from Kryger and closer to the wall where Gorrel's couch was located. She wanted plenty of space to maneuver, where she couldn't be forced into a corner or any obstacle that may impede free movement. She reminded herself that this was her first real empty-handed fight, with death as the only outcome. Curiously, she felt no fear or apprehension; only a deadly calm and the sure knowledge that she wasn't going to stop or give up until she was either dead, or the murderer of her mother and brother lay lifeless her feet.

171

26

The real test, after many years of training, was about to begin. When Quarr stopped about four meters away from the wall, she assumed a casual fighting stance, and quietly went into a state of no-thought in order to empty her mind of all emotion so that her subconscious could respond without interference and to make her responses automatic.

As Quarr mockingly curtsied to him with a pasted-on grin and a show of teeth, Pupaul uttered a mighty bellow of rage, stooped, and rushed in with arms spread wide to grab her in a wrestlers-hold around the waist. His intention was to butt her in the ribs with his head, grab her in a bear's hug, and while she struggled to regain her breath, break her back slowly and agonizingly as she suffocated.

Quarr predicted what he was planning. Just as he grabbed for her and couldn't stop his headlong rush, she made a curious, fast overhead circle from right to left with her arms, palms close together and pointed outward, while she simultaneously shifted her left leg half a step left and swiveled her hips and right leg sharply to her right out of Pupaul's way. It was a fast, skillfully balanced and easy-looking movement, but it took a lot of practice to make it that smooth and effective.

As her right leg landed behind her, her arms completed the fast circle and came almost gently down to push Pupaul's right arm and shoulder past her, so that his momentum carried him right into the concrete wall. He couldn't stop his momentum, but fortunately for him, his extended hands connected first with the solid obstruction before his head did. He wasn't prepared for missing his target and he had expected *her* back to hit the wall. If she had completed the standard move by grabbing and pulling his shoulders to help his headlong rush along, he would have brained himself, but that would have ended the fight too early for her.

Pupaul was stunned by this defense and unexpected turn of events. He hadn't expected a female as strong as this one, able to push him aside without apparent effort. Dazed and bewildered, he fell onto his hands and knees with a roar of frustrated rage, which immediately changed into a scream of utter agony as Quarr shifted and kicked him hard in the crotch from behind.

Quarr stepped out of Pupaul's reach and projected a derisive, *Sorry, uncle. I couldn't resist the temptation! Did you enjoy that? Would you like a replay?* She had forgotten much of the ancient language of her own people, and this time deliberately used mind-speech on a frequency that Gorrel would intercept to keep its awareness off Kryger's gentle probing. The entity's enormous body was now shaking with its horrible, nerve wrecking, gargling laugh.

Pupaul instinctively and defensively rolled over onto his back, clutching his vulnerable spot with one hand. His agony was too great and he couldn't respond.

The gargling noise they interpreted as a laugh showed Gorrel's perverted pleasure in Pupaul's pain and discomfort. It was enjoying the taunting and the unusual way of fighting, and was unaware of Kryger's subtle infiltration in its brain to sift through its memory for useful information.

What Kryger found very strange, however, was that Gorrel was so arrogant and sure of its own power and invulnerability that it wasn't worried about the attacking forces. Also, Quarr's sudden ability to use mind-speech on a frequency it could follow rang no warning bells.

Quarr laughed mockingly. *I'm enjoying this, uncle, but I'm not sure one can call it a fight, because you're an amateur. Were you so occupied with loose women that you didn't have time to learn? But don't worry, I'll wait for you to recover.* She took another step away with a look of mock disgust on her face. She realized that he was a brawler who relied on raw muscle power and intimidation, and that he had no inkling of the fine fighting arts that were developed on ancient, dying Terra.

Gorrel's slimy, gargling laughter was annoying, but didn't distract Quarr's attention from centering on Pupaul. She was taught never to allow anger to impair her judgment, but the thought of the torture her mother had gone through due of this deceitful man's lust for absolute dictatorship made her so vengeful that she wanted to kick him to a pulpy mess without stopping to take a breath. She suppressed the killing lust and took a few deep breaths to calm herself.

Gorrel was a powerful being, physically and mentally, and it had met no real challenge during a very long lifetime. It was bored beyond measure as only an ageless, undeveloped entity, which knew only this crude, primitive type of entertainment, could be. It

173

was both intrigued and distracted by this unusual, fighting female, and it was not aware of the wispy probe that gathered forgotten information from its big brain. It held all non-Hullenii creatures in contempt. Why should it expect a little, soft-looking creature of flesh and bone to challenge its supremacy?

At first, Kryger was surprised. The creature's brain was not in its head as one would expect, but occupied the vast chest area. As Gorrel urged Quarr and Pupaul to get on with the fight, Kryger carefully memorized information from the enormous brain. He learned that the creature was incredibly old—more than twelve thousand years—as calculated by his standards. He found that each individual of this bizarre race owned at least one planet, which it used exclusively for its own pleasures—one of which was to gorge itself on its inhabitants—and each maintained an occasional mind-link to five others in order to pass on new information as it was acquired. Thus, new experiences and information were constantly shared by the entire race. They were emotionally primitive, and therefore indifferently callous toward everything but their own cruel, basic pleasures. He dared not probe the tenuous links, for Gorrel's contacts might become aware of the intrusion.

Quarr taunted her opponent during the couple of minutes she waited for him to recover to keep him unbalanced and to amuse Gorrel. This gave Kryger enough time to access vast volumes of stored and forgotten scientific data. He would remember everything until he had the opportunity to transfer it to Mike. Gorrel's disorderly mind reminded him of a sloppily programmed storage computer, or an encyclopedia without an index. The creature had stored vast volumes of scientific and other information without cross-referencing it. It seemed unaware of most of the data, and it would have to recall everything if it was looking for specific information. *No wonder they had their minions raid a planet when they got wind of a new weapon.*

Kryger thought that it was a good thing that they had this tendency to forget about information as soon as it was stored, for they could overwhelm the galaxy with the number of weapons and vast other technical knowledge they had stored over the centuries. It would be a sad day for all creatures when they learned to access and apply even a *quarter* of the stored knowledge. He wished he had the brain capacity to copy everything. As it was, he had to be very selective. Perhaps he would have other opportunities after he had passed this batch on to Mike. It was a pity that Mike wasn't linked with him right now.

Kryger searched for its guiding intelligence, but found very little, certainly not enough to correlate and use the vast amount of accumulated data. The primitive, savage instinct for self-preservation wasn't surprising. Perhaps it was the reason for its murderous nature, and why it instinctively destroyed anything that might threaten its continued existence, even though it perceived itself as indestructible. And then there was a fierce, vicious, inborn cunning lying dormant just below the surface of its consciousness; unused and mellowed by ages of unchallenged authority and comfortable existence, just waiting to be awakened by the right circumstances. He suddenly had the foreknowledge that, if the existence of their entire race was threatened, they would be forced to develop a method of accessing old knowledge. Kryger shuddered.

If these creatures had the intelligence to use a mere ten percent of the accumulated data, the galaxy might have been conquered or obliterated centuries ago. On the other hand, if these creatures were so inclined, the galaxy could be made a pleasant place for all its inhabitants. Was there yet another species behind the Hullenii? It seemed likely, but he couldn't find a trace of any such knowledge in the short time available to him. These creatures seemed to think that the universe was their playground—created for their exclusive, depraved amusement. When Kryger had absorbed as much information as he could take without overtaxing his brain—and not wanting to alert Gorrel that its mind had been probed—he gently withdrew the subtle probe.

When the excruciating pain in his groin subsided to a tolerable degree, Pupaul let go of his tortured genitals, but he groaned as he painfully rolled over and slowly got to his feet. He was surprised that this despicable bitch was stupid enough not to attack him while he was totally helpless. He thought complacently that this was one of those fatal mistakes softhearted women were capable of making, but who was he to complain? He wouldn't have given her a second chance. Then he went into an eye-blurring shape changing act. His hands changed into claws and his toes into sharp, solid, bony points, capable of ripping her belly open.

It was such a rapid change that Quarr was almost taken by surprise. *He must be well-practiced and adept,* she thought as she suddenly took a fast, gliding step closer and drove a heel into the thigh muscles of his left leg. She jumped away as he fell forward, again in screaming agony when his leg collapsed from the numbing pain.

She admonished him like a mischievous brat. *Naughty! Naughty! Stop crying like a spoilt child. I haven't broken any bones yet, but I will if you don't fight like a man. Oh, what am I talking about! I forgot that you're not a man, but a despicable coward who does things at a distance to ensure his own safety. How does it feel to begin paying for your cowardly, underhanded dealings, and the murder of my mother and brother?*

Suddenly she felt sick. Revenge was one thing, but torture, even in this mild form, was something that gave her no pleasure. It made her feel soiled. This was alien to her nature. On the other hand, he must pay a little for the murder of her mother and brother, albeit only in this small measure. He wouldn't be limping for long, because he was an expert at shape changing. His agony wouldn't last long either—only as long as it took him to distribute the pain and think of another ploy to prolong his treacherous life. He must be pretty desperate by now, for he hadn't landed a single blow. The pleasure Gorrel derived from his pain was even more nauseating for Quarr. She gave Kryger a quick, sideways glance.

He nodded and slashed his throat with a forefinger, indicating that he had long enough to gather the information he wanted from both. He could see that her playing with Pupaul upset her, and would have nodded even if the gathering of information was unfinished. The main principle of unarmed fights hammered into them was: do not play around with an opponent and give him time to sum up your methods and capabilities.

Finish him off before he comes up with something real nasty, he told her on a very low frequency.

Pupaul again distributed the agony of damaged muscles, so that his maneuverability wasn't impaired for long. For him it was a gift that came with the shape changing ability, but he was at a loss of how to proceed, because this unusual kind of fighting with feet was a feat he hadn't even thought about, except for stomping and kicking a victim to death when he was down.

Then cunning came to him—he would watch her feet with half his attention, and grab the foot when it was lifted. He moved in on her again with arms apart to grab and rip with extended claw-hands, circling warily to wait for an opportunity. He would not be caught so easily again a second time. He didn't know that he had left himself wide open for a martial arts expert like Quarr. Rage was also an enemy he did not take into account. He wanted to rip her apart savagely, and involuntary grew a snout and fangs in a matter of moments. Feeling the change, he snarled viciously, fainted with the left hand, and went for her face with his right-hand claw, but he still watched her legs for movement. He couldn't know that playing time was over and he had made a fatal mistake.

Quarr saw his downcast eyes watching her legs and ignored the left hand faint. Its distance would be too short to come anywhere near her body. Instead, she grabbed his extended right arm at the wrist with her left hand, twisted the elbow upward, and broke his arm at the elbow with a rising right forearm block in one smoothly coordinated counter attack. The snapping sound was sickening.

The screams of utter agony that were generated deep within Pupaul's chest, made Gorrel chuckle gleefully. It clapped its two pairs of claw-hands in a weird sequence as a token of appreciation. This was something it had never seen before. It decided that she would be responsible for its future entertainment, for she had a new, strange way of fighting. It was deadly, but entertaining, and it must be taught to others so that entertainment could be enhanced.

Agony engulfed Pupaul and caused him to disregard the fact that he was fighting for his life. He grabbed his broken elbow without thinking, and bending slightly over, pressed the arm against the side of his stomach, in the hope of easing the excruciating pain. How could this female be that vicious of a warrior? It just wasn't normal. As he turned his head upward to scream his agony at the uncaring heavens, his Adam's apple made a prominent target.

Quarr did not hear Gorrel's slimy chuckle and hand clapping as she rapidly shifted one step away from her opponent. She now was totally committed and concentrated on ending the fight as quickly as possible. Although it wasn't her intention to end it this way, her training took over and quick as a striking snake, she buried the outer edge of her right shoe in the exposed throat.

Pupaul's throat and neck snapped with a soggy, sickening crunch. For a brief instant, he was aware that he had flipped over onto his back, and that he couldn't breathe. Then his head flopped loosely sideways in death. Disbelief and surprise was written all over his face. His chest sagged like a deflated bag of wind as his heels drummed a last, brief tattoo.

Gorrel's gargling laugh and clapping clawed hands were ignored by both. Its glee sickened them.

Quarr took one final look at her dead opponent to make sure that he wasn't able to spring a surprise, then turned her back on the carcass. *I should forget what's past and concentrate on the future—the immediate future. Perhaps the act of turning my back on Pupaul will help me to forget this part of the past. Now, the real test comes.*

Both of them intercepted a thought from Gorrel. *If these creatures weren't so dense, I could make them fight each other. That may be prolonged entertainment and fun to watch. I can order her to attack him, since she at least responded to my command to finish off this Pupaul, the arrogant Gwarra creature, who thought that I would spare my ancient enemies. I will order my servants to take this cadaver to my larder…err…the cool room to them … for preservation until I can dispose of it in the usual way. But first I'll have another fight and another cadaver. I'll taste this other cat-creature for supper. The flavor may be different.* Amused by its own humor, it uttered the nauseating gargling laugh again.

Quarr could see by Kryger's tight facial expression that he had had enough of the creature's shameful pleasure in another creature's agony.

27

Kryger dissolved his shield and addressed Gorrel as insultingly as he could convey by thought; and his loathing was scathing. *What's so funny about pain and suffering, bug-face? You're too dense and backward to recognize a mind-shield, even when you stumble over one. You're just an ignorant, oversized bug with an inflated ego!*

He wanted the creature so angry that it wouldn't have time to consider signaling for backup, and he wanted to experience just how strong this giant bug's mind truly was. From what he had gathered in its mind, he believed that his own mind and brainpower was more focused and therefore stronger. The bugs had grown sloppy, because they never had any real opposition except the forever fleeing Gwarra. Kryger was ready to snap his shield into place should it become necessary.

Gorrel jumped to its claws and reared up as if slapped in the face. *Ah! So the cat-faced creature has a mind after all? Be careful how you address me, small-fry! I can crush your puny body and tear it into small pieces, limb by limb, anytime I feel like it. I'll destroy your mind and make you a helpless plaything before I eat you alive, bit by bit.*

I have no doubt that you can tear me to pieces, you stinking bug, but you have to catch me first before you start bragging. As for destroying my mind, your brain is much too feeble.

Kryger readied his mind to reply with a bolt of pure force as he had been taught, but he knew that this time it must be the strongest bolt he could generate. Back on Nevus, they used a mild mind-stun to discourage large felines, but now he would have to use every iota of power he could muster to scramble the powerful, vast brain of this primitive creature. What counted in his favor was that it was unprepared. He hoped he would not be left too weak to make an attempt to escape afterward, but he could depend on Quarr to look after that aspect, even if she had to drag him by his feet.

Strangely, Gorrel became amused, but not angry. It gargle-barked with amusement, and Kryger followed its thoughts. *I might start to like this cheeky little creature that wants to challenge me. Where did it crawl out of? It might be the enemy agent that Pupaul was afraid of, but this is utterly*

179

ridiculous. I might keep both as pets for a while, but this one must be taught to respect me. It would be useless to me if I destroyed its mind, but to make it cringe before me I must show it how powerful I am, even though I might damage its brain a little.

Kryger assumed that the slimy barks that issued from its throat could be interpreted as roaring laughter. It slapped its chest—or its brain case—with all four claw-hands, which made a dull booming sound as if the pounding was done on a thick steel drum filled to capacity with liquid. *Perhaps that's a sign of real amusement,* Kryger thought.

Both you and the female amuse me, but I'll have to teach you some manners. Prepare yourself for a lesson you'll never forget.

Before I contest your intention, may I ask something?

He already had the information, but it may lull the creature into a false sense of security if he asked a few irreverent questions. Kryger was sure that this creature, on his own, was not nearly strong enough to overwhelm his mind, but if it linked with the other five, it could be disastrous. He would get stronger as time went by, and he may be strong enough in the far future to take on a combined pack of them, but right now he was developing, and his only practice was against Quarr. Also, these bugs might not be familiar with mind-bolts, because Gorrel tried to crush his brain with a clamp or something similar.

You may ask, little creature. It amuses me to indulge in your ignorance.

Kryger gathered that Gorrel was supremely confident. Not one of them had ever encountered any creature, or race of creatures, stronger than themselves in mind or body. There had been the Gwarra once, a long time ago, that could have been a threat, but they now existed only in scattered groups after their planet of origin was destroyed. The Hullenii suffered great losses then, but that was irrelevant, as they could reproduce when the urge, or the need for more individuals, became necessary—which was irrelevant as they lived long, and may even be immortal, for none had yet died of natural causes or old age.

How many of you ugly bugs are there? How many planets are you ravaging? He was reading Gorrel's mind without its knowledge, and realized that he must goad it to attack out of sheer rage with its full mind-power, without even thinking to link with its supporting partners. To his surprise, Gorrel once again stayed calm.

I don't like your impertinence, little creature, but I will indulge you for the time being. I don't care to calculate the exact figure, but it's close to eight thousand. We don't breed like vermin as you soft-fleshed human types do. We have no need for superior numbers, for we are very powerful. We each have a planet—or perhaps two or three if we feel like it—to rule as we deem fit. What relevance does this have, and how does it concern you, cat-face? Any last questions while you still can think for yourself, little creature?

The information Kryger had gathered was that the Hullenii numbered *exactly* eight hundred and seventy eight, and that they controlled a thousand planets. Hundreds of planets had been abandoned when they became depopulated because of the indiscriminate need for murderous amusement and bodies, which ultimately fed its uncontrolled gluttony.

Gorrel had wasted eighteen planets so far, and this one, being sparsely populated, was only a very temporary stopover to get rid of the Gwarra, whom they hated above all else. Kryger gathered that they were reluctant to breed, because it was a difficult, protracted process with no enjoyment. Another reason was that they were afraid of starting a war among themselves for territory. There may be millions of livable planets, but not every planet was populated by edible beings.

They were carnivores. Every living thing of flesh and blood was prey, even their slaves and soldiers, but they were extremely circumspect in choosing their prey among useful slaves. No cadaver was ever wasted, except when that entity died of disease. Kryger was aware of the fact that the late Pupaul was destined for Gorrel's larder, which was disguised as a cold storage room from where bodies were supposedly sent at the proper time on to their next life. The not-very-bright slaves, who dragged cadavers to the cold room, were blissfully unaware of each body's final destination. They were brainwashed into believing that they were storing bodies in a civilized manner to be disposed of at an appropriate time, unaware that they, too, were destined to become a lump of bug-excrement when their usefulness expired, but before they became too old and stringy.

No, no more questions, bug-face. I just wanted to know how big a liar a deluded, self-appointed immortal could be. You seem to be ashamed of the devastation you carrion-eating bugs are causing, he replied with as much scathing sarcasm as he could manage.

Kryger's insulting reply at last made Gorrel boil over with rage, although still held in check by its own bizarre sense of humor. It was amused by what it perceived as cheekiness, or false bravado, in a little cat-faced creature. It was thinking about the surprise it had in store for the inferior little feline-faced human, but it was also intrigued by the knowledge of the creature. *Where did it get the information? I must find out before the creature becomes an incoherent idiot with no mind at all,* Gorrel thought.

Quarr would of course be following the exchange of the "amicable" insults. He warned her to withdraw from his and Gorrel's minds, which she did. She didn't want to be hurt in a backlash of uncontrolled power.

Kryger had to know how strong Gorrel was, and whether he could defeat one of them by mind-power alone. Only by using his own natural resources could he develop the necessary skill and confidence to survive future mind-battles. He made sure that the impenetrable shield around his mind was completely collapsed, although it could be instantly regenerated.

Gorrel's self-constraint was at an end. *How dare this little snack insult its master?* Phlegm, produced by rage, dribbled from its mouth and impeded its speaking organs. It switched to mind-to-mind talk, at which it thought it had no equal among the lesser beings. It was still under the impression that the cat-faces understood its spoken language.

So, little feline-face, you think you are clever and humorous? Its thoughts were colder than deep space. *I will now make you tell me where you obtained the information you taunted me with! Before I'm done with you, you'll wish that you were never born, and beg me to eat you alive to be relieved of your pain and misery. Experience the real power of my mind!*

Kryger felt an unbelievably strong force-clamp around his head. He staggered and almost fell to his knees, but resisted and endured. He just barely stopped the forceful probe. Gorrel was an ancient, skilled interrogator with thousands of years of experience—granted, this was against unskilled, unprepared beings—Kryger tried to remind himself. *I have to learn the hard way, fast, for there is no other way if I want to become stronger. Concentrate…focus solely on overcoming this onslaught!*

The momentary distraction to think almost cost him his mind. Another stab so incredibly strong that he couldn't stop it with mind-power alone broke though his defense. Reacting instinctively, he deflected it with a momentarily activation of his mind-shield. He felt Gorrel's surprise—and his own—but he was fighting for his life with every iota of his being, which didn't leave time for thinking, only automatic reflexes. Time ceased to exist. He was defending and not attacking, because he wanted to learn to resist such amazing power before he launched the only mental counter-attack that he could. He began to realize that his mind was strong enough, but not having had any prior experience, he didn't understand how to proceed to the next step without taking time off to think. He could only be on the alert for new tricks and wait for an opportunity to use the bolt of pure energy he had generated and held on to... to destroy Gorrel's mind.

After an indeterminable time, he felt growing amazement and panic in Gorrel's thoughts, and a resolution to shout for help. *How can this creature resist me? We have to know! It's a threat to our existence, the very first in so many thousands of years. I can kill it with a single blow, but we must have all its knowledge before I crush the life out of it. Then we can exterminate the whole race, or lay waste to their planet if necessary.* Then Gorrel made the momentary mistake of stopping its onslaught to yell for assistance.

The instant the awful mental onslaught ceased, Kryger unleashed the mental bolt into Gorrel's brain. Every particle of pure energy he could generate while resisting the awful onslaught was in that bolt. He had never killed this way before, and wasn't sure that it would work, or whether it was powerful enough, but he had to determine if he was strong enough. He had his answer when the entity fell back heavily onto the couch, but its panicky shout for assistance had gone out an instant before its brain fried.

What Kryger didn't know at the time was that, even if the call hadn't gone out, the sudden break of the tenuously maintained link would have registered and been investigated. Gorrel's shocked contacts reluctantly abandoned their individual forms of amusement, linked, and tried to speak to Gorrel. They found a curiously scrambled void that would have been its brain. They could feel that its body was alive and that the link through its secondary brain still existed tenuously, but otherwise their linked minds encountered only an inexplicable, curious emptiness.

Mentally unmatched for ages, they fell into the trap of believing themselves all-powerful. As a direct result, they became lax and unable to immediately respond to this unexpected, shocking challenge. It was an impossible, unbelievable occurrence that one of their species could die at the hands of another creature, but yet was now an accomplished fact. The unthinkable had happened. After a moment's hesitation, they managed a hurried, confused conference, and unwittingly gave Kryger crucial time to recover.

Not knowing where the thought had originated, but thinking it a brilliant inspiration, the youngest of the quintet—by a century—suggested that the obvious course would be to investigate the situation through Gorrel's own eyes. The link was not severed, only inoperative. Perhaps Gorrel had contracted an unknown disease they should be aware of or something similar.

28

The time-weary, invisible onlooker was pleased with her handiwork, but she knew that within seconds another test would come, and she wasn't allowed to intervene. If they perished in the next encounter, they weren't as powerful and resourceful as predicted so many lonely ages ago, and her punishment would have been in vain. She could honestly report that she developed his brain and powers as much as he was capable of handling at the present stage of his evolution.

She loved this brave, honest child of humanity, but she had to let him face the coming challenge alone. It was a challenge she could so easily eliminate, but they would face similar challenges in future, and had to overcome this one on their own in order to learn and develop. If she interfered to save them, even this once, it would nullify the prediction and her exile would be permanent. She could only watch to see the outcome, and then she had to end her three dimensional existence, because her sentence was over when she separated their entangled minds and directed his mind in the right direction.

Kryger was drained of energy. It was the price to pay for a decent mind-bolt, but after a moment, he probed the mind once more to make sure that the bolt had done its work. He withdrew immediately and retched dryly as he encountered only nauseating, dead brain cells. It filled his mind with such loathing that he was off-guard for a moment. At the time, he didn't know that the main brain was used only for storing vast amounts of data, and that the second, small, independent brain in a Hullenii's head, controlled the functions of its complicated body, and actually did the thinking for the little intellectual activity the entity cared to indulge in.

The quintet, linked together, took possession of Gorrel's secondary brain, and through it, its body. They instantly checked Gorrel's functions and assessed the situation. The primary brain was destroyed by mysterious means, but the body was still alive and otherwise intact. It would function with their guidance, and they could see through its eyes. They were astonished by the insignificant size of the two creatures with cat faces, and didn't see any weapons. How could such insignificant creatures have so much power to destroy the mind of one of their kind—and to shield their minds from theirs? Perhaps they possessed a weapon to scramble brains, but it wasn't visible. They must find out and the perpetrators of this horrible crime must be terminated before they escaped.

When Gorrel's head swiveled suddenly, Kryger was caught off-guard. Then he felt the tremendous power of the linked entities reaching out to grab control of his mind, and instinctively generated a shield, because he realized that he was no match for the terrible mental power of the combined entities. It was almost too late and he had to force the shield into place.

That microscopically unguarded moment was long enough to identify him as the killer, but they couldn't understand their instant dismissal from the creature's mind, and their inability to take control of him. They decided that the creature should be killed immediately by physical means.

As the body of Gorrel started to rear up from the couch, Kryger grabbed his belt with his left hand, pulled his pants away from his body and grabbed the MAG with his right hand. He fired instinctively at Gorrel's chest. He didn't know it, but the bolt went right through the armor-plated cavity, through the building, killed three persons who were unfortunately in the wrong place at the wrong time, and went through a Battleship as it was landing for re-arming, which exploded, blocking the runway for other craft. The bolt continued into the sky and out into space.

Despite the neat hole in its chest, Gorrel's body sprang incredibly quickly, but clumsily into action. Kryger dived sideways and rolled away as Gorrel's claw-feet hit the floor with a heavy clang, like metal striking concrete. He jumped to his feet in one practiced movement, although he didn't have much energy. He was trained to react in any manner he could when his life was on the line.

"The head, Kryger, shoot the head! They control it through the *small* brain in the head!" Quarr yelled out loud, for her own mind-shield was also in place.

Quarr's shout penetrated his tired mind, but the speed of the controlled body was astonishing. *The MAG should be recharged by now,* he thought as he aimed the gun at the small head far above him. He squeezed the trigger and dived to the side, away from Quarr, to get out of its path. Only Quarr saw the head snap up and back and then flop loosely forward.

Gorrel's body hit the wall with a tremendous clang, and then reluctantly sagged down as if being slowly deflated, but now it was *truly* dead. Kryger instinctively dropped his shield and shot out a probe to one of the withdrawing minds. He followed the dazed withdrawing wisp of connecting tendril and "read" the location of the planet and the stars when it splashed back into the shocked consciousness. *At least I know more or less where my next victim can be found,* he thought as he fumbled to put the MAG back into concealment.

"Two!" Quarr let him know. "I followed one as well. I know the precise location. I wasn't idle while you were fighting for our lives, demonstrating and bragging with your newly-found mind power," she jokingly added, trying her level best to sound sarcastic. "I have some additional information."

"We have to get out. Fast! I know the location of the damper, and when I send a MAG-bolt through any part of the complex machine, it'll cause a small nuclear explosion. Let's do it from as far away as practicable."

"Let me help you up." She bent over and held out a hand to help him up from the floor. Then she gave him a handful of ration tablets to chew while she led him from the chamber. The encounters with Gorrel and its mates were enacted in total silence, except for the heavy clangs when Gorrel's claw-feet hit the floor and when its body hit the wall. The guards outside the chamber were blissfully unaware that any dramatic changes had taken place.

The tenuous entity's face was aglow with inexplicable joy and elation as she flashed back to the hidden city and her body. The unusual invention that burned a hole in anything wasn't part of the ancient foretelling. She hadn't expected such a weapon at this stage of their evolution, but she was glad as she realized that her wards may not have survived without such a gadget, and they certainly wouldn't have killed the bug. They were well prepared, and only needed the solid, reflective shield to deflect the strong mental attacks. Her long, long exile was over at last, and she could face eternity and her people with a clear conscience. She was joyous and felt no grief as she entered her body and pushed the button that would bring it back to life. She knew that the activation would be too abrupt for the ancient body to adjust to the ages that had passed. She exuberantly faded from the third dimension as her body crumbled to dust.

Quarr addressed the guards using mind-speech and pictures, and she moved her lips as if she was speaking, which left no doubt in their minds that she was talking to them in their own language.

"Lord Gorrel ordered us to evacuate the spaceport buildings as fast as possible, if not sooner. The damper reactor is overloading and could explode at any moment. Sound the alarm and get everyone in every building as far away as quickly as possible. Do it! Do it NOW! That's an order from Lord Gorrel." She sent a mental, fearful compulsion to obey immediately, without question. As the guards, with the self-important officer in the lead, scurried away to do as ordered, she guided Kryger to the exit.

He was mentally completely exhausted, but summoned some of his inherent stubbornness—or as he preferred to call it, his Samurai spirit.

While Kryger chewed on the ration tablets, Quarr guided him with one hand, and hurried toward the same gate they had entered earlier. The alarm started to hoot urgently. The guard at the small gate, not knowing why the evacuation alarm was ringing, stepped in their way and pointed his rifle at them.

"Stop!" he ordered. "Where do you think you're going?"

Lord Gorrel ordered evacuation of the spaceport, Kryger lied. *Can't you hear it? You too, should heed the warning.* He was too exhausted to think coherently and didn't back up his reply with the normal compulsion to obey.

"You are prisoners! Go back! I let no prisoner out. Those are my orders. I'll shoot if you don't comply right now!" He was adamant, certain that he was doing the right thing.

They didn't have time to argue, and they couldn't be delayed by a duty-bound guard. Other dumb and duty-bound promotion seekers might start to question their orders, or summon the courage to pop into Gorrel's audience chamber to verify the order.

Quarr was near enough. She slapped the gun aside and felled the guard with a single punch to the chin. She stopped for a second to collect the gun. She might need it to discourage overzealous soldiers from chasing after them.

After they had passed through the gate, Kryger broke into a tired run and headed for the knoll from where they had watched the spaceport the previous day. Depending on the wind direction, it was far and high enough to offer some protection from the blast and radiation that would follow the destruction of the damper. There wasn't a better vantage point. They could only hope for the best and would have to deal with any consequences later.

According to the information he had retrieved from Pupaul's brain, the installation ran on controlled nuclear power, which would be violently released if the reactor were punctured, but it was a unique, super-small reactor. The complete layout of the bunker beneath the isolated concrete tower was cemented in his mind, as well as the exact location of the reactor. He grinned. It would only take one accurate shot with the MAG to destroy the whole setup together with a few of the surrounding buildings.

He would pass the know-how to build these infernal things on to the scientists of the Golden People. Perhaps they could use the information for peaceful purposes, as they would never build any machine that suppressed the sensitive powers of the mind. As his father and mother had experienced on Nevus in the early days of exploration, these gadgets eventually destroyed the finer senses and people reverted to savages, as the Bikans had. The subspace-scanner would be welcomed as it had a number of possibilities and uses.

He reached the knoll with Quarr at his side, and they turned to look back. People were hurrying away from Gorrel's lair. The blast would only contaminate a small area, but he should give them more time to get clear, because a few nearby buildings may collapse. He sat down and straightened one leg while he fumbled in his pocket for more ration tablets. His mouth was dry, but he managed to chew the tasteless, dry, energy-giving pills. He would need the extra energy for the run back to their cave.

They didn't need speech or silent mind-to-mind exchange when their shields were down, as they still shared minds to some degree, but without interfering with one another's thought processes. They knew that this would change soon enough if one or the other kept a shield on most of the time. They were separate beings with different talents and they already felt a little out of sync.

Quarr shared that particular reflection. "Even if we shared thoughts for the rest of our lives, it wouldn't worry me, Kryger. It's convenient at times, but on the other hand, it will be nice to stay an individual." She raised a tight shield around her brain—or so she thought.

"I agree, and it might be dangerous in times of stress, or when you pass out during a fight. We should get our minds on different wavelengths for safety's sake…but back to the present. The area around the tower seems to be clear. I'm going to destroy the infernal machine before they think of us as escaped prisoners. Take cover behind the knoll. There's going to be one hell of a brilliant flash in a few seconds. Lie on your stomach and cover your eyes and ears. We'll deal with the fallout later."

"I know what to do, dumbbell!" Quarr was obviously annoyed.

"Yeah, I know that you know. I was just thinking aloud for your benefit so that there won't be any mistakes, and I don't want you to get hurt because of *my* negligence. I think I should eliminate the spaceport's main defense systems before I detonate the damper. There are only two, and both are clearly visible."

"You're on the right track. Keep thinking and you may come up with something original."

Kryger knew that she was peeved by his out loud thinking. He disregarded her petulance as he shielded his mind and backed to the edge of the little knoll. He still had a good view of the tower that housed the infernal machine, but the location of the bunker was only visible when he stood upright. He took the MAG out and sent a carefully placed bolt into the center of each emplacement, causing dreadful explosions as the armed missiles blew up, which resulted in destructive chain reactions. Then he turned his attention to the object of their mission.

The small tower was less than a kilometer away, a little closer than the nearest defense system had been. He recalled the layout he stole from Pupaul's mind and calculated the position of the small reactor in relation to his position. *It should be there, about four meters below ground level. Most of the blast will be upward. I'd better aim slightly higher or I'll shoot below the infernal thing.* He steadied his right hand with his left, aimed carefully and then gently squeezed the trigger before he turned around and dived down behind cover without a second's hesitation. He pocketed the MAG as he landed and clamped his hands over his ears and closed his eyes tightly while he wondered if his calculation was correct.

What seemed like an eternity went by. He was just beginning to relax to try again when a clap of thunder made both of them wince and yelp with pain. Although their sensitive ears were covered by their hands, it felt as if their eardrums had ruptured. Even belly-down in the grass below the top of the knoll and facing away from the explosion, they could see the brilliant flash through tightly closed eyes. They waited a full count of thirty seconds before opening their eyes. Both shook their heads and opened their jaws in an effort to clear their ears, but it was to no avail. They closed their nostrils with thumb and forefinger and blew hard as they sometimes did when their ears blocked from a too rapid descent from high altitude. It didn't help.

It seemed that the physical silence would prevail for quite a while, and they could only hope that it wasn't permanent. Their ears ached with a vengeance. When they opened their mind-shields, they quickly closed them again. There was an unbearable mental clamor going on all over the planet.

He touched Quarr's arm. *I feel better. Let's run to our cave. I'm thirsty, and the water may help to clear our ears. The clamor should be less by then and we can then talk to Dad, or whoever is in charge of the attacking force.*

I'll race you. I can't stand this thundering silence, but at least we can use some of our senses to check for an ambush. She kept the sentry's gun, and was away before he could comment on her sudden energy.

They ran as only beings used to a heavier gravitational pull could run. It was a strange experience to run without hearing a sound, even one's own footsteps, but Kryger could feel his footfalls thumping loudly as if his ears were stuffed tightly with cotton wool, though his tread wasn't heavy, because it was a habit to run as lightly as a cat. It was an obnoxious feeling, which had to be endured while it lasted. He was ready to collapse as soon as a decent opportunity presented itself. The destruction of Gorrel's mind took more energy than he had anticipated, and he wished that he could just sleep until he woke up, but he had been trained to fight against that natural and mostly fatal inclination when in enemy territory. He wouldn't succumb to the temptation, even with the incomparable Quarr as a fierce protector, until they reached the safety of the cave. He couldn't let Quarr know just how weak he was.

He caught up with her halfway to the waterfall and kept pace without apparent effort, but it required all of his willpower not to fall over and go to sleep. Their senses were alert and scanned the immediate area for hidden enemies as they were trained to do, but still, the complete absence of normal hearing was aggravating, and the thumping noise of their footfalls on deaf ears was maddening. But the exercise seemed to clear his head a little, or perhaps the energy from the tablets was beginning to have an effect.

His bracelet abruptly began to heat up suddenly, and he realized that Mike, being unable to break into his mind as usual without asking permission, was seeking his attention.

He opened his shield a little: *Hi Mike. You're surprised, huh?*

Very much so, Kryger. You've developed surprisingly well in a short time, as has Quarr. I sensed both of you through your bracelets, and had to draw your attention by turning up the heat. Why were you cut-off?

Watch the ether for prying and spying entities, Mike. The situation is dangerous for Sensitives. Talk to Quarr, I'm exhausted. I'll bring you up to speed later. Who's the cavalry?

Torak and Lerra, and about half of the navy. Mike abruptly broke the connection, as was his wont. Kryger smiled as he saw Quarr jerk her arm up abruptly and look with surprise at her bracelet. He then concentrated on not falling over his own feet.

29

Kryger cupped his hands and greedily drank the cold water scooped from the edge of the waterfall. After their run in the heat of the day, the water felt more chilly than usual, but it was delicious. He washed his face, drank some more, removed his shorts and jacket, folded them neatly and put both down on a rock away from the water before he shucked his shoes. As he quickly stepped through, the icy shock revived him somewhat. He felt his pulse quicken as Quarr's soft, naked body bumped into his back, but he didn't have the energy to spare for spur of the moment impulses. It didn't take much effort to suppress the inclination, and he shook his head to clear the water from his ears. Their ears had cleared somewhat during the run, and now there was a faint sucking sound. He closed his mouth and nose with one hand and blew hard. There was an audible noise, as if air was being squeezed out through his ears, and he was relieved to find that his hearing was back to normal again.

"Feeling better?" Quarr managed to paste a beauteous, teasing, insincere expression on her face, which almost matched her cheery voice for a change.

"Almost!" he replied as he grabbed the packet of ration tablets from his rucksack. "I'm hungry. Even this tasteless concoction tastes like nectar right now." He devoured a handful of the stuff and washed it down with water from his canteen, which he'd half-filled under the waterfall while he chewed. "Not that you can call this a meal, but I need the energy."

She raised a mocking eyebrow. "Yeah, so I see! I'll join you. I could use some energy myself." She took a handful and started chewing as he finished his portion. She took the canteen from him to swallow the paste. "I wish Mike could add some flavor to this mess."

"Ask him. He says that it spoils the ingredients quickly, but I think he's just being sadistic." He gathered their belongings and deposited them outside with their clothes, then sat down on a boulder to dry in the sun. He closed his eyes and sent a mental call on his father's personal wavelength: *Hi Dad. How are you doing? Busy?*

No, Kryger, not for you. Where have you been? We've been calling you for the past hour—since that mind-numbing interference ceased. We were beginning to believe that you'd finally received your come-uppance.

Kryger felt his mother joining, and the relieved concern in both their minds. It was typical of Mike not to bother to inform them that their children were alive and well. He assumed that everyone had access to the same information.

Hi, Mom. I'm glad that both of you came to the rescue. I had to keep my shield on when I smashed the thought-communication damper. The sudden clamor was too much for my tired brain. I'll tell you the story later. How are things going up there?

We're cleaning up the last resistance pockets. I can feel that you're different, son. What's happened to you? How's Quarr? his father said.

She's here and well. It's a long story. Our scout was destroyed and we've finally found our real enemy. I'm very tired. Come and fetch us, please. We may have been exposed to radiation when we destroyed that miserable damper from close-up, since it was powered by a rather sophisticated nuclear device. How soon can you get here?

We're still circling the moon. About two hours, I'd say. It may take a few minutes to install a decontaminator in a shuttle.

Kryger knew that such an installation would take at least an hour, if not more. *Okay, three hours then. Talk to Quarr, please. I'm going to take a nap in the meantime.*

Quarr had partly collapsed her shield in order to follow the conversation. She took over as Kryger sought a level place to lie down. He was in a daze and couldn't fight the mental exhaustion any longer. He dressed, flopped down, and immediately drifted off into a dreamless sleep.

Quarr told their story from beginning to end. It didn't take long, for she flashed pictures from her memory, leaving out only details of more intimate moments. Her foster parents were proud of their son and adopted daughter, and applauded their courage.

Torak, as admiral of the fleet, could marry them, and he told her that he would do so when they came on board before they said a temporary goodbye.

To hell with ceremonies, he thought privately. *Those two kids always seemed inseparable. They will be going after the Hullenii. They might as well forget about having a honeymoon and continue with their trade. It suits their nature and inclination.* Torak smiled to himself and thought with grim humor, *No, that's not quite true. They first must return to Nevus to collect and test the new fighting scout being developed specially for the two of them by the Golden People. Kryger uses up ordinary scouts and fighters as if they are going out of fashion, which may be true now that we know who and what the real enemy is. The personal gravity neutralizer that is being developed by the twins will make life more bearable for Quarr, and the new scout will carry spares and a robot to manufacture spares if necessary. They will finally have a real fighting-scout craft.*

"What thoughts are you hiding from me, Torak?" Beautiful, golden, cat-faced Lerra was still showing signs of the strain she had gone through when Mike, insensibly as usual and without preamble, reported that he had lost contact with Kryger and Quarr.

"I was thinking about our daredevil son and soon-to-be daughter-in-law. It's a good thing that Kryger is what he is, otherwise he could go rogue and out of control. He's now too powerful in body and mind for any group of us to control—never mind keeping him in one place." Torak shook his head as if disbelieving his own words. "I just hope young Dwarrel doesn't take after Kryger. He worships his brother, you know. Now that we've found our lost children, you should consider going home with them."

"You know I had to come. I just couldn't stay home alone with only my thoughts for company, when Mike informed us, in his artificial, *soulless* manner, that contact with Kryger and Quarr had abruptly ceased. We came to avenge them, remember? But I'm okay now. I'll go home with them, don't worry. We have four—no, five—children. I should accept the fact that we might lose two or three in this war.

"We should have had more children. I often wondered why we had no children after Dwarrel, because there's nothing wrong with us and we're not that old yet. Remember that Peter the Pilot said that our children are *vital* for bringing peace to this universe. We've just seen the first proof that he knew what he was talking about. From what Quarr told us, I know of no person, including us, who could have defeated that bug on its own ground. She says that there are another eight hundred and seventy seven of them left on as many planets and solar systems—that is, unless they suddenly start to breed, which, I pray is unlikely, because habit and inborn inclinations are hard to overcome."

Torak thought for a moment, and then continued the line of thought. "Quarr really surprised me. I knew that she was special, but she has a way of blocking any probe to her mind that neither Mike nor anyone else could break through. I'll always be grateful that our daughters became scientists and not fighters. Young as they are, they conceived the principles of the MAG, which we now know is the only weapon that can kill these big bugs—other than a nuclear explosion, which seems a bit drastic. A heavy beam weapon would perhaps be reflected, according to Quarr, by its shiny carapace. I would have liked to take the body back, so that our scientists could examine it, but the explosion would have vaporized it. I'll ask them to bring the next one home. But wait a minute, we'll have to go and fetch it with a battleship. It will take a sturdy crane or anti-gravity lifter, to move a body that huge and heavy. Quarr estimated that it weighed more than a metric ton, and as a scientist she should be able to estimate pretty accurately."

They were still tossing various ideas about when a messenger interrupted. He told Torak that the surface vehicle was ready for takeoff, and asked, "Would the admiral pilot the shuttle himself?"

"Yes, the admiral would." Torak detested this formal form of addressing.

Quarr shook Kryger by the shoulders: "Wake up, snoring beauty! Dad will be here in about twenty minutes. Mom will wait for us aboard the flagship. Go dip your head under the waterfall."

Kryger was trained to be fully alert the instant he was touched or awakened, but this time he reluctantly returned to full consciousness. He still hadn't recovered the energy he had expended in killing Gorrel. Something would have to be done about it, he decided as he sluggishly forced himself to start thinking again. Perhaps Mike, Quarr, or his sisters, could develop a high-energy tablet, or hopefully something more substantial, to restore expended energy force in a hurry—an emergency energy boost, so to speak. He didn't realize that his mind was wide open.

"Yes, it's a thought. I'll think on it, but I don't know much about that branch of science. I'll pass it on to Mike and the twins.

Dad's going to marry us as soon as we're on board!" she added enthusiastically.

That shook him and he was wide-awake in an instant. "What?" he asked sharply, as if he didn't hear correctly. "Oh, that! Okay, I love that idea, but are you sure? I mean, are you sure you want to put up with me for the rest of your life?"

"Of course, stupid. Do you have someone else in mind?" she asked as if not knowing his mind.

"No. You should know that, idiot. We have no secrets, remember? I hope you didn't tell them *all* about us? It might be somewhat embarrassing."

Quarr laughed musically. "Of course I did!" As his face turned crimson, she added "No, I didn't tell them the juicy parts, if that's what you mean. Mom and Dad were very pleased. Almost as if they welcomed or expected it. I'm pleased to inform you that it wasn't a surprise to them."

"Oh? Oh well, let me go and clear the cobwebs from my mind." He proceeded to dip his head under the icy water, and then drank from cupped hands. *Hell,* he thought, *what must a man go through to just get married? I guess I have to learn to keep an impassive face and ignore digs and insinuations.*

"By the way," Quarr continued, "I spoke to Pgabys and Ycagabys. He needs medical attention urgently. Dad said that we can pick them up. There's plenty of space in the shuttle. I sent them a picture of the Shadows and they laughed. Dad said that he had seen worse, and that these two were beautiful by comparison. Pgabys was quite excited at the prospect of attending an alien wedding."

"Good! I was worried about them. What did they have to say about Gorrel's demise?"

"That's why Ycagabys needs medical attention," she said with a twinkle in her eyes. "He was so overjoyed with the news that he started doing something equivalent to a somersault and tore all my careful stitches in the first tumble, which dampened his joy, because his wounds started bleeding afresh. Poor Pgabys did her best to stop the bleeding, but she didn't have the means to do it, nor the knowledge." Quarr's voice was as serious as it could get, tinged with sadness. She could still feel Pgabys's panicky, helpless, desperate emotion, and her fury at the stupidity of her unthinking male mate.

As Quarr spoke, Kryger visualized the incident as if he had observed it in person, including the surprise on Ycagabys's unlovely face when his wounds burst open with a squelching plop as he jumped, and then his surprised mug with wide-open, bulging eyes when he landed. Kryger couldn't control his laughter and Quarr, catching his imaging, joined after a moment's hesitation.

They were still laughing when the shuttle landed. Scores of fighting craft circled the vicinity and took care of the few fighting craft flown by pilots moronic enough to attack such a large, overwhelming force. Only a few with short runway or vertical takeoff capabilities managed to get into the air. The runway was blocked, but they didn't have a chance against the elite fighting force of Nevus. Kryger was glad that he had thought of taking care of the spaceport's heavy defenses when he had the chance.

30

When the shuttle settled down on the more or less level space where they waited, Torak first invited Quarr and then Kryger to enter the one-person decontamination cubicle, which had been fitted just behind the airlock. They went through the usual routine individually, without discarding their none-too-clean clothes. A disinfectant shower wasn't required for nuclear fall-out decontamination. They would also go through the standard decontamination process when they boarded the flagship, for there was no escaping it for anyone returning from planet-side.

Torak was waiting to embrace Quarr when she emerged from the cubicle. She shook hands with the crew with a sincere smile in her eyes. Torak shook his son's hand when he came out of the cubicle, for they didn't need to demonstrate their affection in view of the shuttle's curious six-man gun-crew and a doctor. Kryger shook hands with them all and thanked them for being there.

Torak didn't waste any time on formalities. "Let's go pick up your friends. Quarr, it would be easier for you to find them. Take the pilot's chair, please. Are you okay, Kryger?"

Navigators could fly any spacecraft in an emergency. If a pilot was injured or killed during a fight, the navigator could take them home if he or she was in a condition to do so. Navigators were therefore more highly esteemed than pilots.

Quarr seated herself at the controls without comment and took the shuttle aloft. She contacted Pgabys and sent the craft in the direction of her mind-signal.

"Yes, Dad, the sleep did me a lot of good. I can think coherently again. I still feel a bit tired from that tremendous bolt I sent into the bug's huge brain, but otherwise I'm fine," he assured Torak. "Quarr told you most of our story, but there are a few things I want to add and explain. We need to be prepared for enemies with very, very powerful minds and almost *irresistible* mind-power. Each individual controls its own planet, and its mind is so powerful that it can persuade an attacking force to fight each other, or do other sinister things for amusement."

He switched to a very narrow beam, meant only for Torak. *Quarr's mind, and mine, developed an interesting intricacy after our mind-merge. We developed mind-shields* along the lines of Mike's, which seem to deflect thoughts. I still don't know how, but I know the basics were already in place, just waiting for the right stimulation. Quarr has gained a lot from the merging, and although she already had the ability to withstand the onslaught of a single Hullenii's mind-power, I don't know if she can defeat one on her own right now. She developed our fighting spirit, but she still lacks the singular will of a Samurai, and the hard concentration of purpose and uncompromising determination.

I will show you, Mom, and other Sensitives how to deflect the mind-onslaught of these monsters, but I cannot teach you how to generate the terrible power required for frying a bug's brain, because you may destroy yourselves, as I almost did. Perhaps Quarr can, but I think she'll do better to destroy them with a MAG, as I recommend you do when you have to. Avoid confrontation whenever you can. The power of a bug's mind is indescribably strong and vicious, and I cannot even begin to explain the awful power of their minds when linked with others of their species.

Torak nodded. Son, I believe that you—and Quarr too, perhaps—were born to pursue and exterminate the ultimate enemy of all creatures in this island universe. Maybe your and Quarr's children will continue with the quest, until our galaxy and its various races are safe from these giant predators.

There is a purpose with everyone's life, and we accept what destiny has in mind for you and Quarr, but we don't have to like it. Some are here on holiday, and some are here to perform a specific task or to learn. Mine was to bring the Golden People back to life and sire the likes of you. I now believe that the purpose of the Golden People, and your brother and sisters— and other children, maybe—is to assist you to bring peace to the Galaxy so that all thinking creatures can have peace in which to develop their own talents and face their destinies. Go for it, son. We're behind you all the way. Are you a true Samurai?

Kryger knew what his dad was asking. Yes, Dad, I believe so. I'm prepared to lay down my life in the line of duty, but I'll fight like hell to preserve it while I still have some life left. I know that death is not important, but how I live is important to me. When I die, I want to know that I've given up my life to achieve something of value for all humankind. Some may be unworthy, but there are others who deserve a chance to grow. You can bet everything you own that I will do my level best to *survive against all odds. I have much to live for.*

Torak said, *That is also what I believe, and I agree. I know that you won't sacrifice yourself needlessly. You have too much self-respect and a fighting ability that would have made many of old Earth's martial experts look like raw novices.*

Their conversation was interrupted by the gentle bump of the shuttle landing. Pgabys moved out of the hiding place when Quarr told her to show herself. Her joy at seeing Quarr was obvious. The doctor and Quarr disembarked to take care of Ycagabys's wounds.

Ycagabys emerged gingerly after the treatment and eyed the shuttle with obvious distrust. The Shadows were apprehensive, but they trusted their friends and entered after a few explanations and a little urging. After all, when one shares another entity's thoughts, one can detect an untruth.

The Shadows didn't feel the pressure of takeoff—shuttles were equipped with anti-gravity units to clear a planet's atmosphere at top speed without the accompanying gravitational pressure if the circumstances warranted a quick exit or if it had critically injured persons on board.

The Shadows stared at the view-screens in awe. It was their first flight, and seeing their planet from far above was a novel experience. They were silent and lost in wonder as the huge planetary surface became smaller and then a fast dwindling orb. The humans left them alone so that they could stare as much as they wanted to, which lasted until they docked in the huge flagship.

"I'll take them to sickbay," Quarr volunteered as they finished decontamination. "Pgabys says her baby is due in a few hours, for she started having contractions just before we picked them up. Just think of it! It will be the first Shadow ever born in space, and under human supervision, no less. I'll reassure the nurses that they are intelligent and won't tear them to pieces, and see them settled in before I say hello to Mom."

It's a pity that not all humans are Sensitives yet, she added in an aside to Torak and Kryger. *It would make it so much easier to understand other creatures and not to fear them for their looks.*

"When would you like to resume the attempt to locate your people?" Torak asked. It was an unwritten law that Sensitives must always use speech whenever non-Sensitives were present, so that they wouldn't feel like a separate species of mankind who could be ignored by the gifted whenever convenient. Sensitives were very careful not to step on touchy toes, since those not so gifted didn't trust them to keep out of their minds. It took a lot of self-control not to react to disparaging thoughts that sometimes radiated uncontrolled from undeveloped, envious minds. As a general rule, a Sensitive would not read another mind unless invited to do so in private, or when threatened; and then only the public mind and not the inner thoughts. But, of course, there were the exceptions that fed general distrust.

"I think that dawn tomorrow will be soon enough, if it is convenient. It's nearly dark down there, anyway. I'll sleep in the sickbay tonight, so that I'll be present when Pgabys gives birth. Oh, here comes Mom!" Quarr exclaimed as a stunning, cat-faced golden-skinned woman stepped from the elevator. Quarr, disregarding dignity and stares, rushed forward and embraced her.

"I'm relieved that you both are all right," Lerra said calmly as she tightly embraced and kissed Quarr. "I should have known that you two wouldn't be easy to overcome."

Quarr still marveled at the controlled strength and fortitude of this woman. It was a new experience every time they embraced, full of wonder and love. Lerra was the last living member of her race. The deceitful Bikans, in an ambush thousands of years before, had murdered her people and the Builders—the mind-sensitive race who designed and built Mike. Some of Quarr's thoughts must have slipped past, for she had relaxed her mental barrier somewhat since the demise of Gorrel.

No love, my race lives on in my children, albeit in half-human form, Lerra spoke in her mind. *You, too, will have a few cat-eyed children, especially the girls. I have never spoken to anyone else about it, but I had a glimpse into the future when The Pilot reconstructed my broken body. I didn't understand the vision then, but now I do. As women, we must learn to be strong, or we'll become suffering wrecks when we see our children die because of another being's uncontrolled greediness or selfish ambition. Men are generally more adept at excepting a loss, but as women, we bear the children who will sacrifice themselves to attain peace for others. Have strength, dear heart, as your children must continue the fight against the Hullenii. We'll talk more later, when we have time.*

The tight-beam thought-transfer took less than a second, and Lerra thought that no one else would be the wiser. She smiled brightly when Kryger took her in his arms and held her for a few moments. She felt the controlled strength of his arms, but didn't have the slightest idea of the phenomenal power unchained in his mind. She wouldn't have cared if she had known—he was her firstborn. She would never know that he had involuntary intercepted the tight-beam thoughts she flashed to Quarr, nor that he was still linked with Quarr's mind. Then, even Quarr wasn't aware of it.

The brief exchange shook Kryger. He realized that he had been given a rare glimpse and a deeper understanding of the nature of a mother—something he never gave thought to, or even suspected that such feelings existed. Behind the lovely smile and acceptance of his dangerous career, lay a mother's concern for the safety of her child. He let her feel his deep love, and she hugged him fiercely for a brief moment.

Then Lerra took control. "We'll all go to the sickbay. Let's have the wedding ceremony there, for the benefit of your friends, Kryger. Come on, Torak. Other business can wait a few minutes longer."

Kryger gave his father a sheepish grin and followed his mother amid the good-natured smiles and clapping of hands by the shuttle and docking bay crews. They all loved Lerra as if she were mother to them all. She always had a smile and an encouraging word for even the lowest-ranked among them. The doctor and helpers pushed the gravity bed with Ycagabys into the elevator.

"You sound just like my mother," Torak told Lerra as he stepped into the huge cargo elevator. *I still remember how she made me marry you before we went after the Bikan-murderers.*

She gave him a heart-warming smile. "Of course! Middle level," she instructed the voice-activated elevator. "Someone has to think and take the lead while you irresolute men blunder about, falling over your own feet." The personnel in the lift smiled at the seemingly severe talking-to the admiral was receiving. "Quarr meets her people tomorrow, and they must realize that we—our entire nation—are solidly behind her. She doesn't want to stay with them for the rest of her life, or be forced to rule them. She prefers to be with us and fight with us.

"However, she inherited certain obligations from her mother, and she has to persuade her people to take

203

responsibility for their own future. Kryger, as her husband, will be there to back her up so she won't face them alone. We'll be there as background observers, and we won't interfere or take a hand unless we are left no choice."

"Okay, so that's the real reason behind your insistence that they get married right away. I agree, love of my life. Quarr, you should have told me that you wanted to find your people. We could have tracked them down a long time ago." This was for the benefit of their audience.

"I didn't ask, Dad, because I had an indication of where they might be found. I felt that the time wasn't right to seek them out. I wasn't ready. I also hadn't made up my mind as to what I really wanted. There was the real danger that increased activity might have drawn the bugs attention to Nevus, which must be avoided for as long as possible."

That was answer enough for their audience, and Quarr switched to mind-talk, since she didn't want to include everyone within the elevator. This was a reminder to Kryger, and information meant only for her foster parents. They behaved as if they had nothing more to discuss. *I don't think it can easily be repeated, but Kryger has a unique mind. If it weren't for that factor, we would have been totally helpless after our mind-merge.*

Our minds—I mean those of my people—seem to have a natural defense against the will-force of the Hullenii. We escaped from them some centuries ago. As far as I know, their planet of origin was devastated by a special package delivered by my escaping people as they passed by. Some hundreds escaped though, and they raided planets that had fairly advanced technology. They finally got hold of a planet-busting bomb, which they dropped on our home planet. Many thousands of my people had settled on planets in other solar systems by then, so we escaped extinction.

We were ruthlessly pursued. As soon as we got wind that the Hullenii may have found a trace of us, we moved to another solar system and disguised ourselves. We lost track of other surviving remnants, and finally, my faction settled on this planet, but there may be other scattered colonies all over creation. The ruling of our nation passed through my family, and there were those who said that we made bad decisions, but they were only greedy for personal power. A male named Pupaul— my mother's older brother—aspired to rule us. He was a

204

scientific genius. He rigged my mother's ship so that it would explode on entry into planetary atmosphere, but he miscalculated. I killed him this morning.

I'm sure that there are others like him, and they can be accommodated or defeated in the system I have in mind. It will be the same kind of government The Pilot forced on the Golden People when Dad handed the kingship over to him. It works well on Nevus.

Mind transference only took a few seconds, but something was not complete for Torak's inquiring mind. The question had bothered him the entire afternoon. *How did this Pupaul know that you were coming?* He let out a suppressed breath and then became somewhat embarrassed, for the sickbay personnel were staring at him, unaware that an inaudible conversation was taking place.

At one time, Pupaul had the ability to accurately predict future events, and perhaps he divined my return after we left on our fatal journey. Maybe he still had the ability. I believe he was living in hell, which probably was the incentive to invent the subspace-scanner and the damper. Perhaps my mother sent a message to our people when her ship crashed on Nevus. Anyway, as is the convention, a successor must takes up his or her duties by the age of twenty-five, if there's no active regent.

From what you told me—that they were waiting at your exit point—it makes me believe that he knew the direction from which you would come, if not the location of our planet. He may have passed this information on to Gorrel. I'd better warn the Council to be on the lookout for enemy scouts, and perhaps an invasion force. Now, let's get you married so that Kryger can be free to assist me in my report, Torak replied.

Kryger quickly searched his memory, but couldn't find information in that regard. It was possible that they could know about Nevus if Gorrel knew and hadn't kept the information for his own use, which was a likely possibility. If they knew, would they link him with Nevus? Perhaps, if his mind was powerful enough, he could extract the information from the mind of the bug he had traced after the encounter with Gorrel. He decided that he would transfer his accumulated information to Mike.

31

Torak wasn't one for ceremonies of any kind. He hated them, especially when he had to conduct the ceremony himself, but he endured it when necessary.

In the sickbay, when Ycagabys was made comfortable on an unfamiliar soft bed consisting of four mattresses placed on the floor, Torak made a short speech about matrimony and the responsibilities of both parties, then pronounced them man and wife, on condition that they sign the register to make it official. That took less than five minutes, which suited Kryger.

Lerra parted with her wedding ring and gave it to Kryger. "Here, put it on her finger. She must have something to show off to her people. Quarr, you can return it after you are finished with your people. When we arrive on Nevus, you can pick one to your liking."

"Thanks, Mom. You think of everything. We'll look after it well. I know that the ring is precious to you." Kryger kissed his mom on the cheek—a rare public display of affection.

Pgabys growled an enquiry, as she was both curious and confused, even though she had followed the accompanying thoughts. "Is it your way to mate officially, friend Quarr? Making a speech and making some marks on something you call a register seems useless. What next?" Not knowing how to explain their status at the time they met, Quarr had told her that she and Kryger were not yet officially mated, and what official marriage meant. Pgabys did not really understand, because her people just added the "bys" to their names, which, when translated, roughly meant, "I am mated".

But it was Kryger who growled a reply. "Yes, my friend. Also, when we are back on our home planet, there will be something we call a celebration. We will invite friends and family members to come together with us and have a feast in honor of our binding. Will you come with us to our planet as our guests? We will return you to Okrion again after some time. We may ask you to speak to your people as our representatives." Kryger sent a mind picture to both of them, explaining what the term *representatives* meant.

"It will be a marvelous adventure for us, friend Kryger, to see another planet and the many marvels created by your science. When will we go? Can we hunt there? I'm hungry."

"We'll go as soon as we can, and yes, we can hunt there, but there are a few things we must first do, like rounding up Gorrel's minions and sending them back to wherever they came from. They've been a nuisance long enough."

"Is that monster truly dead? It seems so unbelievable. He was invincible...indestructible!" The Sensitives, including the Shadows, suddenly became aware that the growling language upset the personnel of the sickbay, and they realized that the growling speech sounded threatening. The Shadows looked like threatening monsters to non-sensitive, human beings.

Kryger switched to mind-speech. *Rest assured. Gorrel is as dead as a rock. We'll look in the ruins to see if a few pieces of his body can be found, but I think the blast converted his body to scattered dust. I have to go now. We have a lot do before morning comes. Quarr will stay here with you. If you need anything, just ask her.*

Perhaps we should reconsider coming with you. Your people are afraid of us. They think we are monsters. We are hungry, friend Quarr. What kind of prey do your people hunt in this spaceship?

Kryger laughed uproariously and Quarr's face showed her consternation. He explained, *That is so, my friends, but most of my people cannot mind-speak, and therefore do not know what you are thinking. Be patient with them. They will accept you if you show no aggression. It means that you must not bare your teeth when you look at them. Just show that you are friendly by obeying their speech, because you can read the thoughts behind their words. We don't hunt on a space vessel, but we store food. We'll get you some.*

Ycagabys immediately understood the problems that his species would have to overcome in order to communicate with non-sensitives of another species, but he was intelligent as well as resourceful, and he had learned much from Kryger and Quarr. *We will follow your wisdom in this matter, friend Kryger. Will you thank them for attending to my injuries? It might help toward accepting us beasts as non-threatening.*

Kryger translated, adding a few inventions of his own, and the sickbay personnel accepted the explanation. They'd met aliens before, and their attitude toward the Shadows changed immediately.

To Quarr he said, "There should be chunks of raw, frozen meat that can be thawed quickly. But try to teach them civilized manners. They might find that they like cooked meat served on a trolley better than raw meat on the hoof." He got up to leave and narrowly avoided a vicious kick aimed at his posterior.

Mike, the artificial intelligence complex, was included in the conference. In any case, Mike couldn't be kept out since only two Sensitives wearing his bracelets—Kryger and Quarr—could close their minds completely to his prying, and Quarr was with the Shadows. There was no need for a scribe with Mike in attendance, for he always kept a verbatim record of the proceedings.

With Quarr's warning about the watch on thought-exchanges between the stars in mind, Mike and Kryger kept a part of their minds on the lookout for eavesdroppers, even though Kryger had insisted that the conference be held on a lower band than the Hullenii could access.

After the conference, Kryger transferred all the knowledge he had extracted from Gorrel's and Pupaul's brains to Mike. Kryger would have preferred to deliver the information in person, but so much could happen to him in the interim that it was safer to make sure that the vital information was passed on so that it could be available to scientists who were interested in such data. Gorrel had stored a wealth of unused scientific data in its formidable brain, and Kryger wanted to be sure that his people had all the data before the finer details faded in his mind. The subspace-scanner was an invention that could turn the tide of the war in their favor, for they could now be on the lookout for enemy vessels, and destroy them as they emerged from subspace. The only negative thing was that the enemy may also have the information and make use of it.

After Kryger made his apologies and retired to sleep for a few hours, the debate continued. Torak ordered that a fleet of battleships and fighters be sent to guard this lonely planet against retaliation. The present fleet would stay on until the relief arrived. He insisted that planetary-based defense systems be installed all around the planet and manned, so that the relief-fleet could be free to move when and where required. Torak, as admiral of the fleet, had his way, for as he was quick to point out, this was their first defense against a more terrible enemy than they had dreamed existed.

The cleanup operations continued during the night. No one ever found out how the rumor started, but when Gorrel's occupying forces on Okrion learned that their invincible master was dead, they were numb with shock and offered little or no resistance. The fact was that the invincibility of the Hullenii was now in question, and the first doubts about their godhood entered the minds of the Purnyop race.

32

Kryger and Quarr were in the upper atmosphere in a two-man fighter when dawn came to the canyon continent. Their parents and a squad of elite ground troops followed in the shuttle. They planned to circle the location of the hidden city at a distance, and won't interfere unless Quarr or Kryger called for help. The Gwarra people were an unknown quantity, and not even Quarr could guess what their reaction to her return would be, but both she and Kryger had rested well and were alert and ready for whatever may come their way.

Quarr had extracted the location of the underground city from Pupaul's mind. Kryger told her that Gorrel also knew the location and was contemplating, and savoring, the kind of slow vengeance it would wreak on the Gwarra when it came around to the task, which was the reason it played along with Pupaul as a pet for as long as it did. The Gwarra would never know how close they came to a slow, sure and painful extinction.

They spiraled slowly down to the hidden city, and when they were close Quarr identified herself on a certain frequency and requested permission to land. She couldn't believe the astonishment she'd caused when they responded after a while. She felt waves of welcome and delight; and some of resentment. She expected that her unexpected arrival would upset a few of the power-hungry aspirants. *Let them resent as much as they liked, she thought with wry amusement; they will be even more upset very shortly.*

Quarr almost felt elated because of the surprise she had in store for her people. She carefully shielded her mind although she was confident that no one in the hidden city could equal her power, physically or mentally. She knew that she could have killed Pupaul with mental power alone if the situation had been different.

Ironically, the coordinates led them to the same canyon their scout had blocked when it self-destructed, but about five hundred kilometers farther north to an almost round plateau, which seemed to be solid black rock. Here in the colder north, the sources of the canyon river struggled to form decent brooks.

Without being directed, Kryger set the fighter down on the western side of the plateau, at the more or less level base in front of what looked like a sheer cliff. He already knew, courtesy of Pupaul, about the cunningly camouflaged entrance. "Landing in front of the entrance should surprise them to no end", he told Quarr.

Quarr was surprised to find a mechanically generated thought-screen covering the city, but she easily penetrated the supposedly impenetrable barrier, and after she had ascertained who was in charge, told them who she was. Kryger followed the exchange of thought and speech of the councilors who had hastily assembled when the slowly approaching fighter was detected.

There was a shocked, hasty debate in the council chamber, which they still imagined was thoroughly screened by a separate generator to keep eavesdropping intruders out.

Then, as they already knew from following the Council's exchange, Quarr was told: *You're not alone. Who's in the other craft circling some distance away?*

They're friends; my foster parents, who took me in and raised me as their own child when we crashed on their world. They will withdraw if you feel threatened, or they will land if invited.

Debate again, and Quarr sensed that they were on the verge of confused panic. *No, we can not decide yet. We must first establish your legitimacy. Do you have proof?*

I'm here, right in front of the entrance to your secret city, talking to you, and that's enough evidence. Don't waste your time and mine, for a panicky discussion at a distance will get us nowhere. You have felt my thoughts. Do you repudiate my heritage? Quarr vaguely recollected that an ancient law required that the doubter must challenge her to mortal combat, face to face, in person, if he or she had any claim to the leadership.

Ah! So you know our ancient laws? That's proof enough for now. Let the other craft land and enter after you, for it might attract unwelcome attention from the Hullenii; if it hasn't already. We will meet your foster parents to attest your claim.

Forget about Gorrel and the Hullenii on this planet. We killed Gorrel yesterday, and its slaves are being rounded up. I must say; they are rather stunned that their self-appointed god turned out to be mortal, after all.

The announcement caused astonishment and stunned, disbelieving silence. Quarr made use of the opportunity to flash Torak the invitation to land and enter the city. When the massive gate split in the middle and ponderously rolled aside, both craft

211

slowly entered the wide entrance on gravity-neutralizing propulsion.

Torak was careful, and made sure that all external weapons on the shuttle were retracted; for any show of weapons would indicate lack of confidence. Anyway, the shields could be activated instantly if necessary; and he suspected that heavy weapons would be trained on both craft as a precaution the moment they entered the huge hangar. He ordered the gunners to relax, but to be on ready-standby inside the craft when he and Lerra disembarked.

Kryger popped the fighter's hatch open, unfastened his restraining straps and then jumped the three meters from the cockpit like a boy out to impress his elders; which he did. He landed lightly on his feet, which caused exclamations of surprise from the reception committee, because his bulk belied the lithe gracefulness with which he moved.

Quarr, not to be outdone, did the same. They had left their flying helmets inside the cockpit, but their catlike faces were accepted without comment; for the moment at least. These people were shape changers and it wasn't surprising or anything new.

All seven members of the ruling committee; four females and three males, were present. Quarr vaguely remembered that they constituted the temporary ruling council her mother appointed before she left. A long forgotten name popped into her head when she faced the oldest female, who was ahead of the others.

I was too young when we left to remember all of you, but I recall your name. It's Iño, and you're my mother's older sister. I greet you, aunt. Quarr formed a steeple with the fingers of both hands, pressed the thumbs between her breasts and bowed slightly in the ancient tradition she somehow remembered, albeit vaguely.

The older woman rushed forward and embraced her: *Quarr, it is indeed you. But why the catlike face? Is it to honor your foster mother and your pilot? I assume this beautiful woman is your foster mother?* The assumption came out as an uncertain question.

Quarr pointed her left hand, to indicate the trio one by one, in such a way that her borrowed wedding ring was prominently displayed, and hoped that it was her people's custom to wear a wedding ring. She remembered that her mother had worn a ring.

This is Dad Torak, Mother Lerra; and this is their eldest son Kryger, my pilot and wedded husband.

Her last few words raised a storm of protest from the council members. They protested loudly in their own language, which was unknown to the Nevusians and mostly forgotten by Quarr, but they could sense the thoughts which accompanied the words.

I will explain all in due course, Quarr continued, *but this is neither the place nor the time for it. Please lead on to the audience chamber, and we can proceed from there.* She put command into her projected thoughts, and they obeyed without question. Quarr thought: *A ruler expects to be obeyed without question, doesn't she?*

Refreshments were not long in coming, and Quarr asked if the shuttle crew could be served as well, for they have a long wait ahead of them. Then Quarr started her story: *You can speak orally if you like, because we can all interpret the thoughts behind the words. I will use mind-talk for a number of reasons. First, I don't remember much of our language, for my mother was killed shortly after our craft crash-landed. Second, it would be ill manners to exclude my husband and parents-in-law from the conversation. I came back; not because I want to rule this remnant of our nation, but to make changes so that I'm free to pursue the Hullenii together with my husband. It was he who killed Gorrel yesterday, and...*

She was interrupted by blatant exclamations of astonishment and disbelief. All eyes turned to Kryger, who blushed furiously. He was used to attracting attention because of his unusual looks, and detested the thoughts of disbelief directed at him. Even genuine looks of awe and admiration discomforted him because he disliked attention of any kind.

It's impossible for anyone, especially someone so young, to kill one of them. Their minds are too powerful and even beam-weapons have no effect on them. Do you have a weapon that can drill through their ultra-hard armor plating? And how did you shield your mind, or did you kill it from a distance?

Kryger shifted uncomfortably in his seat and controlled his rising anger, but they sensed his genuine anger when he calmly replied: *We were inside its audience chamber. I destroyed its main brain by mental power, and then killed its controlling brain with a special weapon when its body was used by linked bug-minds. I invite all of you to link and try to get through my shield anytime you feel like it, and without warning. In the meantime, please let Quarr tell her story without interruptions. From what I understand, you're advanced enough to easily detect lies.*

Kryger had a directness and force of mind they found somewhat too direct and unsettling. They didn't like the retort, and their eyes shifted to Quarr. She now had their undivided attention.

I see in your thoughts that you think Pupaul will return to contest my claim. Write him off. He didn't leave here on an information-gathering mission as he told you. He sold his services to Gorrel in exchange for having me intercepted and killed. I defeated the murderer in fair physical combat yesterday in order to distract and amuse Gorrel, so that Kryger could enter its mind to extract information while its attention was occupied by its usual kind of amusement.

She ignored the murmur of uncomfortable astonishment. *Pupaul engineered the death of my biological father, and spread the rumor that my father was still alive so that he could rig our ship to explode on re-entry into atmosphere. But he was a coward and botched the job. Perhaps his guilty conscience made him hurry, or he didn't have enough time, but we prevailed. My little brother starved to death after my mother was tortured and killed by a race called the Bikans; just for the pleasure of it, which is why I killed the traitor in personal combat, without weapons.*

Dispassionately, she pictured and flashed the whole sordid tale to them in a matter of minutes; how they crashed, how her mother was captured and gleefully tortured by the Bikans... Kryger was almost amused by their disgust and finicky nausea.

The Gwarra council only realized the magnitude of Pupaul's betrayal when Quarr came to their narrow escape when they emerged from subspace. Torak and Lerra had received the story of the running fights in an off-hand, "it's nothing unusual" way, and they now realized the rare courage of this unique woman as she pictured her blackouts during violent maneuvers and therefore missed much of the finer details.

As they realized that she frequently blacked out and that Kryger was aware of it, the council, and his parents, turned disapproving, accusing eyes in Kryger's direction. He shrugged unrepentantly and flashed a calm, unemotional explanation to them all: *Its one reason why we prefer scout craft, because they're tough and don't break up easily. I'll do anything within my capabilities and power to keep us alive to fight another day, and Quarr accepted it long ago. She never complained, not even once, and that's why we are here to tell our story. I know what she goes through, because even I blacked out for hours when the battleship with Pupaul's gadget aboard exploded near us.* Quarr had skipped that part of the story as he didn't tell her that he blacked out in that awful explosion.

But Quarr received the quick, calm retort, because her powerful mind was alert to every thought that was being thought; even those supposedly shielded, as she related her unusual tale. She suddenly laughed melodiously and said: "No Dad, Mom; don't even think of climbing down Kryger's throat. He's one of a kind, and I would have picked him as my pilot even if my previous pilot proved to be brilliant rather than average. I somehow intuitively knew that Kryger would be the best that Nevus would produce, and he saved our lives with his uncommon methods on countless occasions. His unexpected dirty tricks and violent maneuvers always confuse the enemy and catch them unprepared. Isn't that why you designed a special scout for us?" She projected the thoughts behind her words to the astonished council members.

She disregarded Torak's growled: "No, and I'll have to have it scrapped and start all over again," and continued with her story. She was aware that the council's disapproving opinion had turned in Kryger's favor.

As she came to the moment of her merging minds with Kryger, the council's mood swung in her favor as they reluctantly realized the fine quality of her courage, and the desperate plight that forced her into taking the chance; and they also began to grasp the extent of Kryger's powerful mind. They no longer had any doubts that she was who she claimed to be, and they took pride in her accomplishments, for not one of their race had ever dared as much. They listened in awe and without interruption to the rest of her story.

Kryger didn't know how she managed to bypass their more intimate moments and the discovery of their self-healing ability. There were some things better left unsaid or unthought-of. When she was finished, the council stood up and embraced them both, one by one.

Old Iño, their spokesman, summed up their decision after a silent, hurried discussion. They didn't realize that Quarr and

Kryger had the ability to follow their silent conversation in every detail, and without their knowledge.

We welcome all of you with open arms, Iño declared. Torak, please tell your troops to disembark and relax. We understand your precaution and approve. We have issued a command that they be made welcome as best we can. It may be somewhat awkward, for strange as it may seem, we've had no guests from outside for hundreds of years. So, as princess Quarr indicated, let us discuss the future of our people. We need allies against this ancient menace. I'm sorry Quarr, but there may be some dissent and challenges from relatives, and perhaps the population. What do you want us to do?

Kryger sensed that old Iño was hoping that there would be many challengers and that one may be successful. He wondered why she would be so anxious to be rid of Quarr. Was it the Pupaul syndrome again? Were they perhaps hand in glove, or was it something else?

Is it possible to assemble all or most of the population somewhere? Then I can answer questions and challenges, all at the same time. I have some changes I want to implement as soon as feasible, and everyone should know about it firsthand. I know that there will be opposition, and I'll deal with it, or them, personally, as and when it occurs. We expect the Hullenii to retaliate viciously, and we must make urgent arrangements to counter that threat. This planet is in dire danger, more than you and the rest of the council realize, aunt Iño, and we must do our level best to prevent it. I don't think there is time to prepare to run again, and we have to stop running, as livable planets where we would be welcome are in short supply.

The easy part is getting the people together. This visit is a unique event, and they will already be gathering in the amphitheatre, which can seat a million people, but we don't number that many yet. We can't run anymore even if we wanted to, so we'll have to fight with whatever means we have available or perish at long last. We only have a couple of old reconnaissance craft, and not enough heavy defense equipment to defend a planet. We haven't had enough time to get to it, and it has taken all our resources to excavate and develop this underground city.

Kryger thought that they were rather lax and shortsighted, or perhaps they were tired of life. Defense should have been the first priority for a people who supposedly had been fighting for centuries.

Torak's thoughts were clear, and if he had the same doubts as Kryger, he kept them well hidden. *We have the resources on our planet to rapidly build fighting spacecraft. We will select a thousand or so of your most able young men, women, boys and girls to train. If they're only half as good as Quarr, they'll be a welcome asset for our forces.*

"Thank you. But how will you select them? We only have a few qualified pilots for our aircraft, and I'm afraid they're not very experienced, for we couldn't let them out since Gorrel's arrival."

We will interview volunteers because we know what qualities to look for. They'll be your best, even if some may fall by the wayside, but let's get this other nonsense over with. It's a waste of time, but I guess it's necessary to satisfy outdated tradition. Torak was brutally frank as usual. He was a no-nonsense fighter, and disliked gatherings and ceremonies of any kind.

Iño produced a sort of knowledgeable smile. "I agree, but it will take about two hours for my people to convene. Let's have refreshments or a meal meanwhile; whatever you prefer. We still have a lot to discuss and some agreements to reach, even if Quarr or Kryger are defeated."

Torak gave her a wolfish grin. *Rest assured that they won't be defeated in a fair fight. Our muscles, including Quarr's, are used to a heavier gravity than this, and in any physical confrontation a contender won't stand much of a chance. That's why it's a waste of valuable time.* Perhaps he chose to misunderstand the momentary, undisguised, disappointed look on her face. *Please don't get me wrong. I know that people won't believe unless they see and experience, because outdated tradition must always be satisfied. I just want to get it over with so that we can get on with more pressing matters. Defending this planet and your people is more urgent than any trivial matters.*

There were silent discussions between the seven council members for some time, which they thought were private. After they had reached some sort of agreement, Iño addressed Torak.

"We like your no-nonsense approach and agree with you. With Quarr's permission, we will help you in any way possible. Unfortunately we've been isolated from other cultures for a long time. We have much to learn, and perhaps we can live in peace to develop together, after the galaxy has been cleared of the monster insects, for although they are a superior kind, the Hullenii are just insects."

Torak suppressed an obvious comment, for she conveyed the impression that the council still suffered from a narrow-minded, "let's run and hide" attitude. Why wait another century or two, until after the galaxy has been cleared of bugs, to develop? But perhaps she just expressed it the wrong way. He shrugged his shoulders and held back an urge to cast his eyes heavenward.

33

En route to the amphitheater, the Nevusians were given a tour of the underground city. They were impressed with the quality of engineering, although the principles were not new to them. Iño explained, unnecessarily, that the huge apartment blocks were cut from the solid rock a block at a time, and to also serve as pillars for the dome.

Iño ceased her incessant prattle when they reached the center of the amphitheater—more or less in the center of the city—by means of a tunnel melted through the rock. The inside was carved into ascending, circular rows of benches, interspersed with dividing walls about two meters high.

Kryger's comment, that he was impressed by the unusual engineering effort that had gone into the construction of the city and amphitheater, was accepted with demure pride. Iño replied that when the planet could be defended, they would gradually move outside, for they felt caged in. She admitted that artificial sunlight was expensive. She explained that the walls, every fifty steps or so, contained huge screens so that everyone could see in detail what went on in the center where all the activities took place. Muffled amplifiers were scattered in such a way that they didn't echo.

It reminded Torak—who used to be a student of what little Earth history remained in old records—of the old Roman Coliseum. He wondered how big it really was in its time, but knew it was certainly not this vast.

Iño importantly announced Quarr's return. Overwhelming applause and cheers resounded from around the amphitheater when the cameras centered on Quarr. She stood up, bowed slightly in appreciation, then delivered a short speech about being glad to be home.

As Quarr started her speech, Kryger expanded his consciousness to include everyone present in the amphitheater. It took some serious concentration, but with his newly developed mind it wasn't much of a problem. He filtered the individual minds so that his thinking processes couldn't be overwhelmed with the deafening clamor and chaotic, uncontrolled mental noise. He then opened his mind to overall impressions, endeavoring to sense the mood of the crowd. Almost all were pleased to see such a beautiful princess returned, and most didn't care for court politics, but were only interested in what had happened to her.

He remembered how Quarr used to enter his mind to *read* his thoughts and kept a careful watch. He expected that one or more would try to get into his mind. He gathered that quite a few of them already had tried just that, and were baffled that their powerful probes were lightly brushed aside. He was checking for hostile intensions and wasn't interested in curious priers.

Because it took a lot of energy to concentrate, and at the same time keep such a multitude of minds from overwhelming his own, Kryger quickly isolated a group of seven individuals who radiated alarm and consternation at Quarr's unexpected return. He closed his shield and only kept feelers on the seven.

Kryger sensed that all of them were nonplussed by their inability to sense Quarr's and his thoughts, even when they combined their minds in a probe. He played with the idea of sending each a mild mind-bolt to upset them, but then decided not to give himself away. He would learn much more by watching their thoughts.

Iño told the crowd that she would relate Quarr's tale of involuntary exile in a few words, leaving out much of the finer details, but it took her about half an hour to do so. She loved attention. She left out the details of the death of Gorrel, only mentioning that he was killed with a specialized weapon, and didn't even mention Pupaul. She concluded dramatically, with just a hint of maliciousness, "Quarr indicated that she will change some of our ancient customs, including that of Queen-ruler and consort, which is to be replaced by a council. The population will be divided into wards, and each ward will choose one representative for the council. There will be a person called *President* to preside over the council. More information will be forthcoming in the coming days, but in the meantime, you can give it some thought and decide who you will choose to represent you. Since the ancient rule still applies, those who oppose and want to challenge Quarr or her consort, do so now, or forever keep your peace."

During her prolonged speech, Kryger subtly examined the minds of the suspects. Only one was a woman. She had nothing to do with the six men and she was honest in her beliefs, but the men had more personal and ambitious motives. They were in league with the late Pupaul and didn't know that he was dead. If they did know, it would only have elated them, because they had plans of their own that excluded him. It was in their minds that if the forceful, arrogant Pupaul returned, he would be assassinated at a convenient moment—in secret, of course.

Kryger synchronized his mind with Quarr's. *Six men have decided that they don't like me, but only five are going to challenge me to personal combat. They have their minds settled on power and control through you. They are associates of the late Pupaul. They've hatched a plot that one of them will assassinate me from a distance during the fight, but I'll deal with it, and them. There's only one woman who will challenge you, but she is honest in her believes. She's an aunt or something of yours. She's young and powerful, but no match for you. There she is.* He indicated her wavelength and Quarr took her from his mind.

The woman, about the same age as Quarr, stepped forward. She was magnificently built and moved with obvious sureness and confidence in her own abilities. Even a shape changer must earn his or her muscles to be as strong as that. Built like a legendary Amazon of ancient Earth, she came forward proudly. She stopped before Quarr. Quarr had to read the woman's thoughts to understand her short speech.

"I'm your Aunt Mokerok, but our age differs by only a few months. I'm your mother's late-born sister. It's my *duty* to contest your claim. You've been away too long and know nothing of our people or responsibilities. I therefore challenge you to fight 'til death decides the victor."

I didn't choose to be absent, Mokerok. Quarr addressed her as an equal, and not as a relative or a subject. *I've been exiled all these years because your elder brother plotted against my mother. He killed my father and sabotaged our craft, which crashed on my husband's planet. The crash led to my mother's death by alien hands.*

The safety of our people was a priority, and killing contenders was to make sure that assassination attempts and plots would be stopped before they began. In my book, that is no longer necessary, or a valid reason. I do not wish your unnecessary death and there can still be a royal family if our people choose to have it so. Would your honor be satisfied if I knocked you out once or twice to show you that I could have killed you anytime I choose to? You may try to kill me, of course. Will you swear before the assembly that you will hold your peace forever if I knock you out the number of times agreeable to your sense of honor?

Quarr was careful to be respectful. She detected qualities in Mokerok's mind that were vital for her intended policy regarding her people to succeed. She would definitely appoint her as the first President. The next council may choose her successor, and to hell with aspirants for total power, like aunt Iño. She would put insurances into place so that no one would ever be able to seize control of the government by legal means to become a dictator.

Iño orally relayed the exchange, word for word, to the audience. It would have been a serious offence for anyone else to follow the exchange of thoughts between the challenger and the challenged.

Mokerok considered the implications of Quarr's words for a few moments. Iño had privately told her, with relish of course, of the demise of their brother by Quarr's hand, almost openly hoping to stimulate enmity. Mokerok had suspected their elder brother's betrayal for quite a while, and she was quite grateful to Quarr for getting rid of him. If Pupaul had been allowed to return by Gorrel, she would have killed the traitor herself. Pupaul was a formidable fighter, and she never was a match for him, for she had fought him many times in friendly workouts. If Quarr had defeated Pupaul in a fair fight, as she claimed, then Mokerok could easily be killed as well. She had no wish to die needlessly for the sake of tradition, and she weighed the facts as she perceived them before she replied.

"Killing you will satisfy my honor. If you can knock me out three times in succession, I'll be convinced that you can kill me if you choose to do so. I have trained my entire life to contest you the right to rule if you ever returned. If you knock me out as stipulated, it will satisfy my sense of duty and honor. In that unlikely event, I'll swear loyalty to you. This I declare before the council and the assembly."

Quarr leaned forward and smiled sweetly. *With respect, Mokerok, I accept your challenge and stipulation of three knockouts. You did not say for how long, but we'll see how long you sleep when it happens.*

She sighed quietly. Perhaps it once served a purpose to sort the strong from the weak, but that was outdated ages ago. No, her decision to do away with old traditions was a better way. The old way of killing possible malcontents to ensure peace was a waste of useful talent that could be put to use for more constructive purposes. She had worn shorts and a T-shirt under the flight suit, for she expected an event such as this. She discarded her booted flight suit, and her magnificent, hard body was displayed from close up on the screens. The crowd whistled and cheered, for they expected a long, bloody fight between these magnificent specimens of their nation. Clearly they were still savages at heart.

Kryger felt rather proud of Quarr's decision to discard the suit, and he had no objection to the display of her magnificent body. She could fight even better in the lightweight flight suit—the boots were lethal weapons. He ignored the two lovely women, and concentrated on his real enemies. He detected admiration, carnal lust, and envy, mixed with anger, greed, and lust for power and prestige.

Quarr assumed a casual fighting stance with her fists loosely clenched and arms held low. Judging from Pupaul's performance, her people had no fighting methods to equal the old fighting arts developed on ancient Earth, and with all those heavy muscles, her opponent would be strong, but not very fast. Mokerok, thinking it an easy opportunity, stepped forward quickly and slammed a powerful punch to Quarr's face. Quarr blocked it casually upward and replied in kind with a devastating punch to her exposed chin, which knocked her out cold. Mokerok fell limply onto her back.

The speed of the punch was so lightning-fast that only Kryger and his parents saw it. There was an angry murmur of protest from thousands of voices.

"FOUL! The use of mental retaliation is not allowed," Iño spoke angrily so that the crowd could hear that she was with them. Quarr and Kryger realized that Iño was pleased, because she had her own private agenda that she'd managed to disguise more or less up to now, and if the people disclaimed Quarr, it would nicely fulfill that purpose. Quarr was not perturbed, however, and took it calmly for she couldn't be faulted. This opportunistic condemnation could be nicely turned against Iño. She made sure that she broadcasted her sarcastic reply, and Kryger helped her to reach everyone.

You assured me that this stupid, unnecessary fight to gratify imagined honor and outdated tradition would be recorded! You can replay the action in very slow motion for analysis, can't you? Please do so while we wait for Mokerok to recover.

Iño blushed crimson and turned her eyes away. She should have thought carefully before she voiced her hasty denouncement, but if a punch *was* delivered, it was unbelievably fast. It just wasn't possible. No one could punch so fast that it couldn't be seen by the naked eye. Well, she *would* show them. She ordered the technician to replay the action, very slowly. There was a hushed, expectant silence—then the crowd cheered lustily as they saw Mokerok's arm seemingly being casually knocked aside, and the slight shoulder movement as Quarr delivered the knockout punch with her other fist, perfectly controlled, just touching Mokerok's chin and her head jerking back slowly as she fell backward in slow motion. Without being asked or ordered, the technician replayed it a second time to make sure that he wasn't seeing things.

Iño's face fell. She shook her head in disbelieve. She thought that no one could intercept her thought. *I don't want to believe it, but I must. The evidence is there.* Then she directed a thought at Quarr. *I can't comprehend it, Quarr. How can anyone be so blindingly fast?*

You start to practice young, as I did, learn control and practice every day, year-in and year-out, dear Aunt. There's no magic involved—only hard work. Quarr didn't even try to be polite.

It's a pity that I'm so old. I would have liked to learn this kind of fighting.

It takes a few years to master. One is never too old to learn, but there are no teachers available, and I won't be here long enough to even teach you the basics. But who knows? There may be a chance later on.

Quarr had no intention of teaching Iño anything except humility. The old hag had entertained the hope that Quarr wouldn't pitch up so that she could retain her authority for the rest of her life. She was unaware of Pupaul's ambition, and had her own plans if Quarr did not return by the time the period traditionally allowed had elapsed. Now she'd try to upset Quarr's plans any way she could—without being caught, of course.

Thanks. I'll remind you.

You haven't got a snowball's chance in hell, and if I

ever feel so inclined, I'll make it as difficult as possible to discourage you with a creaking body that can hardly move from stiffness, Quarr thought maliciously as Mokerok regained consciousness.

Mokerok regarded Quarr warily for a moment before she got to her feet. "I didn't see that punch, but I sure felt it. I accept the knockout, although I think the punch was unfair. The next one won't be so easy," she promised Quarr and assumed a ready-for-more-punishment stance—as Quarr thought of such a primitive fighter's posture.

Quarr was still annoyed by what she had sensed in Iño mind, and Mokerok' words fuelled the flame. *Then how do you see this one?* She punched Mokerok fast and hard, high in the stomach just below the heart.

As Mokerok lost her ability to breathe, she involuntary lowered her hands and arms to protect her ribs, and Quarr kicked her on the side of the chin with the bridge of her right foot's toes—not hard, just a slow, controlled touch, since a kick with full power would have broken her jaw, or worse, her neck.

Mokerok again flopped onto the hard rock floor. It was slow enough not to warrant a replay, but Quarr bypassed Iño and ordered the technician to replay it slowly, because her victim would be out for a few minutes. The crowd was amazed and cheered lustily. They couldn't believe that anyone could kick that high and fast, but to Quarr it was slow motion. *The kick wasn't that hard, and Mokerok should recover in about three or four minutes,* Quarr thought.

No, it's more like five or six minutes, Kryger interjected, *if not longer. If you make your moves a fraction slower, it should compensate for your greater strength.*

Get lost, Kryger. I'm trying my level best not to kill or damage her, which isn't easy. She has the best mind on this planet and I'm trying not to punish her too much for her belief in tradition. I need her to take charge of these people in my absence. Quarr cooled down a bit. *The pinhead is fighting for something she'll receive on a platter anyway, but the platter will be different than the one she's fighting for. What do you think of her?*

Sorry, Quarr, I know you're upset and I didn't mean to preach. Your choice is excellent. I like her. She has courage and a sincere belief in the old customs, but she can be convinced that the old ways are outdated and that she must adapt to a new

225

way of thinking. Now, if I may give you some advice? Try a roundhouse kick, not the fighting mawashi you used just now. Use the instep of your foot to connect behind her head. That would cushion the impact somewhat, and it will look good to the crowd. To her, it will feel as if her neck is being broken, and convince her that you could have killed her anytime you chose. Her neck will be sore for at least a week as evidence. She's good, but has no comeback. If she wakes up too soon, keep her busy for a minute or two so that I can work on aunt Iño. I'm going to literally try to change her mind if I can.

Okay, I'll convince Mokerok. I can make her feel like an untrained child, but I won't.

You're half way to convincing her, but her weird sense of honor must be satisfied. She already feels like a novice. Give her a chance to display her fighting abilities. She'll fight fairly, but she mustn't feel that she's a helpless baby in your hands. She'll resent it and you don't want an enemy.

Thanks for reminding me. You're right, of course. I had my mind on other things.

Quarr waited patiently for Mokerok to recover. It was important that she gained a friend, not an enemy that would seek to oppose the changes she wanted to implement.

Uh, aunt Iño. If you want a practical demonstration of this type of fighting, pay close attention to the next exchange. I'm going to give Mokerok a chance to show her abilities. I won't be playing with her, understand, but I have to see what she is capable of and how well she can handle herself. Give her some water when she comes to. She was careful not to let her real intention slip.

"She is the best female fighter we have and may surprise you." Privately Iño hoped so, and told a surprised steward to be ready with a beaker of water. It was not allowed, but if Quarr wanted to be foolish, why not indulge her?

It was unethical to interfere with another person's personal memories or thoughts, but Kryger felt that right now was the wrong time for any individual to create a hindrance for self-gain given the high stakes. The challengers didn't give a damn about tomorrow and ignored the fact that they had quite recently run from an enemy so powerful that they couldn't resist it, and that their place of retreat was known. Personal ambition was okay in a peaceful world, but must now take a backseat until the enemy was destroyed or held in check.

34

When Mokerok regained consciousness, she thought awhile before she got up and declined the offer for water. She kept her distance, warily circling Quarr just out of reach of her arms and feet, looking for an opportunity to dart in and do some damage.

This suited Quarr. She had assumed the ready stance and turned slowly to face Mokerok all the time. Under normal circumstances, she would have finished off her opponent within five seconds of resuming the fight, and Mokerok would have been no exception, despite her long preparation for this moment. She sensed the expectation from the crowd. They wanted to see blood and death to satisfy their savage instincts.

Kryger hesitated a moment, and then discontinued the tracers on his enemies to focus on Iño. He didn't want to cause irreparable damage to her mind. That would be too obvious for anyone who was a close acquaintance and may lead to questions.

Kryger put Iño into a hypnotic state wherein she would observe and remember the fight, but nothing else. Deceit was uppermost in her mind, and he found the reason easy enough. She'd enjoyed the absolute power she'd held over her faction for so long, and she was intent on clinging to it as long as possible. The outwardly sweet old lady was planning a subtle word-sabotage to undermine Quarr's plans regarding the change of traditions and the governing of her faction.

Did she have murder in mind as well? He didn't have the time to find out, but he could change her mind if he was ruthless enough. He only had a very short time to accomplish such a subtle change without her realizing that it wasn't her own decision. Somehow he was certain that he could do it, although he had never even considered such a thing before. He didn't want to misuse his talent and in the process jeopardize his own ability, but this was a necessary evil for the welfare of an entire nation.

He changed her lust for continued power to a permanent image of weariness of having had to guide the destiny of a faction for too long. He engraved the thought: *I thank the Guiding Intelligence that the wearisome task is just about over,* on her conscience and consciousness. He added a motherly love for the faction and an urge to do whatever was best for the population as a whole, and because time was short and he had to keep tabs on his enemies, he added a feeling of shame for any thoughts of personal gain she might remember or have in the future. It didn't take as long as he thought it would, and he withdrew from Iño's mind before Mokerok started her attack to finish Quarr off.

Kryger quickly reestablished his tracers on the men he had identified as enemies. The sixth member of the conspiracy was in an empty section, assembling a complicated, strange weapon for the underhanded assassination of Kryger from a distance if things went wrong for his fellow conspirators.

Through tight-beam transmission, Kryger quickly explained his observations to his father, and asked him if he would quietly go and grab the would-be assassin. Kryger would be missed the moment he withdrew, and it would alert the conspirators.

With a word of explanation to Lerra, Torak, as if taking a casual stroll to the men's facilities, disappeared into the isles. Past experience and practice taught him that if he created a tight shield to stop thought emanations leaking from his brain, people tended to look past him if he moved slowly or remained motionless. He became invisible for all practical purposes, and the people he passed had their attention riveted on the two magnificent women in the arena.

Mokerok darted in for an attack to Quarr's face. It was fast and powerful enough, but Quarr easily blocked the punches and hurt Mokerok's arms with the power of her blocks in the process. She blocked a clumsy kick to her groin with a fist to Mokerok's shin, and saw her wince with pain. She will be crippled for a minute or two while she, like the late Pupaul, shifted the pain elsewhere.

Quarr suppressed a smile. It was a painful block, but the lesson must be well taught, and the recipient must long remember the lesson. She punched Mokerok a couple of times in the stomach and ribs, careful not to do much damage, but hard enough so that she would feel the power behind the controlled punches.

Mokerok did indeed feel the real power behind Quarr's blows and blocks, and she was beginning to pray that Quarr wasn't going to kill her, despite her assurance to the contrary. The realization suddenly hit her that she didn't want to die. It wasn't really funny, but she realized that she was so sure that she would win, that she never thought of losing or giving Quarr a chance to live. Now that she knew that she didn't really stand a chance to be the victor, she wanted the fight to stop before she was seriously hurt, but she couldn't back out before she was knocked out again. Her sense of honor had been satisfied and above all, she desperately wanted to live. She wondered why Quarr didn't deliver a decisive blow, for she could have followed up a number of times. Then she realized that the kicks and punches were carefully controlled. She knew that Quarr wasn't playing with her, but waiting for an opportunity to knock her out for the third and final time.

Now she knew that Quarr really meant what she said about not killing relatives, because it wasn't necessary. Mokerok felt relieved, but she still tried to land a killing blow. She couldn't just give up and admit defeat, for she would be a dishonored outcast. Her whole body ached. She didn't want to die so young for the sake of primitive, antiquated customs. She knew that she was outmatched, and she very much wanted to be alive at the end of this fight to begin a real, useful life. There were so many things she still wanted to do. Why did she challenge Quarr when she really didn't want to? Did Pupaul influence her for his own sinister purposes? She would think on it seriously after the fight…if Quarr left her alive.

When Kryger flashed her a brief signal that he was finished with Iño, Quarr took half a step back and lifted her supple right leg high in an almost lazy circle kick over Mokerok' defensive fists, and tapped her fairly hard behind the head with the instep of her foot as Kryger had suggested. She withdrew her leg with a fast snap along the same route, and watched her magnificent aunt flop sideways with a faint look of surprise on her face. Two attendants were ready to carry her away on a stretcher.

The crowd roared approval. This was top-shelf entertainment, and fighting methods none of them had even dreamed of. They roared for more contenders, but Quarr was finished. There were no more legitimate challengers. She turned to Iño. *I really detest sensation-seekers! I assume that Kryger will have a few challengers, but you must warn them that they will be facing certain death. There will be no leniency for anyone from him, and challengers must be ready to die for their*

229

misguided intentions.

Iño nodded and raised her arms for the crowd to stop cheering. When relative silence returned, she announced, "There was only one legal challenger for our returned princess, but she lives, as her death would be wasteful of useful talent. Let those who oppose her choice of spouse step forward, but I give contenders fair warning that no quarter will be given or asked. I must emphasize that the ancient rule still applies to male challengers, and the contest will only be concluded by the death of the challengers or the challenged! I also emphasize that *only* the use of natural appendages, skill, and strength is allowed. The use of weapons warrants the death sentence. The offender will be killed on the spot even if he only *holds* such a weapon and does not use it."

Kryger asked her, *Are shoes or boots allowed, or must the contestants fight barefoot?* He also broadcasted the question to the crowd.

Iño wasn't sure and said so, but one of the councilors advised, "It is doubtful that a shoe or boot could be considered a weapon, but to avoid misinterpretation afterward, it is best that the challengers and the defender remove footwear and clothes that may conceal a weapon."

Torak was ready to pounce on the sneaky, would-be assassin as the five challengers confidently stepped forward to formalize their challenge. Their thoughts, wide open to Torak, were full of envy and hatred for a person they had never met. They were ready to kill the dog, for they coveted the dog's beautiful collar. Every one of them was anxious to be first. They would draw lots for the privilege, for they were quite sure that the first contestant would be victorious. Their "backup" was a crack shot, and he would kill Kryger the moment he was knocked down, or at an opportune moment if he was too strong to overcome.

In the absence of the forceful, overbearing Pupaul, one of them would win the throne, with princess Quarr thrown in as a magnificent bonus. According to the ancient laws, she couldn't refuse the one who killed her husband in the contest. Only the strong could rule. The assassin's weapon wouldn't leave a wound to show how the defender was killed, but the deluded fool would be killed to shut his mouth after he had completed his task. The other five contestants weren't aware that their thoughts could be intercepted by the newcomers, and their ignorance would cost them greatly.

Torak dropped the tight mind-shield as he moved in behind his target. It was only then that the miscreant became aware that he wasn't alone. Before he could react, Torak grabbed him from behind the neck with one powerful hand and squeezed, then closed his other hand over the hand that gripped the strange weapon he had armed. As nearby, astonished bystanders, became aware of the brief struggle behind them, there were angry exclamations as they recognized the assassin's weapon. The man squirmed in Torak's powerful grip, but he was held by a big man in an unbreakable hold, and the only thing he could do was soil his pants, which he promptly did when he realized the consequences of foul play in the fight for supremacy, and that he had been caught with the compromising evidence.

Torak was heavier muscled than Kryger, and nearly as strong as a fully-grown lion on his own planet. He lifted the assassin with only the hand, holding his neck as easily as an ordinary person would lift a cat. Accompanied by a dozen furious bystanders, he carried the squirming, crying assassin down to the arena, into sight of everyone as the camera's swung to focus on the unexpected spectacle.

Torak stopped in front of the council and put his captive down on violently trembling legs, then relaxed his hand to allow the weapon to fall out of the would-be assassin's hand before he relaxed his grip on his neck just a little. The weapon fell with a clatter on the floor.

It seems that this coward, Kryger broadcasted to the crowd, *was persuaded to commit murder from a safe distance. Is it permitted to include him with his cowardly fellow conspirators? I will fight all six of them at the same time, and save you the necessity of killing this underhanded assassin.* He couldn't let anyone know that ordinary thought-shields were useless when he or Quarr were around.

"Unfair!" was the immediate response from the crowd. The roar was deafening and the onslaught on his mind was total. He blanked them out and concentrated on one individual mind, and then could make sense of what they shouted. *No one can fight six opponents at the same time and call it a fair fight. Traditionally it must be a one to one fight. You have the right to have them all executed for foul play.*

Kryger again told them what they preferred to hear. *To execute them would spoil the fun, wouldn't it? I'm a complete stranger to you, but like Princess Quarr, I'm a trained fighter. I would deem it unfair if I fought these traitors only one at a time.* He wanted the crowd on his and Quarr's side, and sensed that they would deem him a coward if he backed out now and took the easy way out. The crowd didn't even realize Kryger was using mind-talk. They thought he was using a small microphone.

He sensed the change in the crowd's mood. They liked his recklessness and disregard for odds and protocol. They roared their approval, although most thought him either a braggart or a fool who wanted to impress them with alien bravery.

In the meantime, Torak propelled his victim with considerable force into the challengers, kicked the gun toward the council, and went back to his seat, conscious of the awed attention he was receiving. He ignored the stares.

If there are any others who would like to join this fight, please step forward or forever hold your peace. This is the last opportunity. I will fight any number. The more, the merrier.

Although the crowd thought so, Kryger wasn't bragging. Six eager contestants—each one wanting to be the one who killed him to claim the victory and its rewards—would get into each other's way. This wasn't a new situation. He had fought more than this number on many planets when his single-seat fighter was disabled and he had to crash-land when he couldn't make it back to the Carrier or Battleship. He was much younger then. It was before he had been ordered to transfer to two-man scouts and fighters with Quarr.

He expected no one else to accept the invitation, and nobody stepped forward. Five of the six contestants were quite confident that he would be an easy victim for their combined attack and the sixth smarted under his humiliation by a big alien. He knew that his life was forfeit. He had nothing to lose anyway, so he might as well be reckless and show some imagined bravery.

Torak and Lerra kept their silence and didn't interfere or try to access the thoughts of their son. Even though they were blissfully unaware of the furious, deadly fights and narrow escapes he had experienced on many strange planets, they knew that he was capable of destroying any number of unarmed opponents. He always judged his distance correctly, and

232

controlled his kicks and punches so that he wouldn't injure his own family during practice, but he was not so kindly inclined when confronted with strangers who were after his head.

When Kryger shucked his flight suit and stepped barefoot into the arena clad only in shorts, there was an audible gasp from thousands of throats. They had never seen such a powerfully muscled body. The loose brown shorts did not hamper his legs, and he moved as lithely and gracefully as a young tiger. The supple muscles rippled all over his body as he swung his legs and arms a few times in a number of ways to loosen the kinks. He wasn't displaying his muscles to impress his adversaries or the crowd, but was warming up, as cold muscles hamper fast reflexes. He changed his breathing pattern and bent his legs rapidly a few times as well to get the blood circulating faster. Once his legs were somewhat hairy—an inheritance from his mother's side—but now it was hairless and smooth, courtesy of Mike.

Mokerok, who had recovered and returned as a spectator, found that she was envious of Quarr. *No wonder she grabbed the alien,* she thought. *In her place I would have done the same without thinking twice. One doesn't find such a magnificently developed body every day, and maybe not even in a lifetime, but I sense that he has a wonderfully developed mind as well. Even that cat-eyed face is overwhelmingly strong and determined. I pity those idiots. There are a lot of loose pebbles rattling around in their empty skulls. Even if they will be deemed humiliated and dishonored, they should humbly withdraw their challenges while they can, because they won't live to regret it. I was very lucky, and judging by Quarr's fighting ability, this one is death incarnate. Anyone can see that he is a warrior—very calm and sure of himself. He is experienced in dealing out death.*

As for the six adversaries, they had disregarded Torak's incredible strength. They felt solace in their numbers and were confident that they were equipped to deal with one man, even if he was strong and well trained. Whoever heard of one young man beating six well-trained fighters? They, too, were well muscled and fit, and they had removed all superfluous garments and shoes, but they looked like a pack of starved, emaciated hounds compared to the tiger before them. Kryger didn't want to kill needlessly, and thought that he would make one last attempt to save some lives as he approached them, but it usually had the opposite effect. Their thoughts were anything but friendly.

Except for this lowdown would-be assassin, of course, do any of you have second thoughts and want to withdraw? He broadcasted the invitation to the whole crowd. *Once we start, there will be no time to surrender or a plea for mercy,* he added, knowing that their greed was too rampant for second thoughts, or to consider all relevant facts. He was disgusted by their thoughts, which were not wholly on the fight, but centered each in his own private ignorance and on the fun each would have with Quarr's exquisite body. They were in for a rude awakening. By then it would be too late to concentrate on the fight.

As expected, Kryger heard boos of derision from some, and cheers from others, but it served a purpose. His challengers relaxed and became arrogant, for in their ignorance they thought that the cheers were meant for them. Only a softy and a coward would try to bluff and lessen the odds he himself had invited. Perhaps the braggart's abilities weren't up to his boasting and he was having second thoughts. To express their opinions in recognizable terms, they all simultaneously showed him a rude sign, accompanied by laughter from the masses.

Kryger smiled, shrugged his shoulders, and indicated that he was ready.

35

Mokerok was having second thoughts too. Perhaps she had misjudged the alien's character. He might just be a windbag with a smooth tongue and an inflated ego because of his well-developed body, which was definitely impressive. But still, he survived a full mind-merge with an untrained shape changer, so there could be something in his favor that she might have overlooked. *Okay, I'll wait and see for myself. His mind will be unguarded when he fights,* she decided.

Druta, who was left in charge of the palace conspiracy when Pupaul left, replied sarcastically and loud enough for his words to be picked up, so that everyone would hear his disdainful reply to this braggart's despicable faintheartedness. "Having second thoughts, pretty boy? It was your idea to fight all of us together, remember? We do not ask for your leniency, nor will we spare you any pity."

He addressed his henchmen. "Let's rid our hierarchy of this alien trash so that we can carry on with our lives." He winked at them as one hand changed almost instantly into a sharp, bony spear. The other hand changed into a claw with sharp predator nails. His intention was clearly to stab and claw the big idiot into tattered, bloody ribbons, and blind him at the same time. His henchmen copied the same idea. Four of the remaining five even changed their toes into sharp, bony points. Quarr's effective kicks had given them the idea of using their feet as weapons too.

Kryger bowed mockingly, his feet shoulder-length apart and his hands held together as if in prayer, but he did not take his eyes off of them. *Then let's get on with it. Or do you need more time to add other worthless changes?* He changed smoothly into a fighting stance and shielded his mind to external influences and mind-probes. His challengers may try desperate, illegal measures when things began to go awry for them. They weren't quite a match for him, but he wasn't dim-witted enough to be overconfident. A single misjudgment or wrong move could cost him his life. For some strange reason, he felt a little fear enter his mind. He used it to send the adrenaline coursing through his veins.

Quarr was able to detect his signs of uneasiness. She approved, since it would make him more alert and careful. She was also aware of Mokerok's interest and misgivings, so she sent a tight-beam thought to her. *Watch Kryger closely. You're not going to see anything like this again if you live a thousand years. He's not bragging as you think. He was just giving them a final warning. He does not like to kill for the sake of proving a point.*

It was dangerous to allow the six to form a moving circle around him, but Kryger's hearing was keen, and he could sense their movements. The would-be assassin started his rush from the side. Perhaps he thought to redeem his loss of face by being the first to prove his mettle. He had nothing to lose, for his life was forfeited. Kryger heard him start and saw him out of the corner of his left eye, which was enough. Seemingly oblivious of the attack as he eyed the others, Kryger waited until the assassin was close enough. Then he turned slightly in his direction and kicked his chin with the heel of his left foot so fast that his leg was a blur. There was a sharp crack as the jaw and neck broke.

Being sure of the result, Kryger brought his foot back to his knee to maintain balance and took a quick glance over his shoulder. Logically, the one behind his back would attack while the opportunity was there. He executed a hard back-kick into the groin of the attacker and viciously deflected bony-arm stabs from both sides, still balanced on one leg as he brought the foot back again to his knee. Before the two in front of him could join the rush, he put his foot down, bent his knees slightly, and somersaulted backward high into the air over the line of baffled attackers. He landed a couple of meters behind the man he had kicked in the groin, and who was clutching his oysters with a now un-clawed hand. Kryger recognized their spokesman, Druta, as the recipient. *That should teach him not to be so sneaky*, he thought fleetingly.

He asked, and on impulse included the crowd, *Have you no shame, Druta? You shouldn't play with yourself in public. Where's your decency?*

As the crown roared with laughter, the other four again formed a quick circle around Kryger to allow Druta to quickly rearrange his vital organs elsewhere to get them out of harm's way, and to distribute the pain to a more bearable level. The humiliation was too much for Druta to endure, and he was so desperate that he lost his head. Against the rules, he started a rapid, complete shape change.

Kryger sensed an opponent rushing him from behind. Again he jumped high, but to the front this time. In passing, he kicked the nearest man with the side of one foot in the throat as he looked up and gaped, smashing the man's larynx and knocking him onto his back. Kryger twisted around in the air like a cat, and landed facing the backs of two of his adversaries. As they quickly jumped around, he executed a series of rapid punches, killing both of them. As he took a glance in Druta's direction, he noticed that Druta was changing into a predator. Only two contenders were left to dispose of. It was almost too easy.

The realization passed through his mind that he hadn't received so much as a scratch yet. *Good thing too,* he thought. *My wounds healed almost instantly, and that might be interpreted by a hostile person as cheating in a fair fight to the death.*

As the thought entered Iño's mind to command one of the supervisors to kill Druta for breaking the strict rules of combat to put his adversary at an unfair disadvantage, Quarr put a restraining hand on her shoulder. *Never mind; leave him be. He did not anticipate losing, but he suddenly realized that all of them together weren't a match for Kryger. He doesn't want to die. He thought it would be a quick, easy victory, and now that his delusion is dashed, he will try anything to stay alive. He really put himself at a disadvantage. Sit back and see for yourself.*

The crowd, having thoroughly enjoyed Kryger's strange and devastating kind of fighting, shouted for someone to kill the lawbreaker. Iño silenced them with a few words, explaining that Druta was placing himself at a vulnerable disadvantage, but the crowd didn't believe it, and neither did she. In their belief and experience, a man without a weapon was not a match for a predator.

Kryger quickly scanned the brains of the four he had dispatched to make sure that they were dead and not suffering unduly. He stood, relaxed, hands on his hips, taunting the shape changer. *You're as slow as a snail, Druta! Come on, hurry up. We don't have all day. You should've chosen to imitate a snake. You're poisonous enough, but no, you want to imitate a clumsy little pussycat. Don't forget to spit before you charge. I doubt it will impress anyone, but try it anyway.* He turned his head slightly and saw out of the corner of an eye that the other challenger was creeping up on him from behind.

The newly created predator roared his anger and humiliation. Madness formed in Druta's brain as he realized that he would be killed whether he won or not, but he was past caring and only wanted to destroy the creature responsible for his humiliation and defeat. He was jealous of Kryger's magnificent body, and the demonstrated power of that body. He lost all reasoning power and charged, leaping into the air like the short-tailed Slaplat leopard that he imitated, claws extended and mouth agape to grab and tear his hated adversary to bloody pieces. Druta didn't realize that a predator looked ridiculous in shorts, and hearing the roar of laughter misinterpreted the crowd's merriment.

Kryger waited calmly. Should he play with it first to bring a lesson home, or should he kill it outright? It wasn't his hobby to play games with an enemy—fooling around or showing off with a well-trained attacker usually was a fatal mistake—but this was only an imitation, not the real animal, and Druta was acting against the old rules. Kryger couldn't resist the temptation. Yes, he could afford to fool around cautiously. He should be about twenty times faster than any fighter born in the lighter gravity of this planet, and also faster than a real predator of this planet. He had a lesson to contribute to the education of the shape changers.

He kept track of the man behind him and waited until the last moment. As the claws of the imitation predator reached out for his shoulders, he bent his knees unbelievably fast and took a step forward so that he was under the body. He then assisted the imitation beast in its jump by lifting it with one arm and hand under the ribs, and pushed its rear with the other hand, using the power of his hips as he straightened his legs. The shape changer smashed face first into the wall just below a camera lens, giving the spectators a rare glimpse of a distorted, bewildered, comical predator face with wide eyes. The laughter was uncontrolled. There was no sympathy for the groggy, staggering creature that tried to maintain its imitated form.

Kryger ducked sideways in the same action to avoid the remaining adversary who had charged in low to avoid his flying companion. As the attacker missed the thrust with his bony spear-arm, Kryger grabbed the arm with both hands, twisted and pulled hard, which made the attacker turn head-over-heels. The arm broke at the shoulder, but Kryger showed no mercy. As his attacker landed on his back, Kryger, still holding the arm just behind the created bone-spear, twisted it further and buried it in his attacker's own heart just as the man started to scream.

Kryger never knew that he had been a pleasant surprise to his great-grandfather, who'd made it his life-task to impart his fighting knowledge to his direct descendants. Torak, known as the most deadly fighter on Nevus, knew this, and that he was not a real match for his son in a serious fight, but he still disapproved strongly of Kryger's tactics. One shouldn't fool around with predators, even live imitations, but he wouldn't distract Kryger's attention right now. Afterward he would give him a severe talking to.

Kryger now had a mind unequalled in the galaxy, and he was aware of every thought concerning him. There was time before the last remaining attacker fully recovered, so he answered his father's unspoken rebuke, and included his mother.

No, Dad, that's not quite right. I know you feel like kicking my backside into an elliptical orbit around the moon right now, but I want to bring home a point to these people. I'm not playing with a wild predator with instincts—only a man in animal form. The Gwarra can change into the outward form of animals, but an imitation is not the real thing. An imitator cannot assume or copy a wild animal's basic instincts. He may fool a fearful victim, or himself, but he can never be as ferocious as a real predator. I want them to realize that shape changing won't win a fight or, for that matter, a war. It will be of no use to change into a ball if your disabled fighter is about to crash-land.

Sorry, son, I wasn't thinking. I have had no experience with shape changers—except Quarr, of course, and she never changed once she copied your mother's form.

Exchanging thoughts was almost instantaneous. Kryger didn't allow his attention to be distracted from his remaining opponent. Perhaps he should perform one more demonstration with this would-be predator, but it depended on the method of attack. He could have followed the man's thoughts, but like his father, he would only think it fair if it was life threatening. He waited, balanced and ready for the next attack.

The attack came about half a minute later and was aimed at his lower abdomen. He almost laughed at the inanity of it. He waited, poised, and as the imitation predator came within range, he sidestepped nimbly. As it passed, he kicked it with the ball of his right foot on the snout where it was painful for man or beast. There was a sharp crack as small bones broke.

The imitation beast uttered a human scream. It seemed to sob for a while before slurred words came out of its mouth. "Damn you, you alien bastard. Why must you have an answer to everything I try? What are you that you can kill five of the finest fighting men without even breathing heavily? Even a predator has no chance to touch you."

Kryger heard the words echo from hundreds of speakers and realized that a sensitive microphone was aimed on them. Damn, it was a nuisance not to know a language, but it was a chance he couldn't let go by! It took a lot of energy, but he broadcasted his reply. *Imitating a predator doesn't make you one. Changing your shape doesn't alter your abilities or character. It's only a form of disguise, and you can't copy the basic instincts of the shape you imitate. You would have done better if you had thought before you fought, and then only relied on your training and experience in your real form.*

"I'll show you!" the predator screamed, and it charged again, once again jumping at Kryger's throat, but a little faster this time to catch him off-guard.

Kryger stepped nimbly aside, and as the imitation predator landed, he grabbed a handful of imitation fur and vaulted onto its back. A shape changer is limited to what he or she already has. He can't add extra weight and mighty muscles, and the imitation leopard—which was only as big as Druta's normal body-mass allowed—collapsed under Kryger's weight. The neck, and the angle of the head, was just right where it pressed against the hard rock-floor, and Kryger planted his right fist with all his power just where the head joined the neck. There was a loud crack and the fake predator's body convulsed, then relaxed tiredly. Kryger let out a deep sigh of regret and quickly stood. He moved away as he watched the imitation gradually assume its normal form in death.

A collective sigh issued from the audience. At first they had enjoyed the entertainment, but they were not happy now. It took a stranger no time at all to recognize the obvious, which should have been apparent to them centuries ago.

Their education was just beginning as far as Kryger was concerned. He let them in on his thoughts: that if they were to be of any use in defeating the Hullenii, they had to learn to overcome their basic instincts and learn to *fight* instead of *run*. Shape shifting was of little use in a battle for survival against odds, unless one had the opportunity to hide.

"I feel ashamed, because I only thought of my own ambition and not of our nation as a whole," Mokerok told Quarr a while later. "I envy you your luck in finding a warrior of that caliber for a mate. If there are any more such men, please introduce me." She nodded sincerely. "You were quite right—the chance that I'll see another fight like that in my lifetime is none existent. Kryger thinks of us as a faction only, and he may be right. He saw right through our basic problem—as a faction, we ran so many times that it became instinct. We should have taken time to think about developing weapons to defend ourselves instead of taking to our heels every time we smelled trouble."

Quarr held out her arms to Mokerok, who gladly accepted the invitation and gave her a fierce hug that Quarr kindly returned. This was to the consternation of the whole assembly, for when Mokerok approached, the nearby cameras focused on them out of curiosity to record how two erstwhile enemies were going to react to each other after an almost one-sided fight.

In a narrow beam, directed only at Mokerok, Quarr said, *You deserve to know the truth. I didn't want to kill you, because I sensed the quality of **greatness** in you. We will talk later in private, and I will brief you in detail. I want you to be the first president of our nation and control the direction our faction. Will you accept?*

Mokerok was speechless and let go of Quarr to recover. Her eyes showed shock, but after a moment she started to giggle, and as the humor of the situation finally registered fully, the giggle turned into real, uproarious laughter. Quarr, sharing her thoughts, smiled and took her hand to lead her out of the amphitheater.

I'm glad you knocked some sense into me. Only now do I realize what an enormous task I wanted to take on, but I will accept—after I know what you have in mind. I have two conditions. The first is that you will teach me how to govern. The second is that you must always be ready to help me when I get stuck with a problem. You are wiser than me and you have broader experience.

I thank you, Mokerok. I too, accept, but you'll come with us to learn directly from my mentors. The second condition we'll have to work out, because there will be restrictions.

They passed a lot of people who gaped at the two former adversaries walking hand in hand. Not a single thought leaked, because Quarr shielded both their brains while she transferred the shield's principles to her chosen successor. Mokerok would need it in order to be spy-proof. Already they were forming a bond, as twins do.

36

"We've decided to go back to the ship. Everything seems to be under control," Torak informed his son about four hours later. "Ycagabys informed his people that the reign of terror was over, and he feels that he is strong enough to come down to guide them. Pgabys will accompany him, since she has given birth to the baby—if you can call the lively little monster that—and wants to teach him to hunt, even if he can scarcely control his legs. It's a good idea. The sooner he gets used to real gravity, the better.

"There are still pockets of resistance here and there, but the roundup should be completed within a day or so. A relief force will be here in about three to four weeks, and they will build moon and planetary-based defenses. Unfortunately, we cannot really spare them for long, but we'll see what we can do to speed things up and train the Gwarra to man the weapon-systems. We have to head home after we've completed the handover to the relief force. There isn't anything you can do in the meantime, so you might as well take a few days off to really recover."

"Thanks, Dad. I'd like to take a look around the canyons while Quarr takes care of her business. There's something curious I think I should check out. When I return, if it's okay with you, I'll select a number of possible candidates to take along and train as instructors. I suspect that they have the means to adapt to our higher gravity, because Quarr was able to do so when she arrived on Nevus. If not, Mike can assist while he educates them."

"Yes, that's a good idea. We have the resources to build fighters and battleships, but it'll take a couple of years before they can handle the bigger ships and take care of themselves."

"With respect, Dad, Quarr and I are the only ones at present who can withstand the immense power of the bugs combined minds in close proximity. We should be responsible for searching and extermination, and our forces should do the rounding up afterward, one planet at a time. We already know the location of two to start with. We'll be on our way as soon as the new fighting-scout you mentioned is completed and tested." Another way of killing the giant bugs came to mind. "Perhaps our scientists can create a virus that would only attack the bugs and no other life forms."

"I'll mention the idea to the Golden People, but they'd need a carefully preserved bug for testing. They've been trying to find out who gave the Bikans the idea of poisoning our planet's air thousands of years ago. Perhaps they still had some brains left then. Who knows? Yes, I haven't lost track of the fact that we *lesser mortals* cannot stand up to the bugs, but we can accompany you, stay out of range, and start rounding up their followers as soon as you're done. We'll save time that way, and we'll also keep the gnats out of your hair so that you can focus on the real job. Anyway, we'll plan it in conjunction with the War Council."

"Okay, Dad. I'll go along with the plan. As you'd taught me a long time ago, no detailed plan can always be followed to the letter when circumstances change. It may be a few days before I rejoin you."

Torak suddenly had a premonition, which felt like a shadow moving in on his mind. "Those may be prophetic words, son. I have a feeling that something inimical is going to happen. I've had this intuition before, and it always portended evil events. I feel uneasy all of a sudden. Please Kryger, stay close to transport at all times. I may need you in a hurry."

"Will do, Dad. I'll utilize the fighter you let us have to examine a particular canyon for a span of a few kilometers. I remember seeing a curios effect when Quarr and I flashed over it, and I'd like to investigate. These canyons fascinate me. I have a feeling that some of them conceal more than they reveal. I know that The Pilot would love to explore this canyon continent. You should tell him about it."

"I will. We'll be off in a few minutes. You just have time to say goodbye to Mom while I talk to Quarr and Iño for a minute or two, then I must rush back to get the fleet on fulltime battle alert. I hate the responsibility of command and this sense of urgency. It leaves me no peace of mind, and this feeling of looming disaster is starting to get to me. I don't want to leave anything to chance."

Kryger was troubled by his father's premonition, because Torak had an even finer intuition than Quarr. Also, Quarr's foresight was immediate, whereas his father's was always a few days or weeks ahead. He should have a few days to explore that canyon, as well as the feeling he had of something or someone *calling* him. There was something nagging at the back of his mind, something of a brief glimpse of an anomaly that had registered when they flashed over the terrain, but the urgency of their immediate need to escape had pushed it into the background. In the morning, he would try to follow the same route. Anything could be hidden from sight in the maze of canyons.

Quarr had taken leave of Kryger, because she would be busy half the night setting her guidelines down in writing for the council that would lay down the rules for the faction from now on. She would remain occupied for the rest of her time on Okrion.

Kryger wanted to leave before sunrise. With that in mind, he'd arranged for food for a week, and slept in the fighter.

Quarr tiredly went to a lonely bed well after midnight. She fell into an exhausted sleep just as Kryger became half-awake. Wondering what the matter was, he synchronized his mined with Quarr's frequency. He found that she was asleep and that she was dreaming. Or was it a vision? A sad, beautiful woman was addressing her.

"Quarr my love, I've been granted special dispensation to visit you from the spirit world, for my task is still unfinished because of Pupaul's deceit. I would have spoken to you last night in the ship, but you had very little opportunity to sleep. We, on this side of life, were concerned and wanted you to spare Mokerok's life. She, along with you and Kryger, are vital players in the war against the Hullenii. She, like you, has a quite unique mind. It runs in our line of the family. But you felt her uniqueness and decided to spare her life for your purposes. She is the right one to guide and govern this remnant of our dwindling race. Your decision to spare her may ultimately save the universe.

"At present, Kryger is the only being in the universe capable of defeating the Okur Hullenii *in direct* confrontation. At this stage of his development, he is already powerful enough to defeat two of them linked together, but the bugs will be forced to work together to eliminate him, and if successful, they will strip the galaxy of sentient life in a few short centuries. Kryger may die in one of these battles unless he has adequate resources and help, but there must be those who can continue the fight with intensive training, which is to be your key task in your present life.

"From now on, the Hullenii will spare no humanoid being or planets controlled by humans. This galaxy may become a desolate place if Kryger dies without enough offspring trained and dedicated to the task of exterminating the Hullenii that, through human ignorance, weren't allowed to develop naturally into the role designated for them by the overall plan.

"Your offspring, those of your sister-aunt and perhaps a few others, through your intensive training, should be capable of dealing death to the Hullenii and ultimately exterminate them, but Kryger is the only male who can sire such children. The choice will be his and yours, and he will be very reluctant to mate with her or anyone else, for he loves you with his entire being, but you must try to persuade both of them to have at least one child by telling them what I tell you. Think about it. You will lose nothing in the process. There won't be another opportunity to free the galaxy of these archenemies of life and civilization. Some of the children will die in the fight, just as Kryger may, but some will survive to continue our line, and to fight against the tyranny of the armored, long living bug-like insects and other would-be tyrants that will pop up now and then in the far future. Unfortunately, events in the three dimensional world are only probabilities and can't be predicted precisely, for the acts, choices and preferences of individuals can change the course of events and history. From this side, we are sometimes permitted to give advice, but cannot influence or interfere with three-dimensional affairs.

"My darling daughter, I see that you are confused. You and I have suffered much at the hands of the enemy's minions, but you came out strong and purposeful. Let me briefly describe our history, which was passed on verbally from generation to generation, so that you may understand.

"First, your half-remembered taboo against merging minds with aliens applies only to our line of the family. The ordinary members of our race are free to interbreed with another race whenever they want to, but they elected to follow our rules, which was harmful for the race. There was a valid reason for the restriction, for our line has a unique mind-trait, in that we can *resist the mind control of the* Hullenii without their knowledge. It is the reason we guide our people, which is quite different from ruling them. I did not have the chance to teach you our private history, because you were so very young when my devious brother decided that female rule was old fashioned, and redundant.

"When a female of our line takes the regency, she doesn't kill family members to avoid plots to overthrow her rule. She does so to get rid of the ambitious, lesser minds that are next in line, but don't have the unique trait and inclination to guide our people without personal gain, and who only want to take control to exploit them for personal greed or aggrandizement. Our unique mind-trait must not be weakened in the event that the regent dies childless and another female has to take her place. We don't accept challenges from the stronger minds in our family, and we tell them the reason by tight-beam thought-communication. You must explain this to Mokerok, for she too must know this in the event that you are killed and the plans you have for our nation comes to nothing. We also produce offspring with the strongest males—in mind as well as body—but fighting the consort is rarely permitted, for females were trained to know when brains rather than brawn was required, and love or respect had nothing to with her choice.

"When we choose a mate, we look for strengthening traits. Love must take a backseat to preserve our unique traits. Unwittingly, you recognized this trait in Kryger and my young sister. That's why you didn't hesitate to merge minds with him when he needed it. Given time, information and the opportunity to develop, he would have overcome the lure of the Hullenii's irresistible mind without your help. He was born of parents selected for this purpose by the Higher Powers who plan the fate of the universe, as well as the destiny of mankind and other creations. We are all here for a purpose, and we must fulfill our destinies whether we want to or not, otherwise we are deemed failures and we must return, time after time, to the three dimensional universe until we learn our lessons.

"The Hullenii, from the planet Okur, were not born as the dominant species. Okur is in a solar system a thousand light years away from this planet. Originally they were small—no bigger than small dogs—but they were scientifically enlarged over a period of time by a process that also increased their already long life expectancy to thousands of years. This made them think that they were immortal. The human scientists on Okur found that the big insects had a remarkable capacity for remembering things, and that they had the ability to transfer that knowledge to each other, so that all knew within seconds what any one of them had experienced or learned.

"The intention was to use as them as repositories of knowledge instead of relying on fallible machines. The innocents disregarded the fact that the insect-like creatures were a long-living predator species, and the result was that they developed powerful creatures that were incapable of original thought, and could not be destroyed by the weapons they had at their disposal. Their idiot creators thought it a fortuitous bonus, because they had opposition who foresaw what would happen, and who tried to destroy the bugs. When they were unsuccessful, the opposing part of the population fled the planet.

"The Hullenii can't invent anything, for they are incapable of original thought, but they are great at remembering and copying any useful invention. They can only store the details of what they see and hear, but promptly forget about it unless they know what it is used for and have an immediate use for; and of course, someone who can create the object.

"As they continued to grow bigger, they developed increasingly voracious appetites, and eventually started preying on their creators until their planet was almost devoid of life. Aside from other bugs, they regard every living thing as prey.

"An ill-fated, accidental visit by us, the first space-faring people who landed on that planet, provided them with their first spaceship. They were on the verge of starvation when our ship landed, and simply seized the crew, wrung their minds dry, had them alter their spaceship for the big arthropods to use, and then hung them up in their larder. Then they came to us, the designers of that spaceship, in a nearby system.

"The Hullenii enslaved us and used our peoples' expertise to build starships and weapons of mass destruction for them. We remained their slaves and cattle for thousands of years…but years reckoned by another unit of time than we now are used to. We were always aware of our enforced slave status and were on the lookout for a way out. An unplanned mating with a strong Sensitive male from another humanoid culture, who was brought to us for breeding purposes by our masters, produced a female child who was immune to the mental commands of the insects if she chose to ignore them. The parents, realizing that the child's potential could be the deliverance that everyone was praying for, fled to a remote region, and fortunately, the Hullenii master of our planet was not

248

concerned with a few defectors. The escapees brought up their child and prepared her until she reached maturity.

"The child's name was Gwar, and we, her direct descendants, were known as the Gwarra. Eventually, after our escape, the nation adopted that name out of reverence. When she was ready, she joined the construction workers at the spaceport and studied the Hullenii and other cultures that were brought in as workers to manufacture more and more starships and new weapons. One by one, she taught promising minds to resist the compulsion of the bug that controlled our planet.

"She avoided the lax attention of the Hullenii and became a scientist. When she met a man with exceptional mind-power, she took him as husband. Once he was trained to deflect the mind-power of the bug, they set about inventing a bomb that could devastate a planet. By this time, thousands of our people were trained to resist the control and mind-power of the Hullenii arthropods, and they manufactured more spaceships than the bugs wanted, that were also much larger—without their knowledge, of course.

"We know that the trained minds—many thousands of them—secretly boarded the spaceships under the noses of the unsuspecting bugs, who didn't have the slightest inkling of rebellion. This bug had ruled for a few thousand years and there had never been any resistance. It was a heart-breaking choice, since those who stayed behind knew they were doomed. They expected retaliation from other Hullenii, because the bugs controlled an unknown number of stellar systems by then.

"When they took off, they triggered a nuclear bomb that destroyed the spaceport together with the bugs waiting for their ships to be completed. They fled our home planet in all directions, but Gwar's ship deviated to drop the planet-buster on the insect's home planet in passing. We believe that a good many insects, and their breeding centers, were destroyed with that planet.

"The Hullenii, in turn, laid our home planet to waste. Since then we have played a game of hide and seek. They are forever on the lookout for us and will destroy any planet they find us on to make sure that none escape. We colonized a few systems, but in time we lost contact with the others. We don't know if we're the last surviving colony. We fled every time we smelled one of them, which was often in the beginning, and we dared not keep contact with other colonies by sending mind-messages which could be intercepted.

"Gwar laid down some taboos for our family. Over the centuries, other rules evolved as mistakes were made and corrected. The restrictions were passed on from one generation to the next among females, for we are the direct heirs of Gwar. Female minds usually are more sensitive than male minds. There were males now and then who had this special ability, and controlled inbreeding with relatives was not an exception to the rule when another talented male was not available. As female ruler came to be accepted as natural and unalterable, the males were unfortunately kept in the dark, and that is why my brother wanted to end things as they were. It was a mistake to keep the knowledge from males, but it doesn't matter anymore. In you and Mokerok we have achieved what our ancestors set out to do. And now there's Kryger to share the responsibility of exterminating the bugs.

"Have courage, my love. The road ahead will be long, tough, and filled with sorrow. You didn't have a normal childhood, and the remainder of your life will be mostly hard, for which I apologize. The three of you will make sacrifices to ensure that your children, and those that come after, will have a chance to develop in peace. That knowledge will be the only reward. Although I would have preferred to live to hold you in my arms and see my grandchildren grow into man- and womanhood, the Powers who control our destinies sacrificed me to bring the three of you together in a way that would ensure that our special abilities are fully developed and put to use.

Quarr was tired of putting her life at constant risk. Peace was of utmost importance to her. Constant fear and war only brought out the worst in people, and Kryger might not survive for long. "Yes, mother, I will do what's necessary. I have enough courage and insight to see the logic and the necessity for Kryger's children. I also see why everything happened to develop our abilities, but perhaps the bitterness of your death instilled the will to endure and fight to survive against all odds to avenge your death."

"Thank you, love. When we have lived long enough to be able to look back, we see why we had to suffer and have certain obstacles put in our way to overcome. They may seem so harsh and unnecessary at the time, but they strengthen our character to make us stronger for what we must do and learn, for *that* is what life's about. Most people have a choice of the path they can take, but others are born for a special purpose and have no choice. Although we cannot remember, what we must do, or learn, is decided before we are born, and very few creatures can change their destinies. And if they do not learn what they must, they fail. We are born because we have a purpose, even if it's just to have a child that will pass on certain abilities to her or his offspring. I am content. I must say goodbye, my love. My time is up."

Kryger kept his silence and quickly de-synchronized. He immediately drifted off to sleep and therefore missed the last bit of news, for the nebulous spirit-woman quickly continued.

"I'm grateful that I've been granted this brief opportunity to see and talk to you. Be careful, as you are already carrying your first child. I should mention..." but she vanished before she could complete the sentence. Quarr had so many questions that would now never be answered.

She wearily tried to review the information. What could she say to Kryger and Mokerok to make them understand? It was difficult to think. She was so exhausted, but she concluded there was no urgency to comply with the request. It could wait a few days. She was dead-tired, but sleep just wouldn't return. Already carrying a child? That was good and bad news. What would Kryger do without her? Would he be able to cope alone? What was her mother going to say before her time terminated? The questions repeated themselves over and over in her mind for what seemed like hours, but gradually she drifted off into a fitful sleep, plagued by nagging nightmares.

37

Kryger was long gone when Quarr reluctantly woke up, and she wasn't going to call him before she was fully awake so that she could sense if there were eavesdroppers. She thought that she might as well think some more, talk to Mokerok, and when he returned, tell him in person about her mother's unprecedented visit and what she had said. Perhaps she should first tell her story to Mokerok, and see how she reacted. Right now she just wanted a hot, leisurely bath and a late breakfast. She was not required in the conference room before lunch. The trustees wanted to discuss the implications of her abdication and her plans. Quarr grinned mischievously. Old Iño might disapprove, *emphatically*, when she heard that Mokerok would be heading the council from now on. The foxy old lady may have a yearning to stay in power awhile yet. It was time for her to step aside, unless she was chosen by people to represent them in council.

Intuiting that Quarr needed time to think and come to grips with her mother's suggestions, Kryger departed earlier than planned. The fact that he would have a wife and an occasional mistress disturbed him more than he cared to admit. It went against his disciplined upbringing and customs—but then he thought that if Quarr gave in to her mother's recommendation, Mokerok will more or less be out of reach most of the time, and hopefully she would prefer to be married to someone of her own choice as well.

He would have rejected the proposal immediately, without second thoughts or regrets, if Quarr had told him the story under normal circumstances. She was his ideal woman. He had no thoughts of any other girl, for only Quarr measured up to his standards. It would also upset his family, because it was against their beliefs, but perhaps they would see the necessity of it if it was explained properly. If it came to that, he knew he would take the coward's way out and let Quarr do the explaining. He decided not to give it further thought. Such things had a way of sorting themselves out.

He had the restless spirit of a warrior and an explorer combined, and when he had had a bellyful of fighting, he usually asked for leave to visit a certain, lonely place in the Thirstland to think and calm his restless soul. He would continue to do so when he felt the need, but that lonely desert place was three hundred and some odd light years away at the moment.

He smiled and took the fighter up into space.

Kryger recognized the landmarks he had fleetingly seen during their hectic descend. This time he stayed high in the atmosphere so that he had a better view of the seemingly endless canyon continent. He almost enjoyed the leisurely descent.

Every planet has something unique about it, he thought. *I remember the gigantic, white rock-finger pointing obscenely into the sky. It must be at least five kilometers high. It will be a serious obstacle for aircraft without radar at night. It's like a warning or admonishing finger among the high mountain peaks.* He slowly flew toward it. He remembered passing close to it. He slowed down more after he had passed it, engaged the gravity neutralizers for silent flight, and dropped down as close to ground level as the terrain allowed. He would proceed cautiously from here on, because he wasn't sure what to expect.

He recognized the canyon immediately when he reached it. It started as a broad valley, surrounded by high cliffs, and a few small brooks converged toward the far side to combine and feed the river further down. The small patches of carefully cultivated vegetation, cunningly interspersed and mixed with local vegetation, were only noticeable if you were looking for it with a trained eye. The cultivators had gone to great lengths to blend small fields with natural vegetation. *This isolated community dearly wanted to keep to themselves. I wonder why? Who—or what—are they? Are they humanoid?*

As the fighter flew on almost silently, he surprised a few unwary humanoid harvesters and cultivators. They froze for an instant in shocked surprise and then changed into rocks or animals. He suddenly accelerated to dodge a missile, while simultaneously activating the shields and the automatic defense system. The missile exploded against the canyon-wall before it could turn. He laughed out loud—they were human. He had stumbled across a lost colony of shape changers, and they were very protective of their privacy. He dropped his mind-shield and broadcasted a friendly thought.

Hold your fire! I'm not the enemy. There's another colony of your people nearby! The fighter automatically destroyed another missile. *The time for hiding is over. The*

253

Hullenii know of this planet, and there is no place to flee. We must talk. Who speaks for you?

A timid mind, full of fear and apprehension, replied, *I'm Masipah, and I'm the spokesperson for my people. Who are you? What do you want with us? How did you find us?*

Kryger followed the thought to its source for closer contact, and found a hard breathing, fearful, panicky female mind. He realized that she was on the verge of doing something stupid, or collapsing from panic, but he didn't feel any sympathy. Someone that cowardly shouldn't be in control.

Her mind was numb with horror and unable to think lucidly. She was clearly not used to dealing with outsiders. She thought that the mechanical thought-shield in their underground refuge was impervious. Perhaps it did stop the Hullenii's penetration, but it would have to be a much more effective shield to block his thoughts. He spoke calmly to try and remove her fears.

I'm Kryger. I'm the consort of princess Quarr, the descendent of Gwar. He felt the consternation the mentioning of the name caused. She knew that he knew what he was talking about. He blessed the fact that he was still mind-linked with Quarr and the coincidence that caused him to share Quarr's vision the night before. Before he could state the purpose of his visit, Masipah replied.

Perhaps you should come inside for a face-to-face talk. I'll have the gates opened so that you can fly directly in.

She was so blank from shock and fear that it didn't register that Kryger was following her thoughts, and thus aware of the special reception she planned for him. He shook his head in exasperation and quickly synchronized with Quarr, who was still in the bath.

Quarr was not really surprised that Kryger had found another remnant of her people on this planet. He had the knack of coming up with the unexpected. She somehow expected to meet survivors sooner or later, but right now she was coldly furious. Quarr was amused by Kryger's choice of words.

Listen carefully, lady—if I may call you by that misnomer—this fighter has enough power to destroy this entire mountain that you so foolishly regard as impregnable. You are centuries behind. The pitiful few untrained soldiers you managed to get together to overpower me are hopelessly, pathetically inadequate. Did you feel an earthshaking tremor three or four

*weeks ago? Of course you did! That was a scout exploding
when our enemies thought they were being as clever as you
think you are now. Try to think instead of just reacting, Masipah!
You can hide forever for all I care, unless you have some pride
left and want to defend this—your home—with the rest of us.*

*Don't move! We have a dozen homing missiles trained
on your craft. They will be fired automatically if you move.*

Kryger wasn't amused anymore. Such stupidity could
only end in disaster. He became angry.

*You don't listen at all, do you? I'm talking to you inside
your **impregnable** citadel. I have no wish to destroy you or your
people, but the destruction of those missiles **will** destroy your
people outside and most of your crops. The backlash could
destroy most of you inside as well. Do you want that to happen?
What will you gain? And most importantly, think of what you will
most certainly lose.*

Masipah couldn't think coherently. He waited, for he
was aware that quite a few persons were angry with her
ineptitude and were about to restrain her. In a way, he felt sorry
for her. She may be a good administrator, but she was
unprepared to cope with unexpected visitors.

Poor thing! You were too hard on her. Quarr was full of
mirth at this unexpected turn in events, for she shared
everything with Kryger. *I was just about to climb down her throat,
but you saved me the trouble. Well, why don't you take off, as
you threatened, and leave them to contemplate their peaceful
existence? It's the typical cornered-rat syndrome—drop dead or
fight.*

*Don't be flippant, Quarr. I want to give them a chance,
because I sense that there are a few people with excellent
brains here and they can be utilized in the war against the
Hullenii. When I'm finished with my harassment to force some
guts back into them, you can talk to them if you feel like it.*

Quarr didn't take exception to his somewhat strong
language. Her perception was fully merged with his, and she
saw what he saw and felt what he felt. A strong Sensitive male
interrupted them.

*I apologize for the hostile reception, Kryger. Your
unexpected arrival caught all of us off-balance, and we
apologize for Masipah's panicky reaction. Not all of us fear
discovery, but we have been isolated for so many centuries that
we've become paranoid. We became unused to the idea that we*

eventually would be discovered. The missiles have been deactivated.

Kryger immediately liked this matter-of-fact attitude. *I understand. I apologize for my harsh attitude. I fear that I was forcing an issue, because we can use all the help we can get to fight the Hullenii. I'll land the fighter closer to the entrance so that we can discuss our mutual problems in person. If, however, you prefer to remain in isolation, I'm quite willing to forget that I found you.*

No...it's time that we meet other people. We already are inbred to such an extent that we face extinction. Our problem is that, though we have fighting craft, we've been reluctant to practice except on simulators. Our bodies may be somewhat weak and unused to high-gravity maneuvers, but we still have some pride and fighting spirit left. We'll meet you outside. We've been away from the real sun for far too long. The time has come for us to emerge from our burrows and brave the real world without fear.

When he sensed a group of people moving toward a certain exit, Kryger felt the urge that led him here diminish. He moved the fighter closer. Because he sensed that he could trust the speaker, he deactivated the fighter's automatic defense system. He suddenly remembered that he was not kin to the shape changers, and that his height and well-developed body may intimidate them.

Please don't be intimidated by my strange face and big body. I'm human, but of a different species. I can change my face with an effort for a short while, but I'd prefer not to. I don't speak your language yet either.

Don't worry, Kryger. We're used to all kinds of shapes and faces. We change to amuse each other and ourselves. We don't care about how you look. What counts is that you have a strong mind and honest thoughts, therefore we can be honest with you. You will sense the same in us as well. As much as we respect and love Masipah, we restrained her physically. We sense in you the relentless type of courage inherent in a selfless fighter, and that we admire. We may have grown weak in body, but most of us are strong in mind, and our sciences have progressed. If we can't fight with you, we can grow the food to feed the fighters, and we can design and build fighting craft for those who can fight.

256

38

Just as Kryger jumped down from the cockpit, nine persons emerged from a cunningly camouflaged, narrow door. They froze in numb surprise for a moment, and it wasn't because of his out-of-the-ordinary face. The tallest of them would just be about shoulder-level if they wore very tall shoes. Compared to him, they were emaciated, pale pigmies, although they moved with the grace of well-trained athletes. The leader, who incidentally was also the tallest by about two centimeters, recovered first from the unexpected surprise.

Sorry, Kryger. He was embarrassed. *You're a **big** surprise. When we arrived here, about three centuries ago, we were the only humans on the planet. Although we know that we're not as tall as our race used to be, we've forgotten how tall one **can** be. I'm Paruk, and I'm pleased to meet you.*

He sensed that it also was the custom of Kryger's people to shake hands, and he reluctantly held out his, as if expecting it to be crushed in a vice-like grip. To his surprise and relief, Kryger's grip was firm, but friendly. He immediately felt at ease and introduced the others, who in turn, were surprised at the gentle strength of the giant's hand.

At that stage, Quarr decided to withdraw. *I have to go, love. If they don't have their own transport, bring as many as you can squeeze into the fighter to meet us. I think they've had enough surprises for one day. I'll inform the council so that they won't be stunned when they meet long lost cousins who lived on our doorstep all this time. See you soon. Enjoy!* She disengaged her mind.

Paruk introduced Kryger to everyone. As the last person, a woman named Injani, was introduced as their seeress, he received an astonishing thought-flash. *We must talk privately later. It is important.*

He was used to surprises, so his face remained impassive as he acknowledged her message.

He addressed the committee of nine, but his question was directed at Paruk. *I have the ability to broadcast our conversation to all your people, who seem to number less than a hundred thousand. Do you want to keep this private, or do you wish to include every one?*

Yes, please. Some of them are as apprehensive as

Masipah, so it might be in our interest to include every soul. If you don't mind, a crew with visual equipment will be here in a few minutes to take pictures so that our population can see and get used to the first stranger that we've seen in many, many years. In the meantime, we ask you to briefly tell us how you came to our planet. What happened? How did you find us?

Kryger did. It took him almost twenty minutes. The camera crew came, but weren't intrusive as they activated a *live coverage* of the silent broadcast. Then Paruk told him their history, which wasn't much. They took off every time their seer or seeress found that a bug had settled on their planet of refuge, but when they came here, they knew that it was their last stop. Their spaceship needed major repairs before it could take off again, and they couldn't do them, so they dismantled it. Because they had lost contact with other colonies some centuries before, the faction began to deteriorate physically. When he finished the brief history, he asked Kryger to stay for a few days if he could, so that they would get used to the presence of a stranger before they met their long lost cousins.

The hangar entrance was reportedly big enough to allow his fighter inside, but Kryger decided that it should stay outside in case he had to leave in a hurry. As they entered the secret, camouflaged entrance, the seeress Injani, fell into step next to him. She had unusual blue-gray eyes, which was a deviation from the normal yellow of the Gwarra. He closed his mind to the rest of them.

Ah, thank you Kryger. This conversion must only be between the two of us. I sent the call that led you here, for I did not know how to talk to you directly. I am very sensitive to—what shall I call it? What I mean is that I can receive messages from departed souls, and I can also see them and talk to them. Please bear in mind that it isn't easy for me to tell you, a total stranger, what was asked of me.

The soul of a ruler of our long lost cousins visited me three weeks ago and also briefly last night. She asked me to share my talent with you, because it will save your life a number of times. She told me of our nearby cousins, but now you know why I kept the information to myself. She also showed me a safe, healing sanctuary on this planet, which you should use when you are battle weary and need peace for body and soul. She said that you would need it from time to time. It seems that the Powers who guide our evolution and destinies are on your side and want to keep you alive for as long as possible. You have a destiny so strange and perilous that normal mortals would go mad if they experienced just a small part of it. I certainly don't envy you, and I'll willingly give you what talents I have, if you would allow me to transfer it. To the best of my knowledge, it cannot be taught.

Kryger kept his silence.

I sense your well-suppressed dismay. Yes, it was your wife's mother. Last night she said that you are a marked man, and that bugs and their slaves will arrive soon to destroy this planet in the hopes of killing you. The Hullenii, if they ever get hold of you, have planned a most hideous death for you to avenge Gorrel's murder. There are already a number of spacecraft, large and small, on their way here to try and capture you. They will lay this planet to waste no matter what. She told me that they should arrive in seven to ten days.

I've kept this information to myself because it would cause panic, as well as the fact that I'm already regarded as a bit odd, and it's not because of my uniquely colored eyes. I thought you different as well, because you walk with a step as light as that of a feline. It marks you as different.

I'm an adviser, because of my gift of divining future events. That is one of my abilities, and I will gladly give it to you, for it might help you. But my peculiar ability, which the lady's spirit asked me to give to you, is that I can instantly make my body weightless with the power of my mind. Gravity no longer affects me. I was born with this ability, and although I have tried, it cannot be taught. I cannot fall to my death from any height if I'm awake. I don't know how it works, but it's a form of levitation. Apparently you will need this ability from time to time.

Now comes the part that may be hard to explain. I can only transfer the abilities by a partial merging of our minds. I believe you know what that means. The fact was made quite clear to me that this was my only opportunity to help humanity to survive.

I was shown the special place on Nevus that you visit on occasion. I have seen both only in my astral body of course, but the one on this planet is different and more peaceful, because it is a solid crystal cave and naturally isolated from outside influences. I will take you there as soon as you have made up your mind. We can partially merge minds there, because it is a safe place for you to start practicing. You can

259

only bump your head against the ceiling and not float out into space before you can master the ability.

Kryger was uncomfortable. He didn't know how to take this news or what to make of it. It sounded logical, though. He knew that when Higher Powers decide to take a hand, nothing could be done to shirk the responsibility. He informed her that he couldn't decide right there and then, but would think about it. She didn't take that kindly, but was diplomatic about it.

*You must realize that this isn't about fornication for pleasure. You and I, and a few others, are instruments of greater things. Life as we know it is at stake. The particular genes that a few of us carry must be combined in a way that will serve the purpose for which we were born. That is one of our functions. When we die, our particular genes will die with us, **unless** we have offspring. You must be positive. You will lose nothing through this.*

*It was made clear to me that if I were not willing to share this ability with you, it is probable that you wouldn't live another three months. Your life, and your training, would be wasted. There may only be one unborn child to continue the fight against our enemy—**if** he and his mother survive the coming battle for this planet.*

Do you think this is easy for me? Don't think I made this decision lightly. I have had three weeks to think about the complications. You are a stranger, and if my people could escape or be left alone, we could hide for another century or two without degenerating into useless monsters, but for what purpose? We'll eventually be found and destroyed—as will all life in this galaxy, in time. It's the destiny of mankind—of our people and all the inhabitants of this galaxy—that's at stake.

You'll find the ability to predict the short-term consequences of a decision taken by others and by yourself useful. I'm not talking about a full merge—I'm trained whereas your Quarr wasn't. See? I was told all about you. Husband and wife usually share only traits that clash so that they can live in peace and make a success of their marriage—or at least understand each other. You don't want to cheat on Quarr, so let me have her frequency. I can tell her what I've just told you. I will be truthful and diplomatic, so don't worry about getting into trouble with her.

Kryger was ashamed of his doubts and response. This small woman had nothing to gain, and he sensed that she was sincere, for she spoke the truth. He made a decision. *If Quarr agrees and tells me so, we'll leave at dawn tomorrow. My father expected big trouble that you confirmed is on its way here. I'll take all the help I can get. I know that fights in the future will be relentless, with no quarter given or asked. We, as an intelligent species, have the right to live and decide our own futures. Thank you for your frankness and sacrifice. I know it wasn't an easy decision for you, and I won't forget that. Let's finish this introduction to your people in the meantime.*

Kryger eventually met the fearful Masipah, who screamed and fainted when she saw him. He was tired by this time, but he sensed that she was going insane with fear. He had nothing against her, so he entered her mind and shared a great calmness with her. He soothed her fears.

While he was shown the various facilities that could be useful for the defense of the planet—feeding the defenders, and in time perhaps a few fleets as well—he was kept busy with questions. After a late but adequate meal, he went to bed in the early hours of the morning. Quarr was impatiently waiting for him to be alone.

They have kept you busy, haven't they? I have had an extremely busy day myself, but I retired early and this seeress, Injani, spoke to me about what she told you. My mother came to me in a vision and I believe she wanted to tell me the same thing last night, but her power failed before she could. I had a mind-message later when I was taking a bath, which told me the same thing Injani did, so I had all day to think about it, and I agree only on condition that you let me have those abilities as well. One never knows what will happen. Ask her to also show you how to handle a controlled partial merge, because men should be able to do it as well, and you don't want another full merge, do you? It was as if he could hear her laughter in his ear. He missed her desperately in that moment.

They spoke awhile before she excused herself, because she needed a decent sleep as well. Kryger forced himself into sleep.

He woke up quickly when Injani came to fetch him for breakfast. She directed him to the other side of the continent, to a deep canyon that somehow seemed familiar to him. He thought that he might have seen something similar on one of the many planets he had been on. The usual deep river was only a hot, shallow stream, vomited out by a dying volcano some tens of kilometers upstream, and the perpendicular, glassy, smooth, brownish-black walls were obscured by foggy haziness. Injani explained what signs to look for—the entrance to the well-hidden sanctuary was not obvious, and it couldn't be located or reached by climbing from below or descending from above. His sensitive mind picked up the profound peace and tranquility long before they reached the huge cave, apparently carved out by volcanic action countless years ago at the dawn of this single planet solar system. He felt an inexplicable uplifting of his spirit as he neared the location as if he were coming home.

    He found that the cave, about halfway up the five kilometer high, sheer cliff, could only be reached by a gravity craft, and that the entrance was a low, rough-edged oval, just a couple of meters wider than the fighter's atmospheric wingspan. In the landing lights, the cave shone brightly with many-hues. It dazzled his eyes. He managed to swing the craft around to face the entrance before he landed and switched the lights off. He opened the canopy and helped Injani down, but the light diminished only slightly. The cave stayed illuminated by the embedded and loosely scattered crystals as if they retained the light.

    The wonder and profound peace that filled their souls was indescribable. Kryger cleared a large area around the fighter of debris before they sat down on the uneven floor to take it all in. He inspected the floor and walls, but could not identify any of the crystals. The only name that came to his stunned mind was peace, so he called them *peace gems.* Kryger sensed that the sanctuary could become an addiction, and that one could easily forget one's responsibilities and stay much too long here.

    They didn't bother unpacking any of the provisions they brought along, because they could eat and sleep in the fighter. They merged, and Kryger practiced for the rest of the day and half the night under Injani's guidance before he fully mastered the ability to make himself weightless. The next morning she showed him how to control levitation, because he could so easily soar out into space, or fall to his death, if he *switched off* at the wrong moment and panicked because he hadn't practiced long enough. He trained under her close supervision until she was satisfied that he had the principles under control, but he sustained many bumps and falls. As long as he remained conscious, he could rise or fall any distance without the use of a gravity neutralizer. She advised him to train regularly until the neutralizing was a subconscious process.

The only thing he must always keep in mind was that he had to have breathable air, and enough air-pressure to keep his physical body intact and his blood from boiling out of his nose and ears. They were both changed when they left on the third morning, but Kryger felt that he had a better chance to survive the odds. He now also knew how a partial mind-merge was controlled so that he could pass the two newly acquired abilities on to Quarr.

He stayed with the colony for another two days, paving the way for an alliance that would benefit both colonies in the long run. Then he crammed three delegates into the fighter, two on the navigator's seat, and one on his lap, to deliver to Quarr and her people.

He flew as fast as he safely could to keep discomfort to a minimum.

Just as the delegates thankfully disembarked after the cramped flight, the call to battle came. An armada had just broken into normal space and every pilot was called to report immediately.

Kryger had a premonition that Quarr would not survive the coming engagement if she participated. Not only was she important as a leader, he loved her too much to risk her life if he knew the risk would prove fatal. He didn't need a navigator for a dogfight in a one or two-man fighter this close to a temporary base. He took off immediately.

Quarr was furious when she mind-flashed him. He tried to explain, but she wouldn't let him. He then blocked her out of his mind and contacted his dad to tell him that he was on his way without Quarr, because he had a premonition that she would not survive if she came with him. Before he finished, Torak interrupted him.

Get yourself here as fast as you can! Mom and the three Shadows are on their way down in the shuttle. I've had the same premonition. Explain to Mom so that she can explain to Quarr. We've armed all the one-man fighters. They're ready to depart. I'm just waiting for you to arrive. They will protect you while you deal with the bugs. I have felt the searching probes of two powerful minds, so expect at least two. We have time to install the MAG and to meet the enemy before they reach this solar system. Put some extra power under your rear while you talk to Mom.

Kryger smiled grimly as he streaked upward on full power. He didn't know where the knowledge came from—perhaps it was something Injani had mentioned—but he had a sudden conviction that Quarr would have a son who would carry on after him if he perished today. He briefly spoke to his mother, Lerra, telling her of his premonition and decision to leave Quarr behind. She promised to talk to her and to lock the shuttle so that Quarr would stay grounded for the duration of the battle.

The battle for Okrion is about to begin, Kryger thought. *What else is there to worry about?* His feeling was that they would succeed in stopping the armada, because they just *had* to. Then he realized what he had to do. He would have to pursue the bugs on his own. He asked his father to cancel the escort, because he couldn't isolate their minds, plus his own, from the powerful Hullenii's mind-invasion tactics. They were sneaky and cowardly enough to turn companions against him. They wouldn't take chances now that Gorrel was just a memory with an unexplained death.

From now on he would be a bug-hunter. He must survive. He had seen and felt the Hullenii's contempt for all life forms aside from themselves. He was grimly amused—the bugs would go all out and dare anything to get rid of him. They would do their utmost to find his race, but it wasn't there to find. This would keep them off-balance for some time.

39

"If the bugs think about it Dad, they will turn us against each other. If I to go in alone with my mind isolated, I may accomplish what I must. I checked where the two Hullenii are. One is on this battleship—" Kryger pointed to the display on the battle-screen. "The other one is in this smaller ship—let's call it a luxury yacht—way behind the fleet. Your feeling of disaster was right. This battleship carries a planet-buster, which they started to assemble when they came out of subspace. From what I could glean from their minds, it should be ready in another two hours, which doesn't leave me much time to intercept and destroy that ship."

The news evoked exclamations of surprise and anger from the assembled pilots. Torak's face went white, but Kryger continued. "I suggest that I sneak around behind them in a scout and first disable the Hullenii in the yacht. Then I'll try to explode the bomb in the battleship, which as you can see, is bringing up the rear end of the formation. How I will do it is irrelevant." Torak knew about the top-secret MAG, but the others didn't, and what they didn't know, the Hullenii couldn't extract from their minds. "When it becomes necessary—I'll let you know when—keep their attention away from me as much as possible."

Because of the threat of the bomb, there wasn't enough time to manufacture and test the special equipment for holding and aiming the little weapon, and Kryger would aim the MAG by hand toward the minds of the scientists working around the bomb. It would have to be done by opening the cockpit canopy partway, and aiming with mind and eye. It would be difficult to explode the bomb that way, except by sheer chance, but he would keep on trying by going closer and closer. That bomb and battleship must explode far away from the planet. He would put the spare coil in while the scout was being made ready, and he was determined to keep on pulling the trigger until the MAG was empty. He knew that Torak would sacrifice himself and his flagship with everyone aboard to destroy the planet-buster if he failed. Lerra was that precious to him.

Kryger told his father what he wanted—the computer programming wizard whom he knew was on board, and the fastest scout. When the programmer genius and scout were made available in record time, Kryger told the programmer what he wanted, and without the man's knowledge, sent him a picture of exactly what he meant—a program to jump short distances in subspace to get behind the approaching enemy ships. He had made a rough calculation to save time. "Make the jump kick-in automatically at twenty thousand km/h, stay on for just two seconds, and then bring me out immediately, regardless of speed. That's all I want—except a button that will do the same for half a second after the initial jump if I'm not behind the enemy."

"Almost impossible with the time available," the programmer replied, "but I can get you behind that yacht with half an hour's work. You'll have to turn the scout yourself though, and it'll be traveling faster than the old proverbial bat with its ass ablaze. No wonder they say that it's your hobby to write scouts and fighters off in just about every battle."

"I hope it doesn't come to that again. Please make it as fast as you can, but take into account that in half an hour they will be *much* closer, and that I will need another six or seven minutes to achieve that speed at full blast."

The new gift talent from Injani was not yet fully developed, but he had an insistent urge to take extra oxygen tanks. He asked his old friend, the store-master, for four two-hour oxygen cylinders, filled to capacity, and to have them cross connected and fastened together in a very strong harness to strap to his body. If it couldn't be done within fifteen minutes, Kryger would be dead within the hour.

He pre-flight checked the scout, and was relieved when the extra tanks were installed at the pilot's seat in just over fifteen minutes. Just after they were finished, the programmer told him that the program changes were completed. He added, "You'll overshoot the target by a couple of thousand kilometers because of the constantly closing distance. I can't keep adjusting the FTL speed all the time."

Kryger shook his hand. "Thanks Mor. I knew I was asking the impossible, but it provides me with the element of surprise. Please keep working on the principle to make short jumps lasting for one to five seconds at the push of a button or the flip of a switch. It will help in battles to come if one is hurt and needs to instantly get some distance away." He mentally told his dad that he was ready to fly.

"It's a brilliant idea that someone should have thought of long ago, but I will think it over afterward. We have to survive first."

"Some of us must survive to carry on. There is no other choice," Kryger replied. The *clear deck* hooter sounded as he entered the cockpit. He closed the canopy from the pilot's seat, then moved and strapped himself into the navigator's seat. He couldn't endure the planned acceleration from the pilot's seat. The extra oxygen bottles made it extremely uncomfortable. The navigation equipment could only be handled from the navigator's cabin, but the scout could be piloted from there as well. Permission to be ejected from the ship was granted immediately and he was away on full, crushing power. He turned the scout on the correct course as soon as he was out of the ship.

When he was at the correct programmed speed, the newly installed program automatically kicked in and took control of the scout. Mor had done an excellent job, and the disorientation had scarcely begun when he was back in normal space again, far behind the invaders. He didn't even check the scout's speed. He blacked out when he turned the scout in a tight half circle. He expected that, because the scout could easily take more than forty gravities, even if he couldn't, and he would lose consciousness ten times over if it would save Quarr, his beloved mother, and the planet.

He came back to consciousness within seconds and straightened his flight-path toward the enemy vessels. He slammed the throttles to maximum power and again felt the exhilarating, powerful forward surge. With the scout quickly settled at max, he moved forward to the pilot's seat where he would have better control of its weapons, but first he strapped the awkward harness with the extra oxygen cylinders to his body, and connected his suit to it.

He sent a tenuous probe toward the vessels ahead and identified the Hullenii yacht. It was way behind the other craft, which was supposed to be the safest place for an *observer*. He grinned wolfishly and slightly changed course toward it while he kept a probe on the occupant. He didn't try to enter its brain, but he would sense any thoughts it transmitted. When he was an estimated ten kilometers behind the yacht and closing, he popped the canopy open and sighted the MAG. He fired twice, once at the insect, and when that entity's thoughts ceased, he aimed at the fiery exhaust tube of the yacht and pulled the trigger again. One shot up the rear and the yacht drifted quietly to be collected later—if there *was* a later.

He established a tight link with Torak without asking permission. *Dad, this bug and his yacht at the rear was easy. It was supposed to keep watch on our thought exchanges. Its brain is dead, but its body might stay alive without air. Take a fix on it. I'm going after the battleship. I think you should get the planet or the moon between it and our fleet as fast as possible. There may be one hell of an explosion if the bomb is fully assembled. The bug may think that you're running away, and that should take their attention away from the rear until it misses its pal. You don't have long. I'm already sneaking up closer, and I don't want any of our own people needlessly killed in the blast.*

He dropped the link. Torak would immediately act on his advice. He was lucky that he could disable his first quarry with only two shots, but it had been under the impression that it was quite safe so far behind. Scientists would have a complete body to dissect and study at their leisure if it wasn't destroyed or blown too far away if the planet-busting bomb exploded.

It was time to stop speculating. The difficult part of his lone mission was about to begin. He must be aware of all that was going on around him, and concentrate as never before to reach and destroy the heavily guarded battleship. The planet was already a small black dot to the naked eye, and he pushed the throttles to see if he couldn't get them past the solid stop to coax a little extra speed out of the howling scout.

While he was at it, he subtly probed the mind of the remaining Hullenii. He found its mind in a state of rage, confusion, and incomprehension.

How could a detested companion ignore him if he asked for its opinion, or did it inexplicably die all of a sudden? No matter, this planet would die soon, with or without the aid of another Hullenii. Those damned slow-moving idiots who called themselves scientists! Perhaps he should brain a couple of them so that the others would hurry up the assembly to escape the same fate. Granted, a pre-assembled and armed planet-busting bomb would have exploded in subspace, but they should have had the components close together, not stashed in different parts of the ship. It accessed their minds. What a surprise! The bomb was almost ready.

Having followed the bug's mind-probes, Kryger also switched his attention to the minds of the assemblers. They were not real scientists, because he now knew that the bugs destroyed anyone who could think for themselves. They were afraid that their cattle would rebel against them if they were smart enough to put two and two together. Any being capable of original thought was a menace to their self-proclaimed godhood, and therefore were destroyed as soon as he or she came to notice; if that person was "innocent" enough to draw attention.

The battleship was surrounded by a thick layer of defense and attack craft, but he would have to get within a hundred kilometers of it to be reasonably accurate with his aim. If he scored a direct hit on the bomb that close, his chances of coming out alive were a big, fat zero. Two hundred kilometers might give him a slightly better chance of surviving the explosion, but no one had seen such an explosion before, so this was guesswork.

They were still about three to four million kilometers away from the planet when Kryger snuck up to within five hundred kilometers of the battleship. Then half the defender-screen turned and headed his way. He thought that perhaps the MAG's range was more than the estimated three hundred kilometers. Raising the canopy just high enough to push his hand through, he aimed at the battleship and pulled the trigger three times for luck. The scout rushed along at maximum speed, and he wondered if it was fast enough to catch up with the bolts. He didn't really want to find out, so he changed his course slightly. At close to the speed of light, the bolts, if they didn't dissipate too much, would catch the battleship within a second or so.

Nothing happened for two or three seconds, and the fighters were closing fast and forming an O-formation as they approached. Kryger closed the canopy fast, and aiming at the battleship, fired one nuclear missile. The second followed less than two seconds after the first. The fighting craft and other gunners had a good chance of destroying the first missile, but he hoped that the second one would get through the cordon that guarded the battleship.

The first missile exploded almost in the center of the O-formation as they continued to concentrate their combined force-beams on it—as he hoped they would—and the force of the nuclear explosion destroyed them all. The gunners on the battleship destroyed the second missile within thirty kilometers of the ship. They were seasoned warriors, not the amateurs he had to deal with a few weeks ago.

He started the special breathing pattern to induce weightlessness, which, he hoped, would partly or fully protect his body against the full impact of the explosion. When the scout was past the three-hundred-kilometer limit from the battleship, and still at full speed, he popped the canopy open again. Of course, never having experienced or even heard of the force of a planet-busting bomb before, he didn't know what to expect, except that it must be extremely powerful to rip an entire planet to pieces. He didn't know what his chances of survival were so close to the expected explosion, but it was his life against that of everyone he held dear. He didn't hesitate.

He aimed at the minds of the bomb-assemblers and triggered three shots before he saw the battleship falter and a slight flicker beginning, then he sharply angled the scout away and turned the belly of the scout toward the ship. At the same time he slammed the canopy closed and activated the shields just as he saw a brilliant flash in the rear-view panel that blinded him.

As he felt the effect of the special exercise taking hold of his body, the irresistible force of the exploding bomb hit the belly of the scout. It felt as if a billion sledgehammers were aimed at him and the scout, and all landed in the same place at the same time. The scout faltered as if it had run into a solid wall. Just as unconsciousness started to take hold of his brain, he vaguely felt himself being crushed like a doll, and then being ripped apart together with the scout. *Not even three weeks!* he heard himself shout from a long distance away. He didn't know that his broken, unconscious body was propelled away with the pilot's section of the cockpit, at an angle away from the far-off planet, and that by some miracle, the harness holding the precious oxygen cylinders remained intact.

Kryger groaned. Finding satisfaction and relief in the action, he groaned again. Then he wondered why he was groaning. As he became conscious of the pain that wracked his body, he groaned again, this time involuntarily. He grimaced and thought, *I must have survived the explosion, otherwise there would have been no pain. Grandma assured me that there is no pain in the afterlife, but she could have been wrong.*

"No, she wasn't wrong," his father's strong voice assured him. "We thought you were gone, because we couldn't detect you or your thoughts, but Mike told us that your bracelet was still functioning, which meant you were still breathing. You were traveling away from the solar system like a meteor. He led us to you while the rest of the fleet rounded up what little remained of the scattered invaders. You had us worried for a few hours. It might interest you to know that you still had enough oxygen left for twenty minutes when we caught up with you."

Kryger tried to speak and then gave up as only croaks came out. He asked, *How long ago?* It didn't really matter, but he wanted to know. Something nagged at the back of his mind.

"We picked you up three days ago, about five hours after the explosion. Hell, what an awful great-grandmother of all the grandmothers of an explosion it was! It even rocked the planet about three million kilometers away. We were behind the planet and the ship still tumbled. Mike, as ever, watching your doings closely, said that the shields held just long enough to save your life. Most of the enemy ships were destroyed, but none of ours. I've never seen a planet-buster in action, and I never again want to. Even the far away explosion in space was blindingly spectacular.

"Son, you saved a hell of a lot of lives. Remarkably, you had no wounds or broken bones. You have a constitution like a rubber doll, and the doctor says that you will only take a few weeks to fully recover. Your body took a severe beating and it was full of odd dents and markings. It's a wonder that you're still alive, but we're not complaining. Mom and Quarr were here, but there's a lot of unfinished business down there for Quarr, and Mom is helping her to get it on the way as quickly as feasible."

Torak seldom used strong language, but Kryger felt the deep emotion behind the words. He would risk his life again to save his parents, Quarr, and—he put a clamp on his thoughts. Some secrets must remain secret.

I have a request, Dad. Please take us home when Quarr has completed what she needs to do. I need to listen to the dripping fountain in the desert before I hunt bugs again. Did you recover the bug-body, or was it blown away too? He received the affirmative. *Okay, so you have one deceased bug-body to study and I won't have to be careful to preserve another one.*

His body throbbed all over with pain, and he privately wondered what he looked like before he was rescued. This wonderful healing ability may have worked overtime, because he vaguely remembered that he felt broken when he lost consciousness. No wonder he felt so drained of energy. He idly wondered how many times in the future this self-healing gift would save his life. He wasn't looking forward to the next experience. What mattered now was that he recovered completely so that he could prove the dire predictions wrong. He had much to live for, but he wasn't afraid to fight with everything he had to come out alive after every fight. There was this conviction that he had much to learn and that his end would be different than expected.

www.ingramcontent.com/pod-product-compliance
Lightning Source LLC
Chambersburg PA
CBHW061554170626
46811CB00001B/195